CW09751725

PRAISE FOR TH
WI

Haunting. Horrific. Highly recommended.

— TJ DALLAS, AUTHOR OF *THE BARTENDER'S PRIDE*

Dark and violent, with exquisite tension and beautiful attention to details... You won't be disappointed.

— KATHLEEN DE PLUME, AUTHOR OF *DRAGON QUEENS*

If you like dark stories with a romantic element, I cannot recommend this book enough. It does not shy away from blood, gore, or feels.

— MEGAN JOHNSON, GOODREADS

Readers are given a choice to choose our own ending and take sides. I chose my "perfect" ending. Which would you choose?

— @PIPSQUEAKREVIEWS, INSTAGRAM

An amazing dark fantasy... Do not expect fluffy or warm and fuzzy. Lianyu Tan will show you no mercy.

— VICTORIA TSAO, GOODREADS

# THE WICKED AND THE WILLING

AN F/F GOTHIC HORROR VAMPIRE NOVEL

## LIANYU TAN

This is a work of fiction. Names, characters, places, and incidents either are the product of the author's imagination or are used fictitiously. Any resemblance to actual persons, living or dead, events, or locales is entirely coincidental.

Copyright © 2022 by Lianyu Tan

lianyutan.com

All rights reserved. No part of this book may be reproduced or used in any manner without written permission of the copyright owner except for the use of quotations in a book review. For permission requests, write to lianyu@lianyutan.com.

First paperback edition May 2022

Cover Design by Story Wrappers (storywrappers.com)

Edited by Silvia's Reading Corner (silviasreading.webs.com) and Emily A. Lawrence (lawrenceediting.com)

ISBN 9780648994831 (ebook)

ISBN 9780648994848 (paperback)

ISBN 978-0-6489948-7-9 (hardback)

ISBN 978-0-6489948-8-6 (audiobook)

Shattered Scepter Press

20221105

*For my wife
and for everyone who's ever been
a stranger in their land of residence.*

**红颜薄命**
*Beautiful women suffer unhappy fates.*
Chinese idiom from a Yuan dynasty drama, 鸳鸯被.

This standalone gothic horror vampire novel is set in Singapore in the late 1920s. At that time Singapore and parts of now-Malaysia were collectively known as the Straits Settlements, a British Crown colony.

Due to the mature content and dark themes, this book is intended for adult readers only. It contains potentially disturbing content including graphic rape, racism, torture, suicide, self-harm, and adult characters who are survivors of childhood sexual abuse. Further content warnings are available from the author's website: lianyutan.com.

This book adopts the spelling and naming conventions of its setting.

# WARNING

This F/F gothic horror novel contains potentially disturbing content including graphic rape, racism, torture, suicide, self-harm, and adult characters who are survivors of childhood sexual abuse. Visit lianyutan.com for more information.

# PART ONE

1927

# CHAPTER 1

# MOVING OUT

## GEAN CHOO

*Saturday, 12 March 1927*

On the day when everything changed, Gean Choo sold the last of her mother's belongings: a silver hairpin adorned with a butterfly. Warmth suffused the jewellery shop, lamps hovering over a wealth of riches in burnished gold and silver, trapped beneath glass. The clerk was a Eurasian man with wide dark brows and curly hair, skin a shade of bronze. He was leaning over a ledger on the counter, pen in hand, but straightened when he saw her.

"Back again?" he asked in English.

Ordinarily she would've smiled at him, dropping her voice to a soft and hesitant near-whisper, but not today. The woman on the pallet opposite her own had kept her up all night by coughing, bad enough it'd sounded like she'd been trying to hack up a piece of her lung.

Gean Choo drew the hairpin from her head, ripping out a few hairs along with it. When she held it out upon her palms, the lace butterfly shivered its wings. "How much?"

The clerk set out his scales and loupe. There was no one else in the shop, so he took his time with the assessment, making a small mark in his notebook.

Gean Choo stared at the width of the butterfly's thorax and the tiny bumps of its eyes. A woman wore her wealth on her person; it was her security against a future with no sons to nurture her, no family to serve as her bulwark and shield. In happier times, the pin had shone against her mother's hair, silver against black, the slightest movement making the wings quiver as though about to take flight. It was charming, but nothing so glamorous as her mother's pieces of gold and jade. Its humble nature had perhaps saved it from her father's unending appetites. He'd probably forgotten all about it.

"Three dollars, seventy-two cents," the clerk said.

"You must think I'm bodoh."

"It's not even sterling."

"I'll go to Little Chung's," she said, naming a shop down the road.

"Be my guest."

Little Chung would speak kindly to her, call her "sister," and offer condolences for her recent loss. She'd be lucky if she could bargain him up to three dollars.

She didn't have time for this. "Four-fifty," she countered.

He wasn't having it. Perhaps she wore her desperation too openly, like a layer of dirt she couldn't slough off. Perhaps it clung to her like the grease in her long plait or the grime around her collar.

She left the store with three dollars and seventy-two cents tucked into the pocket sewn in her sleeve. Outside, the midday sun blazed down upon the asphalt. A Sikh traffic warden stood at the intersection, over-sized white mittens on his hands for visibility, rattan "wings" enlarging his profile. She followed a bare-chested hawker across the road, keeping close behind one of the large, covered baskets he balanced across his back.

A few blocks away, she bought a new shirt and trousers, along with a pair of cloth shoes. When interviewing for this position, the woman on the phone had said she'd be some kind of lady's companion. These plain clothes were unlikely to suffice for such a job, but they would have to do.

She returned to her lodging house in the early afternoon. The narrow alleyway was dusty with red laterite, crowded with long poles hanging out of windows, sagging with laundry. Voices called out in a handful of languages over the clatter of steel pans and the sizzling of hot oil, the air pungent with raw sewerage and burnt grease.

A man stopped her beneath the shadow of an awning, his face lightly splintered with wrinkles, graced with a gap-toothed grin, hair shaved close to his head to reveal the outline of his skull. In those last awful few weeks, she'd seen him enough to recognise him. He'd been one of those men hovering about her father, speaking to him in hushed tones, waiting for the old man to drop.

"Teo's little girl, isn't it? My deepest condolences for your loss," he said in Hokkien.

Sim Lai Hock was being facetious. She was already nineteen, an age when most women were married with one child on the hip and another on the way. "Thank you. You're too kind."

He shook his head. "I shed a tear when I heard about your father. But what a life, no? Drink all day, smoke all night. Not a bad way to end."

Somewhere distant came the thud of a mosque drum, summoning the faithful to prayer. A quick series of beats at first, leading into an extended rhythm like a pulse. It was already over an hour past midday.

"I should go—"

His hand shot out, grabbing her elbow and pulling her in close. He'd eaten. There was a sliver of green clinging to one tooth, the odour of something decaying on his breath. "Why the hurry?" His nails dug into her skin. "Did Papa tell you about his debts? His passion for cards? Did he tell you how much he owes me?"

"How much?"

"Nine hundred."

"You're joking."

His eyes gleamed with avarice, like two black buttons. "You think this is funny? Think I want to wait all day for Teo's little whore to show her face? Ha. Ha. Ha." His spittle arced across her cheek like the first brush of monsoonal rain.

"I don't have that much."

He let her go at last. "Not yet. I heard you took a job. Tanjong Katong? House on the sea. Expensive lah."

She massaged her elbow with her other hand. She'd only accepted the job the day before and had told no one, save her lodging sisters. Clearly a mistake. "I can't get that much. Not right away. I'll have to pay by instalments—"

"Big house, big opportunity. No money? All right. Lai Hock understands. You find another way. Maybe your mem has rings, diamonds, silverware..." He grinned, revealing a missing front tooth. "First edition books."

A rickshaw rattled past, then abruptly stopped, disgorging its passengers—two men in sarongs. Gean Choo lowered her voice to a hiss. "I can't rob my employer! I'll hang!"

"Then don't get caught. Maybe there's an accident. Maybe the whole house goes up in a fire—oh, so sad," he said, vowels dripping with false sorrow.

Her teeth ached from clenching her jaw.

Lai Hock reached out and took her left hand before she could protest. "You won't scream, will you?" he asked as a smile curled on his face like a cat in a sunbeam. With his other hand, he reached into his pocket and pulled out a knife, unfolding it with a flick of his thumb. He turned her palm face up. There was something glacial about his eyes.

She should've screamed. Should've hit him, should've run, should've done *something*.

But she couldn't move; she could scarcely even breathe. She did nothing, said nothing, thought nothing... for she was nothing.

Lai Hock pressed the tip of the knife against her skin. It didn't hurt, not at first. There was a sharp sting, no worse than a bee. He drew three lines to make a shape like an inverted "U," two strokes inside and a final line to seal the box. The cuts were shallow, but they bled all the same, red beading up from her skin like a lotus emerging from a swamp, pooling in the hollow of her palm.

"Here you go, little sister. A reminder. Can't read? It says 'four,'" he said. 'Four,' a near-homophone for 'death.' "I give you four weeks, then we talk again."

Four weeks was nothing. She wouldn't rob anyone—not for him. Not for this.

He wiped his blade clean against the shoulder of her tunic. "Why so sad? A pretty face has no trouble making money here."

Her cheeks flushed an angry red. She didn't trust herself to speak, instead fishing out her handkerchief, using it to bind her palm, holding the edge in her teeth to pull the knot tight.

By the time she glanced up, Lai Hock was gone.

THE INSIDE of Gean Choo's lodging house offered a hot, foetid darkness, redolent with mingled odours of urine, garlic, and belacan. The light from the outside fell in narrow slices through the bars of the door, turning her shadow into a looming monstrosity.

She navigated the creaking steps to the upstairs floor, where the landlady's daughter stopped her in the corridor. "Shopping?" Bee Leng asked in Hokkien, glancing down at the cloth bag hanging from Gean Choo's shoulder, speaking around a mouthful of betel nut. "You can afford new things, but not rent?"

They said Bee Leng's mother had run off with a Malay, evidence of her mixed parentage in the shape of her eyes, the shade of her skin, which was darker than her mother's warm beige. They said her father had left them before she'd been born.

People said a lot of things.

Gean Choo reached into her sleeve pocket and pulled out her few remaining coins, offering them with both palms out, her bandaged left hand below the right. "I can pay this much today. I'll come back with the rest next month."

"Huh." Bee Leng took the coins. "It's not much."

Gean Choo tamped down her instinct to snap. She folded her anger into neat triangles and stashed it away in a forgotten pit, never to be recovered.

The corridor was narrow, the walls serving as storage, leaning in on either side with stacked firewood, sleeping pallets, clothes, cooking utensils, and baskets, all crowding in upon the walkway. A cockroach scuttled from the base of one wall to the other, followed by its friend, both unafraid to be seen in the open. Gean Choo couldn't reach the rest of her things until Bee Leng moved—which Bee Leng knew. Yet she stood there, jaw moving mechanically, betel nut glazing her teeth red.

"Please," Gean Choo said. "I'll be late."

"Late for what?"

The other women hadn't told her, but they'd told Lai Hock. "I'm taking a job. Moving out."

"What job?"

"The Edevane house."

Bee Leng continued to stare, her red mouth like a gash across her face. Then she laughed, a half-suppressed snort followed by a giggle. "Really? The cursed house, with the English widow who dances all night?"

"That's not—" Gean Choo gestured with her palm, the movement pulling at the wound where she'd been cut. "That's ridiculous. It's just a house."

"Simply Asiatic superstition," Bee Leng said, momentarily switching to English, adopting the British accent of a colonialist. She giggled again.

This was doing nothing for Gean Choo's nerves, nor her temper. "I will pay your honourable mother within the month," she said. How she would do that, exactly, was another matter, particularly with Lai Hock breathing down her neck. She'd manage. Somehow.

Bee Leng finally flattened herself against the wall, allowing her to pass. "Ma says you're two months overdue."

"I'll repay her with interest." Gean Choo entered the shared room where she kept her things. It was situated in the middle of the townhouse, lacking a window. Inside were two women engaged in hushed conversation on the floor, though neither looked up as Gean Choo went to her bed —a narrow wooden shelf affixed to the wall above another woman's pallet. Bee Leng followed her in, leaning against the doorframe with her arms crossed.

"Live-in job? Needs a fortnight's notice."

"I'll cover the extra two weeks." Gean Choo pulled herself up onto her bunk, ducking to avoid banging her head against the hanging baskets used to keep foodstuff away from vermin. She put aside her new clothes and threw everything else she owned into the empty bag: some personal items and another set of clothing, just as threadbare and discoloured as the shirt she was wearing. She wrapped the one photograph she had of her parents, taken on their wedding day, in a handkerchief. Then she changed into her new clothes with no concern for modesty, the starched collar rough against her skin.

"Address? So Ma can reach you when you miss the date. Again."

"It's—" Gean Choo paused. It was somewhere in Tanjong Katong, along the east coast, a ways distant from the town centre. She went through her old shirt, reaching inside the pocket. Miss Skelford had given her a slip of paper with four digits and the Edevane name written upon it. "That's their telephone number." She handed it to Bee Leng, then picked up her bag. "Please, if your mother wants to get paid, I must go."

As she took her first step down the narrow staircase, Bee Leng called out, "Hey. How will you pay if some hantu takes you?"

*Just send the invoice to hell*, was the first thought that came to mind, but she turned and smiled, eyes lowered in contrition. "If hantu are there, I'll beg for mercy. 'Let me pay up before I die,' I'll say. 'I still owe Koh Bee Leng's mother.'"

Bee Leng laughed. "Please. You'd run away screaming."

And so would anyone else.

THE CAR WASN'T OUTSIDE when she left the lodging house. Gean Choo loitered, bag dangling from her hands. Bee Leng had just been teasing. The girl had nothing better to do than to invent ghost stories.

A steady stream of traffic flowed, kicking up clouds of dust. Most of the rickshaws had their hoods down against the heat of the sun, their curved carapaces like the shells of insects. Some of the rickshaw coolies ran bare-chested, ribs visible against their skin, straw hats pulled low over their faces.

Her palm itched.

An oxen cart rumbled past, wheels crunching over the dirt, and then a sleek black sedan pulled up by the wayside. The driver leaned across the console towards her. "Teo Gean Choo?" He was a wiry Malay man of some indeterminate age between forty and sixty, his face colonised by fine wrinkles and age spots. He was dressed in a cream jacket, its weave pure and new.

"Yes." She stood in a hurry, then repeated the word in Malay, blushing. Her knowledge of Malay was abysmal.

The man got out of the car. He walked with a limp, favouring his left leg as he came around and took hold of her bag, stowing it in the footwell of the back seat. He wore no shoes, his feet appearing even more calloused than her own.

The car's cream leather seat sighed when Gean Choo slid onto it, with an exhalation of polish and something else, like the whiff of dollar bills. The driver got back into his side. Gean Choo hadn't quite shut her door when he pulled away into traffic.

"I'm Zaid."

She closed the door. "Thank you for coming."

As he drove, a noise rose around them, a roar like hundreds of voices raised, though she couldn't quite make out the words. Above that came the beat of drums. They'd only passed two blocks when they hit a wall of traffic, vehicles crammed throughout the street. Rickshaws, motorcycles, and pedestrians broke away from the jam and circled back the other way.

She leaned forwards, though it did little to help her make sense of all the chaos. Drivers yelled and honked their horns. Zaid slapped the steering wheel in frustration, muttering a curse under his breath. Seeing an opening, he began to turn, but then came a series of loud pops, like firecrackers setting off at New Year's. Yells pierced the general hubbub as people ran and pedestrians crammed together in the crowded streets. A man slammed against the side of the car, making Gean Choo jump. Blood oozed from a cut on his forehead. He slapped a crimson palm against her door, leaning heavily against the car for a moment before the crowd pushed him on and he vanished into the thick of them.

"Close the window," Zaid snapped.

"How?" She'd never been in a car with movable windows.

Zaid leaned across her lap and tapped the small crank set into the door. She wound it, her face blushing hot. He managed to turn the car around, but it was still slow going amidst the press of traffic, made even more miserable by the confined stuffiness of the car. She kept the top inch of the window wound down for the chance of a breeze. Poor Zaid seemed just as uncomfortable as she was, sweat beading on his face.

South Bridge Road was an impassable mess. A rickshaw puller darted out too close to the car, and her heart leapt into her throat. She pressed herself into her seat, her new clothes sticking to her skin. All that effort, only to appear rumpled when they finally reached their destination. Given half the chance, she'd rather have kept her mother's pin. No point worrying about it now.

"I'm sorry," she said. "I could have walked."

Zaid clucked his tongue like a disapproving auntie. "It's not good for young women to walk so far."

"Where is the house?"

"Meyer Road."

She settled herself more comfortably in her seat. While the traffic jam was certainly unusual, there was no reason to think it was a sign, a message meant only for her. But Bee Leng's warning wouldn't stop ringing in her head, and despite the heat of the afternoon, she shivered.

# CHAPTER 2

## AMBROSIA HALL

### GEAN CHOO

*Saturday, 12 March 1927*

The traffic cleared once they'd bypassed South Bridge Road. Zaid clung to the coastline, driving down a wide street framed by large, spreading Angsana trees, their leaves dappling the sunlight.

It was less picturesque outside of town, a landscape of big industrial sheds and smoke billowing from tall chimneys. Boats crowded the Kalang River, with wooden, attap-roofed houses built over the water's edge, resting on spindly stilts. A group of barefooted boys stared at them from outside one of the houses, some in tunics and pants, some only wearing sarongs, round eyes sparkling in their brown faces.

The industrial buildings fell away as they drove farther east. Enormous palm trees soared high above the road, fronds waving. Traffic was lighter in this distant part of the settlement, rickshaws disappearing, the road now the domain of motorcars, pedestrians, and a single mosquito bus, this one a black Ford remodelled to seat seven, the bus conductor hanging off the back, his hair whipping across his face in the breeze. Off the coast, ships and boats crowded the harbour, masts rising from their decks like white bony fingers reaching up from the grave.

The houses were scattered far apart as if they loathed company, free-standing bungalows both squat and sprawling. Zaid pulled near one, drawing close to a pair of looming wrought-iron gates. The sign over the gate read "Ambrosia Hall" in curly English letters.

"No guards," Gean Choo said. "Robbers? What then?"

Zaid chuckled. "The mem isn't afraid of robbers." He paused outside the gates and got out of the car, using a cane this time. His left ankle was turned slightly out, the foot dragging with each step as he approached the gate and unlocked it with a key. The metal creaked as he pulled each side open, anchoring them to the ground before getting back inside the car.

Gean Choo hesitated as they passed through the gates. "Should I close them?"

"It's all right."

On the other side, he limped out again and repeated the process in reverse, leaving the car to idle as he locked the gates. As the car rolled on, the estate greeted her with an impression of lush and serene symmetry. A broad driveway framed with stone columns and palm trees dancing overhead led down to the main house, which was two stories tall and all in white, with a red terracotta roof. Short pillars raised the ground floor to prevent flooding and the verandahs enclosing both floors had carved balustrades, decorated with geometric shapes and flowers.

Mother had said they'd once lived in a house just as grand, though Gean Choo's memories of that time were indistinct and unreliable. She'd had her own amah, hadn't she? Some kind young woman, her voice soft and low.

Zaid pulled into a garage at the side of the house.

"Thank you," Gean Choo said.

He grunted. "Close your window."

She'd forgotten all about it and dutifully wound up the glass before getting out, taking her bag from the back. Her legs ached after being cooped up for so long.

"Come, let's find the boss," Zaid said.

She followed him. There were more buildings towards the back of the estate in the same style, one with the kitchen and presumably, the servants' quarters, and a smaller one for storage or perhaps even sheltering a generator. A covered jetty led into the ocean, and there was another small structure built above the water, against which two sampans were moored. Flowering bushes filled the gardens, lining a crushed gravel path. Where the paths converged stood a fountain with a statue of a naked woman pouring water into the receptacle below. The crease at her waist seemed so lifelike, Gean Choo almost longed to run her fingers over it.

They passed a stand of single-petalled lilies with deep black flowers. These she touched, brushing the smooth, velvet skin of their petals. The plant drew away from her hand, the flowers furling tight as buds. She continued to stare at them until Zaid snapped his fingers and she moved on.

A pair of workmen stood perched on ladders, re-painting the white finish on the back of the house. Watching them was a man—no, a woman —perhaps in her thirties, standing beneath the shade of a broad tree, smoking a cigarette. She had the look of a hero from a Yue opera, broad-shouldered and flat-chested, though her hair was cropped short above the ears. Her skin was a paler shade of beige than Gean Choo's, her nose broad, cheekbones high-set. She wore a loose, long-sleeved blue jacket and black pants.

Gean Choo caught herself staring at the shape made by the woman's full lips as she exhaled, breathing a cloud of smoke into the air. It wasn't just the haircut or the ambiguous clothing. Something about her... maybe it was the way she stood, unapologetically taking up space as if she had a right to be here, with no fathers or uncles or brothers or husbands to tell her no. Gean Choo had never seen a woman look so self-possessed.

As they approached, the stranger turned her attention away from the workmen, her gaze narrowing in on Gean Choo, pinning her like an insect to a board. Her eyelids were smooth from lash to brow. "You're late," she said in Malay, presumably for Zaid's benefit.

Gean Choo lowered her eyes in contrition, staring at her new shoes. "I'm very sorry."

"There was trouble in town. Bad traffic," Zaid said.

Gean Choo tossed him a look of gratitude.

"Mm." The woman jerked her head to one side, and off he went, heading towards the servants' quarters. She switched to Hokkien. "I'm San Po Lam. You've met Zaid; he drives for Mrs. Edevane. I'll introduce you to the rest of the staff and show you to your room."

"Thank you." Her room. As in... she wouldn't have to share? Gean Choo couldn't let herself hope.

As they started walking, Po Lam turned towards the main house and called out to one of the workmen, "Hey! This part between the windows needs another coat."

Balanced precariously on the spindly ladder, the man glanced across at his work. "It's all right, it looks different only because the paint is still wet—"

"No. Another coat."

The man grumbled under his breath, but he picked up the paint can and climbed down the ladder, dragging it back to the section Po Lam had indicated. Gean Choo followed her to the servants' quarters. There was a covered walkway connecting it to the main house, tiled in matching terracotta. Above them, sleek dark cables ran along the inside of the walkway roof.

"Does this house have electric?" Gean Choo asked.

"Yes. The generator's over there." Po Lam pointed out the small, shed-like building with the hand holding the cigarette. "Drops out occasionally."

"Oh." What did the tuan do to afford all this? Plantations, probably, or perhaps tin.

Po Lam took her shoes off before entering the building and Gean Choo followed suit, pleased to do so since a blister was already forming on her right toe. They stepped into a kitchen filled with the warm, dense aroma of something earthy. Mushrooms? A woman stood with her back to them, whisking something in a bowl with a pair of chopsticks.

"Auntie Seok Eng, this is Teo Gean Choo," Po Lam said, raising her voice to be heard over the clatter of the whisking.

"Eh?" Seok Eng partially turned from the bench top. She had a kind, round face, her forehead dripping with sweat, cheeks red from the sweltering heat of the kitchen. She was perhaps in her fifties, with a towel thrown over her shoulder. The once white towel, now with a yellowish tinge from constant use, was embroidered in red with the sentiment "Good morning," in English, and presumably, in Chinese characters.

"Oh! Welcome!" Seok Eng said in a tone that set Gean Choo on edge. It was too sympathetic by halves, as if Gean Choo had lost a bet instead of securing a prized job. "Makan in twenty minutes, all right?"

"Thank you," Po Lam said, and they continued. She led Gean Choo down a hallway, opening a door, its hinges creaking in protest. "This is your room. The bathroom's down there if you need to wash before dinner. Don't be late."

Gean Choo touched her hair. Perhaps she was less presentable than she'd imagined. "Of course. Thank you. I mean... I won't be."

"What's wrong with your hand?"

The cut didn't even hurt anymore. "It's nothing. A scratch."

"Recent?"

"This afternoon."

"Wait here."

Po Lam left her for a moment and then came back with a battered tea caddy, the words "Gold Leaf" still visible in faded letters. She handed it over. "Wash and redress the wound. If it's still bleeding, wrap it again, properly this time. Use two rolls of bandages."

"It's really just a scratch—"

"Mrs. Edevane is sensitive to smells." Po Lam clicked her tongue. "Particularly the smell of blood. If I'd known, you wouldn't be here."

She was so close. She'd been assigned a room—a whole room!—and Po Lam had introduced her to the others. She couldn't let this be her undoing. "Is it... is it because of her faith? I'm not menstruating—"

"So you said."

They'd spoken about the embarrassing matter at some length when Po Lam had interviewed her over the phone, which was to say they'd exchanged more than half a dozen words on the subject. Po Lam had said that if her courses arrived, she'd have to leave the premises until they were over. It seemed an unlikely problem since she hadn't bled for some months now, even though she was in no danger of being with child.

"I'll wrap my hand carefully," she promised. "Thank you."

Po Lam left her to settle in. The air in the room was warm and stifling, so she opened the window to let in the breeze. Almost immediately, it began to rain, forcing her to shut the window in a hurry.

The bathroom down the hall was almost as large as the room she'd shared with eight others at the lodging house. The door locked behind her with a satisfying click. Gean Choo leaned against the door and stared at the tiles. They were blue, white, and teal, with rhomboids arranged in a star-like pattern. The bold colours were almost hypnotic if she stared at them for too long. She glanced reflexively under the sink for rat droppings but found none, and even the basin was free of dust.

The old tea caddy held rolls of bandages and a bottle of Mercurochrome, its label stained, blotches shading from bright to dark red. She unwrapped her hand, the handkerchief sticking to the wound. The cuts stared at her accusingly, and when she sluiced them, it turned the sink crimson.

Four weeks.

The Mercurochrome stung. The thin crust of antiseptic on the applicator stained her fingers, turning the dry skin around her nails red. It seemed a pity to waste bandages, but she didn't dare disobey Po Lam and used two full rolls, wrapping until her hand was as puffy and white as a steamed bun.

With her good hand, she washed her face and brushed her hair. A mirror would've been nice, but she shouldn't be so vain. She re-tied her hair into its long, single plait and took the comb back to her room. Fifteen minutes had passed, maybe.

The room was plain and clean, large enough to fit nine pallets on the floor without overlapping. There was a bed and a nightstand in pale wood, and a rattan chest the width of the bed. The room's window faced the garden, overlooking the big tree, the grey line of the fence in the distance.

Gean Choo flopped onto the bed and pressed her face into the pillow, inhaling the scent of soap. The rough-spun cotton was wonderfully clean beneath her fingertips, bleached to a crisp white, and there was even a soft muslin mosquito net, currently tied to one side. She stretched out her hands and feet, spreading herself wide like a starfish, luxuriating in the emptiness, the privacy. There was nothing adorning the walls, nothing crowded against the ceiling. The simplicity made the already large space look bigger. Outside, the rain pattered against the tiles, the ocean gurgled along the shore, and gulls called overhead. Much closer, a gecko chirped, almost bird-like in tone.

She could get used to this.

Scents of ginger and green onion wafted from the kitchen. She smoothed the front of her shirt, making sure none of the buttons had popped loose, then went back to the main part of the building. Others were already seated around a large, round table. In addition to Po Lam and Seok Eng, there were a pair of older Chinese men, so alike they must've been twins. Zaid wasn't there, but perhaps he ate separately.

Seok Eng nudged out a seat for her, still wearing the same kindly smile. She sat.

Po Lam put down her chopsticks for a moment to introduce her to the other two men.

Gean Choo smiled nervously. "Good evening."

Conversations happened around her in a mix of Hokkien, Hainanese, and Cantonese. Seok Eng had a niece who was getting married. The two houseboys in their fifties were indeed twins, so similar she couldn't tell them apart at first glance. The eldest one had a wife nagging him to return to Hainan, but he already had a concubine and another son in town. He had to be doing well for himself if he could maintain two families.

"Slow down," the youngest brother muttered to her. "You'll choke."

Gean Choo paused with chopsticks halfway raised to her lips. She set them down, swallowed, and smiled politely. "It's because Auntie's food is so delicious, I can't help myself."

Seok Eng picked up a clump of noodles and fried tofu and dumped them into Gean Choo's bowl, as if she were an honoured guest and not her junior. "Don't embarrass the girl. She's a skinny little thing only."

Gean Choo took a sip of tea and burnt her tongue. It was probably unbecoming to eat this much, but her stomach didn't care. "Does everyone live on the estate?" she asked.

"Only yourself, Zaid, and I," Po Lam said. "The day staff don't live here."

"Day staff?"

"The rest of us," Seok Eng said. "We'll be heading home soon, but we'll be back in the morning. There's Alif also, the gardener. You'll meet him tomorrow."

"Is the mem an insomniac?" Gean Choo asked.

"She keeps odd hours, rising at seven in the evening and going to bed around six in the morning," Po Lam said. "Starting tomorrow, you'll match those hours."

Eleven hours on duty. That didn't seem so terrible, even if they weren't daylight hours. "Is she ill?"

A delicate pause fell over the table, like a carpet of flowers settling over an empty street. "She values her privacy," Po Lam said. "Her health is a matter for herself and her doctor."

Once the meal was over, the eldest brother disappeared and the younger began clearing the dishes. Gean Choo stood. "Uncle, should I help clean up?"

"No," Po Lam said before he could answer. She took out a pocket watch, flipped open the lid, and examined it. "The mem should be up soon."

How strange to lie abed until this late in the day. She glanced out the window. It was growing darker outside, probably close to seven by now.

A series of bells were mounted on the board above the stove in the kitchen, labelled with various rooms—bed, study, drawing, sitting. Wires connecting the bells ran alongside the boundary of the ceiling, leading towards the covered walkway. One of the bells rang, and Seok Eng glanced at the board. "The bedroom. She must be awake already."

"Good. Gean Choo, bring the mem's dinner with you," Po Lam said.

Seok Eng handed her a tray with a single bowl on it, noodle soup swimming in a clear broth, along with delicate slices of fatty pork offset by blanched greens and a sprinkle of aromatic coriander. Squares of opaque, mauve jelly were stacked to one side, half-submerged in the broth.

"What's this part?" Gean Choo asked, tilting her head towards the jellied squares.

"Blood tofu. It's very nutritious," Seok Eng said.

"Come along." Po Lam was already standing by the door.

Gean Choo followed her out, setting the tray down for a moment to put on her shoes. Po Lam kept a quick pace, forcing Gean Choo to hurry, eyes downcast as she focussed on keeping the tray steady to stop the soup from sloshing over the sides of the bowl. Electric lights illuminated the walkway, insects swarming around them.

"It's good she rang," Po Lam said. "Some days she doesn't get up until late. Never try to wake her if she's still abed. Do you understand?"

"I understand. Are there children?"

"No."

"Oh." How sad to be left here all alone. Mrs. Edevane probably didn't even have any other family close by for comfort.

"The shutters upstairs must always be opened after sunset and closed before sunrise. The mem has priceless antiques, sensitive to sunlight."

"It's bad for mould," Gean Choo said. And it would make the room excessively hot. Wasn't the mem already sick?

"It's not for discussion. And never touch the shutters in the mem's bedroom. If she wants them open, she'll do it herself."

"I see."

"You'll have one day's leave per month. We'll go over the calendar tomorrow. No guests on the property—men or women."

As if beaus would be chasing her out along the east coast. "That won't be a problem."

"Good."

The walkway connected with the main house's back verandah. Po Lam stepped inside without removing her shoes, so Gean Choo followed suit, wiping her soles on a mat. They passed through a dining room, and Po Lam had to turn on the light to help navigate around the furniture. It was all made of dark wood, heavily gilded like something from another era, the chairs upholstered in damask, their frames carved with scrolls and rosettes of European design.

They stepped into a foyer where the light was already on, illuminating the white marble floor. A glittering chandelier hung in the atrium above, so out of place it must've come from overseas, along with some of the furniture. The chandelier was fitted with electric lights, switched on in an extravagant display of excess in this empty house, every facet sparkling, throwing tiny rainbows across the walls.

A thought occurred to her, sudden and vicious. She was the only ugly thing in this entire estate.

A grandfather clock stood below the staircase, made from wood carved with intricate birds, the clock face inlaid with mother-of-pearl. It was almost seven o'clock. The minute hand ticked to twelve.

The clock tolled the hour with a deep, sonorous chime. Once the last bell had rung out, leaving only a faint ticking to fill the silence, the mem of the house appeared on the first-floor landing.

## CHAPTER 3

# ENGLISH ROSE

## GEAN CHOO

*Saturday, 12 March 1927*

This was probably what they meant in the novels by "English rose." Mrs. Edevane's pale, even skin was clear and smooth, the colour of soft tofu. Her complexion was nothing at all like the steamed-prawn red of some mems who'd lived in the tropics for too long, acquiring a permanent blotchy countenance and weathered skin like pebbly crepe. The mem was a slight, tall woman in T-bar heels and a green silk dress, iridescent beneath the chandelier like a peacock's wing, shading from green to blue to black. Her eyes were deeply hooded and free from paint, her long yellow hair rolled outward about the nape of her neck. She smiled at Gean Choo, her jewel-encrusted hand resting on the balustrade, her cheeks graced with dimples.

"You must be the new girl," she said, her voice betraying an English accent. She raised her hands in a graceful gesture that encompassed their surroundings. "Welcome to my humble abode."

For a moment, Gean Choo didn't know what to say. The air seemed to crackle with static between them, electric. She was probably staring like an idiot as Mrs. Edevane descended the stairs, the tiny beads on her dress glittering under the chandelier.

*Don't just look at her like a mute. Say something.*

"I'm pleased to be of service to you, Mem," she managed, three steps later, Mrs. Edevane's heels clicking as she navigated the wide staircase.

It was just past seven o'clock, and from what Po Lam had said, the mem stirred herself at this hour every day. What did she do for the rest of the time? Perhaps she was an invalid, suffering from some sort of tropical disease that affected only Europeans?

Near the bottom of the stairs, Mrs. Edevane stopped a few paces away from her. The mem was perhaps a head taller than herself, eyes serene as the river on a calm day. There was something odd about her smile, something sharp, as though it didn't quite match the delicate curves of her face. "You don't know how long I've been waiting for you."

Waiting for... was she late? Yes, but even had she arrived in the early afternoon as scheduled, Mrs. Edevane would've been abed, anyway. And she'd only been offered the position the day before, so she couldn't possibly have started earlier in the week. Whatever could Mrs. Edevane mean?

Before she could say something stupid, like ask the mem to enlighten her, Mrs. Edevane sighed and seemed to crumple, reaching out to grab the balustrade as a shudder wracked her body, her other hand closing into a fist pressed against her stomach. Gean Choo didn't think; she dropped the tray, leaving it to fall with a liquid splatter and the crash of breaking porcelain, and rushed forwards to offer her support. Mrs. Edevane grabbed onto her, hands icy, and Gean Choo staggered beneath her weight, helping her into a seated position on the steps. She was heavier than she'd first appeared, or maybe Gean Choo was weaker than she'd imagined. The mem's skin was cold beneath that silk dress. Was she really ill? And if so, was it something contagious? Perhaps the day staff had the right of it, not staying on the estate at night.

"What a sweet girl you are," Mrs. Edevane breathed, as if she could barely summon enough energy to speak. "What's your name?"

"Teo Gean Choo, Mem."

"*Ghee-en Chew*. Did I get that right?"

Gean Choo nodded, although she had not. It was close enough.

Mrs. Edevane's eyes were a colourless grey, startling to look at, like the eyes of a kitten she'd once found lurking behind her father's house. Though she wore a gentle smile, pain creased her smooth, youthful face.

"Mem. Can you stand?"

Po Lam's voice made Gean Choo startle. Mrs. Edevane twisted in her arms, then leaned against the step, holding herself upright without assistance.

"It must be time for your medicine," Po Lam said. Mrs. Edevane nodded, closing her eyes in pain or exhaustion. Maybe both. She held out her arms, and Po Lam leaned down and picked her up as though she weighed no more than a child. Po Lam carried her up the steps with Mrs. Edevane's hands wrapped behind her neck, her head resting against Po Lam's shoulder, as though they had done this many times before.

It was true what they said, wasn't it? Without one's health, one had nothing. "The widow who dances all night"? Why had she ever listened, even for a moment, to Bee Leng's ridiculous gossip? Mrs. Edevane could barely support her own weight, the poor woman!

# CHAPTER 4

## SIMPLY UNBEARABLE

### VERITY

*Saturday, 12 March 1927*
*Twenty-five nights since last meal*

Po Lam deposited her on the smoking couch in the bedroom, handling her with characteristic gentleness. Verity pressed the back of her hand against her forehead. If she were human, she would be burning with fever, but as she was not, and had not been for some time, she only touched the cool expanse of her skin and the faint murmur of her night-time pulse.

Po Lam straightened. "Is there anything you need, Mem?"

Verity paused a moment. "There is... there is something you could do for me, if you'd be so kind."

Po Lam didn't answer right away. Into that empty silence yawned all the ways in which Verity needed her—needed someone like her. Or perhaps she'd just grown accustomed to Po Lam's face? Yes, that was it. Her dear, grim, unsmiling face; inscrutable at best and disapproving at worst. Well. Verity was trying so very hard—couldn't anyone see that?

"You're not due for a few days yet, Mem."

Verity brought her knees together and compelled herself to sit up, grabbing the back of the sofa for support. "That might be so, but the wait is… It's simply unbearable." She took a breath and exhaled slowly. "Please."

The ability to command prey with but a word was not one of Verity's gifts, but Po Lam inclined her head all the same. "I'll see what I can do."

In a burst of sentimentality, Verity longed to take her hand in gratitude, to feel the grip of her fingers, the strength of her arm… to feel something, anything besides the gnawing pain of her stomach. But she restrained herself. "I know I can rely on you."

After Po Lam left, she smoothed out her dress and settled herself more comfortably on the couch, gently patting her hair to ensure everything was in order. She was a bundle of nerves tonight. Silly, really. Why ought she feel apprehensive? But finding good staff was so very hard, and she was so tired of being disappointed.

The new girl seemed short and small. They were always so frail before Cookie had the chance to fatten them up, but frail or not, she'd leapt admirably to Verity's rescue. Charming, really. She shuddered. How warm the girl's hands had been; how strong her pulse. How delightful to see a new face. One grew so tired of hearing the same old voices, day in and day out. Would this one be quicker on the mark than the last, or would she deny the evidence of her own eyes until the very end? Verity couldn't tell. Not yet. And the not-knowing made the dance so exquisitely delightful.

# CHAPTER 5

# JUST A SCRATCH

## GEAN CHOO

*Saturday, 12 March 1927*

Mrs. Edevane's spoiled dinner lay in a spreading puddle on the marble, mixed with shards of porcelain. Gean Choo rushed back to the servants' quarters, hoping to find Seok Eng or one of the houseboys, but they were nowhere to be found, no doubt done working for the night. Even Zaid wasn't there, or at least, didn't answer when she called, but she discovered the storeroom with spare cloths, buckets, broom, and a metal dustpan made from half an empty fuel can. There was also an ice box. She opened it, grabbing a handful of greens and more of the mauve stuff, already jellied. Hopefully, Seok Eng hadn't been saving it for another purpose. She'd have to explain her mistake in the morning.

Gean Choo sliced the blood tofu and set it to simmer with a fistful of noodles, then returned to the foyer and cleaned up the mess. When Po Lam came back downstairs, she was still on her knees.

"Is she all right?" Gean Choo asked.

"She's fine."

Did Mrs. Edevane fall often? Did she have a doctor? If Po Lam hadn't been nearby, what was Gean Choo meant to do? She couldn't have carried Mrs. Edevane, especially not up all those steps. It wouldn't have been fair to ask Zaid, either, because of his bad leg. But she didn't ask any of those questions. "I put more noodles to simmer."

"Good. You might as well take it up to the mem's room. It's the last one on the left."

Back in the kitchen, Gean Choo washed the greens, arranged the condiments, and dithered over the placement of crockery on the tray, folding a napkin into a neat triangle instead of the crown-like shape Seok Eng had used. She'd have to ask her to demonstrate in the morning. Po Lam had left her unsupervised, displaying either her trust or her indifference, and so Gean Choo was all alone by the time she went back to the foyer and up the steps.

The air upstairs was dense with heat, suffocating due to the shutters being closed all day. Gean Choo went to the third door on the left and transferred the tray to one arm, rapping on the door with her free hand. "Mem? I brought supper."

"Come in."

The air in the mem's bedroom was even more stifling, if that were possible. Mrs. Edevane reclined on a smoking couch next to a table with a lit opium lamp, a pipe resting in one hand. The room was large, containing an imposing four-poster bed, the couch, a dressing table and stool, and a few smaller tables. Curtains canopied and enclosed the bed with deep purple velvet drapes.

There was no clean surface upon which to set the tray. "May I move your books, Mem?"

"Go right ahead."

The books on the side table were bound in leather and stamped in gilt. Gean Choo closed them and stacked them to one side, leaving enough room to place the tray. "I'm sorry I dropped your dinner. I'll ask Seok Eng to teach me to prepare this the way you'd prefer."

Mrs. Edevane adjusted the lamp, the flame growing smaller, reflecting blue against the beadwork on her dress. The silk looked difficult to press, fussy with pleats and littered with trim. Hopefully she didn't wear dresses like this all the time, or it was going to make laundering impossible.

"How thoughtful of you. Do you smoke?" Mrs. Edevane asked.

Should she be insulted, or was this some kind of test? "No, but my father did. I can cook for you if you'd like."

Mrs. Edevane waved her over.

Gean Choo crouched beside the table and inspected Mrs. Edevane's paraphernalia. Her opium was of a higher grade than Gean Choo was used to, consisting of a dark, smooth paste wrapped in small squares of wax paper. "How many pipes would you like me to cook?"

"A quarter square will do. I have to run an errand tonight."

Gean Choo glanced at her face, then looked away. Mrs. Edevane didn't seem healthy enough to be running any errands. Her skin was waxy and pale, her eyes heavy-lidded, face lined with fatigue. Her hand shook when she held the pipe, and when she sighed, the prominence of her ribs stood out beneath the thin green silk.

But it wasn't her place to comment. Gean Choo picked up two steel tools and used them to pinch off a piece of the opium, holding it between the needle points. It was a little awkward with one hand partly immobilised by bandages, but she could do this by rote. She brought the paste over the lamp and began kneading it, rotating it constantly to prevent it from burning. As she cooked, the mem continued talking.

"I won't need you for the rest of the night, so you might as well unpack after this." Mrs. Edevane reached over the table and picked up a glass apothecary bottle, shaking a few brown pills into her palm and swallowing them without the benefit of tea or water.

"As you'd like, Mem," Gean Choo said, even though she had already laid out all her possessions, so there was nothing left to unpack.

"Your English is quite good."

"Thank you, Mem."

"Where did you learn? Here or overseas?"

As if her father could've afforded to send her anywhere for her education. Perhaps once, before his habits had proven his downfall. But even if he'd had the funds, he wouldn't have wasted them on a mere girl. "Here, Mem."

"You're one of Miss Skelford's girls."

She hadn't been a schoolgirl for some years now. Would Miss Skelford always have a claim on her? "Yes, Mem. She used to teach, although I understand she no longer does."

"Quite. Are you Straits-born?"

"No, Mem. My family's from Amoy. My father... thought it important for me to learn English."

And how she'd cried for him to leave her be. The girls from down the street didn't have to go to school, so why did she? The other pupils had all been proficient already, forming bonds and groups, but none with room for her. She'd been so shy the first few months the headmistress had implied she was a mute.

"We're both expatriates, then." Mrs. Edevane smiled, forming dimples in her cheeks, her eyes warm yet pained. She was lovely in her suffering, like a venerated saint. Gean Choo bit her tongue; how awful for her to think that! The poor mem all alone in this big empty house, and to be sick on top of that, too.

Yet Mrs. Edevane was still beautiful. There were many European bachelors on the island; some even came without attachments, without concubines still living in a kampong, pale-faced children in tow. Surely she must have callers.

But perhaps she'd loved Mr. Edevane very much.

"What happened to your hand?"

Gean Choo looked at the bandages. "A little accident. Just a scratch."

"Are you accident-prone by nature, or circumstance?"

Gean Choo blushed and glanced up, her mouth suddenly dry.

"I'm just teasing," Mrs. Edevane said. "But you must take care of yourself."

"I will, Mem."

The opium was ready, having turned from a black blob into golden brown taffy. Gean Choo set it down on a little plate, then took a pinch of it using the point of a needle. Mrs. Edevane handed her the pipe, and Gean Choo carefully inserted the single dose, her hands trembling, unlike the last time she'd cooked for someone.

The mem took back the pipe and held it over the lamp. When she breathed in, it was a practised, full breath. She thoughtfully exhaled in the opposite direction, away from Gean Choo's face. The bittersweet cloud was cloying, hovering bluish-white in the dimly lit room.

They repeated the process until all the opium had been smoked. The mem lay back on the couch with her eyes closed, the tension in her face gradually easing. As the last cloud dissipated, Mrs. Edevane tilted her head to one side, looked straight at Gean Choo, and said, "You're a pretty little thing, aren't you?"

Unspoken was the aside "for an Oriental," implicit in her tone and in the way her gaze lingered, consumed, her pupils tiny pinpoints in those colourless eyes.

Gean Choo froze. Everyone had called Mrs. Edevane a widow, but perhaps she had a beau around the house. She couldn't afford to be seen as a liability, a seductress of the East. So many mems were hesitant to have young women working for them, considering them temptations for their husbands. "I'll cut my hair if it displeases you."

"You mistake my meaning." Mrs. Edevane reached out and grasped Gean Choo's chin in her hand, holding it firmly, her red-lacquered finger-nails digging into her flesh. "I like being surrounded by pretty things."

This early in the relationship was the time to set boundaries, to assert all the ways in which she could not be bought. But Mrs. Edevane hadn't beaten her, hadn't insulted her. And if she was a little eccentric, well... what rich person wasn't?

Still with Gean Choo's chin in her hand, Mrs. Edevane extended a finger and stroked her cheek, her nail brushing the side of Gean Choo's mouth. Her touch was cold, startlingly so in the muggy heat of the too-dark room.

Gean Choo dropped her gaze and held her tongue. A rap at the door made her startle, and the mem finally released her.

"The room's ready for you, Mem," Po Lam called from behind the door.

Mrs. Edevane offered Gean Choo a wan smile. "It seems we must be off. Help me downstairs, would you?"

They ended up with Mrs. Edevane's arm around her shoulder and

Gean Choo's hand upon her waist, steadying her. They walked downstairs in this fashion, Mrs. Edevane's pale, narrow hand gripping the banister with white-knuckled intensity. Mrs. Edevane didn't seem well enough to leave the house, but Po Lam didn't seem concerned about the mem's health.

They went through to the back verandah, where Po Lam took over supporting Mrs. Edevane. The two of them navigated the steps down to the garden path, moving with tortuous slowness. They paused long enough for Mrs. Edevane to glance over her shoulder. "I'm quite fine. Go to bed."

Where were they going? The garage was in the other direction. Po Lam had said the mem's room was ready. What room? Maybe the structure at the end of the pier? Perhaps the hush of the ocean soothed her spirit.

There were fewer lights this far from town, which only accentuated the vastness of the night sky and the endless sea. When she gazed above into that star-speckled void, it felt as though she were falling.

When she walked back to the kitchen, the empty pot reminded her that Mrs. Edevane hadn't touched her dinner. Should she fetch the bowl? She probably wasn't meant to enter Mrs. Edevane's room without invitation. But what if there were rats? She shuddered at the thought.

All the lights were still on in the main house when she returned, but of course, no one was there. She went and retrieved the tray without lingering, only stopping to confirm the opium lamp was out.

In the hallway, she considered the food. It would only go to waste, so she tried a little. The soft texture of the blood tofu wasn't bad, each mouthful salty and rich, though it would've been better piping hot in the aromatic broth Seok Eng had made.

After cleaning up in the kitchen, she held her warm, clammy palm to her face. She could still feel the press of Mrs. Edevane's fingers upon her cheek.

## CHAPTER 6

# AFRAID OF THE DARK
### PO LAM

*Saturday, 12 March 1927*
*Ninety minutes ago*

Po Lam drove down Sheik Madersah Lane at a crawl, her window lowered, a cap pulled over her face. Mrs. Edevane didn't like the women she brought home from here—they were too old and diseased to take up a valuable brothel bed, plying their wares in the open, miserable and wretched—but she'd given Po Lam no advance notice. She hadn't been due for a week. Now one broken bowl and the whiff of new blood, and she was already going back on her word.

The headlights caught a pair of naked knees, a woman tugging her sarong down. She walked to Po Lam's window and peered in. Her weathered face, speckled with age spots, was missing half her teeth. "One dollar ten minutes, two dollars half an hour."

"I'll give you ten if we go back to my house."

She held out her hand. "Pay first."

Po Lam gave her five. "The rest after."

The woman tucked the note into her shirt and got in the car, reeking of hard living—unwashed hair and stale beer, clothes crusty with sweat. "Your boss not want to come here? Too good for that?"

"Maybe."

The woman leaned back against her seat as if relaxing. Po Lam would have to tell Zaid to go over them with the polish again. "Any cigarettes?" the woman asked.

"No," Po Lam said, even though the edge of her cigarette case dug into her hip when she shifted her weight. Although the mem smoked, she preferred her women to abstain.

They drove the rest of the way in silence. At the estate, Po Lam led the woman to the servants' quarters. She pulled a fresh towel and clothing from the storeroom, then handed them over. "Wash yourself and your hair, then put these on."

"So fussy," the woman said, her voice hoarse, but she took the clothes eagerly. "Want to join me?"

"I'll wait outside."

The woman went into the bathroom and shut the door behind her.

Po Lam leaned against the wall and took out a cigarette, lighting it. Maybe it was time to ask Mrs. Edevane for another raise. Po Lam's youngest sister had just finished her confinement—twins!—and the next oldest was due again. She'd probably given birth by now, come to think of it, though the news wouldn't reach Po Lam for some time. Their husbands couldn't be relied upon to provide for them. Life back home was indifferently cruel, even for women who'd done everything right. It wasn't fair, but the world never was.

She'd finished her cigarette and was contemplating another when the bathroom door creaked open. The woman appeared with the towel draped around her neck. She smelled infinitely better. "Happy?" she asked.

Po Lam jerked her head towards the door. "Come with me." She took them down the back of the garden, where the grass gave way to sand and a covered jetty led out over the water, ending in a pavilion raised on stilts over the sea. Inside, the single light failed to turn on when Po Lam flicked its switch. The furniture consisted of two sofas, covered by dust cloths, their shapes lumpy and shadowed in the dark. Po Lam felt around near the windows and opened the shutters by touch, revealing what would've been a panoramic view of the ocean, had there been enough daylight to see it.

The woman sat on one of the sofas, making it creak. "You got a lamp?"

"Afraid of the dark?"

The woman rasped a laugh. The faint starlight streaming in through the shutters was enough to catch the gleam of her lips, the shine of her eyes. "Only of what's in the dark."

"Wait here," Po Lam said. "I'll get your client."

The woman made a vague noise of assent. "Hey," she said as Po Lam reached the door, "you've been kind to me tonight. What's your name?"

There was no reason to lie. "Po Lam."

"I'm Lei Heung."

This was the worst part, when they tried to humanise themselves. If only she could forget they even shared the same species at all.

"I'm from Tsungfa," the woman went on. "You know it?"

"No," Po Lam lied.

The woman was probably not much older than Po Lam's thirty-three years, but she wore each of those years in the wrinkles fracturing her face and in the stoop of her shoulders. "Hard life, there. Then this man, funny, handsome, tells me I can make all sorts of money overseas. Good work. Washing, cleaning. You know?"

Po Lam said nothing. She knew the woman's story because it'd once been her story, too. Oh, the details were different, but the theme remained the same—to be born a poor woman was to live a life of misery. She couldn't let her sisters endure that, not when she had the means to help them.

"Wish I could find him again. I'd stick an awl through his eye," the woman said, sighing in pleasure as if imagining the slide of the spike going in.

She'd never get that chance. Po Lam closed the door and locked it behind her, then went to fetch the mem.

*Now*

Mrs. Edevane came out of the pavilion, patting a handkerchief against her lips. She could stand without assistance, clacking away in her heels with a spring in her step. She fished inside her purse and brought out a compact, leaning against the railing as she reapplied powder and lipstick by touch, pressing her lips together several times to even out the paint.

Po Lam tried not to look at her. Freshly satiated, the mem was radiant, her complexion glowing, her smile infectious. It was easier to deal with her when the edge had worn off.

"How do I look?" Mrs. Edevane asked.

Po Lam drew out her handkerchief and lightly dabbed at the side of the mem's mouth, soaking up a spot of blood. "All right."

Mrs. Edevane laughed and closed her compact with a snap. "Oh, come now, you can do better than that." She dropped her voice to a conspiratorial whisper. "I'm sure our new girl would've said I looked divine."

Yes, she probably would have. The last maid had lasted a year. This one could go faster. She had the look of someone dazzled by the lure of imperial finery, by the promise of easy living, and a dozen little luxuries. And why not? After all, the newborn calf had no fear of the tiger.

Mrs. Edevane put her cosmetics away and walked down the length of the pier. The wind picked up, pressing her skirts to her legs, teasing out curls of her hair. In the next moment, she was gone. A faint cloud of smoke hung where she'd stood, dissipating on the breeze.

Po Lam opened the door to the pavilion and got to work.

ZAID WAITED BY THE BOAT, ankle-deep in wet sand as Po Lam deposited the body into the sampan. Together, they wrestled the limp limbs into a hessian sack. Po Lam went to the garden shed and picked up a stack of terracotta tiles, dislodging a pair of lizards that scuttled off into the night. Back at the boat, she slipped the tiles into the sack one by one.

Zaid climbed into the sampan, taking up the oars. Po Lam pushed the boat off the sandbar then climbed in herself, dripping seawater.

They didn't speak. A small oil lamp hung at the front of the sampan, glimmering over the waves. They took turns rowing until the lights from the house were lost from view, then Po Lam holstered the oars and seized one end of the sack, Zaid taking the other.

As they lifted the sack over the edge of the boat, the hessian moved beneath her grip. A strange sound, like a groan, emanated from the bag. "Stop!" She dropped her end of the bag, but it was too late. Zaid's half was already over the side, and now the boat was tipping, water spilling over the edge and drowning their feet. Zaid scrambled to toss the heavy sack into the ocean, the boat rocking violently when the weight finally dropped into the sea.

The sack was a dark shape, quickly sinking beneath the waves. The water and the night distorted everything, but maybe—just maybe—it was still moving...

Po Lam took a deep breath and dove in, ignoring Zaid's alarmed yell. She swam quickly, reaching out into the dark. By some quirk of fate, her hand closed around the hessian, but it slipped from her grasp. Kicking harder, she reached out again, securing it. She groped in her pocket for a switchblade and sawed through the ribbon holding the bag shut. She fumbled with the cloth, clumsy in the dark, in the depths, her lungs burning for air. The switchblade fell from her hand as she grabbed Lei Heung under the arms, hauling her up towards the surface.

When her head broke water, she'd not taken more than half a breath before a wave swept over her, momentarily dunking her under. For a moment, she couldn't see the boat and dread crept down her spine. Lei Heung's weight against her shoulder was an unmoving, limp mass. She turned counter-clockwise, found the light from the sampan, and called out, waving one arm as the waves rocked her up and down, dragging her farther from the boat.

Some merciful ancestor must've been smiling down, for the light grew brighter. She swam towards it, dragging Lei Heung with her. When she drew near, Zaid's oar almost clipped her on the shoulder.

"Why did you do that?" Zaid asked, grimacing as Po Lam gestured to her burden. "You want to follow her, too?"

Despite his grumbling, he helped drag Lei Heung back into the boat, and then extended his hand to Po Lam. Once she was onboard, they both stared at the body sprawled against the hull, limbs all akimbo.

Po Lam unhooked the lantern and brought it over. Lei Heung was cold, her neck stiff, and her eyes were unresponsive to touch or light.

"Dead for sure lah," Zaid said.

Perhaps she hadn't been a few minutes ago? Had they drowned a live woman? But her skin was so cold and pale, the jagged gash across her neck white with scar tissue. Po Lam sat down, tepid water sloshing around her ankles, the lantern braced on her knees. Something had moved in the sack.

It had.

Hadn't it?

Zaid stared at her oddly. "You're not feeling well?"

She fixed the lantern back near the prow and took up the oars, even though her arms still burned from her impromptu dive.

"What're we doing?" Zaid asked.

"We need a new shroud. And more weights."

"We're out so far already; might as well finish now."

Part of her wanted to agree. It was the gleam over Lei Heung's eyes, open forever. If they left her in the ocean, at least Po Lam wouldn't have to look at her for much longer. "You want her to wash up on the tide like this? What would the neighbours say?"

"One dead whore, anyone could've killed her like that. No one cries for poor women."

No. Po Lam wouldn't cry for her, either.

But she'd row back to shore to cover Lei Heung's face and save her eyeballs from the gulls.

"You don't have to come with me the second trip," she said, blinking away a stinging trail of saltwater as it dripped from her hairline.

"Who's going to save you next time?" Zaid shook his head as he took the oars from her, slicing through the water in long, smooth motions.

Her shoulders ached and her heart was still pounding from the swim. She grabbed the front of her shirt and wrung it out, though it did little good when the rest of her was still wet. When was the last time she'd done anything that stupid?

"All right?" Zaid asked.

"Yes," she said, and tried not to look at the body in the boat, with its blank, uncaring face open to the sky.

# CHAPTER 7

## THE MEM EATS THIS?

### GEAN CHOO

*Sunday, 13 March 1927*

Gean Choo slept poorly. It was far too quiet with just Po Lam and Zaid around. She was used to someone hacking up their lungs in the middle of the night, or people getting up to relieve themselves. The ever-present need to diagnose every single itch or tingle —was it a cockroach or a mouse?

She woke once, when Mrs. Edevane returned from whatever business she'd had, humming some unfamiliar tune as she passed through the garden. Was Gean Choo dreaming? Those footsteps seemed far too quick to belong to the sickly mem.

By mid-morning, she'd given up on sleep. She'd missed breakfast, but as she stumbled into the kitchen, she found a plate had been left for her, covered to ward off vermin. Underneath was thick-cut bread generously spread with kaya and two eggs still in their shells.

She was still eating when Seok Eng breezed in, baskets hanging from her arms, the curved rattan digging into her skin as she carried a wooden crate with "Cold Storage" stamped on the side. Gean Choo stood. "Let me help you."

Seok Eng passed her the crate, and she staggered under the weight of it. "Ice box in storeroom, all right?" Seok Eng said.

The crate was so big it obscured her view, but she made it into the storeroom, only banging her elbow against the wall once. She set down the crate and took the used tray of melted water from the icebox, throwing it on the lawn outside. Bits of sawdust clung to the grass.

"I'm sorry I slept in," she said to Seok Eng, who was now emptying several apothecary bottles into a mortar. "Thank you for leaving me breakfast."

"You should nap later," Seok Eng said, putting an empty bottle back on the counter. "Or you can help me if you can't sleep."

"I'd be happy to. Oh! And... I broke a bowl last night. I'm sorry."

"It's all right."

Gean Choo went back to the storeroom to unpack, brushing the sawdust off a large block of ice in the crate. She placed it in the tray and fitted the tray back onto the top shelf of the icebox, then proceeded to unload the rest, liquid blood in jars and an armful of vegetables.

Back in the kitchen, she ate the last of her toast, savouring the sticky rich sweetness and licking her fingers. She took the plate to the wash bucket to clean up. "Does the mem take blood very often?"

Seok Eng shrugged with one shoulder. "All the time. I say, variety is good, better for the body, wouldn't you agree? But she's stubborn. It doesn't matter—rice, toast, she always has to have this on the side."

"Could you show me how to make it some time?"

"Stir together salt and blood only, then simmer. It's not hard." Seok Eng lit the oven, adding an additional burden to the already hot day. There was only a slight breeze moving through the opened windows. How awful the first floor must be right now, muggy and warm, closed up like a tomb.

Yet the mem's hands had felt like ice, hadn't they? It must've been her imagination; no one could possibly live in this climate and still feel so cold. But then there'd been Miss Skelford, too. When Gean Choo had kissed her goodbye a few days ago, her mouth had barely felt tepid, like kissing a dead thing.

Seok Eng unpacked the rest of her purchase, a jar filled with more blood.

"Are we making blood tofu?" Gean Choo asked.

"No." Seok Eng took several metal trays from a cupboard and poured blood into each one before sliding them into the oven.

"And the mem... eats this?"

"Not like that. When it's all dry, I crush it together with these and make new tablets," Seok Eng said, picking out an apothecary bottle of opaque amber glass from her basket.

The label only had Chinese characters, which Gean Choo couldn't read. "Mrs. Edevane must be quite sick if she needs so much medicine."

Seok Eng frowned. "With the hot weather and being so humid, many ang mo get sick like that."

"I know we're not supposed to talk about it, but why—"

"If you know, you know." Seok Eng handed Gean Choo the bottle of pills, showing her the mortar with pink residue still clinging to its sides and a bowl half-filled with pink powder. "Make sure to get it fine. No lumps, all right?"

Gean Choo picked up the mortar and pestle, hugging its weight close to her chest, the marble reassuringly solid against her ribs. She sat on the floor, hooking her leg around the mortar to hold it close, and poured in a handful of pills. They were pale pink, the width of her smallest fingernail. When she crushed them, little puffs of powder spurted up from beneath the pestle.

She was halfway through the first bottle when Po Lam walked into the kitchen. Po Lam leaned against the wall, her feet bare beneath a pair of loose pants. "Afternoon."

Gean Choo looked up for a moment and almost crushed her finger from inattention. There was a stillness about Po Lam in the way she held herself, in the terseness of her sentences, conveying only what was needed and nothing more. As if she had to keep herself distant. In control.

What would it take to see that control unmoored?

"Thought you'd still be sleeping," Seok Eng said.

"If only." Po Lam looked at Gean Choo. "She's got you hard at work."

"This one volunteered," Seok Eng protested.

"I'm always happy to help Auntie," Gean Choo said, almost catching her finger again. Clearly, she couldn't sneak glances at Po Lam and crush pills at the same time.

"I'll be outside if she wakes early," Po Lam said, with no need to specify who "she" was.

What kind of business needed fragile Mrs. Edevane's attention so late at night? The question was on the tip of her tongue, but she held it as Po Lam left the kitchen. She continued working the pestle until the pills were all reduced to a fine pink powder. "I've finished, Auntie."

"Good, good. Would you fetch some coriander? It's down the western side, past the generator shed."

Gean Choo left the kitchen and slipped on her shoes. Alif, the young Malay gardener, was standing along the fence line by the herb garden, chatting to someone on the other side.

She froze. Was it too late to turn away? No. Yes. He'd recognised her.

"Hey, Teo's girl. What a surprise to see you here." Lai Hock was leaning with elbows resting over the fence, cropped hair gleaming in the sunlight, mouth pulled wide in a grin. His gaze dropped to her outrageously over-bandaged hand. "What's the matter? Hurt yourself?"

She covered the bandages with her other hand. "I'm fine." She walked closer and picked the coriander, the stalks releasing the sharp scent of sap.

"I was just in the neighbourhood, making a delivery. Maybe I'll see you around some time again, eh?"

She turned her back and walked away, green stems clenched in her fist. Mrs. Edevane had no guards, no security. It was Gean Choo's duty to warn her. At the very least, she had to warn Po Lam. Or could she pay him off before he ever made good on his threats?

Seok Eng glanced up as she approached. "You find it?" She tutted as Gean Choo handed over the coriander. "This part is all crushed some more."

"Sorry, Auntie."

"Finish that bottle. I've another two after it."

They both got back to work. The pestle made a rhythmic thudding noise, but it couldn't distract Gean Choo from the thoughts clouding her mind.

Nine hundred dollars.

Four weeks.

She was utterly out of her depth.

# CHAPTER 8

# MY LORD

## VERITY

*Monday, 21 March 1927*
*Nine nights since last meal*

Verity took her time getting dressed, picking out an airy white frock in silk organza. White wasn't her colour, but it didn't matter. She was making a point.

She was obliged to do her own hair. It took so long to train a girl, and she hadn't yet managed with this new one. Once she'd slid the last bobby pin into place by feel, it was time to attend to her make-up.

One cruelty of her condition was the impossibility of seeing her face. She'd tried, in vain, all sorts of contraptions. Mirrors, of course. Silverware. Nothing produced an image, not even the camera, when it had come along—and she'd been compelled to drain the darkroom clerk. Artists were her last bastion of hope, but they could never be trusted.

So she kept things simple. Powder and a light swipe of blush. And her lips, by feel, in an inoffensive pink close enough to her natural colour to make any mistakes less obvious. But oh, how she longed for the new liberties given to this generation, for bold carmine and scarlet, for burgundy and magenta.

She rose from her toilette and glanced at the opium pipe before choosing to swallow a few of Cookie's little magic pills. They were getting harder to procure, with the damn government insisting on meddling in everything these days. The taste was awful—non-human blood and bitter quinine, strychnine, caffeine, and heroin... plus whatever else the apothecary had included as filler.

No matter. It was enough that she could consume it at all, that she'd found something to tide her over in between proper meals. It was a pity pharmaceuticals didn't affect her kind the same way it did humans—a pity or a blessing. They provided little benefit for her, besides taking the edge off the night, but she didn't crave them, either.

That was probably for the best.

The new girl was rearranging cushions on the drawing room couches downstairs. Verity walked over to her and the girl startled, holding a cushion against her chest as if that could protect her from anything.

"Mem. Good evening," the girl said. "You look well."

"Thank you." Verity smiled to show her teeth. "I'm feeling much better."

It wouldn't last, of course. Not for the whole, empty month, another three long weeks without a decent feed... but now? Now warmth filled her veins, buoying her with pulsing wings.

Mingled scents of motor oil, dirt, soap, and sweat heralded Po Lam's presence before the woman came inside. Not entirely unpleasant. "Good evening, Mem. I've placed the latest reports in your study."

"Anything that should concern me?"

Po Lam shook her head. "The manager thinks they'll be on track to meet quotas by the end of the year."

"How marvellous." Verity flicked the end of her scarf over her shoulder and spoke to the new girl. "When you're done with that, give my sheets a turn. You'll find fresh ones in the hallway closet."

"Yes, Mem."

"Will you be needing me tonight?" Po Lam asked, her face blank and devoid of emotion as usual.

"Yes." Verity glanced at the clock. "I'm due at Cottesley's in an hour. I suppose I should eat. Bring it upstairs, would you?"

Po Lam nodded and Verity left them, heading back to her study.

A KNOCK CAME at the door a few minutes later, too hesitant to be Po Lam. "Come in."

The new girl entered with a tray full of blood jelly on rice and a cup of undrinkable tea. At Verity's waved hand, she placed them down on the desk, away from her paperwork. She was wearing the same off-white shirt and black pants as yesterday, or a set so alike that Verity could not tell them apart. "Are all your clothes like that?"

The girl glanced down at herself. "Yes."

Verity put her books to one side and rose from her desk. "Come with me."

She went down the hallway and stopped at the linen closet, rising on her toes to grab a pile of soft, well-worn clothes. She handed them to the girl.

"You're about her height. I think these should do," she said. The new girl came up to just below Verity's chin. Maybe a little shorter than Jade.

"Thank you," the girl said, her voice lowered to a whisper.

Verity waved her off. "Well, go change, then."

The girl dropped into an awkward half-bow and left. She really was hopeless.

Alone in her study, Verity rearranged the items on her plate, gnawed on her blood jelly, and skimmed her books. Even warmed, the foodstuff bore almost no resemblance to the real thing—springy in texture, mauve in colour and unappetising on the tongue. It was palatable only to the most indiscriminating consumer.

Three more weeks.

She read her plantation manager's report until it was time to leave. Po Lam had been right, since everything seemed in order. Her discovery of Po Lam had been a blessing. A good servant needed only three things—loyalty, competence, and mortality—and Po Lam had all three. So far. It wouldn't last. Verity was approaching the second century of her undeath, and the only enduring truth—besides herself and the existence of politics—was that good help didn't stay good for long. They always wanted more: holidays, unrealistic salary increases, eternal life. Po Lam had been with her for almost two decades, and she was getting to that point in life when humans became nervous about mortality. But Po Lam had not made any such demands. Yet.

Downstairs, Verity almost collided with the new girl, who was carrying her sheets away. She'd put on one of Jade's old dresses, the one in sky blue, with a fashionably dropped waist and the hemline falling just under the knee. Her bare calf made it obvious she needed hose. That, and new shoes; something prettier than the cloth disasters she wore.

"Much better," Verity said, because any improvement was worth praising, at least in the beginning.

The girl blushed and stammered her thanks. Verity left her to work, heading into the garage where Po Lam was waiting.

"What's the new girl's name again?" Verity asked as she slid into the back seat, wrinkling her nose at the scent of unwashed whore. No matter how carefully the car was cleaned afterwards, there was always something amiss. She ought to get another vehicle just for pickups.

"Gean Choo."

It sounded like a sneeze. "Take her to town next month to get her hair cut." The delay was in case she ran. No point prettying up a girl who didn't have the nerve. "And she'll need hose and shoes... probably underwear, as well. The usual."

Po Lam hesitated. "There's no reason Zaid couldn't do it—"

"Nonsense! I can't possibly allow a young woman to go off with a man she's barely acquainted with. Besides, he'd be useless at the modiste." One of them might as well take advantage of the newest styles. If Verity tried to keep her hair in a real bob, she'd need it to be cut every time she woke up. No one had time for that, not in this wretched place with fewer than twelve hours of true night.

It was a shame she'd never see the shopping district in the daytime. This decade was a delight after years of stays and coutil, of hemlines caked in filth and impossible skirts. Good riddance to all that ridiculous froth.

Po Lam drove her to Bukit Timah. The night was clear for a change, the stars bright. Not the right constellations, all of them turned sideways and barely recognisable. Verity braced her arm against the door and leant her chin in her hand, staring into the night.

Damn this exile. Charming and rustic as it was, she'd had enough of short nights and perpetual mould, of narrow-eyed Chinamen and their slim-hipped daughters. She'd been floating about the Straits Settlements for what... almost ninety years?

Long enough for tempers to cool and hearts to change.

But their new overseer seemed disinclined to mercy. Lord Kalon Cottesley had only been here since February. The council had shipped him out from a sojourn in India, where he'd apparently struck fear in the hearts of both the governing humans and the vampiric population.

His stay was meant to be temporary. He'd achieved the council's objective of investigating the murder of his predecessor, the easy-going and much-mourned Winston Lawrence. But that was all weeks in the past, now.

Perhaps she'd be lucky; perhaps this party was Kalon's means of announcing his retirement from island life.

She didn't feel lucky.

A FEW DOZEN kindred milled inside Kalon's home; the men in dark suits, the women in glittering gowns. Everyone was aggressively cheerful, smiles too brittle, laughter too high-pitched, washing away the memories of their last gathering with glasses sourced from Kalon's own household.

Daphne Ainsworth approached her, stunning as always in a bronze metallic frock that made the most of her long legs. She'd cut her brown hair into a bob, her bangs blunt across the front.

They exchanged air kisses. "Darling, you're late." Daphne dropped her voice to a whisper. "You know how this new one loathes a laggard."

She knew. She knew, but she couldn't quite bring herself to care. Council lapdogs were all the same: all bark and no bite. "I trust you covered for me?" They couldn't hope to be inconspicuous standing together, not with Daphne being taller than most men and her gown glimmering like a beacon. Verity glanced around the room. Their host seemed to be absent. Perhaps he wouldn't notice her tardiness.

"It wounds me that you feel obliged to ask," Daphne said, pressing a cream-gloved hand over her heart in mock consternation. They'd first met in the 1800s, in Toulouse, back when Daphne had been going by a different name, favouring suits over frocks.

A man approached Daphne from behind, slapping her shoulder hard enough that blood sloshed from her glass and spattered all over her gloves. "Oh! Dreadfully sorry, M—" he caught himself in time, "Mrs. Ainsworth."

"Accidents happen," Daphne said, passing the half-empty glass to a servant and stripping off her gloves. "But I daresay you owe me a new pair of gloves, Mr. Haywarde."

Freddie Haywarde was a round-faced, obnoxiously cheerful man, who still wore muttonchops, even though it was so last century. He laughed, his cheeks flushing, a sign he'd definitely been drinking too much. "Of course, of course." He spied someone from across the room and waved her over. "Mrs. Ainsworth, Mrs. Edevane, have you met my youngest, Miss Justine Skelford?"

Youngest referred only to the order in which he'd sired her, not the age of the poor woman at undeath. Justine must've been pushing forty-five or thereabouts, with a faint tracery of wrinkles around her eyes and mouth, now permanently etched. She was a mousy brunette, newly fledged, her blood so thin she had to ward off mosquitoes by hand. How Freddie had ever secured approval to make her was beyond Verity's understanding. She was so, so very common.

Justine exchanged greetings with Daphne, then turned a fawning smile to Freddie. "I've actually met Mrs. Edevane before, and I had the pleasure of sourcing her latest amah. Do tell me, Mrs. Edevane, how is she working out for you?"

"She's just delightful." Easy on the eyes, at least, and charming in how she startled every time Verity walked into the room. As if she could sense what Verity was. What she wanted.

Maybe she could.

"A new girl? Again? You go through those like I go through husbands," Daphne said.

Jade's death was still an abscess in Verity's soul, raw and oozing. "The most precious blossoms are the ones that bloom but for a day."

There was a change in the air, a prickle that set the fine hairs on the back of Verity's neck tingling. The hush came a moment later, rippling through the crowd, people breaking off mid-laugh. Verity checked her expression, fixing it into an amiable mask, bracing herself not to lose her composure, no matter what might happen. Surely he wouldn't repeat the events of his last gathering. There weren't that many bad apples left to flay.

As if reading her mind, Daphne glanced towards the verandah, in the direction of the garden. Verity suppressed her shudder.

Once upon a time, a kindred's death wouldn't have caused such a fuss. Centuries ago, before the Code and before the council, they'd killed each other with impunity. Inter-bloodline wars, entire families wiped out in a single night. Of course, back then humans had still believed in ghosts and ghouls, and so the fallout from such rash displays of power hadn't held the same consequence as they now did in this modern age, with the world made small by motorcars and telephones.

The Code classified murdering their own kind as a capital offence. And so Kalon had claimed his pound of flesh, and more, besides.

The sight of their lord, in the end, was almost anti-climactic—just a clean-shaven man in a suit. He had a lean, pensive face, nose slightly upturned as though he were perpetually cognisant of an unpleasant smell.

The hum of conversation began again as Kalon made his way through his guests. Since Verity had been among the last to arrive, they were still huddled near the front of the room and had to amuse themselves with stilted, vapid conversation until he deigned to grace them with his company.

"Is it true you haven't availed yourself of human blood since the Great War, Mrs. Edevane? What a sacrifice!" Justine said.

"Dear Verity is such a martyr," Daphne said dryly before drinking from a freshly-tapped glass of blood. The smell of it—oh, that smell, coppery-rich and salty, heady and seductive. It was both the worst and the best part of these horrible little get-togethers, being surrounded by that miasma, but unable to make herself partake in it. But it smelled better than it would taste. Thrall blood always came with a trace of bitterness; something like guilt.

Her stomach clenched with a wrenching spasm, her empty hands aching for a cigarette. But of course, Kalon didn't allow smoking inside. Such an ascetic. "I can't help but pity the thralls. Some fates are worse than death, would you not agree, Miss Skelford?" Verity asked.

"Yes, yes, of course, but to not own a single thrall? I can't imagine it. I must say, your trick with the blood... jelly is ingenious. But don't you miss it? The real thing, I mean," Justine asked.

Freddie clapped his fledgling on the shoulder. "Everyone misses it, my dear. Not so long ago, a raw human wasn't considered indecorous."

Even Daphne nodded. Fancy that, a subject they all agreed upon. Verity missed those days like she missed the first touch of real sunshine after a long, dark winter. Those gluttonous feasts where the halls echoed with screams, where the body count necessitated a dozen trips by the coachmen to clear out the dead.

Nothing like that ever happened now. The Great War had certainly flustered the Powers That Be, the sudden realisation that humans could muster such extreme firepower en masse. What if they discovered the monsters hiding in their midst? They'd certainly be better armed than the vampire-hunters of old.

Thus, the amendments to the Code. No more leisurely dining in the open, leaving a corpse behind each night. No more terrorising a village or two, just for the sheer thrill of it.

No more fun.

Of course, life happened more slowly in the colonies. Rules were interpreted laterally—at least, they had been, under dear dead Winston.

Since his successor had taken over, all the humans came peacefully, like lambs to the slaughter, and none died, unless one was careless.

And no one was ever careless twice in Lord Cottesley's house.

The man himself circled around to their group. In her mind, she always imagined him to be taller. He was still taller than she, around the same height as Daphne. They took turns greeting him. Verity went last, sinking to her knees before him with practised ease and brushing her lips against the knuckles of his outstretched hand. She struggled not to flinch at the unexpected warmth of his skin. He'd wasted blood to put heat into his touch, making it seem almost... human.

He stared at her, unsmiling, his blue eyes boring into her own. She ought to say something light-hearted, perhaps compliment his pearl-white, perfectly pressed waistcoat, but the words died in her throat. She couldn't forget the sight of him from their last gathering, his sleeves rolled back, bloodied up to the elbows, candlelight flickering gold and orange across the hunting knife dripping in his hand.

Did he know? He couldn't know. How? Besides, killing humans was a misdemeanour, not a capital offence. The worst she'd suffer would be a slap on the wrist.

He tucked a lock of hair behind her ear. She shivered, fighting the urge to bare her throat. Upon his arrival in the Straits, she'd been obliged, like the rest of them, to swear fealty with her breath and her blood. Their kind depended on hierarchy, were unfairly obsessed with it. Human revolutions had done nothing to shake the core of the vampiric aristocracy.

In the end, it didn't matter that she'd lost her appetite for small talk because Kalon spent the next few minutes conducting a strangely one-sided conversation with Justine of all people. Verity rose to her feet, biting back her frown, and smoothed down her skirts.

"I was glad to hear your health improved post-rebirth, Miss Skelford. Particularly your cough. Would you say the incidence of coughing has improved a little? A lot?" Kalon asked without any preamble or word for the rest of them. His voice was a smooth tenor, perfectly modulated. His bloodline was able to compel humans with the faintest whisper or the most vehement shout. Speakers swore they could do nothing against another kindred, but Verity had her doubts.

Justine glanced around, wide-eyed, fidgeting with her strands of faux pearls. "Th-thank you, my lord. I've not experienced any coughing since..." She glanced at Freddie.

"Since your rebirth," Freddie finished for her. "Yes, now that you mention it, I believe that's right."

Kalon didn't acknowledge him. "And you still smoke, Miss Skelford?"

Justine pursed her lips, as if considering whether to lie. Everyone knew Kalon found smoking a filthy habit, too human by halves. Verity silently willed her to do it.

"Yes, my lord," Justine said to everyone's disappointment, except perhaps Freddie's.

"And you haven't noticed any ill effects? Chest pain, sore throat, hoarseness of voice?"

Justine shook her head, trying not to show her surprise at this line of questioning. "I understand the rebirth differs for everyone, but I certainly can't complain. I mean, I'm terribly grateful, of course," she said, looping her arm with Freddie's and leaning into him.

"You're welcome, my dear," Freddie said.

A servant came up and whispered to Kalon, who turned back to their little group with a smile on his face. "The band is ready for us. Shall we adjourn to the ballroom?"

THE REST of the night passed with music and dancing and drinking—so much drinking, all around her, from elegant crystal glasses filled by blank-faced servants. Verity had to step away from it all, her head pounding with the beginning of a migraine.

She hadn't gone far enough.

"Mem? Mem. Excuse me. The tuan says no smoking in here."

Verity's cigarette holder was already halfway raised to her lips. She completed its arc, inhaled, then exhaled towards Kalon's unfortunate boy. The servant grimaced, his pinched, weathered face scrunching up tight.

Part of her couldn't help but marvel at Kalon's control over his thralls. The boy had probably smoked like a chimney before entering Kalon's service, yet here he was, sharing his master's deep disapproval, as though he'd never smoked a day in his life.

"It's all right. I'm heading outdoors," Verity said.

Kalon had amused himself by filling the back of the estate with topiaries. Where had he found so many hedges on such short notice? His gardeners were skilled at their craft. There was a cyclops, looming ten feet tall, with an axe in one hand and a shield in the other, and a glorious phoenix, her tail an enormous swathe of green. Other monsters, both beautiful and hideous, lined the wide pathway leading to the obligatory tennis court and a freshwater pool.

At least the air was clean here, without the all-too-tempting miasma of freshly-drained blood. It would be another three weeks or so before she could feed again. She groped in her purse for some of Cookie's pills and swallowed them, wincing as they battered her dry throat. The schedule gave her only the bare minimum she needed to survive. Every one of these horrible get-togethers was a reminder, a slap in the face, that she needn't be so stubborn. She could drink her fill if she wanted, fill her household with an entire stable of thralls. She'd probably need a larger estate.

If she wanted. If she could condemn those poor souls to a twilight half-existence, neither dead nor unalive nor undead. Awful.

The occasional corpse was a small price to pay in comparison.

One of Kalon's servants came up to her, a Sikh man wearing a pure white turban, contrasting with his navy tunic and pants. "Excuse me. My lord wishes to speak with you," he said in lovely, though accented, English.

Verity flicked out her spent cigarette butt and stamped it into the ground. "Whatever for?" she asked, but of course the man didn't respond. Instead, he gestured her towards the house.

INSIDE, the smell seemed even worse than before, that cloying miasma of fresh blood, human and warm. Verity's hunger choked her like the hangman's noose. It was all she could do to keep walking, to move as if she didn't care, to smile as if she weren't starving.

The lord himself was in the billiard room, standing with glass in hand, surrounded by a handful of kindred. Enormous paintings dominated two of the walls, one of Leda and the swan, and another of an unfortunate maiden being harried by a death's head figure in a tattered cloak, ravens circling overhead.

The scent of blood was worse in this room, for all that no one had been drinking upon her arrival. Kalon turned towards her as she entered. He had his arm around the shoulders of Emiel Thyssen, a short, stocky man of Dutch extraction, a century old, formerly of the East Indies. Emiel had a vague grimace on his face, as though he shared Verity's discomfort.

"Mr. Thyssen was just explaining the multi-sire hypothesis to us. Are you familiar, Mrs. Edevane?" Kalon asked.

"I'm afraid I am not."

"Leofric Greenwood had this theory," Kalon released Emiel, leaving both hands free to gesticulate, "that one could combine bloodlines in a fledgling. The same as two parents contributing to create a single child."

She glanced at Emiel for help, but the man only shrugged. Useless. "But that's impossible."

"Conventional wisdom says so. Greenwood did not endear himself to his local kindred—something about using their progeny as test subjects. Someone staked him about a century ago, but his papers lived on. They were even expanded upon to postulate that if one could create a fledgling with multiple bloodlines, what about a vampire already in their prime? What if one person could have several gifts, several inheritances? Wouldn't they be... unstoppable?" Kalon said the last word with a kind of reverence, as if he really believed such a thing could be so.

It would upend the order of precedence. It would change everything. "The council would never allow it."

"You're right, Mrs. Edevane. Of course." His smile curved on his face, teeth white and gleaming. Was this a test? Did he know about her killings, her minor deviations from the Code?

He was the council's attack dog. Everything was a test.

Kalon cleared his throat, making her tense, and waved everyone else out of the room. When they'd all gone, Kalon ushered her to a lounge and sat. "Please. Sit. I'd offer you someone to drink, but..." he raised his shoulders in a shrug, "I fear they wouldn't meet your ethical standards."

Verity sat on the sofa perpendicular to him. "I've eaten, thank you."

"You are an inspiration to us all." He took a glass from a side table, raised it, and drained it in a few long gulps.

Verity held her hands perfectly still on her lap, her nails digging into her thighs.

Kalon smiled, a sheen of red marring the perfect white of his teeth. "I know how these soirées bore you, so I shan't keep you long." He reached into his pocket, pulled out a notebook, and flipped it open. "The tecoma should be blooming now. I was hoping you might oblige me with your company. Would you care to take a drive with me... say, the ninth of April?"

A drive? To where? And for what? Verity swallowed, her dry throat making it feel as though she were swallowing glass. "If my lord wills it."

"Splendid! I look forward to it."

Sometime later, Verity stumbled out of the house, requiring Po Lam's assistance to lead her to the car. Without her presence, it was quite possible she'd have tried to climb into someone else's vehicle.

What on earth could he possibly want?

# CHAPTER 9

## DOES SHE HAVE A BEAU?

### GEAN CHOO

*Monday, 4 April 1927*

Gean Choo was getting used to sleeping in late. She woke around lunchtime, after a restless night spent in uneasy terror, alert to any sound that vaguely resembled a knock or a voice. As she sat up, the hollows of the unmade bed called back to her. She'd already grown used to the softness, but she had work to do.

It'd been over three weeks since she'd left the lodging house and Lai Hock's deadline was fast approaching. At least her palm had healed over. Though it held faint traces of a scar, that too would only fade more with time. Perhaps she should wait him out, call his bluff. Surely he wouldn't dare come for her in this house? But he'd already proven how close he could get.

It was her duty to tell someone. But Gean Choo had never been all that virtuous.

She put on her new clothes again that afternoon, ignoring the faint whiff of naphthalene as she shook them out—the lemon-yellow dress, with its floppy bow at the collar. Her legs felt strange and bare. She smoothed down the fabric. Had its previous owner been around her age? Shared her fears, her wants?

Most likely, she'd met some kind of bad end. Perhaps Mrs. Edevane was the sort of mem who became angry when drunk, the sort who struck her servants a little too hard. Po Lam was clearly strong enough to handle a corpse. The verdant backyard could be growing lush over a pile of bodies, bone and blood feeding the earth.

*Stop it, Teo Gean Choo.*

One of the houseboys had made it clear that the mem's laundry was Gean Choo's responsibility, and that she might as well take care of everyone else's, too. Her hours didn't make it easy. Mrs. Edevane didn't usually care for her presence at night, apart from the dinner service, but Gean Choo was always on edge, primed for the bell that would summon her to the mem's study or her drawing room or, just once after that first night, to her bedroom to prepare her opium pipe.

The sky appeared clear, but such appearances were often deceptive. If it rained, she planned to move the drying rack beneath the covered verandah. It had room enough for a six-seater lounge set, but like the deserted tennis court and the empty upstairs verandah, it was devoid of furnishings that would make it a liveable space.

She added her clothes into the wash barrel, with the sheets and other servants' laundry making for a heavy load. She set the mem's silk dresses aside for the dry cleaners, but the green one from that first night was perhaps a lost cause. The hem appeared to have been trailed in mud, and even if that were salvageable, it had another brownish stain near the collar.

She eyed the gardener as she hung the clothes out to dry. Alif, the Malay boy, was round-cheeked, large-eyed, narrow-chested, and wiry. He remained "boy" in her mind, even though he was probably as old as she. When he smiled, which was often, his mouth revealed a gap in the bottom row of teeth. He had strong arms, cords of muscle visible as he wrestled piles of trimmed palm leaves from the ground to the wheelbarrow.

Her father had expressed awful views about Malay people, sentiments she didn't care to repeat, even in the privacy of her own mind. She'd never corrected him during his diatribes. Did that make her complicit? Maybe something of his vitriol had passed down to her, an unwanted inheritance like her too-large feet or her tendency to daydream.

Alif seemed not to notice the labyrinth of her thoughts. She watched him work, his shirt taut over his spine as he leaned to one side. His collar sagged, loose and dark with sweat.

"Gean Choo."

She dropped the wet shirt she'd been holding, then picked it up. At least it was one of her own, now speckled with dirt. She shook it out. "Good afternoon," she said, trying not to blush.

"Are you almost done with the laundry?" Po Lam's hardened gaze drifted to Alif, suggesting she was in a slightly worse mood than usual.

"Yes. Is there something you'd like me to do next? I noticed the upstairs needed dusting, but perhaps one of the others intended to—"

"The mem wanted me to take you to town. To go," her voice dropped a few notes in distaste, "marketing."

Gean Choo spread out the last pillowcase, emptying her basket. "Of course. Let me put this away and I'll be right with you."

She could think of few things that gave her more anxiety—the prospect of being trapped in a car and then in a shop for possibly hours on end with Po Lam, but there was nothing for it. On the drive down, she squeezed her hands in her lap, trying to give herself courage. Start with the easy questions. "What are we buying?"

"Shoes. Clothes. A haircut."

"For me?" Her mind skipped back to that first day when Mrs. Edevane's fingers had dug into her jaw. Perhaps the mem wanted to mar her appearance after all. An irrational flash of vanity arced through her like lightning, grief and outrage all in one. "Does she have a beau?"

"What?" Po Lam scowled. "No."

"Who was she seeing the other night, then? And the night before?" The car had hummed down the driveway both times, not arriving back until late.

"It's none of your concern."

It both was and wasn't. She'd have to corner Seok Eng. The older woman seemed more inclined to gossip.

At least there were no serious traffic problems that day, although there were a few more policemen walking the street than before.

They stopped by the shoe store first. When she sat down to be measured, she tried to avoid looking at her feet, calloused and worn from months spent barefoot. They left the store with two boxes, one tan to match everything, and the other black.

The dress shop was next. Po Lam sat in a corner, flicking through a sample book while Gean Choo stripped down to her underwear and an assistant measured her. Was Po Lam glancing her way? No. Every time she looked up, Po Lam was studiously examining the samples, testing a piece of fabric between her thumb and forefinger.

They left the dressmaker's with what seemed to be an excessive amount of underwear, sleepwear, and hosiery. And there was still the order they'd placed for later.

"You have an eye for colour," she said as they walked to their next destination, boxes and clothing in hand.

"One of my uncles is a tailor," Po Lam said grudgingly, as if to speak of her past was to chip away a small part of herself.

Gean Choo couldn't let it go. "Does he live here?"

"No."

"Did you come here when you were young or were you born here?"

"We've arrived," Po Lam said.

The dry cleaners stank of solvent, overpowering the street smells of frying garlic and raw sewerage from open drains. They left Mrs. Edevane's gowns, though the green one was probably unsalvageable.

It was a relief to be back on the street, breathing in the relatively fresh air. Gean Choo could've used a drink and something to eat, but instead, Po Lam walked her to a hairdresser.

The hairdresser was a steely-eyed auntie, plying her business along the five-foot way, the covered walkway outside a row of shop houses. She'd plastered posters on the wall behind her with glamorous models, their curls lush and shining, the posters sun-faded and peeling at the corners.

Gean Choo sat on a venerable and splitting wooden stool. She wouldn't cry when she saw her hair on the concrete. If the mem wanted her shorn, then it was a paltry sum to pay. And perhaps the hairdresser would give her something for the offcuts, as well. It was long enough for wig-making.

The hairdresser tugged at her braid. "What would you like?"

"How about that?" Po Lam pointed to a poster of a woman with short hair set in waves. The text below the drawing was selling spring-lock curlers.

So Mrs. Edevane wasn't trying to punish her? Gean Choo shouldn't have cared either way. Vanity was such a petty sin, something Miss Skelford had always said she should strive to cut out of her character.

The blades of the scissors were cold against the back of her neck. She was distantly aware of Po Lam's presence, leaning her weight against a column.

"Look straight," the hairdresser said, adjusting her head.

Gean Choo managed to sit still for the remainder of the ordeal. Afterwards, the hairdresser ran some kind of lotion through her hair, rubbing it in all over. She combed it through and spent the next several minutes placing silver clips on either side of her head.

"Will I have to do this every day?" Gean Choo asked. She should've been paying more attention.

"Yes." The hairdresser swished a bristle brush at the back of her neck, pressing too hard. "Done," she said. "Keep the clips in until it dries." She plucked a small mirror from an apron pocket and handed it over.

Gean Choo glanced at her reflection. When was the last time she'd seen her face? There hadn't been a single mirror in the mem's house. Strange, especially since Mrs. Edevane seemed like the sort of woman who'd appreciate a looking glass.

She didn't look anything like the girl in the poster—just herself, but with silverware all over her head. Maybe it would be nicer once it dried. Would Mrs. Edevane be disappointed? She couldn't afford to let that happen.

Po Lam straightened and assessed her with one look, probably coming to the same conclusion. She picked up extra clips, combs, hair pomade, and the mirror, paying the hairdresser before gesturing to Gean Choo to come along.

The afternoon trade was bustling with bicyclists overtaking rickshaws, cars zooming around both, and the occasional oxen-pulled wagon. Street hawkers offered economy rice and mee siam from little carts, their woks sizzling on portable gas stoves. A Chettiar strolled down the five-foot way, head closely shaved, bare-chested, the folds of his white, winding garment like a sarong bulging around the expanse of his stomach.

One of the rickshaw drivers was having a heated conversation with a hawker—something about owed money. The reminder sent a chill down her spine. She'd already spent half the trip staring every man in the face, looking for Sim Lai Hock. She hadn't seen him since that day by the fence, but she couldn't shake the feeling he was stalking her. Perhaps he even could sense that she'd left the secure confines of the house.

Gean Choo hurried to match Po Lam's long stride. She kept bringing her hand up to feel the bounce of the blunt, too-short ends of her hair. But she couldn't let it distract her.

Once they got into the car, there would only be the drive back to the house. And though the mem might not get up until sunset, Gean Choo often had the odd sensation the house itself was watching her. If she wanted answers, she'd have to ask the questions now, on this busy street with people all around them.

"You know..." Gean Choo began, picking up her steps to circle around a beggar.

"What?"

"It must be tiring, doing all these chores. Are you hungry?" She looked from Po Lam to a nearby hawker stand and back.

Po Lam hesitated, glancing down the road, towards the car. "There's food at home."

"I know, but it's Auntie Seok Eng's day off, isn't it? And the kitchen is so hot," she said, fanning her face with her hand.

Po Lam grimaced, but she must've agreed because they were soon squatting by the road, bowls in hand. The cheap wooden chopsticks were darkened at the tips from use. Grease gilded the noodles red and gold, and Gean Choo's hunger made it taste even better.

Halfway through the meal, she summoned her courage. "You asked me a strange question when I rang about the position."

Chewing slowly, Po Lam finished her mouthful of noodles. "Did I?"

"You asked me when I'd last menstruated."

Po Lam lowered her chopsticks. "You can't work in the house when you have your period. You won't receive a wage, but Mrs. Edevane will pay for you to stay at a lodging house for however long it takes."

"Why can't I work?"

Po Lam shrugged. "Religious taboo."

The mem did not seem like the kind of foreigner who was moved by spiritual concerns. If any of the rooms held a Bible or a prayer book, Gean Choo had not yet found it, and she'd seen no other accoutrements of a devotional life. "She's Christian?"

"Not exactly." Po Lam eyed her over the noodles. "And you're late."

"I'm sorry?"

"On the phone, you said your last period had been a fortnight ago. It's been three weeks since. So five weeks. Are you pregnant?"

"No!"

"Have you ever had one?" Po Lam asked. "A period, that is."

"Yes."

"Do you want to see a doctor?"

Gean Choo blushed and glanced away. "No, thank you. It's not necessary." She tried to return the conversation to Mrs. Edevane. "The mem... she's really very sick, isn't she?"

"I said it's not for discussion."

"Is there anything I can do to help?"

Po Lam paused, staring down at her bowl. "Do your job. Follow the rules."

"But there are so many rules—"

"When you make a mistake, I'll be sure to let you know."

Gean Choo shifted her weight. She'd tried Seok Eng; she'd tried Po Lam. Her Malay wasn't good enough to ask Alif delicate questions, and the twins might betray her to Po Lam if she kept nagging them for answers.

So that only left Mrs. Edevane herself as a source of information.

Gean Choo needed a plan. She only had four days left until her father's debts were due. The cuts on her palm might've faded, but their memory hadn't. She desperately needed to know if she could throw herself on her mem's mercy and beg her for aid. Or should she help herself, as Lai Hock had suggested? There were probably enough items she could steal if she were truly desperate. The jewellery, for one, if it were real, which she suspected it might be.

Aside from stealing, she had few options. Would Lai Hock try to kill her if she couldn't pay? Why not? He had a reputation to uphold. If he could appear next door, he could find his way into the servants' quarters and learn where she slept. It was no secret.

She ought to tell Po Lam. No, she couldn't. If she told her now, it'd look like she'd been keeping secrets for a month... which she had been.

She stirred around the dregs of her bowl and changed the subject. "What happened to the last amah? Did she make a mistake? Break the rules?"

Po Lam's eyes were deep brown and unflinching, half-shadowed by her smooth lids. "She followed a new family to India."

"Why?"

"Got a better offer, why else?"

That was hard to believe. Mrs. Edevane's rates were outrageously generous as it was, not even counting the clothing. Still, Po Lam held her gaze, making Gean Choo the first to look away.

"Finish your food," Po Lam said. "We should get back."

She forced herself to gulp down the rest of her bowl before following Po Lam to the car, carrying her shoeboxes under one arm. It started raining as they walked, an almost welcome distraction from the sweat plastering her dress against her spine.

The car seats were warm with radiating heat, so warm, that for a moment, they almost seemed cold. As they started moving, Gean Choo spoke up. "I'll do my best here, I promise."

Po Lam's response was disappointingly unenthused. "All right," she said, as if she didn't believe her.

Maybe Gean Choo didn't believe herself.

# CHAPTER 10

# YOU DON'T LOOK YOUR AGE

## GEAN CHOO

*Wednesday, 6 April 1927*

Her four weeks were almost up since Lai Hock expected payment on Friday. Begging for more time seemed futile. Maybe he'd died. He could've had an accident. Or perhaps one of his other marks had turned upon him.

She pinched the inside of her elbow until her skin turned white. She ought not to hope for that. Never again.

She went upstairs to the study after dinner. The sun had set. Every bit of free wall space was lined with shelves, stacked with books. Doors led to the verandah, creaking when she opened them. The accumulated heat slowly leached out with the breeze. It wasn't raining, though the air was pregnant with moisture. The palm trees were tall sentinels in the dark, the empty tennis court like a hole cut from a tapestry.

The study held a desk and chair, a reading couch, and a few small tables. A human skeleton stood in one corner. The first time she'd seen it, she'd turned on the light and gasped at the sight of its hollow eye sockets, its eternal grin. But then she'd marvelled at the structure of the skull, the delicate places where the bone wore thin. Its mouth was missing a few teeth. Someone had inhabited it once. Moved those limbs, touched the world through those hands. Now she simply avoided looking at it, as if it wasn't there.

The mem's account books were scattered across the room, seeming to rest where they'd been placed. She cleared a space for them on a lower shelf and began arranging them by date.

The latest book wouldn't lie flat. She opened it to find two earrings between the pages—gold, with dark crimson stones, ornamented with tiny seed pearls. She stared at them for a long time.

Mrs. Edevane had so many jewels. And it was so easy to lose earrings, especially when they were attached with wire instead of a secure screw back.

She probably wouldn't even miss them.

Gean Choo's heart raced as she hooked the delicate ear wires in the seam on the inside of her skirt before folding the fabric back the right way and smoothing her hand over it. The textured metal of the earrings stood out accusingly beneath her fingertips, but when she rose, she couldn't see anything amiss.

She bent again to grab the book and put it away. Downstairs, the grandfather clock began to chime. The study door yawned as it opened wider, admitting more light from the hall.

"Good evening," Mrs. Edevane said.

Gean Choo couldn't stop her flush or how her heart leapt faster. Her hand wanted to drift to her skirt, but she arrested its movement at her hip. This was how innocent people stood, wasn't it? She was being utterly normal. "Evening, Mem."

Mrs. Edevane was dressed in a teal suit with a blouse and matching pleated skirt. Gean Choo couldn't look at her, in case guilt was written all over her face.

"How have you been getting on?" Mrs. Edevane asked.

"Very well, I think. Everyone's been so kind to me, Mem."

"I'm glad to hear it. Keeping yourself occupied, I hope? You're not too bored?"

"Not at all, Mem."

"You can read, can't you?" Mrs. Edevane gestured, encompassing the shelf-lined walls. "Feel free to borrow anything you'd like. I promise, most of these are more interesting than those dreary ledgers."

"Th-thank you, Mem."

Mrs. Edevane drifted away from her towards the desk where Po Lam had left a cardboard box, papered over with a mosaic of postage stamps. She took a penknife from a desk drawer and cut through the string and tape.

Gean Choo glanced at the door. "Will you be wanting your dinner?"

"Not just yet, thank you."

The knife made an awful sound on the cardboard, dry and hollow. The box opened at last, and Mrs. Edevane lifted out a large square envelope, dusting it free of wood shavings. A smaller card fell loose, and she picked it up, turning it over and glancing down for a moment, inhaling sharply, before dropping it back in the box. "Wind up the gramophone, would you?" she asked in a distracted voice.

The gramophone was a portable one, housed in a neat black box. Gean Choo checked the needle, then set about winding it.

Mrs. Edevane brought over a record, tossing the empty envelope to the floor, and affixed it to the gramophone before lowering the needle. An orchestral tune started up with an abrupt burst of strings. The mem swayed to the music, her eyes closed. "I once saw this conducted by the composer himself, sung by Bianca Bianchi. A divine voice. If I'd had the chance, I would've locked her up and never let her go." She opened her eyes and smiled to show she was jesting.

Gean Choo glanced at the record cover. Johann Strauss, the second. Perhaps she was misremembering her music lessons, but hadn't he died last century? Assuming she'd been an adult when she'd watched him, that would make Mrs. Edevane fifty years old, at least. Gean Choo had to be mistaken. "You don't look your age, Mem."

Mrs. Edevane fluttered her lashes. "How old do you think I am?"

As questions went, it was an obvious trap. "Twenty-one," she said, deducting a few years from her real estimate.

Mrs. Edevane laughed. "Oh, to be twenty-one again! How gay that would be."

"How old are you, Mem?"

"You should never ask a lady her age. It's very rude."

"I'm sorry," Gean Choo said, cringing inside. Of course, she ought not to. Yet, Mrs. Edevane couldn't be older than twenty-seven, surely. English brides, on the whole, appeared to wed at a later age; she could still make a good match.

"It's quite all right. I'm positively ancient. Venerable, if one were to be kind." The record stopped, and Mrs. Edevane moved the needle away. She picked up the gramophone with the record still in place. "Come with me."

After another longing glance down the staircase, Gean Choo followed her to the verandah. Save for a pair of decorative plinths, it was relatively devoid of furniture. Mrs. Edevane placed the gramophone on one of the plinths and set the song to play again, its sound muted in the open space.

It was a clear night. The verandah overlooked the back of the estate, with its empty tennis court and the stretch of the ocean reaching out into forever, the waves endless and dark.

"Dance with me," Mrs. Edevane said.

Gean Choo blanched. She couldn't dance. More to the point, the movement might upset the delicate position of the earrings, tucked in only by their wire hooks. "Mem, the others might need help in the kitchen—"

"They can spare you for five minutes."

"But I don't know how to—"

"It's easy. Hold out your arms, like this." Mrs. Edevane demonstrated, crooking her left arm, her right arm placed higher as if holding an invisible partner. Gean Choo tried to copy her.

Mrs. Edevane laughed. "No, silly—" She stepped inside Gean Choo's hold and repositioned her hands, left on Mrs. Edevane's shoulder, right in Mrs. Edevane's grasp. The mem's right hand settled upon Gean Choo's waist.

"Move your right foot to start." Mrs. Edevane danced them into a square, her steps long. "Keep your head level and your arms firm. One, two, three—see how I'm shifting my weight?"

They were too close. Mrs. Edevane wore some kind of heady

perfume, with a faint whiff of old paper beneath the florals and woodsy heart.

Mrs. Edevane showed her how to turn a corner, and then how to follow a simple twirl. Gean Choo's skirt flew out with the motion. It was dark, but maybe the slight weight of the earrings was ruining the line of the fabric. Maybe it was obvious. Surely Mrs. Edevane could see the truth on her flushed face.

By this time, the gramophone had long gone silent. "That's enough practise," Mrs. Edevane said. "Put the record on again, would you?"

Gean Choo released Mrs. Edevane's hand. As usual, the mem's touch was cold despite the tropical heat. She wiped her palm across the front of her dress as she went to the gramophone, winding it slowly to give herself more time. Her fingers itched to run over her seam, but she managed to restrain herself.

When the strings started up again, Mrs. Edevane counted them in under her breath and then pressed her weight forwards, giving Gean Choo no choice but to retreat.

"One, two, three..."

The beat was too quick. She wasn't meant for this. Gean Choo stared over Mrs. Edevane's shoulder, not knowing where else to look. Mrs. Edevane had smeared on a red tint today, just on the centre of her lips, but it made them appear fuller.

The verandah was wide and long, offering plenty of space as they made a circuit. Perhaps, under different circumstances, she might've enjoyed this. The first beat wasn't so much a step as a glide. Did it look right? She'd never done this before. Mrs. Edevane managed to make her feel elegant, somehow, connected in that tight framework of arms and legs, the push and pull guiding her to know her mem's mind, when she wanted to go forwards or back, or left or right.

She had to know about the earrings, didn't she? No. Why would she suspect anything?

The light didn't quite reach the far end of the verandah. It must've been a trick of the darkness, for there seemed to be a red glint to Mrs. Edevane's eyes. The mem moved as if she were dancing on a cloud, every step effortless, every shift in weight or slight pressure of her hand in time with the music, floating like a goddess. Gean Choo couldn't ruin this like she'd ruined everything else.

When the last notes of the song died down, Mrs. Edevane tugged her back in from a twirl. She held Gean Choo close, leaning forwards, forcing her to bend in a dip. She smiled, the gleam of her teeth a pale sliver between red lips, her colourless eyes turned dark and large beneath the night sky.

They were almost close enough to brush noses, to... kiss. In that moment limned by moonlight, Gean Choo wouldn't have minded that at all.

Mrs. Edevane's arm trembled against her back with the effort of holding her in place. Her lower lip quivered, her gaze dropping from Gean Choo's eyes to a point somewhere below her jaw. All at once, she pulled Gean Choo upright and released her, stepping away as Gean Choo stumbled to find her balance.

Mrs. Edevane paid her no mind. She had already turned and was walking back into the house, her skirt gusting out behind her in a swirl of teal. "My pipe. I need my pipe. Come cook for me."

# CHAPTER 11

# DON'T MAKE ME

## PO LAM

*Thursday, 7 April 1927*

P o Lam woke to find mail slipped under her door. The contents of the letters made her sigh.

*Big Sis, our youngest is very sick...*

*...doesn't trust me and it would mean so much if you could...*

*...heard the factory is closing...*

*...haven't received anything from you in a while? Perhaps the mail got lost...*

She had three younger sisters, all married, and no brothers. If they knew how she made her money, would they still write to her with hunger on the page? Or would they cast her out like the murderer she was?

If it were up to her, they'd never know.

She put the letters aside and was ill-tempered all throughout dinner. She'd dreamed of the ocean again, crashing waves and stinging salt, the curl of a dead hand around her ankle.

She was still picking over her food when Gean Choo came back from serving Mrs. Edevane's dinner. "The mem's asked for you," Gean Choo said.

Po Lam almost called her by the wrong name. In those clothes, she resembled Mrs. Edevane's previous girl. The mem certainly had a type—young, but not so young to be scandalous; pretty, but not so pretty that they couldn't be cut down with a few choice words.

Suckling pigs, ready for the slaughter.

"Where?" Po Lam asked.

"Study."

She found Mrs. Edevane seated at her desk, surrounded by books on all sides, her plate of blood tofu only half-eaten. It had been almost four weeks since the prostitute, and she had to be starving by now.

Not the best time for Po Lam to get on her bad side.

"What do you think of the new girl?" Mrs. Edevane asked, her fork dangling from her fingertips. She set it down and pushed the plate to one side, displacing a book, which thumped when it hit the floor.

"She's fine."

"Oh, come on. You must have more of an opinion than that."

She was young. She was dumb. She was just like the others. "She's curious," Po Lam said. "Asks questions."

"You think that's a problem?" Mrs. Edevane leaned back in the chair and crossed her legs. Po Lam averted her eyes, since Mrs. Edevane didn't always wear knickers.

"She'll want answers." It was bad enough with the streetwalkers, the tin miners, the plantation workers. At least Po Lam only saw them alive for one night. It was different when the game was played slow, when she had to watch them fade, week after week. Like the difference between a predator killing to eat and killing for play.

Mrs. Edevane rubbed her fingernail over her bottom lip. "I haven't decided yet, but I would like to get on with that gazebo. And she ought to help you."

*That fucking gazebo again.* "Help?"

Mrs. Edevane stood and wandered to the bookshelves, plucking out a sheaf of bound papers. "I know we shelved this after Jade... well. It would look lovely in the garden. It still needs a feature down the back there, don't you think?"

She tossed the papers onto her desk. Po Lam leafed through architectural plans and pamphlets on tile patterns, doorknobs, and other design elements.

"Try not to bother me with the details. I just want it to be... pretty. And all glass, of course."

"All of it?"

"Well, not the framing, obviously, and not the floor. But yes. Like a greenhouse, but clearer." She flopped onto the settee, sinking in among the cushions. "I'd like to put a cot down and gaze up at the night sky." She waved her hand in an arc, her jewelled fingers glittering.

"You'd get a better view from the boat."

Mrs. Edevane clucked her tongue. "All that rocking! I'd get seasick."

What would the mem throw up? Could she even do such a thing? Maybe vomit like black coffee grounds, tarry and stinking.

Mrs. Edevane closed her eyes and pressed the back of her hand against her forehead. "Fetch me my pills, would you? And turn off the light. It's too much."

Po Lam switched off the lights. The vents built into the tops of the walls still emitted some illumination from the hallway, but since Mrs. Edevane didn't complain, she left the hallway lights on. She found the pills by her bedside and brought them back. Mrs. Edevane took the bottle and shook out a few, swallowing them dry.

"Should I find someone for the weekend? Not like before," Po Lam said, before Mrs. Edevane could protest, "someone younger."

Mrs. Edevane lowered her hand and laboriously propped herself into a sitting position. "No," she said, her voice suddenly cold, "I don't think that will be necessary, do you?"

"She's only been here four weeks, Mem."

Mrs. Edevane brought her knuckles to her mouth and bit them, gnawing at the skin. It was hard to see in the dim light, but the flesh would regenerate, faster than the mem could destroy it. "She's a smart girl. Educated. She'll know what to do."

That prediction was probably right.

Gean Choo seemed considerably more enthused about the mem's project than Po Lam could ever convince herself to be. They were back in the servants' quarters, seated around the big round table. The rain pattered down, pinging against the roof and the covered walkway. Zaid was out in the seaside pavilion, fixing the light since another globe had blown again. The mem was safely ensconced in the house, and Gean Choo had already finished her dinner service. The other servants had left for their own accommodations, so it was just her and Gean Choo and the rain.

Po Lam watched her shuffle the papers. She was probably mentally picking out fabric patterns for the furnishings and considering how best to match the exterior with the rest of the buildings, all details that bored Po Lam to death.

It wouldn't be a struggle to wrestle Gean Choo's limp body into the sampan, given her slight stature. Was Po Lam prepared to do that? Could she really do this again, harden her heart for another cycle, another girl, on and on and on until her body broke from the strain of it all? She'd promised herself she'd leave after the last one. She'd promised—but once again, she could never keep a vow she'd made to herself.

Gean Choo pointed to a page filled with tile designs. "This one would coordinate well with the patterns on the verandah, but this one echoes the starburst in the entryway—"

"Don't make me."

Gean Choo lowered the pamphlet, her cheeks pink with colour. "What?"

It had been a near slip of the tongue. *Don't make me watch you die.* "The mem. She's not the... She's dangerous," Po Lam said, censoring herself out of habit rather than need. Mrs. Edevane's hearing was good, but it certainly wasn't that good, and she'd never shown any evidence of understanding Hokkien.

"What do you mean? She's a sick woman all on her own. How could she be dangerous?"

"Listen to me. You'll die if you stay here. You have to get out. Tomorrow, at dawn. Zaid can drive you into town; he owes me—"

"Is this a joke?"

"This sounds like a joke, does it?" Po Lam had to give her more information. She had to make her understand, make her believe.

But she'd never spoken out against Mrs. Edevane before. Force of habit made her tongue lie heavy in her mouth, useless as lead.

"It's so kind of you to care about me," Gean Choo said, her eyes large and liquid, her mouth soft. She slid her hand over Po Lam's.

Po Lam snatched her hand away. "You don't understand—"

"I think I do."

"You don't!" Po Lam leapt to her feet, paced towards the windows, pressing her fist against her chest.

"Help me understand, then." Gean Choo's chair scraped as she stood with a rustle of fabric. "You're the eldest in your family, aren't you? Auntie Seok Eng told me."

*You can still walk away. Don't get involved. Just think of her as already dead. A corpse on two legs. That's the most sensible thing to do.* She stared out into the rain, into the dark. She ought to know what to say to the mem's girls by now. There'd been enough of them, hadn't there?

But she'd never tried to intervene before. Not like this. Why now? What was different about this girl?

Maybe she wasn't different. Maybe it was Po Lam who'd changed.

She turned. Gean Choo stood in her fashionable dress and bare feet, her hair in dishevelled waves that started too high and ended too early.

"The mem's not sick," Po Lam said. "She's... she's a monster."

There was a long pause. Gean Choo blinked, her gaze flitting from her face to the door and back again. "Do you really expect me to think—"

"It doesn't matter what you think," she snapped, "as long as you leave."

Gean Choo tilted her head slightly. "How long have you been working here?"

"...Nineteen years."

"Oh. When you started, I might not have been born."

That was an odd thought. She'd been fourteen at the time, at an age when most women were looking towards marriage.

"You must trust her," Gean Choo said.

"That's not true."

"You respect her, then."

Only the kind of respect that came with a healthy dose of fear.

"How many amahs did you have in that time?"

"Too many." She couldn't remember all their names. After a while, they all blurred into one. "There's still a chance," Po Lam said. "She hasn't... You can still leave her. Save yourself—"

Gean Choo started walking towards her. "Save myself from what? What would you rather have me do? Should I serve opium? Serve food? Serve myself? What else do you think I'm qualified for?" Her cheeks were flushed.

"You must have family—uncles, grandparents," Po Lam said. "Let them find you a good match—"

"Yes, I could serve my husband. Hope he doesn't drink or smoke or gamble or beat me. Have four babies before I'm twenty-five and say I'm blessed if two live to adulthood. Bury the rest from starvation or miscarriage, illness or injury, or my heaven-blessed husband shaking one too hard when he gets home late and they won't stop crying. You think that's the better choice?"

Gean Choo's eyes held Po Lam's reflection—a broad-shouldered figure in a loose white shirt and black pants. She hadn't been given a choice, but none of those options had seemed appealing to her, either.

But the difference was that Mrs. Edevane didn't see her as food.

"I'm sorry," Gean Choo said. "I'm not going anywhere. If you want me to leave, you'll have to dismiss me. Will you do that?"

She could. She could make her leave, then whip up a story for Mrs. Edevane, tell her she'd caught Gean Choo bringing a man on the property, perhaps. The mem would be furious. Maybe even vindictive. That scenario couldn't end well for any of them.

"No," Po Lam said.

"All right." Gean Choo exhaled. She went back to the table and sat down again, spreading out the papers. "Definitely this one." She pointed to a design as if they'd only ever been talking about colours and shapes and nothing else.

After a moment, Po Lam sat next to her and tried not to think about how she'd look, shrouded in a hessian sack and lying limp across the bottom of a boat.

# CHAPTER 12
## YOUR INFINITE MERCY
### GEAN CHOO

*Friday, 8 April 1927*

Despite all that dancing, the earrings had made their way safely back to her room. She'd looked at them again in the early morning light, running a fingertip over the faceted gems, her nail enormous next to the seed beads. The red stones had seemed lit by an inner fire, taking on the warmth of the gold around them. She'd hidden them through a small hole in the corner of her mattress.

That had been two days ago. Now, at least, she had something to offer Lai Hock when he came, something to buy herself more time. He was meant to call on her today. It'd been four weeks, hadn't it? Or it would be, by midnight. Maybe he was giving her a day's grace. Maybe he'd meant to come tomorrow—

The sound of the bell made her spring to her feet. Dining room. Maybe Mrs. Edevane was calling her to take her plate away. No, she'd already done that. Perhaps she wanted a cup of tea? She'd never asked for one before.

Miss Skelford had preferred hers with milk and one sugar, though she'd seldom had fresh milk on hand. Maybe Mrs. Edevane—

The bell rang again, making her flinch. She hurried to the door, slipping on her shoes, and went to the house.

The dining room held just the big table and chairs, and a few sideboards in gilt-edged wood. The table seated eight, or twelve when extended. She'd never seen it configured at its full length. Mrs. Edevane didn't appear to entertain, or at least, she hadn't for as long as Gean Choo had been working. The light hanging above the table was on the fritz, flickering on and off with no discernible pattern. Perhaps the mem had called to have the bulb changed? The flashing light was giving Gean Choo a headache.

Mrs. Edevane was seated at the table, smoking, her cigarette fitted to a long ivory holder. She glanced up when Gean Choo appeared. "Oh, finally. Sit," she said, gesturing with the holder.

Gean Choo pulled out a chair, lifting it so the legs wouldn't scrape against the marble. She'd never sat at this table before. She did so gingerly, as if the furniture would reject her weight and send her sprawling.

"I think," Mrs. Edevane began, "you have something to tell me."

A bead of sweat rolled down her spine. "About what, Mem?"

Mrs. Edevane waved her free hand before her but said nothing more. Her eyes were cool, her face stern, but occasionally her lips twitched as though she were holding back a laugh. The light flickered off for a second, leaving her face in shadow. The afterglow must've been affecting Gean Choo's sight, because there was that suggestion of red in Mrs. Edevane's eyes again.

"I don't know what to say, Mem." Her nails dug into her clammy palms.

"Tell me what's making your heart beat so, as if you'd just run a mile."

"My heart's not racing."

Mrs. Edevane sighed. "You're a very poor liar. And I can't abide a liar." She propped her cigarette against an ashtray, stood, circled around the table, and grabbed Gean Choo by the ear. She was far stronger than she looked. Was this the same sickly woman who'd collapsed down the stairs that first night? How? Gean Choo had to stand to ease the pressure.

Once she was out of her seat, Mrs. Edevane shoved her with a hand like an iron bat swinging into her clavicle.

Gean Choo stumbled to the floor, her ear stinging. She pressed a hand to it. All her blood had rushed to that one extremity, radiating heat.

"That's better," Mrs. Edevane said and seated herself, brushing down her skirts with a sigh. "Try again."

"Mem, I really couldn't think—"

Mrs. Edevane shook her head. "No. As droll as this is, my patience wears thin. Again. The truth, this time, if you'd please."

Droll? She'd have to look up that word later. Gean Choo shifted her weight, knees pressed together and tucked to one side. Everything she'd worked for in the past month was slipping away from her—the security, the respectability. She could say goodbye to her hopes for a good reference. A jail cell awaited her, or... or the noose, if Mrs. Edevane were feeling particularly vindictive. She could always say Gean Choo attacked her, attempted to kill her in the midst of a robbery. The evidence would be thin, but it'd be a European woman's word against her own, and by that scale, her word meant nothing—

"Out with it," Mrs. Edevane snapped.

"Mem, I... I stole from you," Gean Choo said in a near whisper.

"Finally! Now, was that so hard?"

Only one of the hardest things she'd ever done.

"Fetch it and bring it here."

"Mem?"

"The thing you stole from me. Or things, as it may be."

Gean Choo moved from her knees and fled the house. The air outside was cool and moist, filled with the soft whirring call of a nightjar.

She could run now. Just take her things and head off by foot. Little Chung wouldn't ask where she'd found the jewellery if she accepted an outrageously low offer—

She was so sick of running, though. And then... and then what? She'd have to leave Singapore, of course, maybe even leave the peninsula entirely. And there was no guarantee that Little Chung would give her enough for a train ticket, plus lodging, plus meals for however long it took her to find her feet.

Did she trust Mrs. Edevane? She did not. But surely she had a woman's tender heart. If Gean Choo threw herself on her mercy, then maybe, maybe…

She went back to her room and felt around in the mattress, her questing fingers failing to grasp anything. Had she moved them and just forgotten? Surely not. No, there they were, finally. She exhaled as she pulled out first one, then the other.

They seemed so small to warrant such a fuss, not more than one and a quarter inches in length from the top of the ear wires to the bottom of the big pearl drop. She clutched them in her hand and stared down the path that led to the driveway before turning and heading towards the main house.

Inside the dining room, Mrs. Edevane had finished her cigarette but was still toying with the holder, spinning it between her fingertips. She looked down when Gean Choo held out the earrings in her palm, her left hand cupped below her right. "Is that all? They're just garnets. Hardly worth losing one's liberty over, are they?"

Mrs. Edevane hadn't even known what she'd taken. She'd probably never even looked for the earrings, perhaps hadn't realised they were missing. Was the whole thing just a bluff? Gean Choo ought to have tried harder, protested her innocence, but instead, she was stuck here, heart still racing, unable to contemplate what the next hour might bring. "Mrs. Edevane, please, I'll never—"

Mrs. Edevane plucked the earrings from her hand. "Sit down first. No," she said, as Gean Choo reached for a chair, "where you were before was perfectly fine."

She deserved it. The floor was cool against her skin and the hardness was no burden. She'd slept on a wooden plank for months.

"Tell me your sad story," Mrs. Edevane said, fitting another cigarette into her holder. "Tell me why I ought to be forgiving. Make my heart bleed for you." A match flared beneath her cupped hands as she lit it, orange flames reflecting against her face. Her attention was briefly distracted from Gean Choo, but the reprieve was short-lived. On her exhale, she returned her gaze to the girl before her.

At least she didn't seem angry. That was a good sign, wasn't it? There was nothing for it now. She just had to throw herself on the mem's mercy and hope for the best.

"I'm an orphan, Mrs. Edevane. My father passed away recently, before the New Year."

"I hope that's not all you've got."

"N-no, Mem. When he died, he... he had debts. Large debts."

The smoke drifted like incense from Mrs. Edevane's pursed lips. "And whom did he owe?"

Telling her everything seemed so easy, so natural, she scarcely thought to lie. Besides, surely Mrs. Edevane would know either way. "A man named Sim Lai Hock. He—"

"A secret society man?"

Gean Choo shifted uncomfortably. "I'm not sure, Mem. Maybe."

Mrs. Edevane rested her cigarette against the ashtray and steepled her fingers, pressing them against her lips. Her eyes closed for a moment, as if pained. She reached into the purse sitting atop the table and pulled out a bottle of pills, shaking a few into her palm and throwing them back with a dramatic jerk of her head. "How much does he want?"

"Well... nine hundred, Mem."

Mrs. Edevane exhaled with a sharp puff of breath, somewhere between a cough and a laugh. "What did your father do? Before, I mean."

"He traded spices for a while, but then he... he had to sell the business."

"And you think a gambling broker or opium dealer or whatever your... your—"

"Lai Hock."

"—whatever he was, you think he'd lend a—I'm sorry—a failed businessman that much?" She laughed, throaty and low. "I daresay he's having you on."

Hadn't she thought as much herself? But hearing someone else say it made it so much worse. When Lai Hock had presented her with that outrageous figure, she'd frozen and had made no attempt to talk back. Mrs. Edevane just didn't understand. How could she? This was a settlement governed by her kind, a British colony. Its society and laws were arranged in such a fashion to protect the virtue and safety of women just like her. Not people like Gean Choo.

"Do you know the punishment for theft?" Mrs. Edevane asked.

Her breath stuck in her throat. She couldn't speak. The light was stuttering again, on, off, on, off. "Imprisonment. A fine."

"Yes. And I rather doubt a young woman like yourself has the tenacity needed to survive prison life."

The prison wardens. Her fellow inmates. The squalid conditions... Mrs. Edevane was right. She wouldn't survive such an ordeal. "Mem, I've made a terrible mistake, I'm so sorry—"

Mrs. Edevane moved her chair away from the table and turned so she was facing out. "Come here and apologise properly, like the Indians do. No, don't get up. Crawl."

Gean Choo had no room left for shame. She shuffled forwards on her hands and knees, like an animal, until she was a yard away from Mrs. Edevane.

"Closer. Do you ever pay attention? Maybe that's why you're in this situation in the first place."

Gean Choo inched forwards until she was almost on top of the mem, her breath brushing against Mrs. Edevane's skirted knees.

"Cry," Mrs. Edevane said. "Beg for mercy, that's a good girl."

"Please, Mrs. Edevane. I promise I'll never do it again; please, have mercy on—"

"No, no, no!" Mrs. Edevane's hand descended, slapping her ear. "Not like that. Like you mean it. Really think. Think about what I could do to you. What you'd suffer."

Her ear smarted with a hot pain, sharp and ringing. She couldn't just cry on command. Or could she? She focussed on her deep shame, the one mistake she couldn't unwind. She was no one. Worse than no one. Everyone would've been better off if she hadn't been born.

"Please," she said, hoping and praying the tears would come. "Please,

Mem. This wretched girl has made a terrible mistake and throws herself upon your infinite mercy—"

"Come, girl. Try harder. Surely losing your freedom is something worth crying about?"

Had she ever really been free? Were any of them free? The thought derailed her for a moment, and Mrs. Edevane's hand tensed as if to strike her again.

She'd never been kissed by someone she cared for. There, that was something worth crying about.

"Please," she said, pressing her palms over her chest, her head bowed. "This miserable slave will accept your gracious punishment. Please don't give her to the authorities. Please don't let them lock her away—"

Now the tears came at long last, burning hot at the corners of her eyes and sliding down the planes of her face, gumming up her throat.

Mrs. Edevane opened her arms. "You poor dear. Come rest your head," she said, hands beckoning.

Nothing could be more unappealing in that moment, but she obeyed, laying her head on Mrs. Edevane's lap like a convict going to the guillotine. She was still crying, shaking with the force of her sobs. Mrs. Edevane placed her hands on Gean Choo's head, stroking her hair. The gentleness with which she did so made Gean Choo cry harder.

"My poor little lamb," Mrs. Edevane said, her voice warm and breathy as smoke. "You really aren't very bright, are you?"

She'd been top of the class in most subjects at school, an unfortunate position, making her the target of suspicion and derision by the other girls. Having someone tell her she was, in fact, an idiot, was something of a relief. There, at least, was a reason for her many failures since leaving school. If she were simply stupid, then it meant none of this was her fault.

"I'm sorry," she sniffled.

Mrs. Edevane's knees and hands were cold, her fingertips lingering on the back of Gean Choo's neck, brushing through the soft down at her hairline. She pinched Gean Choo's naked earlobe. "All right. That's enough."

Once she'd started crying, it was hard to stop. She sat upright and gulped back her tears, hiccoughing. She badly needed to wipe her face, but couldn't find her handkerchief.

Mrs. Edevane offered hers, waving it while glancing away. "Go fetch your sewing kit. And an oil lamp."

Gean Choo pressed the handkerchief to her face. She didn't trust herself to speak, but she nodded.

The things Mrs. Edevane had asked for were in the storage room. The walk calmed her. That, and the cool night air, blowing in from the ocean. She wiped her face and splashed water on it in the bathroom. The handkerchief was embroidered, V J M. Perhaps the M was Mrs. Edevane's maiden name. She'd seen the J in some of her letters, addressed to "Verity Josephine Edevane."

She was halfway back to the main house when it occurred to her that she could've run then, too. She hadn't even thought about it. Surely Mrs. Edevane wouldn't turn her in now. Not after all that. But still, her steps were halting when she approached the dining room and grew even more so the closer she came. The light globe had given out at last, leaving Mrs. Edevane in the dark. She was a still, unmoving shape, so still that at first, Gean Choo mistook her for furniture.

"Mem! Please, let me change the bulb—"

"Later. You have a lamp, after all."

Yes. Of course she did. Gean Choo felt for the table and placed down her items. She lit the lamp with trembling fingers, fumbling with the first match, but getting it on the second try.

"Why are you shaking? There's nothing inherently frightening about the dark. But the lost souls who dwell within it—well, perhaps they're something to be feared."

Gean Choo glanced at her. Mrs. Edevane had curled up in the chair, one knee tucked to her chest, her head cradled in one hand. It didn't look particularly comfortable. Her eyes glittered with a gleam of reflected orange flame.

She'd forgotten to blow out the match. It licked at her fingertips, and she dropped it, yelping, then bent to retrieve it.

"Bring those things over," Mrs. Edevane said. "Now, pull up a chair. Facing me. That's right. Sit."

As Gean Choo did so, Mrs. Edevane rifled through the sewing tin, plucking out two large-eyed embroidery needles. She unscrewed the glass top of the lamp and held a needle within the flame, using only her bare fingers.

"Mem," Gean Choo began, "may I say again how very sorry—"

"I'm quite aware," Mrs. Edevane said. "Head in my lap. Left side up. No, *left*. That's the one. Goodness, what did they teach you at school?"

Things she'd rather not have known. "Mem—"

"That's enough talking. I haven't actually done this before, you know."

With her other hand, Mrs. Edevane gripped the bottom of Gean Choo's earlobe. Gean Choo couldn't see the needle coming down, but she felt it, a sharp bright sting entering her flesh, another sting when it came out the other side. Mrs. Edevane left it there for a moment while she did something over the table. She came back, removed the needle, and replaced it with one of the earrings. The metal felt warm.

Mrs. Edevane pressed her fingertips against her own lips, then pinched the earring wire. Her hand trembled, sending shivers across Gean Choo's neck.

"Mem! Are you unwell?"

Mrs. Edevane brought her hand to her mouth and closed her eyes, going still, not even seeming to breathe. In a pained whisper, she said, "I'm fine. Other side now."

She didn't look fine, her forehead creased with strain, lips forming a thin line. But nevertheless, Gean Choo straightened and then lay down the other way, moving as though in a dream. Perhaps she was dreaming or hallucinating. How else could she make sense of this?

Mrs. Edevane pressed the heel of her palm against Gean Choo's head. "Keep still."

It hurt less the second time, maybe because she was expecting it, or maybe because she was sufficiently distracting herself with questions of *why* and *why her* and *what did this mean?*

After the earring was in, Mrs. Edevane's hand tightened in her hair, gripping it so fiercely it felt like she'd tear out a chunk. Gean Choo cried out. A sharp gust of wind rattled the windows and blew out the lamp.

Mrs. Edevane leaned over and a flat, cold, wet thing worried the lobe of Gean Choo's ear. A tongue. Was she... was this a kiss? But—

Mrs. Edevane stood, throwing Gean Choo off her lap in one fluid motion. Gean Choo landed heavily on her hip, sprawling across the marble, her elbow jolting into the tile, sending a sharp tremor of pain up to her shoulder. She bit her tongue to stifle her cry.

Mrs. Edevane walked to the table and unerringly found the matches, even though Gean Choo's eyes had not yet adjusted to the dark. She relit the lamp, the glow illuminating her face, then turned and looked at Gean Choo expectantly. "What do you say?"

Gean Choo raised her hands to her ears, brushing her thumbs over where the wires disappeared into her throbbing skin. The damning evidence of her guilt trembled at the slightest motion. "I... Thank you, Mrs. Edevane. You've shown me such mercy and kindness, I don't—" Her eyes welled with tears again, unbidden this time. She couldn't cry now. She'd already added Mrs. Edevane's handkerchief to the laundry basket.

"I'll spot you the money, too," Mrs. Edevane said. "The full amount, as an advance against your wages. You'll pay it off in...?"

Gean Choo couldn't believe what she was hearing. "A year?" she offered, uncertain if that was right. It didn't sound right, but Mrs. Edevane's rates were unusually high, enough to support a man. A Eurasian man, even.

"Yes. Well done," Mrs. Edevane said, somewhat patronisingly, as if surprised she was capable of basic arithmetic. "And you can keep the earrings. They suit you."

Gean Choo shuffled over, took Mrs. Edevane's hands and leaned over them until her forehead grazed Mrs. Edevane's knuckles, ignoring their chill. "Oh, thank you, Mem. Thank you so much. You don't know how much this means to me—"

"I might have some idea." Mrs. Edevane took her hand back and traced her fingertips through Gean Choo's hair, circling around over her ear and trailing down against her jaw. "I can't bear to see you distressed. You'll let me know, won't you, if someone tries to bully you again?"

"Yes," she lied. She'd die of shame first.

"Good. I'm going to take care of you. And you'll take care of me. Won't you, dear?"

"Yes, Mem." She had to be worthy of this generosity, this second chance. "Of course. Anything you want."

Mrs. Edevane smiled, and the lamplight flickered red across her eyes.

## CHAPTER 13

# KEEN TO KNOW ME

### VERITY

*Saturday, 9 April 1927*
*Twenty-eight nights since last meal*

On Saturday evening, Kalon's Sikh driver picked up Verity at half-past nine. They'd met before, at Kalon's estate. What had he been doing then? Not serving drinks. Perhaps he held some position of note among Kalon's staff. The man was silent as they purred along the stretch of road, the ocean to their left crowded with ships.

Verity glanced out the window. "This isn't the way to Lord Cottesley's."

"He'll meet you at Mount Faber, Mem."

There was a sick feeling in her stomach, a welcome distraction from its typical pit of emptiness. Did Kalon know about her killings? Maybe. But in that case, why not simply censure her when they'd last met, make an example of her in front of the others instead of drawing this out? Was he trying to blackmail her? Why? That couldn't possibly grant him any benefit on top of the ones he already possessed, by virtue of being her liege.

Verity was at a disadvantage. Her least favourite position.

The car halted midway up the road to Mount Faber. A moment later, Kalon opened the door opposite her and climbed into the back seat.

The car started up again. Kalon was wearing a black dinner suit and wouldn't have looked underdressed at White's. It made Verity regret her more casual choice of dark floral linen.

"Good evening," Kalon said.

"My lord."

His chestnut-brown hair was suspiciously damp, as if he'd come straight from a bath. At least he didn't smell of blood. There was only the soap and solvents used by the laundress, and cologne—sandalwood and tangerines.

They reached the top of Mount Faber. A car was already parked there, a Rover in black or maroon. It was hard to tell with the scant light.

Kalon huffed. "Oh, blast. This spot is usually so quiet, too."

His driver spoke up. "Tuan, would you like me to—"

"No, no. I'll speak with them."

Kalon got out, walked over, and leant down at the driver's side of the other car. The occupant wound down their window. She couldn't hear what he'd said to them, but a man got out of the passenger's side and ran away screaming. Kalon stepped back, and the driver soon followed his passenger.

Kalon circled around and opened the door for her. The night air was fresh, slightly cooler at this altitude. Below them was Keppel Harbour to the southeast, vague suggestions of islands in the distance. The boats were a confusion of masts and sails, the ocean a glimmering sheet of inky black. The town was spread out in lights to the northeast, a constellation of civilisation painstakingly carved from dense forest and swamp. Insects sang to each other with clicks, whines, and chirrups, while a nightjar whirred in the trees above.

Kalon's eyes were blue in the light, but his driver had turned the headlights off, leaving them in the dark. His irises reflected a flash of red as he glanced down the slope towards the runners. "Would you hunt with me, Mrs. Edevane?"

Verity looked at the Rover's doors, left hanging wide open in the couple's haste to take flight. "Two on two? That's not very sporting."

"Five minutes' head start is sporting enough."

"If you're not keeping them for anything, there hardly seems to be any point."

"Of course there's a point. Gives us a chance to stretch our legs. Exercise is good for the soul."

He watched her deliberate, his gaze cool and impassive. Did he know about her small white lie, the truth about her eating habits? He must know. "As you'd like."

He unbuttoned his dinner jacket and removed it, handing it to his driver. Kalon rolled his neck from side to side, joints creaking with a cartilaginous pop. "I think that's time enough."

He started down the slope, Verity following close by his side. It was easy enough to tell where the two men had gone—snapped twigs, muddy footprints, the lingering acrid odour of fear. It had rained not long ago. The encroaching trees and green shrubs around them were still damp, her satin shoes unbearably soaking up the mud.

The breeze brushed her skin and stirred her hair. If she closed her eyes, it was almost like old times. Hunting over a brae in the Scottish summer, though the air was still too warm, the city lights too bright. How dare he make her remember.

They caught up with the men easily enough, closing in on their panting breath, their pounding footsteps. Verity seized one, and Kalon the other. Her mark tried to kick her until she twisted his arms behind his back, her voice in his ear.

"Don't be a ninny, there's a good sport," she said. She hadn't Kalon's talents and couldn't command with a word, but he froze all the same. She'd nabbed the passenger, a Eurasian man of indeterminate origins, curly dark hair plastered to his forehead with sweat. His eyes showed the whites, rolling with fear, and his heart thudded frantically in his chest, allegro. Verity had to swallow to keep her teeth from emerging. He was so unreasonably warm, the veins popping out of his neck as if they'd been limned with radium paint.

Kalon said something to the driver, who slumped over, collapsing. He came up to Verity's prisoner, gazing down at the man with a smile, his eyes flashing red. "You came to Mount Faber with your lover. When he stopped the car, you had a fight. He made you walk home in the dark. You don't remember anything else. Sleep."

The man went limp in her arms. Verity dropped him, eager to put some distance between herself and that too tempting sack of warm blood.

"Well, that was bracing." Kalon stuck his hands into his pockets and gazed out at the harbour. "The port that never sleeps... it's rather pretty from a distance, don't you think? When one can't see the filth."

"It's a city." What did he want? What could she possibly give him? Maybe she didn't want to know.

They began a slow walk back to the car. She'd made a mistake agreeing to meet him this far into her feeding cycle. Her jaw ached. Pins and needles covered every part of her body, her limbs still jittery from the sudden exertion. She wanted to scream. Her right hand wouldn't stop trembling, even when she clasped it with her left.

"Are you quite all right?" Kalon asked.

She dropped her hands, lowering them to her sides. "I'm perfectly fine."

He glanced at her sceptically, but decided not to comment. "This evening has been most illuminating, my dear Mrs. Edevane. Allow me to thank you for your time." He held out his hand, and when she placed her fingers within his, he bent over and pressed his warm lips against her skin. Her flesh crawled. She wished for a folding fan to hide her mouth, to hide the sudden visceral distaste she was certain was leaking into her expression. But instead, she smiled the gawkish smile of the ingénue.

He watched her. "I'd love to see you again. Next month? My residence this time?"

*Love.* Was he looking for an excuse to execute her like his last victim? She'd only broken the periphery of the Code, not its heart. "As you wish, my lord."

He reached into his pocket and pulled out a notebook, riffling through its pages. "How about the sixteenth? And bring your new amah. I'd love to meet her. It'll help me understand what you find so captivating about the local population."

He said it nonchalantly, as if she wouldn't sense the threat. As if she wouldn't wonder why he knew so much about her household. Would he care that none of them were thralls? The Code said he was meant to care, but that was subject to considerable discretion. What else did he know about her?

"Why?" she asked.

"One can tell a lot about a person from how they treat their servants."

"If you're so keen to know me, my lord, you simply have to ask."

He closed his book and smiled at her, his pale eyes like the most delicate glaze of cobalt blue on porcelain. "I am asking. Bring your amah."

# CHAPTER 14

## NEVER DESIST

### GEAN CHOO

*Monday, 11 April 1927*

The other servants didn't comment on Gean Choo's new earrings, even though she wore them all the time. She looked at them often, using the little hand mirror when she was fixing her hair. They'd healed perfectly the night of their piercing.

Part of her wished they hadn't. If they'd been infected and closed over of their own accord, Mrs. Edevane would surely have to pierce her again —and while she never wanted to repeat the mortifying events leading up to that occurrence, she wouldn't have said no to placing her head on the mem's knee. To having Mrs. Edevane's hand running through her hair.

Just thinking about it sent a tingle down the back of her neck.

It was rare she even saw another soul around the house most nights. Zaid would leave, taking Mrs. Edevane with him. Po Lam would... Po Lam would do whatever she did at night.

Gean Choo was never entirely idle, but occasionally, there was not enough work to fill every hour. There were only so many times she could sweep the same floors or dust the same shelves.

This left her with hours alone, only her thoughts keeping her company. Had she really imagined that flash of red in Mrs. Edevane's eyes that night on the verandah, and again, in the dining room? The unnatural chill of her skin?

Maybe she was just scaring herself, primed by Bee Leng's mocking stories. But Mrs. Edevane was such a confusion of fragility and strength, of mercy and severity. Was that eccentricity? Or was there something more sinister at play?

She'd taken advantage of Mrs. Edevane's generosity, sneaking in a few hours of reading here and there. Mrs. Edevane's study was well-stocked with everything she might possibly want to know about music history, philosophy, and anatomy. There were travelogues, memoirs, books in other European tongues.

But it was the mem's fiction that drew her: Austen. The Brontë sisters. Wharton. The monsters: Dr. Frankenstein. Mr. Hyde. The Phantom of the Opera.

Dracula.

It was silly, perhaps, to be frightened by a book, but Mrs. Edevane was only up at night and didn't seem to own any mirrors. Her flesh was cold as the grave and almost as pale. Had she ever even eaten anything that wasn't the blood tofu or those odd brown pills? Her plates were returned every evening half-full.

It would mean Po Lam had lied to her. It would mean hantu were real.

On Monday, she crept back to the study after dinner. The shutters on this floor were still closed, leaving the room stifling with trapped heat and pregnant with repressed secrets. When she switched on the light, it flickered for a moment before humming and settling upon an orange, steady glow, illuminating Mrs. Edevane's hoard of books, the shelves heavy with the aroma of old paper and cured leather.

The skirts of her new dress whispered against her legs when she walked to the nearest shelf, the rasp of the fabric still foreign and unsettling. She smoothed her hands over her hips. In her right she held a feather duster, although there was no need to use it. The twins kept this room spotless.

She picked up a crimson, cloth-bound book and flicked through the pages. The clock downstairs had read half-past six. She didn't have much time before Mrs. Edevane woke up.

There was plenty of nonsense about needles and heaving breasts, soft kisses and trembling embraces. She skimmed the pages to read it again, embedding the passages into her brain like she was cramming for a test: *complained of extreme languor... appalling dreams... horrible lust for living blood...*

Her fingers trembled where she held open the book. *It will never desist until it has satiated its passion, and drained the very life of its coveted victim.*

Po Lam had lied to her, but she'd also tried to warn her. She'd called Mrs. Edevane a monster. Was she? But she'd been so kind. Could one be a monster and still be good?

She turned the page. A shadow fell upon it, and a voice spoke behind her.

Gean Choo screamed.

# CHAPTER 15

# DEXTER OR SINISTER?

## VERITY

*Monday, 11 April 1927*
*Thirty nights since last meal*

Verity was ravenous.

The pipe helped, a little, as did the pills, taking the edge off the night. The blood jelly she ate in delicate bites, forcing each one down as if it were the finest blancmange.

It was impossible to concentrate when she was in such a state. The world seemed less vibrant, more sinister. Reading tired her and even music became dull. She took herself dancing a few times, just for the joy of it and to feel the breeze on her calves, but colonists were, on the whole, a rather boring lot, and it had only made her miss London all the more. Give her the cut-crystal elegance of Claridge's or Brown's. Give her the fog, even, and the haze; give her the streets filled with carriages.

No. It would be motorcars now.

A city of alleyways, of dark corners and darker hearts. A smorgasbord of pale, creamy necks hidden by ruffled lace.

Her city.

Instead, she was stuck here, on the other side of the world, abandoned by anyone of consequence. She was bored. Worse yet, she was becoming boring.

Her temper wasn't at all improved by nagging doubts about Kalon's demand. What was he planning? Why did he care a whit about how she managed her affairs?

The Code said domestics had to be managed, had to be secured to protect the secrets of vampiric existence. The exact language was open to interpretation. Dear, dead departed Winston certainly had never enforced widespread thraldom. Besides, everyone in the colonies knew the Code was more of a... guideline.

Perhaps Kalon hadn't received that memo.

On Monday, she woke in a state of drowsy half-somnolence that indicated the sun had not quite set. She dozed in her bed with the sheets thrown back. She had lost the ability to suffer from fluctuations in climate, a definite plus in these sultry lands.

Something had woken her. What was it?

She rose, threw on a peignoir over her nightgown, and cracked open her door to the shuttered gloom. A half-circle of light emanated from the stairwell, which she avoided, creeping around to the open door of her study.

The girl stood by Verity's desk, outlined by the orange glow of electric light gleaming upon the buttons on her dress, the garnets hanging from her ears. A feather duster dangled from the tip of one hand, forgotten. In the other she held a book, her lips moving occasionally to sound out the words.

She seemed utterly unconscious of the fact she was being watched. Her pulse was adagio, inviting. Scents clung to her—soap and sweat, shoe polish and pomade.

Verity's mouth watered in response, her fingers curling by her sides. How pretty she'd looked on her knees, trembling and begging for mercy. How easy it would've been to tear open her throat that night; the sharp, sudden scent of blood from the piercings almost too much to bear.

Not now, though. They'd healed well enough. The girl had nothing to fear from her.

Verity crossed the room and glanced down at the open page. "Le Fanu. He had quite the imagination, didn't he?"

Gean Choo shrieked, dropped the book and the duster, then pressed her palms over her chest. Her pulse jumped to allegretto. "M-mem. Good evening. I'm sorry, I was just—"

"Dusting, I know."

If she touched her now, the girl would shrink from her, heart rate spiking again. She was not too sun-browned, the veins in her neck shining from beneath her skin.

Gean Choo bent and picked up the fallen objects. She held the book delicately, by the tips of her fingers, as if it were like to bite her.

Verity gave the girl space, circling around the desk and flopping down on the sofa, the flimsy silk of her robe draping over the edge. "Did you get to the good parts? Read page one hundred and forty-three. That's my favourite."

Gean Choo set down the duster so she could open the book with both hands. It was an older edition with a red cloth cover, *In a Glass Darkly* embossed in gilt along the binding. Had she bought it in London or Edinburgh? All her years blurred together.

The girl turned to the requested page, the rasp of old paper sending a delightful shiver down Verity's spine.

"'...love is always selfish; the more ardent the more selfish. How jealous I am you cannot know. You must come with me, loving me, to death; or else hate me, and still come with me, and *hating* me through death and after. There is no such word as indifference in my ah... apa—'" she stumbled over the word.

"Apathetic."

"'—in my apathetic nature,'" Gean Choo concluded in her beautifully modulated voice, the Chinese twang almost completely beaten out of her. She was trembling a little, breathing a bit too fast, but she hadn't run.

Verity could work with that. "Put the book down and come here."

Gean Choo came and stopped a good two yards away from the sofa. She'd done a bit better with her waves today, managing to put some interest into her otherwise straight black hair. The cut suited her. A little paint and she'd be presentable enough for Kalon, at least.

"'Gean Choo.' What does that mean?"

The girl raised her eyes, widening them a bit. Her mouth moved, but no sound came out. She coughed into her sleeve and tried again. "Beautiful pearl," she said and blushed.

"Pearl." Verity smiled without showing her teeth. "You don't mind if I call you 'Pearl,' do you?"

She shook her head.

Verity patted her dress for her cigarette case, but she was still in her nightgown. She silently cursed. "Come sit," she said, tilting her head towards the end of the sofa. It sat three comfortably, though Verity was taking up two thirds, her feet dangling over the edge.

Pearl put down the book, went and sat, perched with hands on her lap, back rigidly straight. She looked ready to bolt.

"Do you suppose everything you read in books is real?" Verity asked, holding Pearl's gaze. Pearl's irises were thin rings of brown around her enormous pupils, her chest trembling as it rose and fell.

"No, Mem."

"And yet, there's a kernel of truth there, somewhere, if one looks hard enough." Verity reached out and brushed the ends of Pearl's hair, her fingers naturally falling to cup the girl's chin. Her lips were slightly parted, lush and pink. She froze beneath Verity's touch.

"What sort of truth do you mean, Mem?"

"About who I am. What I am."

Pearl's pulse beat softly. Living with humans was so distracting—the constant noise, the rasp of her breath, every little rustle as Pearl shifted her weight. Sometimes it was a wonder she didn't go mad and slaughter them all.

"What are you, Mem?"

Verity's next word came as a whisper. "Hungry." Her teeth gnawed at the inside of her lip. If Pearl ran, she'd have to kill her. That would be a waste. It was so very hard to get blood out of the rugs.

Pearl's breath stuttered in her throat when Verity brushed the side of her neck, when Verity clasped the curve of her shoulder through the dress. Her pulse was like a beacon, allegro, maddening.

Verity touched her nose behind Pearl's ear and inhaled her terror, placing one palm on her hip to stop her from inching away. The girl was rigid, her flesh warm beneath Verity's fingertips. "If you'd just let me have you," she murmured, her lips against Pearl's ear, "hold you. Taste you... I can show you the depths where pain becomes pleasure."

A bead of sweat slid down the back of Pearl's neck. Verity moved her head and kissed away its salt.

"Mem."

"Yes, dear?"

Pearl's hand opened and closed into a fist. "I feel you've hired me on false pretences."

Verity laughed. "You wouldn't have believed me if I'd told you the truth, you silly girl."

Pearl tried to move away, but Verity's hold on her was iron. Had she come on a little too strong? No. Beneath the sharp, sour scent of fear was the unmistakable musk of arousal.

Pearl closed her eyes then opened them, and glanced somewhere over Verity's shoulder. "I said I'd do anything for you, Mem."

"You did." Verity brought her hand back to Pearl's cheek, tilted her face up to look at her. Pearl's eyes were larger than Po Lam's, with a visible crease. Verity brushed her thumb over her mouth, and the girl's lips parted. "Are we in agreement?"

There was only the sound of Pearl's breathing, and from downstairs, the ticking of the grandfather clock. The light bulb hummed overhead, stuttering once.

"Yes," Pearl whispered and glanced away, her cheeks flaming red.

Verity let the word linger in the air, as though it were a meal she could savour. "Dexter or sinister?"

"Pardon?"

"Are you right-handed, dear?"

She nodded.

Verity took Pearl's left hand and pressed a kiss upon her palm, ignoring the resulting shiver. She held Pearl's knuckles to her cheek, entwining their fingers, then sighed, blinking away a tear. She was growing sentimental in her old age, that was her problem.

"Mem... do you..."

"Don't rush me, dear."

The girl fell silent. Her right hand clawed at her knee, nails digging into flesh, judging by the white of her knuckles.

Pearl's sleeve had three small buttons on the cuff. Verity undid them one by one, tugging gently as not to damage the narrow chiffon loops. She rolled the sleeve back to the elbow, baring the soft beige skin underneath.

Verity sighed again, her canines lengthening. She turned the girl's hand to reveal the faint tracery of veins, the paler ribbons of her tendons. She brought Pearl's wrist to her mouth and bit.

Pearl made a strangled noise, somewhere in between a cry and a moan, and tried to pull away. Verity grabbed her elbow with her other hand, steadying her. She would not be moved now—not by tears, not by pleas, not by the devil Himself.

Pearl clutched at her with her right hand, her mouth moving. Whatever she said, Verity couldn't hear it. She was lost in the heat filling her mouth, the velvet coppery slide of it down her throat, the ratcheting pulse that joined them. Pearl was an untapped well and Verity was her mistress. Both of them were exactly where they needed to be.

When the flow began to ebb, she had to fight the impulse to keep going. *Not enough*, her soul whispered. *Never enough.* But Verity was not a monster.

Her canines shrank back to their usual shape, and she swallowed for the last time, then pressed a kiss against Pearl's wrist. She held her hand, clasped against her cheek, reluctant to let go all at once. A stray drop of blood hovered on her lip, which she licked clean, not intending for anything to go to waste.

Pearl drooped, wilting on the sofa. Her breathing was shallow, her pulse spiking. Verity smoothed the hair back from her face and pressed a kiss to Pearl's forehead. "That wasn't so bad, was it? You performed admirably well, considering it was your first time."

Pearl drew her hand back and cradled it in her lap, thumbing over the newly healed bit of skin that marked the underside of her wrist. "Thank you, Mem. It wasn't so bad."

Her eyes told a different story, half-lidded and brimming with tears. But she didn't cry. She didn't cry.

Verity paused at the doorway and glanced back at the sofa. Pearl hadn't moved. Her eyes were closed, but from the sound and the subtle movement of her dress, she was still breathing.

Ah, well. She'd get used to it.

They all did, in time.

# CHAPTER 16

## YOU DON'T APPROVE

### GEAN CHOO

*Monday, 11 April 1927*

Gean Choo must have dozed off at some point, for she roused on the sofa with Po Lam shaking her awake.

"Hey," Po Lam said, hovering too close to her face, "get up."

Her mouth had gaped open as she'd slept, and a trickle of drool wet her cheek. She blushed hotly, wiping it away, but Po Lam was no longer looking at her face. Her gaze had dropped to her wrist, which sported a white strip of scar tissue, newly healed. Not the delicate pinpricks of legend, but a gash, sealed over by whatever dark magic kept Mrs. Edevane upright and moving through the world like a human. Po Lam didn't look surprised. If anything, that furrow in her brow, the tightness in her lips was that of resignation. She was quiet, closed-off. Professional.

"Can you walk?"

Gean Choo rose to her feet. The room spun and she staggered, forcing Po Lam to catch her. Her arms were solid and warm, a far cry from the freezing touch of Mrs. Edevane's fingers. "Thank you."

Po Lam silently helped her out of the study, across the dark corridor, and down the stairs. Outside, a light drizzle pinged against the roof of the walkway connecting the servants' quarters.

"Did the mem leave for the night?" Gean Choo asked. The house felt different when she wasn't around, holding all the melancholy of a deflated balloon.

"Yes."

"Without the car?"

"She took her own transport."

They reached Gean Choo's room and she collapsed onto the bed, her legs no longer willing to support her weight. Po Lam came back sometime later with a steaming pot of tea and leftover congee from their breakfast.

"I'm not sick," Gean Choo said.

"I know." Po Lam hovered in the doorway, her face unreadable, until Gean Choo made the effort to sit up and try a mouthful of food. As soon as it touched her lips, she scarcely stopped until the whole bowl was empty.

"You don't approve," Gean Choo said as she sipped the tea. She wanted to say, *You lied to me.*

"It's none of my business." Po Lam walked over, her jaw clenched, stiffness in the set of her shoulders.

Gean Choo clutched her teacup as if it could offer her any protection, but Po Lam merely leaned over to pick up the empty bowl from the side table. She took it to the doorway, then glanced over her shoulder, the mirror of her eyes reflecting the gold of the electric light. "Rest as long as you'd like tomorrow. The mem won't expect you to return to your duties until after Easter."

Easter was still a few days away.

Po Lam went on, "I'll say this once. Don't talk to anyone about what happened here tonight, about the nature of the mem's existence. You haven't seen her temper."

"I'd never betray her."

"Good." Po Lam left her room, softly closing the door behind her.

Gean Choo slumped back in bed. Rain trickled down the side of the window, spattering the floor beneath the open shutters. She ought to close them, but the cool breeze was welcome after the stuffiness of the first floor.

She examined her wrist, turning it towards the light as she traced over the scar. There was no pain, not now, but then? She shuddered to think of Mrs. Edevane's face, rapturous and devouring all at once, the cold bite of her fingers, the eager curve of her mouth.

All those ghost stories were real. That meant—

She staggered out of bed to undress and turn off the light, then crawled back into it. Her arm throbbed with a phantom ache, but she was fine, just fine. She'd seen the healed scar with her own eyes.

How queerly Mrs. Edevane had looked at her, with mingled longing and elation. How gently she'd touched her, with soft, elegant hands, as if she were something precious, as if... as if Gean Choo were giving her the whole world.

She could get used to that.

# CHAPTER 17

## INCAPABLE OF LOVE

### PO LAM

*Thursday, 21 April 1927*

Po Lam couldn't help but notice Gean Choo's restlessness over the course of the previous few weeks. Her mind seemed to wander. Po Lam often found her staring aimlessly into the garden or not watching where she walked. This distraction had consequences—she'd broken another plate and had come close to smashing a vase when crossing the foyer.

Was it the shock of discovering the truth about Mrs. Edevane? Or something to do with her family? Miss Skelford had said she was an orphan, but perhaps she had siblings nearby or other relatives. Po Lam would've asked, but then she'd be giving the impression that she cared. And she didn't. She couldn't. But whatever trouble the girl was in, it was spoiling her work, and that was something Po Lam did care about.

"I'm sure she wouldn't want to buy any. No, thank you. Goodbye." Gean Choo put down the telephone, absent-mindedly tucking a stray lock of hair behind her ear. She was wearing a coral-red dress today, the colour of ripening lychees... or the colour of her cheeks whenever she blushed. Which seemed to be often. Including right now. "Oh! You startled me,"

Gean Choo said as she turned, catching sight of Po Lam. Why was she blushing? Maybe she grew flustered with everyone. No, that wasn't true. She gossiped earnestly enough with Seok Eng, was sickeningly doting upon Alif, and even the twins didn't perturb her.

What Po Lam was about to say probably wouldn't help. "We should talk."

"What about?"

"You've been a little clumsy recently. That plate the other day, and the near miss with the vase. Is there something going on? Something I should know about?"

Gean Choo stared down at her hands clasped before her. "I'm very sorry. I was in a hurry, I suppose, and... these skirts still trip me up sometimes—"

"Are you in some kind of trouble?"

"It's not... no—"

Po Lam tried to summon all her patience. "I can't help if you don't tell me what's wrong."

Gean Choo smoothed down her skirts. "There's nothing wrong." She met Po Lam's eyes at last, her gaze defiant. The impression only lasted for a moment as she spoiled it in the next by getting down on her knees before Po Lam and pressing her forehead against the floor. "I can't afford... I need this job, please, I beg of you—"

"No need for that. You can get up."

She straightened, brushing a bit of sand from her forehead. Her lips parted as if she were going to say something, but then she shook her head. "I've just been clumsy. I'll be more careful in future, I promise."

"All right." She was still hiding something, but it was clear Po Lam wouldn't get any further tonight. "Did you get in touch with the architect?"

"Yes. They're sending someone out tomorrow. A Mr. Maclaren? At four o'clock."

If the mem wanted her gazebo, she'd get her stupid gazebo. "Good."

*Friday, 22 April 1927*

Mr. Maclaren was late. By the time they'd finished discussing specifics, it was already six o'clock. He was a spindly man with rheumy eyes and a hacking cough. Po Lam tried not to stand too close, even when they had to go over the plans together.

After he was gone, Gean Choo came over to stare at the empty site. "It'll be beautiful."

It sounded like a nightmare to keep clean, but that would be the twins' problem, not hers. "As long as Mrs. Edevane is happy." She'd not meant anything by it, but Gean Choo stiffened next to her.

"Do you think she's unhappy? Right now?"

"Not any more than usual. Why?"

Gean Choo lowered her gaze. "She hasn't..." She touched the inside of her wrist, with its pale band of scar tissue.

"It's not safe to drink from the same person so often. She'll summon you when she thinks you're healthy enough."

It'd only been ten nights since Mrs. Edevane had fed from Gean Choo, and a further thirty nights since Lei Heung, the woman from Sheik Madersah Lane. One body a month was manageable. That had been Mrs. Edevane's norm for several years now, though she'd briefly had a period of abstinence during the Spanish Flu. Those years had been horrifying for everyone, including Po Lam, who'd been twenty-four at the time. Mrs. Edevane had scarcely moved, lying in bed all night with the curtains drawn, her flesh wasting away until she'd been little more than bones. The threat of illness had haunted her, even though Po Lam was quite sure Mrs. Edevane's kind were immune to human disease.

Those years had been awful, but the months directly after the pandemic had been even worse. Mrs. Edevane had entered a period of frantic consumption, as if making amends for lost time. Bodies had piled up. They'd moved house from Bukit Timah to Tanjong Katong to be close to the sea and its vast, unmarked depths. The perfect grave. Mrs. Edevane had lost her corpse-like visage and gradually curbed her appetite.

And Po Lam had learned something new. Mrs. Edevane didn't always have to restrain herself. She chose to. And as long as she did that, as long as she was trying, somehow, to control her hunger, Po Lam could accept that. After all, even monsters had to eat.

"Oh," Gean Choo said, rubbing at her wrist. "She must be hungry, I suppose."

"Auntie Seok Eng feeds her. You mustn't feel sorry for her."

Gean Choo glanced up, her eyes wide. "But she hates that stuff. It's nothing alike. When she's—" She glanced away, her cheeks flushing red.

Po Lam needed no reminders about how much the mem enjoyed feeding. "Don't pity her. She's not like you or I, understand? She's not human. She doesn't deserve your—" Devotion. Loyalty.

Love.

"—kindness," Po Lam finished inadequately.

"But she's been nothing but kind to me."

Po Lam couldn't listen to this anymore. "Don't forget to write down the dates Mr. Maclaren agreed to begin construction."

"Yes," Gean Choo said, subdued.

Po Lam was turning to leave when she spoke again.

"Has she ever bitten you?"

"No."

"Haven't you ever wanted her to?"

Po Lam stared at her without speaking. After a moment, Gean Choo dropped her gaze. "No," Po Lam said, barely concealing her shudder of revulsion.

"Do you... do you think what I'm doing is wrong?"

Po Lam heaved an exasperated sigh. "I'm not your mother. Are you Christian? You could see a priest if it bothers you that much. Or visit a temple. I don't care what you do with her as long as it doesn't interfere with the rest of your job."

Gean Choo gnawed at her lip. "I see," she said. "Thank you." She made it sound as if Po Lam had given her blessing, when she'd intended nothing of the sort.

"Just don't... don't expect too much from her. She's incapable of love."

"I understand."

She didn't. She wouldn't. And by the time she realised how very wrong she'd been, it'd be too late. Could Po Lam really stand by and watch it happen again?

# CHAPTER 18

## YOU'RE MY FAMILY

### VERITY

*Friday, 22 April 1927*
*Eleven nights since last meal*

Verity slept poorly, waking up far earlier than she'd intended. Instead of trying to drowse back into the velvet darkness, she sat up, fumbling to remove the sleep mask covering her eyes.

That noise—

Oh. A girl's laughter.

She put on a robe, gloves, and dark glasses, then wrapped her head and neck in a scarf, leaving only the smallest slit for her eyes. The windows in her room were constructed in such a way to permit airflow but not light, so she went to the end of the hallway and opened the shutters just an inch, hissing as the faint sliver of light turned every patch of exposed skin red-raw.

Down in the yard below, Pearl was speaking with the gardener, leaning in rather too closely to supervise his planting of the flower beds, her modest chest almost in his face. Verity rolled her eyes behind the glasses.

Pearl disappeared for a moment into the kitchen and reappeared with a tumbler. Verity could imagine the condensation beading on its surface. As she handed it over, their fingers seemed to touch. He smiled at her.

Verity snapped the shutters closed and returned to the safe, dark womb of her bedroom. She tore at her ridiculous getup, throwing the scarf and glasses onto the bed and sat at her dressing room table, tapping cold cream delicately over her sunburn. It stung, as though the top layers of her skin were peeling off. They were.

She found her pill bottle and dry-swallowed a handful, massaging the unburnt skin of her temples. Forget the gardener. Her real problem, her only problem, was Kalon.

It would be naïve at best to assume he bore no ill intent. Maybe he didn't know or care about her killings. Fine. But still, there remained his odd request to meet her amah. Him, meeting her servant? She'd made discreet inquiries and learnt that none of the others were being subjected to such scrutiny.

Maintaining a household of unbroken humans wasn't a crime. Not a crime, though it skirted the edges of respectability. And she had to be more than that. She had to be irreproachable, prove she could be trusted, that she held their secrets, her human sympathies aside. A council enforcer like Kalon would demand nothing less. He probably had a quota, didn't he? Some imaginary number of souls to stake, crimes to punish. How else could one end up with such a reputation as a kin-killer?

She wouldn't be anyone's statistic. She wouldn't let herself end up as some spectacle, a mere cautionary tale.

Verity twined a lock of hair around her fingers and chewed on the ends. She was too old for this nonsense. Kalon was almost certainly her junior, yet they'd placed him in charge of this admittedly provincial little backwater, instead of her. All because he had a cock, or because he'd let the right bloodsucker bite him. Things that shouldn't matter always did.

Verity rose and dressed, choosing a blood-red suit with a pleated skirt. The clothes bore that unsettling hint of mildew and naphthalene she'd forever associate with the tropics.

Downstairs, Po Lam greeted her with the day's newspaper, twelve hours hopelessly out of date. Pearl was nowhere to be seen. Was she off courting the gardener? On paid time?

Verity settled at the dining table, condemned once more to eating the unappetising mauve slabs that constituted the majority of her diet. Kalon, no doubt, would be deciding which of his myriad thralls to sup on tonight. He'd probably choke before letting a sliver of animal blood past his lips.

The text of *The Straits Times* crawled before her eyes like ants on a leaf. Po Lam hovered somewhere in the room, invisible, vigilant.

"Where's Pearl?" she asked.

"Helping in the kitchen."

Verity glanced down, trying to concentrate on a newspaper article. Something about the price of rubber. She missed Jade, Pearl's predecessor, more than she could say. She had nothing left of her, save a lock of hair. Photography was so cheap these days, there'd been no reason to go without, yet she'd never made the time.

"Are the orchids in bloom?" At Po Lam's blank face, she continued, "The ones in the back garden by the fountain."

"Yes, Mem."

"Gather up a bunch, would you? I'd like to pay my respects to Jade."

Po Lam nodded and left the room. Verity picked up another slice of her dinner, grimaced, and swallowed it down while barely chewing. Some emperors had possessed harems two, three hundred deep. One could drink their fill and not touch the same vessel for months with a stable that large.

It was awful, surrounding oneself with so many humans. En masse, they resembled nothing so much as a mob. Thralls were perhaps even worse, eerily quiet, disturbingly mechanical in look and deportment. She didn't know how anyone could stand them... like automatons activated with a key. They were positively ghastly.

Po Lam came back with a bouquet of orchids tied with string. She'd surrounded the flowers with smooth flat leaves, their deep green setting off the white blossoms.

"You have quite the eye," Verity said.

"Thank you, Mem. Would you like me to fetch Zaid?"

Pearl still hadn't emerged to say good evening, and the slight rankled Verity like a sore tooth. This was her house, after all. "You're here. Let's just go."

They drove down the long, straight roads to the cemetery in Bidadari. The place was deserted this time of night, the wrought-iron gates locked. Po Lam simply walked to the side where the fencing was shorter and scaled them, agile in her loose pants and flat shoes. Verity set down the bouquet and briefly made herself insubstantial, shuddering at the effort it required as she re-solidified on the other side. She bent down and picked up the bouquet, sliding it between the bars of the gate.

Perhaps that little movement was too much because her vision spun. She clutched the bars, closing her eyes and leaning her head against them.

Po Lam appeared by her side. "Mem?"

She gripped Po Lam's sleeve and then the firm muscle of her arm. The woman's heartbeat ticking away was slower than Pearl's resting pace. She'd never touched her. Edibility wasn't a criterion she considered when training a majordomo.

But tonight, with her empty stomach twisting upon itself in knots, she probably could've managed. But then she'd have to find a new house-keeper, and good ones were even rarer than girls in this horrible colony with its two men for every woman.

Po Lam's neck was half-hidden by the stiff collar of her shirt. Sensing her regard, she met Verity's gaze, her dark eyes betraying not a hint of fear. "Mem? Do you need to sit down?"

Verity pulled herself upright, using Po Lam's arm as support. "No. I'm fine."

She leant on Po Lam for the rest of the walk. Jade's plot was on a pleasant rise, one small marker in a sea of others, indistinguishable until one took a closer look. Po Lam set down her lantern and exhumed the encroaching weeds with her hands. She took Verity's bouquet and propped it against the marker.

The lantern's light reflected yellow against the grey stone, bouncing off names and dates, the odd statue of a guardian angel. If Kalon found out she still came here, he'd use the knowledge against her somehow. Sentimentality? Over meat?

But Verity had always loved too deeply, that was her problem.

They stood for a few minutes in silent contemplation, Verity with her hands folded before her and her feet planted solidly on the grass, this foreign soil so far from home, she might as well have been living on the moon.

When they were walking back to the car, the heavens opened up, forcing them to hurry, Po Lam's lantern swinging by her side, the light bouncing off sprawling trees and mausoleums, and finally, the iron fence surrounding the cemetery.

Back in the car, they hummed along for a few miles before Verity spoke. "How is your youngest sister? Did she have a good birth?"

"Yes, thank you, Mem. She had a son."

"Another nephew! How wonderful for the family. I must send her something as my congratulations."

"That's kind of you, Mem."

The car's yellow spotlights streaked the road, a little blaze of light burning across the darkness. Nights could be so miserable, the endless tedium of unchanging gloom. "Is she still living in Canton? Perhaps we should visit sometime."

The change was subtle, Verity might've even missed it if she hadn't been watching. Po Lam's grip tightened upon the wheel. "If you'd like, Mem. But there are more Europeans living in Hong Kong, I believe."

"More nosferatu as well, from what I understand." Verity yawned, covering her mouth with the back of her hand. "Sometimes I despise my own kind. It's like having a big family where you all hate each other, but everyone is too polite to say so most of the time."

"If the family lives in harmony, all will prosper."

"You're my family," Verity said in a rush of sentiment, what Kalon might call weakness. "You and Cookie, and I suppose even little Pearl." She bolted upright in her seat. "Is she fucking the gardener?"

Po Lam's reaction was immediate. "What? No, Mem. She would never disrespect your house like that."

"Well, good. I still want him gone, though. Find someone more experienced."

"Yes, Mem."

Back home, she found Pearl at last, polishing the brass handrail on the main staircase. She was wearing one of her new dresses in cream muslin with a boat neckline, displaying a few brown freckles scattered across her beige skin.

"Good evening, Mem," she said, lowering her eyes in deference, heat rushing to her cheeks. Her skin was as soft as it looked. Verity could practically taste it.

"Pearl," she said curtly and brushed past, placing fresh fingerprints on the newly-burnished handrail as she headed upstairs. She felt Pearl's wounded eyes follow her all the way.

Verity went into her study and wound up the gramophone, putting on the waltz they'd danced to on the verandah. The record had been a gift from Kalon; a lucky guess, perhaps, picking one of her favourite composers.

Pearl's weight in her arms was a phantom presence, the pressure of her warm, sweaty palm against Verity's own. If they danced again and she leant in to kiss her, Pearl wouldn't flinch away, she was sure of it.

Maybe Verity ought to dismiss her, tell Kalon she'd run off instead of letting him meet her. But that was as good as signing the girl's death warrant; he didn't seem the sort who'd leave loose ends dangling.

She could manage Kalon. Prove to him that Pearl wasn't a threat, thrall or no thrall. Make him see reason.

If such a man could be reasoned with.

# CHAPTER 19

## THE MEM'S SUPERIOR

### GEAN CHOO

*Monday, 25 April 1927*

It was hard to think it'd been two weeks since that night... that strange and terrible night when she'd learned the truth.

Had it all been some silly fever dream? Was the ache in her wrist merely base superstition? No. It had to be real, hadn't it? The lack of mirrors in the house. The way Mrs. Edevane only ate one thing, swirling the rest of her food around on the plate but never consuming it.

It'd all been so strange. The pale pink rose of Mrs. Edevane's nipples beneath the lace trim of her nightgown, the lantern sleeves of her robe like an insect's wings.

Some spiders ate their mates.

Sim Lai Hock still hadn't called upon her. It'd been over three weeks since she'd expected him to come, demanding his payment. Was it so terrible that part of her wished he were dead, wiping her debt clean? Yes. She shuddered and curled the fingers of her right hand, focussing on counting her breaths until she imagined all her loathsome thoughts flowing out of her. She couldn't think like that. Never again.

Mrs. Edevane seemed to grow more agitated towards the end of the month. She snapped at Seok Eng that her blood tofu was too cold, even though steam visibly rose from it, and berated Zaid over a tiny scratch on one of the car doors. Gean Choo did her best to keep out of her way, which wasn't difficult since Mrs. Edevane spent much of her time away from the house.

One night, shortly after she'd served the mem's dinner and they were all expecting a few minutes of peace, the bell rang from the parlour room. Gean Choo was elbow-deep in dishwater, cleaning out the big saucepan Seok Eng had used to simmer noodles.

"You'd better see what she wants," Seok Eng said.

Gean Choo shook water from her hands and dried them, leaving her kitchen towel on a hook before heading to the main house. It was raining again, so she kept to the centre of the covered walkway, narrowly avoiding stepping on a beetle as it scuttled across the path.

Behind her, the bell rang once more in the kitchen, jangling angrily, and she hurried her steps.

She found Mrs. Edevane in the parlour, her supper half-eaten on the settee table. Mrs. Edevane had abandoned her usual fastidious appearance tonight, her long hair bound up in a careless bun, her face devoid of paint. Even unaccented, her features seemed very fine—the large expressive eyes, that curious shade of pale grey; the small, narrow lips, peach-pink in their natural state. Her nose was thin and pointed, her cheekbones prominent.

"Did your parents beat you, Pearl?" she asked without preamble. She was swathed in a man's over-sized dressing gown, made of red-and-white cotton in a chequered pattern. Her hands were shoved in the pockets as she stood by the piano, lean and pale and utterly refined.

"Seldom, but—"

"Then I suppose you're not very much acquainted with pain. True pain, the sort where the sheer weight of memory wakes you up screaming at night."

She'd done that plenty of times. Well, not the screaming part. Screaming was a luxury reserved for people with sprawling bungalows and private bedrooms.

Mrs. Edevane took a seat at the piano. Her dressing gown was belted only at the waist, and when she placed her feet on the pedals, the robe's edges slid loose, revealing her knee and the bared top of her thigh. She began to play and continued speaking, which was a pity, since the music was lovely enough to be enjoyed without interruption. "My... my *superior*," she said, her mouth twisting at the word, "would like to meet you."

Cold lanced through Gean Choo. "Why?"

"There are some who believe we can never coexist peacefully with humans. Not truly. And so they seek control in the name of safety. For the preservation of life, you must understand. Yours and ours."

Gean Choo didn't follow, but she nodded anyway.

"Some of us don't approve of... freemen."

"I'm sorry?"

"Like you and Po Lam and Cookie, dear. You can think for yourself, can't you? And you do, which is delightful. But if the council had their way, I would staff my household with nothing but thralls." Mrs. Edevane's right hand did some complicated little trill, almost reaching the highest notes on the piano.

"Thralls?"

"Yes, it's like... a very obedient servant. Oh, I know you try your best, but this is something else." Mrs. Edevane stopped playing in the middle of a bar and pulled her fingers from the keys. The last notes rang in the air, begging for a major triad. She closed the cover on the piano, came over, and slapped her.

Gean Choo yelped, pressing her hand to her burning skin.

"See? If you were a thrall, that wouldn't have bothered you. I could cut off your arm and there'd be nary a whimper."

"I'm sorry," Gean Choo said, rubbing her cheek. Hopefully, Mrs. Edevane didn't intend to dismember her to prove a point.

Mrs. Edevane rolled her eyes. "Well, I suppose there's no use fretting over it." She reached inside her robe and fished out a cigarette case, pulling one out and lighting it. When she exhaled, she stared at the smoke as if it held the answers she was seeking.

"Who is your superior, Mem? And what does he want with me?"

Mrs. Edevane fixed her with her gaze. "He's an absolute arse. And I have no idea what he wants."

*Wednesday, 27 April 1927*

IF THE MEM wouldn't tell her what she needed to know, she'd have to find some other way. One morning after Mrs. Edevane had gone to bed, she cornered Po Lam along the walkway to the servants' quarters.

"Who is the mem's superior?"

Po Lam slouched against a column, hands thrust into her trouser pockets. She fished out a hand-rolled cigarette and lit it, offering it first to Gean Choo, then took a drag at her refusal. She exhaled, her full, sensuous lips pursed. Gean Choo shouldn't have noticed them, but she did. "In general? Or here? Her sire is Duchess Bennesbrook."

"Here. And she was talking about a man."

"Lord Cottesley, then," Po Lam said, as if that were self-evident. "He arrived a few months back. She's not particularly fond of him."

"He wants to meet me."

That caught Po Lam's attention. "Why?"

"She doesn't know."

"Did you forget what I said about keeping the mem's secrets? Have you seen someone? Telephoned anyone?"

"No... no!"

Po Lam stared at her. It was hard to hold her gaze, even though she'd done nothing wrong.

"You know I haven't left the house by myself. Who would I tell? It's not like anyone would believe me, anyway!" People never did. Let them scold her, beat her, harm her... as long as they didn't call her a liar. "Do you believe me?" Gean Choo asked, trying, and failing, to keep the piteous whine from her voice.

After a moment, Po Lam said, "I'd like to. The mem believes you."

"How can you tell?"

"Because you're alive."

Gean Choo shuddered. Did she believe Mrs. Edevane was a murderer? Carmilla had been, in the book. On reflection, it wasn't hard to imagine Mrs. Edevane's teeth gnawing through muscle, spilling bright, arterial blood.

"In any case, you can't lie to Lord Cottesley," Po Lam said. "He's dangerous. Worse than the others. When he talks... he can make people do things."

"What do you mean?"

"The other vampires call him a Speaker. He's part of some special bloodline that can make people obey just by giving an order."

The thought made her shiver. "Can Mrs. Edevane..."

"No. No, I don't think she can."

How would she know the difference? Was some part of her fascination with Mrs. Edevane involuntary? Or was she grasping at straws, trying to excuse herself from her own incomprehensible behaviour? "What do you suppose he wants from me?"

A gust of wind toppled over the ash column at the end of Po Lam's cigarette. She stubbed it out against a pillar, flecking the white stone. "I don't know. You must be careful. Don't antagonise him."

"Of course. I'll be on my best behaviour."

"Is Mrs. Edevane..." Po Lam trailed off, making it uncertain what she'd been trying to say.

Mrs. Edevane seemed fine, albeit somewhat distracted. She hadn't even asked Gean Choo for anything, although she watched her sometimes with a look that bordered on lust, her colourless eyes honing in on the pulse in Gean Choo's neck.

"She seems a little nervous," Gean Choo said, forcing the admission through her teeth.

"He frightens her."

"I didn't think anything could frighten her!"

"Now you know what sort of person he is."

She didn't, not really, except anyone who could frighten the mem could certainly frighten Gean Choo.

"He frightens all of them," Po Lam added. "They say he can't be bribed. That he betrayed his own sire to feed his ambitions."

"A sire is the vampire who made him?"

Po Lam nodded.

At least that was one thing the books had gotten right. "How do you know all this?"

"Some vampires still work with normal humans, not just thralls. Servants talk. It's the only thing we can do to keep each other sa... to help one another," Po Lam said.

That made sense. "I appreciate you telling me all this."

They'd spent so long talking that the first drift of sunlight reached the house, touching the weathervane with long fingers of rose gold. If only she could meet him here in the dawn light, with the shadows growing shorter, inch by inch.

Gean Choo nodded towards the sunrise. "We should try to get some sleep."

"You go on ahead." Po Lam pulled another cigarette from her pocket and lit it, the end briefly glowing red.

Gean Choo approached the servants' quarters. When she reached the door, she glanced back to see Po Lam standing with the cigarette dangling from her fingertips, looking at her. Their eyes met, and something... She was imagining things. She glanced away as if the brush of Po Lam's gaze had pained her, like touching a hot pan. Her stomach clenched, and she hurried inside, growing the distance between them. It was easier than trying to distance herself from the sentimentality she wasn't allowed to feel.

# CHAPTER 20

# PLEASE LEAVE

## GEAN CHOO

*Sunday, 15 May 1927*

P o Lam left the house for a few nights unannounced. Gean Choo had accumulated two days' leave herself, though she hadn't made any plans. Where would she go? Who would she see? The estate felt safer than town—spacious, familiar, the air clean and tinged with salt.

During the day, the sound of the new gardener's shears and the screeching of seagulls had Gean Choo tossing and turning, trying in vain to sleep while the sun shone high overhead. She missed Alif, even though they'd scarcely been able to communicate with each other. This new man was older, Indian. She wasn't sure of the specifics, since he was barely responsive to any of her attempts at light conversation. Maybe he'd been instructed not to chat on the job, or perhaps none of their languages overlapped to a sufficient degree.

Zaid tried to cheer her up, strangely, by telling her ghost stories. They'd started making the most of their language differences, with her asking questions in English and him responding in Malay. It was clear he knew about Mrs. Edevane's true nature. Had everyone known? Was she just an idiot?

"The day staff don't know," he said, holding a finger to his lips.

They were sitting on the pier, enjoying the last two hours before sundown. Gean Choo ought to have headed into the kitchen to help Seok Eng prepare dinner, but the breeze over the water was so refreshing that she couldn't bring herself to move. "Are there other creatures like the mem?"

Zaid nodded. "Many. The penanggalan are witches who can free their heads from their bodies. Their heads fly around at night, looking for blood, with their spinal column and intestines dangling. To destroy her, you must find the headless body and fill the cavity with glass shards or burn it."

Gean Choo shuddered. "You've seen one?"

He hesitated, then lowered his voice. "No... but I've seen a pontianak."

"Pontianak?"

"Beautiful women." His hands made a shape in the air, curving in and out. "Died in childbirth, or while pregnant. Or in some legends, they were stillborn themselves. She prefers to hunt men who've wronged her. During the day, she lives in the forest or in a banana tree."

"And can you save her?"

He grinned, revealing a row of teeth stained reddish-brown by betel nut. "Drive a nail in the back of her neck, and she'll make a good wife."

"That's what you should've done then," Gean Choo said, teasing. "Aren't you still a bachelor?"

Zaid fiercely shook his head. "And I'm happy to stay that way!"

ON THE PREVIOUS MONDAY Mrs. Edevane had summoned her for the first time since that night in the study. They'd sat in the big sunroom on the pier, Mrs. Edevane running her long fingers down Gean Choo's arm. She'd taken her left wrist again, and Gean Choo had been able to remain conscious the whole time, horribly aware of Mrs. Edevane's cold mouth upon her flesh, the steel in her grip. Afterwards, they'd talked about nothing in particular, or rather, Mrs. Edevane had talked and Gean Choo had listened, half-drowsing in a state of extreme languor.

She'd been quicker to recover this time, which ought to have pleased Mrs. Edevane, but the mem just seemed more irritable without Po Lam around. It was all this business with Lord Cottesley, wasn't it? It had to be. Gean Choo had done nothing to warrant the mem's discontent.

Mrs. Edevane wore an evening dress tonight, a sleeveless magenta gown spangled with beads, the skirts glittering where they caught the light. Perhaps that meant she'd be out the whole night, leaving Gean Choo in peace at last.

Mrs. Edevane fished out a pocket watch from a matching bag and consulted it, tutting at the time. "Can you drive?"

Gean Choo shook her head.

"Really, it is too inconvenient," Mrs. Edevane huffed, replacing the watch and closing her bag with a snap. "I suppose one must do everything oneself!"

Gean Choo chose not to articulate all the things Mrs. Edevane had not, in fact, done for herself that evening, including cooking her dinner, serving it, and cleaning up afterwards, cooking her pipe, repairing a loose paillette on her shoe, washing the hose she wore or the linens she'd slept upon. There was simply no point.

Mrs. Edevane tugged on a pull-cord, bouncing her foot against her calf until Zaid arrived, his cane tapping against the floor.

"Mem?" He leaned more heavily on his right side than usual. His leg must pain him today.

"I'm going out." Mrs. Edevane shrugged on a light wrap and disappeared with Zaid out the back door. The noise of the engine and the crunch of tyres on gravel sounded a moment later.

Gean Choo had been left all alone in the house before, but this felt different. The tick of the big clock in the foyer seemed too loud, the hands pointing to just after eleven o'clock. She stifled a yawn with the back of her hand. She could take a nap in the living room and no one would know.

But then Mrs. Edevane's nightgown would go unmended, her buttons unsewn. She resigned herself to sitting down with the mending basket and spent the next hour making repairs.

Midway through her chores, someone rapped on the door—three knocks, one after the other, evenly spaced like a triplet. Gean Choo jumped and clutched a shirt to her chest, wondering if she'd imagined it.

The knocks came again, louder this time, giving her no choice but to believe in them.

She set aside the mending and glanced at the clock, which began to chime. Midnight. Halfway through the hour of the rat. An hour for brigands and witches, for ghouls and those unfortunate enough to serve them.

This time, it sounded like someone was trying to wear a hole through the door.

*Bang. Bang. Bang.*

It could be a traveller who'd blown a tyre and needed help. The porch light was broken, and no one had gotten around to replacing it yet. The person at the door was standing in the dark, a suggestion of movement behind the glass panels flanking either side of the door.

One of those panels shattered. Gean Choo screamed as glass rained down over the white marble. A black-clothed leg emerged from the frame, the wood studded with jagged glass like broken teeth. The leg was followed by a sawn-off shotgun, and then the man holding the gun.

Gean Choo braced her hand on the table, standing. The phone had an extension in the servants' quarters. She wanted to go to it, to force herself to move, but she couldn't. Her body only knew one way to keep her safe, and that was to freeze. That might've worked with some jungle beast, an animal too simple to tell live prey from dead, but man was another kind of predator altogether.

Sim Lai Hock raised the gun, his finger on the trigger. "Stay there. That's a good girl."

She slowly raised her hands to chest height to show they were empty. That was the right thing to do, wasn't it? Miss Skelford had taken her to the cinema once as a treat. The seats had been so soft, like the plush darkness, punctuated by the light of the projector. The men in that film, what

Miss Skelford had called a Western, had done the same thing when staring down the barrel of a gun.

A second man strode through the newly smashed window, taller than Lai Hock, his hairline receding. He held only a pistol, its barrel pointed aimlessly at the floor as he craned his neck, taking in the glittering monstrosity of the chandelier.

"The lady got taste hor," he said, reaching out and caressing a marble statuette, eyeing it from all angles. It was a nude of a woman bathing, small enough to fit in a suitcase.

"You don't have to do this," Gean Choo said. "I have your money." Her head felt dizzy, pounding with fear. How was she meant to explain away the broken window and the fresh mud tracking all over the floor?

"Let's see it, then," Lai Hock said.

Gean Choo's hand went to her pocket, to the precious slip of paper she kept upon her person at all times. She opened the envelope she'd placed it in and took it out, offering the cheque to Lai Hock with both hands.

He grabbed it and held it up to the light. Reading the English words, he snorted and waved it in her face. "A cheque? Really?"

"It's good money," Gean Choo said. It was the first cheque she'd ever touched. She tried to take it back, but Lai Hock waved her off with the barrel of the shotgun and slipped it into the front of his jacket.

He tilted his head towards his companion, who ceased his admiration of the statue and started walking towards them, his shoes crunching over the broken glass.

"My father's debt has been paid," Gean Choo said. "Please leave."

The shotgun, previously idle, snapped back into position, pointing directly at her chest. "We've come all this way and haven't seen the rest of the house. That's not very hospitable of you. Eh, Kim Seng?"

"Your ma would be ashamed," Kim Seng said. He was only half paying attention, his covetous eyes running over the furniture, the clock, even the gleaming piano.

Lai Hock gestured with the barrel of the gun. "Hands up. Higher. Walk backwards to the stairs, then get on the floor."

Gean Choo hesitated a moment. What would Mrs. Edevane do if she found blood splattered all over her pure white floor? Would she be devastated by the violation of her belongings, the loss of all those precious curios painstakingly moved from the old world? Or would she get down on all fours, heedless of the wreckage, and lick Gean Choo's drying blood from the ruin of her chest?

"Don't be stupid," Lai Hock said.

It didn't matter either way. Last ditch heroics only worked in books and movies. Gean Choo was not so enamoured of her chances that she thought she could take on two armed men and survive.

She did as he'd asked. Kim Seng holstered his pistol and procured a rope from his satchel, using it to tie her arms behind her, then tethered her to the stair railing. He had to hunch to do so, close enough to smell the garlic on his breath. Was that poisonous to Mrs. Edevane? She'd never thought to ask. She'd never... and now she might never get the chance to—

Hot tears trembled on her lashes, welling up and sliding down her face. She sniffled.

"Don't make so much noise like that," Kim Seng said, pulling a knot tight, making her arms twitch.

Were Mrs. Edevane's neighbours awake? Would they hear her over the distance, the background hush of the ocean, the creak of cicadas in the night?

Gean Choo drew in her breath and screamed. Kim Seng punched her face, snapping her head to the left. He drew the pistol, holding it by the barrel, and rained blows over her skull and cheeks. Her nose broke with an audible crunch.

There was no room to move, no dark corner for her to cower in. She had to breathe through her mouth, through the pain, through the blood that dripped into her eyes and down her face. Kim Seng set the pistol aside for a moment and gagged her with a length of rope, its coarse fibres digging into her swollen lips. Her whole face was a throbbing mass of pain. One of her eyes refused to open while her other eye blinked madly, darting from side to side, as if seeing what was coming could do anything to stop it.

"What's this?" Kim Seng reached towards her and unhooked her earrings, jerking them out none-too-gently. He placed one of them between his teeth, then examined it under the light. "You have a good life here, don't you?"

Gean Choo couldn't say anything, wouldn't have said anything. It hurt to breathe. The light caught the facets of the garnets as if they were glowing. Swallow the pain. Think about how it'd soon be over—the shame, the futility of life. Nothing ahead, save judgement. All her sins, catalogued and tallied, with stealing among the very least of them.

Kim Seng slipped the earrings into his pocket and stood.

"We have work to do. Hurry up!" Lai Hock said.

"Don't worry so much. The mem won't be back for hours."

"We don't know that."

They'd been watching the house, making note of the mem's movements. How long had they been planning this?

Wincing, Gean Choo gingerly moved her head as far left as it would go and glanced at the clock. Fifteen minutes past midnight. The mem might not get back until closer to six. What damage could they do in six hours? Neither of them had bothered to disguise themselves.

They didn't plan to leave witnesses.

Kim Seng headed upstairs, his footsteps creaking, while Lai Hock swept the ground floor. Cabinets opened and shut, and something crunched like porcelain shattering as they ransacked the house.

She closed her eyes. At least Po Lam wasn't here; she might've done something stupid. At least this way, Gean Choo didn't have to watch her die.

Kim Seng traipsed down the stairs, holding a bulging sack. He stepped out the broken window and came back with an empty bag.

They probably had a car parked outside. Gean Choo stared at the telephone sitting in its alcove. It could've been a million miles away for all the good it could do her.

Lai Hock made two trips out the broken side panel onto the porch, and Kim Seng made three, the last one carrying the mem's gramophone. It wasn't even worth that much, but the sight of it made her chest ache.

They didn't bother going to the servants' quarters, at least, likely figuring that any savings made by a servant would be too infinitesimal to bother with. At least that meant Po Lam's things would go untouched.

"That it?" Lai Hock asked his accomplice.

"Uh-huh. Oh, weird thing... There was a big box full of dirt under the bed. Dirt! No one ever tidy there or what?"

"All right. Let's clean up, then we'll go." Lai Hock reached into a pocket and pulled out a knife, jerking the blade open with a snap. He strode up to her, spinning the blade around his fingers as he walked, the flashing silver like the fluttering wings of a butterfly. He leaned down, hands on his knees. "Say hello to your pa for me." His smirk was crooked, his eyes eager. His fist twisted in her hair, pulling her head back. The chandelier glittered in her vision, a thousand points of light sparkling, overlapping and refracting.

Cold. Beautiful. Infinite.

A door slammed open. Air buffeted her face, like a motorcar passing at high speed. The pressure left her scalp and her head dropped back, allowing her to see Mrs. Edevane holding Lai Hock by the neck, lifting him one-handed so his feet dangled an inch above the floor. The knife clattered out of his grasp as he fumbled at her grip.

Mrs. Edevane cocked her head to one side and stared at him as though eyeing a lamb for slaughter. "I'm meant to be on a diet, but I suppose I could make an exception."

A shot rang out. Mrs. Edevane staggered back a step, still holding Lai Hock, and turned her head. Even from a distance, her expression turned Gean Choo's blood to ice, her lips pressed tight in an irritated line. She held a palm against her side, and with a flick of her hand, broke Lai Hock's neck, as if she were butchering a chicken for supper.

His limp body fell to the floor, but she was already moving—had moved so quickly she appeared as a blur. Her arm encircled Kim Seng from behind, her other hand twisting in his hair, pulling back his head to bare his neck. Her teeth glinted. She met Gean Choo's gaze and smiled, sharp-fanged and red-lipped, and tore into his throat.

Gean Choo's wrist throbbed with a sympathetic pain. Bright arterial blood spurted out, and Mrs. Edevane caught it with her mouth. Kim Seng's eyes rolled back in his head and he sagged against her, the pistol falling from loose fingers.

Mrs. Edevane wasn't gentle with him. His body spasmed near the end, legs twitching as he twisted in her grasp, face sallow and puckered, like a piece of jackfruit leather. She let him drop to the floor then bent over, hands on her knees, blood dripping down her chin. Her tongue darted to the side of her lips, and she brushed the back of her hand over her mouth, smearing red all over her jaw. The spray had caught part of her dress, the blood appearing black against the magenta.

She knelt over his body, dug her fingers into his chest, and tore open his ribs, the cracking of bone almost as loud as the gunshot. She plunged her hand in and fished around, tearing out his heart. She held it high above her head and her fist closed around it, squeezing blood directly into her open mouth, her eyes fluttering shut with ecstasy.

Gean Choo couldn't breathe. She pulled against the rope again, but it held fast, preventing her from disappearing. Forget the knife, the guns. Po Lam was right. Mrs. Edevane was the most dangerous thing in this house.

Mrs. Edevane licked her fingers clean as she straightened, the heart dropping with a wet splat into the remains of Kim Seng's chest cavity. She seemed to look around herself for the first time, sighing at all the wreckage. The broken panel with its teeth of jagged glass. The two bodies, one clean with a snapped neck, the other a grotesque mess, oozing blood. The ruins of the grandfather clock, part of its face shattered by the gunshot, hands forever stuck near eleven and one.

Mrs. Edevane leaned to one side, smoothing out her bloodstained dress, and wriggled her finger through a hole in the fabric, tutting. Kim Seng had shot her. Kim Seng had *shot* her, and she was still here, upright and walking towards Gean Choo with a lightness to her step, as though she were strolling in time with some unheard music, still covered in gore from wrists to elbows.

She crouched beside Gean Choo, examining her face. "What a mess. My poor lamb." Her voice was soft and low, with all the warmth of burnished brass. It seemed a voice so tender should not be wed to the blood-spattered canvas of her face, red gleaming on her teeth.

She reached behind Gean Choo. The gag tightened for a moment, then loosened. Gean Choo spat it from her mouth, along with one of her teeth.

Mrs. Edevane pressed her fingers against the pain-filled vista that was Gean Choo's face. "Hold still for a moment," she said, as if Gean Choo had been doing nothing but holding still for the last... How long had it been? An hour?

Mrs. Edevane moved her hands and Gean Choo's nose slid back into place with a horrible crunch of cartilage, too quick for her to even scream. Immediately, Mrs. Edevane leaned in and she—she *kissed her face*, starting with her nose then branching out, her fingers cool against the back of Gean Choo's head. When Mrs. Edevane's lips passed over her eyelid, the swelling went down, followed by the pain. She moved on, pressing kisses against her forehead, her cheek, that sticky patch in her hair.

What was this? Magic. But it didn't feel that way. It felt far less impersonal, something tender, thrilling, taboo...

"There, now," Mrs. Edevane said. "Does anywhere else hurt?"

Only the pulpy hollow in her gum and the ache in her limbs from being stuck in the same place for so long, but those were minor concerns, easily forgotten. Gean Choo shook her head. "He shot you. Do you need a..." she was almost about to say doctor, "care, Mem?"

"I'm quite fine." Mrs. Edevane handled her delicately, as though she were made of cut paper tissue, apt to crumple at the slightest misuse. She pressed her cold, dead hand against Gean Choo's healed cheek, turning her face. Gean Choo moved with her, leaning into her touch. She owed Mrs. Edevane her life. She owed her everything.

Mrs. Edevane leaned down and their lips met. She tasted of copper and death. Gean Choo ought to have pulled back, ought to have recoiled with revulsion, but instead, she melted into the kiss, into the strange, cool softness that was Mrs. Edevane's mouth.

Mrs. Edevane's tongue found a gash on Gean Choo's lip. She sucked on it, causing it to throb.

Gean Choo stifled a moan. Mrs. Edevane had only come to her twice, counting that first night in the study. How curious it had been, the strange sensation of being tethered in such an intimate position, the mem's terrifying strength holding her in place. With foreknowledge, the act had lost some of its horror. She'd have welcomed Mrs. Edevane's fangs that night, sprawled in the grand wreckage of the foyer. At least then she could've been useful for something.

Who was she fooling? She'd have done anything for her saviour in that moment, giddy for her narrow escape from death's door. She'd been forgiven. Freed. Reborn. The rush was transcendent.

Mrs. Edevane ran her tongue over Gean Choo's lip, sealing the wound, her skin crawling and itching as it knitted together. She strained against the rope, desperately needing to be free.

Mrs. Edevane only chuckled. "They made those knots nice and tight, did they?" She traced her hands over Gean Choo's shoulders and down her bound arms, then began tugging at the rope. She must have used a blade, or perhaps even a broken shard of glass, because the rope snapped, allowing her to pull away and shift her shoulders more easily, though her wrists remained tied to each other.

Perhaps the light was playing tricks on her eyes, because Mrs. Edevane's fingertips appeared almost black for a second as she brought her hands back to her sides.

"Thank you," Gean Choo said, waiting for Mrs. Edevane to finish untying her. She trembled with unspent nerves, her knees aching from the hard unyielding floor, trying not to let her gaze drift to the two lumps that had been human only minutes ago.

"Were these your creditors, Pearl?"

She hung her head in shame. "Y-yes, Mem. They came here because of me. I'm so sorry—"

"I see. Well, no harm done. No need to tell the others, I suppose. This can be our little secret, can't it?"

What a gift she was offering her. The gift of silence. Of face. No need to weather Po Lam's contempt, nor have the brothers blame her for all the extra work they would be forced to do. No one else need know her shame —the debt, the threats, her complete failure to give prior warning of Lai Hock's attentions.

Tears welled up in her eyes now that the worst was over. She'd come so close to death and Mrs. Edevane hadn't just saved her; she'd healed her, held her, and held her secret. She didn't deserve this. She didn't deserve any of it.

"Shh, shh. Don't cry, my pet." Mrs. Edevane gathered her close, resting her head against her shoulder. Gean Choo inhaled the powdery dry down of her fragrance, something woodsy and green. She longed to reach out, to tentatively wrap her arms around Mrs. Edevane in return, but she couldn't. Her wrists were still tied. She tried to stop her sobbing, at least, which resulted in streaks of crying punctuated by moments when she held her breath.

"Perhaps you misunderstand me," Mrs. Edevane said, drawing back, her fingers digging into Gean Choo's hip. "I really cannot abide a crier. You'll have to learn to turn that off."

Gean Choo gulped in air. She could stop herself from crying. *Just stop.* "Mem, please. You're hurting me."

Mrs. Edevane released her. "Sometimes I forget my own strength," she murmured, though not quite an apology. She stood and left, crossing to another room, but came back a moment later. "I rang the bell. Zaid will be with you shortly, to help," she gestured with a flick of her wrist, "clean up this mess."

She still hadn't unbound her. "Thank you, Mem."

Mrs. Edevane peered at the blood beneath her fingernails and sighed. "What a disaster. I'll be in the bath," she said, and hummed as she walked upstairs, practically floating, her feet light.

Later, when examining her memories, Gean Choo could almost believe she'd imagined the mem's forceful touch, some distorted figment of stress and fear leading her astray. But she wore the bruises where Mrs. Edevane's fingers had pressed into her hip—five small ovals, like the paw print of some unknowable beast.

# CHAPTER 21

# A BORING LIFE

## PO LAM

*Monday, 16 May 1927*

When Po Lam returned, sometime after midnight, the house was in complete disarray. From Gean Choo's garbled explanation, it seemed clear that Mrs. Edevane had foiled an attempted robbery, leaving quite a mess for them. Between Zaid and herself, they hauled the bodies to the boat, shrouding them in hessian and weighing them down with bricks. The garden shed was running low on heavy objects.

They rowed out to sea and dropped off their grisly cargo, then rowed back. Zaid watched her all the while with studied indifference.

"What?" Po Lam said.

"Glad it went all right."

Glad she wasn't imagining things. Glad her conscience wasn't taking over.

"Sorry I wasn't there," Zaid said.

Gean Choo could've died if the burglars had been serious about not leaving a witness. A clean death, though; an honest one. Was it worse that she'd survived?

They made it back to the pier in record time. She needed to get rid of the robbers' car. In the morning, she'd call a glazier to replace the panel by the door, and maybe to install steel bars. The mess made it apparent that Mrs. Edevane had fed, eschewing her usual fussiness about men. That would buy Po Lam time to source her next meal.

Back at the house, Gean Choo had cleaned up the blood and glass and was putting the stolen loot back in their proper places. There was a pinkish stain on the marble she hadn't quite been able to remove. The twins would have to do their best with it when they arrived later that morning.

Po Lam brushed the damp hair from her face. Her arms ached from the row. She was already bone tired and it was only—she pulled out her pocket watch—half-past two. "The mem upstairs?" she asked.

"Yes," Gean Choo said.

"I'll move the car. I'll be back in a few hours."

"Wait!" Gean Choo reached out and grabbed her sleeve.

Po Lam glanced down at her hand, fisted in the white fabric. Gean Choo released her.

"Take me with you. Zaid is still here, isn't he? He can tell her where we've gone."

"I won't be long. You'll be fine on your own."

"Please," she said, her palms pressed together, raised to chest height.

Po Lam glanced around at all the things not yet done. Several sacks still filled with looted knickknacks, not yet put back into place. The broken grandfather clock, its debris swept up but its hands still unmoving at eleven and one. "Fine. Wait by the robbers' car."

"Oh, thank you, thank you!"

Po Lam found Zaid on the verandah of the servants' quarters, smoking. "I'm dropping off the car. Mem's upstairs."

"All right. Everything fine?"

She hesitated a moment. "Yes. Do what you can with the mess. We won't be long."

The girl was already in the car when she returned. Po Lam slid into the driver's seat and placed her hands upon the unfamiliar controls, starting the ignition.

"This one looks different to the mem's car," Gean Choo said, glancing down at the control panel.

"That one has an adjustment for Zaid. The clutch has a hand control instead," Po Lam said, pulling out into the driveway.

"Because of his leg?"

"Yes."

"What happened to him?"

"You should ask him." The estate gates were wide open. "No one came about the gunshots?"

Gean Choo shook her head. "There was only one shot. Maybe they were all asleep." She got out to close the gates once Po Lam was through, though she couldn't lock them. The mechanism had been broken, yet another thing to fix in the morning. Gean Choo climbed back in. "Where are we going?"

"An empty lot, north. We'll have to walk back, all right?"

"As long as I'm with you, it's fine. I mean... I'm happy not to be on my own."

Thank the heavens for the cover of night, for the darkness that cloaked Po Lam's face. She ought not to be moved by that. She wasn't the sort of person anyone should rely upon.

The streets were quiet at this hour, with only the odd lorry passing, headlights momentarily blinding. It was a while before Gean Choo spoke again.

"How many people has the mem killed?"

She could lie. Not to protect the mem, but to protect herself. Mrs. Edevane could get sentimental about her girls, their recent visit to the cemetery a case in point. If Gean Choo were to compromise them, she couldn't count on Mrs. Edevane to act in a rational manner.

"More in England, I've heard," Po Lam said.

Mrs. Edevane managed her appetites, more or less. She'd only lost control after the Great Flu had burnt its way through the colony. Po Lam shuddered to remember it. If the mem ever got to that point again, she'd leave. No more making excuses. The moment she touched Seok Eng, or

Zaid, or—ancestors forbid—Po Lam herself, she'd have no choice but to leave.

Gean Choo, on the other hand, was a lost cause.

"Do you think..." Gean Choo rubbed at her throat, which remained unblemished for now. As if realising what she was doing, she dropped her hands in her lap, fingers curved over her empty palms like the legs of a dying spider. "Never mind."

"If you're going to speak, then speak."

Perhaps Po Lam's tone had been harsher than intended, because Gean Choo flinched. "I just... Mrs. Edevane's already paid me for a year. If I leave at the end of it... then everything will be all right, won't it?"

"Return the money. Then you can leave whenever you like." Or the smarter thing to do would be to keep the money, use it to start a new life, with a new name. No one would know her in Penang or Ipoh.

And most of all, if she left now, she'd be alive.

"I couldn't."

That was how Mrs. Edevane hooked them, with kindness, with the promise of a better life. What had Gean Choo been running from that made Mrs. Edevane feel like the safer choice?

"Hey," Gean Choo said softly. Po Lam took her attention off the road for a second to glance at her, at those defenceless eyes, so deep and brown and open. Gean Choo stared blindly at the road, one hand pressed against the car door, as though to anchor herself in its solidity. She'd looked at Alif that way, hadn't she? And the mem. Never at Po Lam.

"What?"

"Thank you for tonight. For letting me come with you. I didn't want to stay in that big house after... after something like that."

When Po Lam glanced back at the road, what she saw made her slam on the brakes.

Gean Choo screamed.

The car lurched to a halt, throwing Po Lam against the steering wheel and Gean Choo against the windscreen. Gean Choo went straight through the glass, rolling across the bonnet and tumbling down onto the road.

Po Lam ran out of the car and went to her body, at the far boundary of the headlights. They were the only souls on the road, the car's beams the sole points of nearby light aside from the stars.

When she rolled Gean Choo over, she came away with blood on her hands.

"Teo Gean Choo!"

She coughed, trying to rise onto her side. Po Lam helped her, smearing blood on her shirt. Beads of it rolled down Gean Choo's cheeks and Po Lam suppressed a shudder.

"I'm fine." Gean Choo gripped Po Lam's arm with trembling hands. "Help me up."

"You're bleeding," Po Lam said, her voice hoarse. She tried to look for any other obvious signs of injury, but it was too dark. "What hurts?"

"I said I'm fine. Just bruised, I think." She pulled on Po Lam's shirt. "Come on, we can't stay in the middle of the road like this."

They staggered back to the car, Gean Choo's arm looped around Po Lam's neck. Once inside, Po Lam passed Gean Choo a clean handkerchief. "To stop the bleeding," she said.

Gean Choo leaned her head back against the seat and held the cloth to her face with her eyes closed.

"Don't fall asleep," Po Lam said. She got up again to sweep the excess glass from the bonnet so a stray piece wouldn't blow back at them while driving. When she started the car, she began at a crawl, no longer trusting her instincts nor her judgement. She turned the car in a wide circle, heading in the opposite direction. A walk of several hours was now out of the question.

"What was that you saw on the road?" Gean Choo asked, her words slightly slurred. "Was it an animal?"

How could she say it was a ghost, a phantom? Or worse still, that she was simply going mad? She'd seen... something. A woman, maybe, in a white shift, long black hair tangled in the breeze. But when she'd gotten out, there'd just been Gean Choo on the road.

"Yes. I'm sorry."

"I forgive you."

Po Lam winced. Gean Choo slumped against her seat, head falling towards the driver's side, her mouth ajar.

"Hey. Hey, wake up!"

"'m not asleep."

"Can you walk five minutes? We'll have to find some place to sleep."

Gean Choo sat up, then groaned as she jostled some unseen hurt. "We're not going home?"

"You can't go with an open wound."

"We have to go back."

It was hard to see where the path met the road in the dark. Po Lam missed her turn, cursed, and circled back around. "You're bleeding."

"That shouldn't matter. She... she kissed my face earlier, when it was hurt."

Po Lam had not needed to know that, but now the image burned into her mind like a lithograph. She found the right road, and the car shuddered as it crossed the uneven ground. "She'd only just fed. You can't be in the house with a big cut like that."

"It doesn't matter! She took a bullet for me, and I just left her!"

Po Lam made herself speak in her most soothing voice. "Remember the rules. No blood in the house."

"No blood in the house," Gean Choo echoed, her brows two wings of consternation. "But—"

"You'll see her tomorrow night. That will have to do."

The path ran out, the forest encroaching until there was nowhere left to drive. She parked and got out, going to the back seat where she'd left a lamp and a canteen of water. She lit the lamp, then picked up both items. When she circled around to the passenger's side and offered a hand, Gean Choo waved her away.

"I'm feeling better," she said, and peeled the handkerchief away from her face. There was one large cut diagonally across her forehead and some smaller ones. The large one began to seep blood.

Sailing through a car window and hitting the road was the sort of accident that most people didn't walk away from. Was there some symbiotic benefit to Mrs. Edevane's consumption, casting a protective spell over those she fed upon?

"It's not yet clotted. You should leave it on."

Gean Choo's fumbling hands struggled with the task, forcing Po Lam to help her. When she accidentally grazed Gean Choo's arm, her skin seemed cold and clammy.

Shock, or close enough to it. Po Lam gripped her elbow and led them through the damp grass. They walked a short distance from the car and stopped outside a shack, no more than four walls and a roof, raised off the ground on stilts. There were many empty buildings like this in the area. Perhaps they'd been used as workers' lodgings back when this plantation had been operational, but now it lay abandoned, a gaping hole in the roof open to the night sky.

"I'm thirsty," Gean Choo said.

Po Lam passed her the canteen. Her lamp wavered over the walls of the shack, the scuffed dirt-covered flooring, the puddle of brown water pooled beneath the hole in the roof.

Gean Choo drank, then passed the canteen back. "Do we have to stay here? What if there are... hantu?"

"What hantu? We've left all that behind us. You're the one who wanted to leave the house."

The thought seemed to calm her, but only for a moment. "What if she misses us?"

Po Lam had to fight not to grimace. Mrs. Edevane, missing them? Perhaps she'd be inconvenienced by their absence if she wanted to smoke or... or something else. But to truly miss someone, one had to care for them first.

Gean Choo had apparently resigned herself to staying, lying down away from the puddle, uncaring of the dirt and the unforgiving stiffness of the floorboards. The handkerchief was dark across her face with blood.

"Sit up. It's dangerous to sleep so soon after a head injury."

Gean Choo rolled onto her back, blinking resentfully. Po Lam peeled the handkerchief from her forehead, and Gean Choo flinched.

"Do you have a spare?" Po Lam asked, holding out the bloodied handkerchief.

Gean Choo patted her pockets, then handed her one. Po Lam used some of the water from the canteen to wet the cloth, then gently patted at her forehead, holding up the lantern with her other hand to check for glass. No shards had been left in the cut, or at least none she could see. She moved the lantern from side to side to examine the wound from different angles. "You're very lucky."

"Lucky," Gean Choo echoed.

"I don't think this will scar. Here, hold this for a moment." Po Lam indicated the handkerchief and waited until Gean Choo had applied pressure before letting go. She took a step back and began unbuttoning her shirt.

"What're you doing?"

"You need a bandage. I'll take the sleeves off."

"You can use my dress."

"It's been on the road." How could she forget the awful screech of tyres, the crash of shattering glass, the endless seconds until she'd confirmed Gean Choo was still breathing?

"I'll turn it inside out."

"The mem bought it. Use mine," Po Lam added after a moment's hesitation.

"All right."

Po Lam shrugged out of her shirt, which was long-sleeved with knot buttons. The material did not want to come apart until she caught a loop of thread with her teeth and snapped it, making the rest of the seam easier to unravel.

Gean Choo stared at her. Po Lam still wore loose pants with their deep pockets. The top half of her vest was showing—a tight, sleeveless undergarment with small buttons all down the front, flattening her chest. "What?" she said, her ears hot.

"Your arms are so pale," Gean Choo said. "I suppose you're always wearing long sleeves."

Po Lam turned her attention back to the wound. When she'd finished arranging Gean Choo's hair over the bandage, it didn't look half-bad.

Perhaps she should've taken them to a hospital, but at this time of the night? It would only raise questions she didn't want to answer.

"We'll find a chemist in the morning and re-dress it," Po Lam said. She still had to leave the car somewhere. It was far more likely they could catch a ride back to the house if they started their trip downtown, rather than out in the near wilderness.

Gean Choo reached up and patted the knots in the bandage, tied over her ears so she could still lie on her back to sleep. "I'm sure it's fine." She hesitated. "I still don't see why we couldn't have gone home. The mem can heal wounds."

Po Lam inhaled sharply. "This is not my idea of fun, either."

"I'm sorry." Gean Choo rolled over, bracing her head on one arm. "Shouldn't you sleep, too?"

She should. It wasn't as if anyone was about to rob them, not out here in this cesspit. Po Lam crouched down and laid herself out on the hard wooden floor. She must've gone soft to be squeamish about a little dirt. "For the sake of your head, you should probably stay awake for a while."

"Come keep me awake, then." Gean Choo blushed crimson to her ears. "Not like that."

How was she meant to interpret that? The blush, and the way her own insides twisted. Gean Choo's eyes fell upon her as she stared at the hole in the roof, the patch of stars showing through. At least it wasn't raining.

"Tell me about your family. You weren't born in the Straits, were you?" Gean Choo asked.

"No. My family's from Shiuhing."

"An immigrant like me! But my family's from Amoy." Gean Choo went on, describing her parents and the years of their deaths, 1918 for her mother and only a few months ago for her father. "I never had a sibling. I would've liked a sister, I think. I always meant to ask Pa why he didn't take a second wife, but he never told me."

"So you have no family here?" Po Lam asked. "In the Straits, that is."

"None."

That explained why she'd accepted Mrs. Edevane's job offer. The better lodging houses had to be alert to her reputation by now, discouraging their girls from the inauspicious estate in Tanjong Katong. "You didn't want to go back to Amoy?"

Gean Choo was silent for so long that perhaps she'd fallen asleep. Po Lam was about to shake her when Gean Choo spoke. "I can't go back. I never told them... They still think father's alive."

That confession took Po Lam's breath away. What could be less filial than to let one's own father go unmourned, unable to take his place at the altar of ancestors? But if she never told them, if she still sent them letters stamped with his chop, no one would expect her to return home, to serve the family, to wed someone of their choosing.

"Not forever," Gean Choo went on. "It was never to be forever. I thought... I thought if I were married already, I wouldn't have to go back."

"I thought you didn't want to get married?"

Gean Choo blew out air from between pursed lips. "But I should want to, shouldn't I?

"What do you actually want?"

Gean Choo rolled over, leaning her weight on her elbows, eyes gleaming like polished mahogany. "For someone to really need me. To be the centre of their world. That's selfish, isn't it?"

"No. I'm sure it's something most people want."

"What do you want?"

Now it was Po Lam's turn to be silent. Her work left very little space for socialising, courting, *wooing*... she wouldn't even know where to start. She didn't seem destined for a future that included those things. "A boring life."

"Whatever do you mean?"

"I mean just that. Boring. No murders, no late-night accidents on deserted streets. I'd like to wake up with the sun for once and sleep through the night."

"I understand. But I'm glad you came back tonight."

Po Lam could've easily found Mrs. Edevane absent and Gean Choo's body sprawled in the foyer, her brains blown out against the far wall. She shuddered. How different things might've been.

Gean Choo shifted, twisting to pillow her head against her hands. "Your undergarment... it's like a bandeau, isn't it? My mother used to wear something like that. A 'little vest,' she called it. I remember..." she trailed off. "You have the perfect silhouette."

She meant flat. Boyish. "I doubt anyone would ever call me fashionable." And Po Lam hadn't had fashion on her mind when she'd told the seamstress what she'd wanted. It'd made things easier, though. The woman had pointed out the colourful posters of young girls in tight vests over loose-sleeved tunics, their cheeks pink, torsos straight and narrow.

Gean Choo laughed. It was pleasant to hear her laugh. She wanted to hear it again.

"It's like... have you ever wrapped a skirt so tight it was hard to walk?" Po Lam asked, and Gean Choo nodded. "That's how I feel when I don't have this on. But it's not just uncomfortable. It's also that I'm not... right."

"But sometimes... I mean, do people call you 'brother' by mistake?"

"When I started working for the mem, there were so few women that dressing as a man was easy enough. I even wore my hair in a queue for a while. People didn't expect to find a woman, so they didn't see one. I got better with practise. It's never been safe to be a woman walking alone at night."

"Do you think..." Gean Choo swallowed and lowered her voice. "Do you think the heavens made a mistake by not making you a boy?"

It was the wrong sort of question to be asking on such a night, the moon almost full, far from everything, surrounded by the damp and verdant forest. On such a night, one could believe the gods were listening.

"It is what it is," Po Lam said firmly, to put an end to the conversation. No matter how she cut her hair or lowered her voice, "eldest sister" was a role she could never walk away from, not even here, an ocean away from her family.

"I heard a story," Gean Choo said, as if Po Lam had invited her to continue, "a myth about a husband who wanted a son—"

"Every husband, you mean?"

"His wife had a daughter instead, but she raised the girl, Iphis, as a boy. Iphis fell in love with a woman, but they could not wed. Bereft, Iphis prayed to her goddess, who turned her into a man so she might stay with her beloved." Gean Choo looked at her expectantly.

Po Lam didn't have to answer. She owed her nothing. She answered, all the same, "Have you read a book called 'Flowers in the Mirror'? It describes a country where women are magistrates and scholars, and men are considered the vacuous ones, ineffectual and weak. If we're to make wishes, I'd wish to have been born there."

"I've never thought of you as weak."

At least the darkness hid Po Lam's blush.

Gean Choo fumbled with her hair, smoothing a lock behind her ear. "The mem says in some places in Europe it's... well, if not common, then unremarkable, that some men dress like women and some women like men. And the Bugis recognise five types of people, not just male and female." She said it like she was reciting a fact for school, as if she expected Po Lam to affirm her cleverness, to give her a pat on the head. Her words catalogued Po Lam, dissected her, labelled her in a neat box filled with European degenerates, actresses, and pirates.

"Don't do that," Po Lam said.

"What?"

Everything. Nothing. Po Lam was cruelly aware of the heat of her, the curve of her lips, the folds of her dress as it clung to her thighs. "Talk about things you don't understand."

Gean Choo shifted, raising her head. Her eyes softened as she met Po Lam's gaze. "But I want to understand."

Some might have called that a gift from the heavens. What else could it be? A girl alone in the dark, wounded and blithely unconcerned, desperate for connection. Trusting. Po Lam had to turn her head aside, stare at the far wall, at some indeterminable brown stain darkening the wood. "Let's talk about something else."

Gean Choo blew out a sigh. "All right." She left her in silence for a few moments, which stretched out for so long that maybe she'd given up on conversation, but then she piped up again. "Sometimes the way you talk about the mem, during the day... it makes it sound like you hate her. Why do you still work for her?"

"Same reason as you."

Gean Choo shifted her head but didn't speak, waiting her out.

Po Lam caved. She owed Mrs. Edevane everything. "She paid for all my sisters to go to school. One even went on to university," she said, a near-impossibility for a woman from a poor family. The day she'd heard the news, she'd had to take five minutes behind the generator to cry tears of pride. "And... she taught me. Well, hired tutors for me. Writing, dialects, arithmetic... the basics."

It was impractical, Po Lam had argued, so many years ago, for Mrs. Edevane to hire a separate interpreter, one who might grow to suspect her true nature. It was far more sensible to train Po Lam to do the job herself.

So, by Mrs. Edevane's side, she'd crammed her head full of knowledge and her belly full of food. How could she judge Gean Choo for making the same choice?

Po Lam took a breath. "I don't hate her. She devours, that's all. It's in her nature. Never forget that."

"But I suppose some deserved it. Like those men tonight."

The last girl hadn't deserved it, nor the prostitute, nor the plantation worker from Johor, or the opium server before her. But to say more would implicate herself, and Po Lam wasn't ready to have Gean Choo's horror turned towards her. Not just yet.

She was weak.

Gean Choo yawned, pressing her hand to her mouth. "Has that been awake enough? I'd like to sleep."

Po Lam turned up the lantern to consult her pocket watch. "Four-fifteen. Yes, you should try to rest."

Gean Choo exhaled in relief and turned away, shuffling to get comfortable. "Good night," she mumbled sleepily. "Thank you for looking after me."

It was her delusion that had sent Gean Choo through the window in the first place. She wasn't doing anything extraordinary. "Good night," Po Lam said, and blew out the lantern.

# CHAPTER 22

## I OWE HER

### GEAN CHOO

*Monday, 16 May 1927*

Gean Choo slept through the dawn, despite the sunlight streaming in overhead, forming a spotlight from the hole in the ceiling. She'd woken in the middle of the night, arms around Po Lam, heart filled with this strange, foreign longing. Perhaps she'd imagined it, dreamed it. The feeling evaporated when she woke, insubstantial as incense.

"We need to leave," Po Lam said. "I'll drop the car off in town, and we can find our way back from there."

"Mm." She reached up and gently patted her bandage. Her head still throbbed, and her hips and spine longed for the soft comfort of her bed. She'd have welcomed anything that shortened the walk home.

She shuffled back into the car, dusting off her dress before getting in, cringing at the friction of grit between her clothes and the seat, even though none of that mattered. It wasn't the mem's car.

Po Lam drove them into town, the breeze gusting through the jagged remains of the windshield. Passing motorists stared at them oddly. Po Lam kept to the side streets before pulling into an alleyway.

She took her canteen but left the lantern in the back of the car.

"Come on," she said, not bothering to look back before rushing to the next street.

Gean Choo had to hurry to keep up. At the next intersection, Po Lam stopped, causing Gean Choo to almost collide with her.

"Isn't your lodging house around here?" Po Lam asked.

Gean Choo glanced around, recognising the drugstore on the corner. "Two blocks away. Why?"

"There's a bank there too, isn't there? Do you have papers?" Po Lam asked, still walking.

Her mother had never thought to register her birth. It had never mattered. If she'd ever had other papers, they'd been lost in the flurry of her father's descent into narcotic bliss. "No."

"Ask Mrs. Edevane to give it to you in cash, then. Why did you need it all at once, anyhow?"

Po Lam had watched her retrieve the cheque from Lai Hock's body, so she could hardly deny its existence. "I-I wanted to send some home... to my family," she lied.

"It'd be easier to deal with in cash. Send back what you'd like, then bury the rest somewhere in the garden. Keep the knowledge of where it is up here," Po Lam pointed to her head, "and don't tell anyone. Not me, not the other staff, not Mrs. Edevane."

"Thank you. I will." Gean Choo had never had an elder sister, a real one, looking out for her safety or her future. Po Lam made her wish for that. For something like that. But if she were being honest with herself, her feelings about Po Lam weren't sisterly at all.

They came to her old lodging house, the narrow street crowded on either side with shop signs, rickshaws, and pedestrians.

"How much do you owe?" Po Lam asked.

"Seven dollars," Gean Choo said, blushing. "But I don't have it on me—"

"I'll lend it. After what happened, we shouldn't leave any of your old debts standing. It's bad luck. Do you have others?"

Gean Choo shook her head. "I shouldn't ask this of you. I can come back once I've got—"

"You're not asking me; I'm telling you." Po Lam reached into her pants pocket and pulled out a billfold, handing over eight crumpled Straits dollars. "The extra is for the delay. I'll wait for you here." She fished out a cigarette and lit it, inhaling deeply and breathing out a cloud of smoke. "Well?" She jerked her head towards the building. "Go on, then."

Repay this debt, but form a new one between herself and Po Lam. She'd pay her back, of course, as soon as she could. That should only take a week, or however long Mrs. Edevane took to offer her yet another favour. Would it change her luck? The thought clung to her, irrational, that her debt to Po Lam would bind them, like a cheat's way of creating a red string of fate, one made by lien. But it was only a thought.

She climbed the dark, creaking stairs, wrinkling her nose at the smell of mould, sweat, and raw sewerage. She'd lodged here for months, and now she couldn't imagine condemning a dog to live like this.

"Hello?" she called out when she reached the landing. She peeked into her room. Her old bunk had been claimed, with someone else's belongings now stored all around it.

"Ah, it's you. Your mem throw you out already?"

Gean Choo turned to find Bee Leng staring at her, eyes reddened from too little sleep or crying, or both. A lit cigarette dangled from her fingers and smoke wafted as she gestured. "What happened to your head?"

"A little accident. It's nothing," Gean Choo said, smoothing down her hair over the bandage. She reached into her waistband and took out Po Lam's money, offering it with both hands. "For your ma. I came to repay my debt."

Bee Leng stabbed her cigarette into the corner of her mouth and took the cash, counting it with practised ease. She shoved it into a pocket. "Well. You must be doing fine, then." Her cool, assessing stare took in the cut of Gean Choo's hair, the crumpled line of her dress, the bloodstains around the neckline from her head wound. She glanced towards the windows. "Your gentleman friend is handsome."

"She's my colleague... and a woman." In Hokkien, "she" and "he" were perfect homophones, so she had to elaborate.

If anything, that made Bee Leng's acquisitive stare even more appreciative. "Hmm. Does your mem need another amah? A cook? I can wash and sew, too." She flicked ash onto the floor, the end of her cigarette pink from her lipstick. "I'm not just a pretty face."

"I'll ask her. And I'll put in a good word for you," Gean Choo said, the lie coming easily to her lips. "If you're not afraid of hantu."

"You've managed. It can't be so haunted, can it?"

The crack of his ribs. The oozing squelch of his heart, crushed between Mrs. Edevane's fingers.

"I suppose not. Take care," Gean Choo said.

When she made her way back to the glaring sunshine on the street, Po Lam was waiting impatiently, hands thrust into her pockets. "What took so long? There's so much to do before dusk."

"I know. I'm sorry." They'd left the house in a terrible state. The mem would be sleeping now because of the daylight hours, but when she woke that night, everything had to be in order. The other servants would be justifiably upset with all the extra tasks they'd left them.

They caught a mosquito bus to Kalang Road, joining an older woman wearing hijab. She paid them no mind, her head bent low over her crochet. The bus rattled and shuddered over the laterite road, disgorging them near the golf course.

They walked the rest of the way. The sun beat down mercilessly, doing nothing for Gean Choo's headache. Still, it seemed pointless to complain, so she kept her mouth shut. At least she hadn't ruined her dress. Poor Po Lam, bare-armed in her torn shirt, like she didn't have a wife at home to sew the edges neat. She had such fine arms though, paler than her hands and firm with muscle. Po Lam caught her looking. Gean Choo smiled. Po Lam glanced away. Did she think she was teasing? She wasn't. Not really. But would it matter if she were?

"About last night," Gean Choo began.

"Forget it." Po Lam walked a little faster, forcing her to hurry.

"I just wanted to say I'm sorry. I shouldn't have asked so many personal questions. I didn't mean to, but I did—did ask, I mean—and so I'm sorry." Gean Choo paused to take a breath, but hurried on before she could be interrupted. "I just wanted to say that how you dress is your business, and it doesn't change—I mean, I won't mention—that is, it's what's on the inside that counts. Inside your heart. And I think you try to be cold because you feel you have to be. But you've been nothing but kind to me, and for that, I'm grateful." She pressed her fingertips together and bowed over them without breaking her stride.

Po Lam stopped short. Gean Choo kept walking, oblivious, until she turned her head to find Po Lam wasn't there.

"All right," Po Lam said softly.

Gean Choo should've kissed her last night. Why hadn't she? Concussion. But though her head ached fiercely this morning, it wasn't the only reason.

When they reached the house, approaching from the back verandah out of habit, it was clear the other servants had been busy. All the mess had vanished, even the smashed clock. The glass panel near the door had been replaced, leaving nothing to show for that eventful night. Even the sacks of stolen goods had been removed, causing Gean Choo's heart to race, until she found them in their rightful places upstairs—the books, the record player, even the lewd jade figurines with their creative uses of anatomy.

"It seems we can safely get some sleep," Po Lam said from behind her. "I'll thank the others when I see them."

Was it late enough that she should expect to find Seok Eng in the kitchen, preparing Mrs. Edevane's blood tablets in the oven? What day was it, anyway? Gean Choo hurried out of the study, brushing past Po Lam on the way out. She closed the door between the hallway and the stairwell, flicking on the corridor light to compensate for shutting off the upper floor's last source of daylight.

"Don't," Po Lam said.

Gean Choo didn't want to think too hard about the way she said it, with mingled frustration and fear. "She took a bullet for me. A bullet! I didn't even say 'good dawn' to her. I never miss that, ever."

"You can tell her yourself when she wakes up tonight."

"What if no one checked? What if she hit her head in the bath and drowned?"

"Do you realise how ridiculous you're being?" Po Lam hissed.

"I have to. I owe her," she couldn't explain how she owed her, "so much," she finished. "She healed me. She saved my life." She'd literally saved her face, and not so literally, too. Gean Choo pressed her finger to her lips. She slipped into Mrs. Edevane's room, shutting out Po Lam, and turned on the light. A bulb flickered on overhead, diffused by frosted glass, revealing the Persian rug, the dressing table with its mirror painted over with a pastoral scene of lambs in a meadow, their shepherdess in the background. Like the study, everything was in order, the drawers all shut, the counter littered with perfume bottles, cosmetics, and brushes.

The door handle turned. She pressed her weight against the door, holding it shut, then locked it.

The handle rattled and Po Lam rapped on the other side. "Teo Gean Choo, get out of there right now! That's an order!"

She had to know. One quick look, and then she'd go. She murmured an apology to Po Lam under her breath and dropped the key onto a side table.

The light flickered out overhead, plunging her into darkness for a moment. She stood still, suddenly blind. In the dark, a tokay called out with its rhythmic squeak: *to-kay, to-kay*. When the generator kicked in again, the light sputtering back on, she looked for the spotted lizard among the furniture and across the ceiling, but if it was there, she couldn't see it.

The bed was a four poster, canopied and veiled on every side by thick velvet curtains, blocking out the light. The heat was trapped in the room with the window shutters closed.

Gean Choo twitched aside one of the curtains, bridging the boundaries of the bed, the last bastion of her mem's privacy invaded—foolish, impudent, wrong. Her body displaced the drapes, permitting in a thin sliver of the weak electric light. Was that shapeless mass a person, or a pile of bolsters and pillows?

The meagre light caught the gleam of eyes watching her. Gean Choo jumped, pressing her hand to her chest. The overwhelming urge to be away, to run, washed over her like the tide dragging over the shore. "I just came to make sure you're all right, Mem. I'm sorry to disturb you."

Mrs. Edevane lifted her thin, pale hand and curled her fingers. Gean Choo had to lean in close to hear her. "Come lie with me."

Lie? A word that could mean many different things. Sweat plastered Gean Choo's dress to her spine. "I should let you rest, Mem—"

"We'll rest. Together." Mrs. Edevane turned back the covers and shifted to one side, leaving room for Gean Choo. The bed was large, so they wouldn't be touching.

Gean Choo was still in the same dusty dress from the night before and didn't want to get dirt on the sheets, but she wasn't about to undress before her employer. She removed her shoes, then slipped into bed, calculating the hours of remaining daylight. It was somewhere around two, perhaps? So maybe five daylight hours left. Long enough for the mem to fall asleep again, and for her to creep out.

The mattress was a welcome relief, colder than the surrounding air. The sheets were smooth and thick, soft against her skin.

"Where were you?" Mrs. Edevane asked, still in a whisper, her voice dry and liable to cut, like a stack of paper being shuffled. "What if more men had come back? It's impossible for a woman to feel safe alone."

"I'm sorry. The car... Someone might've asked questions. We had to get rid of it."

Mrs. Edevane's hand crept towards Gean Choo's forehead. She slid a finger under the bandages, peeling them off. Her nostrils flared. "You were hurt."

"It's fine. I'm fine."

The daylight hours were not kind to Mrs. Edevane's beauty. Her skin was stretched taut over her forehead, her eyes deeply sunken, cheekbones sharp, the fat deposits melted away to give an overall appearance that Gean Choo could only call cadaverous.

She was in bed with a corpse.

She'd sat vigil over her mother when she'd caught the great flu; held her father's hand when he'd succumbed to opium dross, spittle trailing down his chin, mouth curved and smiling. Corpses could not hurt her. Most corpses, at least.

"Come hold me, Pearl. I'm still frightened."

Gean Choo put her arms around the mem's bony shoulders. Her entire body was cold, far colder than the surrounding air. She'd searched for the word in one of the mem's books. Endothermic. Mrs. Edevane shifted, returning the embrace, entwining their legs, her knee between Gean Choo's, her palms pressed against Gean Choo's back. She wore a lace-trimmed nightgown in mint-coloured silk, the fabric with its fine tooth cool to the touch. Surely Gean Choo couldn't sleep, not in this heat, but the tangle of the mem's limbs formed a balm that soothed her fevered skin. Mrs. Edevane's teeth gleamed white in her mouth, her face unbreathing, alien, wrong, her pulse unnaturally slow. The hidden strength in her arms made her grip feel like a cage.

"Let Po Lam handle the clean-up next time. I like to see a friendly face before dawn."

There wouldn't be a next time, would there? "Yes, Mem."

Mrs. Edevane shifted, placing her hand on the back of Gean Choo's neck, cold radiating through her skin and down her spine. She could not suppress a little cry when Mrs. Edevane kissed her cheek. "Sleep well, dearest."

# CHAPTER 23

# PERFECTLY WELL

## GEAN CHOO

**M**iss Skelford's teeth were stained nicotine-yellow, the fingers of her right hand similarly affected. Gean Choo couldn't see those details from her seat in the middle of the classroom, but she could imagine them, and the reek of perfume that failed to cover-up the underlying smoke.

Their teacher wore a long-sleeved blouse and skirt, nipped in at the waist. Probably stifling in the humid, tropical air. She paced the little rectangle of open space before the blackboard, chalk gleaming white between her fingertips.

Gean Choo glanced down at her desk to check her notes, but when she looked up again, she was no longer in the classroom. Instead, she sat in Miss Skelford's drawing room. There was her low table, with its neat pile of papers, her pens, her books, the leather satchel with its brass clasps.

Behind her came the creak of the door closing, the clatter of shutters being lowered. Miss Skelford's heels clicked against the floorboards as she stepped, one, two, three, and her manicured hand with its nicotine stains descended on Gean Choo's shoulder. The curve of her bosom, preserved in crisp poplin and buttressed by her brassiere, brushed the back of Gean Choo's skull as she leaned over. "Let's keep this to ourselves, Miss Teo."

*Monday, 16 May 1927*

A ROLLING SHUDDER ripped its way through Gean Choo, and she writhed on the sheets, gasping for air. Had she gone blind? There was nothing but velvet darkness above and to either side, but it was simply the mem's boudoir curtains shielding her from daylight.

And surely those were the mem's fingers, cradling the back of her head, and down below, pressed between her thighs—

Mrs. Edevane's mouth was at her throat, her lips coming together to kiss her unbroken skin. Soft, so soft. For now. Her knees rested on either side of Gean Choo's. She did something with her fingers, swiping them to either side of her—of her—

*Clitoris*, her inner schoolgirl voice supplied, devoid of affect. Though Miss Skelford hadn't called it that. She'd said, "A pearl for a Pearl," and smiled at her own cleverness.

Gean Choo peaked, pressing up against the mem's fingers. Out of habit, she held her tongue and didn't cry. She was a Brave Girl.

Mrs. Edevane stroked her again, in the dark, and she made a soft noise of protest. She wasn't fully undressed. Her knickers were gone, her dress unbuttoned only to the waist, skirt ruched up over her hips. The silk satin of the mem's nightgown rasped against her bare thighs.

Mrs. Edevane gently turned Gean Choo's head to the side and pressed her fingers against her lips. Gean Choo opened her mouth and tasted musk and salt, the weight of unspeakable secrets.

"Darling, why are you crying? Didn't you like that? I was so careful to be gentle. I know you humans are delicate."

The nails of her other hand stroked Gean Choo's bared throat. She couldn't move. Mrs. Edevane's lips went to her collarbone, gliding up. She grazed her teeth against Gean Choo's skin—

"It's the sixteenth," Gean Choo said, trying to sink deeper into the pillow, to catch her breath, to try to make sense of everything that was happening. Had she seemed awake? Talked in her sleep? Why else... why? "Monday? You promised Lord Cottesley you'd see him tonight."

Silence for a moment, then a sound like a growl, like the vocalisation of some wild animal, a leopard or tiger. Gean Choo flinched. If she hadn't been in the same room, she'd have sworn that such a noise could never have come from Mrs. Edevane's slender throat.

"Fuck him," Mrs. Edevane said, but she sat up. She threw back one of the curtains and stood, the resulting breeze providing a brief moment of relief from the stuffy heat. It let in the light and Gean Choo had to shield her eyes, blinking in the sudden glare.

The bed was only cool where Mrs. Edevane had leaned her weight. Without her near, the air was stifling. Gean Choo hastened to fix her clothing, attending to the clasp on her brassiere and re-buttoning her dress. Her fingers were clumsy this evening, this simple task requiring several attempts.

"I want you to wear the red dress tonight, and the earrings," Mrs. Edevane said, bringing a brush to her hair and tugging it savagely. "And then come and do my make-up. Twenty minutes, do you hear?"

"Yes, Mem."

She all but ran downstairs, out the back door, across the covered walkway, her heart hammering. She hadn't had a nightmare like that in years. She wasn't a schoolgirl anymore, ignorant and helpless and disgusting. She was done with that life, or it was done with her. Both. Neither.

She ran into Po Lam in the corridor, literally, their elbows colliding as they met around a corner. She sprang back and Po Lam's gaze descended upon her, knowing, assessing.

"Excuse me. I have to get changed," Gean Choo said.

She couldn't bear to look at her face. Po Lam's hand reached into her pocket, pulled out that damnable watch, and flipped it open. "You're not due at Lord Cottesley's for another three hours."

"Well, the mem's toilette takes a while." Gean Choo tried to slide past, but the corridor was too narrow.

"Did she hurt you?"

Gean Choo took a breath, held it, then released it. "I'm perfectly well, thank you," she said in her best English, raising her eyes and holding Po Lam's gaze, daring her to say otherwise.

"Don't forget to bring her dinner," she said in Hokkien. "She always forgets to eat before going out and complains on the way home." Po Lam brushed past her, heading towards the kitchen. Gean Choo watched her retreating back, the high line of her shoulders.

Twenty minutes.

She locked herself in the bathroom and ran water into a bucket. Peeling off her clothes, she kicked them into a pile and washed herself, trying to keep her gaze focussed on the algae-limned tiles, at the water sluicing down the drain, looking anywhere apart from her naked limbs.

She dried herself off and went to her room. The red dress was a silk cheongsam, hem falling to mid-calf, the sides slit daringly to the thigh. One was probably meant to wear it over pants, but she didn't have any that matched. Red for marriage, for joy, for the new year.

Red for blood.

After the shapeless cut of her dropped-waist dresses, the cheongsam seemed a distractingly tight fit, although at least the sleeves were loose. Perhaps she'd put on weight. Seok Eng certainly fed her well enough.

She smoothed extra pomade into her already greasy hair—there hadn't been enough time to wash it—and secured her finger waves with clips, sliding them in one by one. She grabbed her tan shoes and brought them with her.

By the time she reached the kitchen, one of the house bells was ringing for attention, the one for the bedroom. It couldn't have been twenty minutes.

Po Lam stood over a steaming pot on the stove. She ladled out the blood tofu with a slotted spoon and handed the plate over. "Make sure she eats at least half." She hesitated a moment. "And be careful."

"Thank you," Gean Choo said inadequately. Were they always doomed to speak in circles around one another?

The little bell rang out again.

## CHAPTER 24

# EVER SO DEAR

### VERITY

*Monday, 16 May 1927*
*One night since last meal*

"There you are, Pearl. My, you look a vision."

Verity didn't have to reach far for a compliment. Dressing Pearl in red had been the right choice. It would set off her own dress—a little beaded number in cream—quite nicely. Like they were characters out of a fairy tale, Snow White and Rose Red.

With nightfall, she begrudged herself to open the shutters. Really, it should've been Pearl's job but the poor girl had seemed so exhausted, Verity hadn't had the heart to wake her. Well, not at first, anyhow.

The evening air stirred the curtains dramatically, turning them into billowing waves of white chiffon. It was all rather romantic, with the moonlight bathing the verandah in its cool glow.

Pearl walked in with a plate of revolting blood tofu. Verity accepted it, forcing herself to swallow the disgusting lumps of warm gelatinous goop as Pearl brushed out her hair.

"You remember how to behave in front of Lord Cottesley?" Verity prompted, wincing when the brush hit a snag.

"Yes, Mem."

"And you'll remember what to say if he asks how you feel about your service?"

"I'll say I'm perfectly content with my employment."

"Good girl." Verity closed her eyes. Pearl's heart had beaten a little faster when she'd issued that compliment. She could practically smell the blush on her cheeks, the richness of blood just beneath the skin. She hadn't tasted her in so long. Too long. Time to correct that once this was all over.

"How would you like your hair tonight, Mem?"

"Rolled and pinned up, if you please. Just like we practised."

Verity's hair still fell to mid-back, impossible to keep short. Achieving her desired look involved rolling up the ends of the hair and pinning them in place, which was time-consuming, but still quicker and less messy than a haircut every night. Long hair would come into vogue again. Fashion always did run in circles.

Pearl slid in another pin, then smoothed the hair down with her hand. "All done, Mem."

She needed a mirror. Seeing herself through the eyes of someone else just wasn't the same. Pearl did her make-up, tweezing her eyebrows into narrow lines before accenting them with a pencil. She worked through the rest of it—face powder, blusher, eyeshadow, carmine. At least her hands were steady and sure, unlike the first time.

"Now let me do yours," Verity said.

"Mine?" Pearl seemed to startle, as if waking from a dream.

Verity snapped her fingers. "Your lips, at least. Come, sit down. We'll swap." She stood and patted the newly-vacated stool. After a moment, Pearl sat.

She gave her a little powder to give the paint something to stick to. Her colour wasn't half-bad; more beige than yellow. The carmine went beautifully on her lips, highlighting her Cupid's bow.

Verity pulled out a handkerchief and folded it over, offering the edge. "And now blot. Press your lips over the cloth."

"But it'll stain."

"Women have to make sacrifices for beauty, Pearl. It's always been that way."

Pearl obediently closed her mouth over the handkerchief, gazing up as she did so. The angle made the most of her short, thin lashes, her eyes appearing larger. Verity picked up a pinch of pomade and ran her fingers over a few strands of Pearl's hair, forming it into a kiss-curl. Powder clung to the down on her cheek, giving her skin a velvety texture.

Verity had consumed the entire plate of blood tofu, but it wasn't enough. Could never be enough. Her stomach throbbed with a disconsolate ache, driving her to distraction. She strode across the room and reached for her pills on the side table, shaking out five and scooping them into her mouth. Their dry edges rubbed against her throat as they went down.

"Did I spoil my lips?" she asked, turning back to Pearl. The girl shook her head. "Good." She shrugged off her robe. "Come help me dress."

She sat with Pearl in the back seat of the car, passing through the cool serenity of the night. It had newly rained, giving the world that earthy, fecund smell. So many green and growing things here, vestiges of jungle still encroaching upon settled land.

She drew her pills from her evening bag, letting one dissolve on her tongue like a rather dry and bitter lozenge. She ought to have asked Po Lam to find her a girl the night before. The man who'd shot her had been all right. Killed in haste, though, which spoilt things. And he'd had a few pipes of third-rate dross circulating in his system, which always made Verity jittery. She ought not to have let Pearl go so easily when she'd woken earlier that evening.

Ought to have done a lot of things, really.

Verity leant her elbow against the glass, lights from passing motorists bouncing off the beads adorning her dress. Six weeks stuck on a steamer from Paris, then another four weeks at the postal office, trapped in some forgotten corner before she'd finally received her gown, for an order she'd placed in December! It was really a wonder how anyone in the tropics could aspire to be à la mode at all.

"Mem?" Pearl began, sotto voce.

"Mm?"

"I'm sorry we were late coming back. It was my fault. There was an accident on the road—"

"I suppose you mean this little thing," Verity said, touching her fingertips to Pearl's forehead. She'd avoided powdering directly over the cut. The scab was dark red, almost purple.

"Yes, Mem."

"Next time, just come home. I am more than capable of exerting a modicum of self-control. Aren't I, Pearl?"

"Yes, Mem."

Verity leant back in her seat and adjusted Pearl's hair, smoothing down a stray lock. Pearl's earrings glimmered gold and red. They'd been a gift from Kalon, one of many trinkets he'd sent since that party where he'd appeared ever so concerned with Justine's health. The whole situation with him was honestly a little embarrassing. "If I went back to England, would you like to come? Most amahs travel with their families."

Pearl's hands twisted in her lap. She stared at them, then out the window, then back at her hands. "England is very far away, Mem."

"Oh, I know. And cold, too. You'd look ever so dear in a winter coat."

Pearl smiled, but the smile was faltering. She couldn't imagine, perhaps, being so cold as to require woollens and furs, so cold one's hands went numb, and frost made filigree on the windowpane. She'd look fine sprawled on a fur rug, an orange fire crackling in the background, not a stitch of clothing upon her, head thrown back to expose the fine lines of her neck. Or perhaps Verity would reach instead for a tributary of the great saphenous vein and all its intimate possibilities.

"You've grown dear to me, Pearl. You know that, don't you?"

That startled her enough to look up. "Mem, I..."

The car rolled to a stop before Kalon's gate, a wrought iron affair topped with rearing lions. Zaid stuck his head out the window. "Mrs. Edevane and guest, by invitation of Lord Cottesley."

The gatekeeper opened the way for them. Rain struck the car, and Zaid put on the wipers, their rubber edges groaning against the glass.

Verity grabbed Pearl's hand and squeezed. *Let this be brief. Let him be reasonable.*

Behind them, the gates creaked shut, and the car rolled onwards into the dark.

# CHAPTER 25

# HANTU

## GEAN CHOO

*Monday, 16 May 1927*

L ord Cottesley's estate was vast, at least twice the size of Mrs. Edevane's. The house was alight from top to bottom, glowing like a beacon in the dark, a great, squat shape three stories tall. Even the paths were lit, lest any mem trip in her impractical heels. All the illumination made it hard to see the stars. Perhaps the overall effect ought to have been cheery, but Gean Choo couldn't shake the disturbing sense that the house itself was watching her.

Zaid stopped under the carriage porch, saving them from the rain. He went around to the mem's side, opening her door and helping her out. For one brief, silly moment, Gean Choo waited, as if she were deserving of the same treatment. She silently scolded herself and stepped out before anyone appeared to notice.

Her first glimpse of Lord Cottesley's servants was innocuous, a Sikh man in a navy kurta and trousers, escorting Zaid away, presumably to the servants' quarters. A Chinese woman, also in navy, led the way into the house.

The interior was filled with clean, geometric shapes, arched walkways, and very little that might be called ornate or cluttered. In all directions were flat, bare surfaces and smooth lines. It seemed unnatural. Soulless.

They walked out the back to the huge verandah that extended the full length of the building, just like Mrs. Edevane's. Grotesque shapes loomed from the darkness of the garden. A second glance proved they weren't nine-foot-tall monsters, but merely topiaries, bestial faces rendered mute and frozen in verdant green.

Gean Choo minded her manners. She was calm and not at all distracted by Lord Cottesley's considerable army of eerie, blank-faced servants. Their tunics were collarless, the lights illuminating the pink and red scar tissue at their necks and wrists.

The lord himself met them on the verandah, seated on a rattan lounge chair. He was a European man, lanky, seemingly in his twenties, with hair the colour of coconut husks, immaculate despite the humidity. He wore a dove-grey suit, his eyes the pale blue of an impending storm.

"Mrs. Edevane," he said, rising. His voice was deeper than his narrow chest had implied. "Luminous as ever, my dear."

Mrs. Edevane's smile was bright, but there was a certain tension in the way she gazed up at him, her brow furrowed. "You flatter me, my lord."

He gestured for Mrs. Edevane to sit, and she did so, taking the chair opposite him. Gean Choo remained standing, one step behind and to the left of Mrs. Edevane. A houseboy stayed nearby, his posture impeccable, hands clasped loosely behind his back.

Another servant brought in two teapots and twin cups, pouring out dark red fluid from each pot. From the way it clung to the pottery, viscous and thick, it was clearly not tea. The servant leaned over, the tray steady in her hands as she proffered the drinks. Mrs. Edevane, staring into the smooth flat mirror of her teacup, suppressed a genteel shudder.

"I know you're being ethical, so I had yours sent up from the butcher. Pig's and duck's blood," Lord Cottesley said.

"How thoughtful of you."

They both drank. Mrs. Edevane took the merest sip before moving the cup away from her lips.

The servant stepped back with her empty tray, taking her place with the houseboy at the top of the verandah. They both had the same vacant, dull expressions. So that was a thrall. Were they even still human?

Lord Cottesley waved and his servants moved, bringing out a high stool and matching round table. On the table, they placed a mirror and a candle.

"If you would be so kind," Lord Cottesley said, still speaking to Mrs. Edevane.

"Pearl, go sit." Mrs. Edevane wasn't looking at her. One of her knees was bouncing, restless beneath the cream drape of her skirt. Gean Choo longed to place her hand on her arm, to soothe her, but she couldn't.

She went and took her seat, coming face to face with her reflection in the glass, seeing her make-up for the first time. Mrs. Edevane had changed the shape of her mouth, making it rounder in the centre and smaller at the edges, like one of those posters on the walls of the hair salon, advertising eau de toilette and cold cream and things that fashionable young girls were meant to want.

Lord Cottesley did not appear in the glass, but his presence stirred the air behind her. He wore a spicy cologne, notes of sandalwood and citrus. It made her stomach roil.

Mrs. Edevane stood too, somewhere behind her and to the side, the weight of her gaze a pressure at the back of her skull. *He frightens her*, Po Lam had said.

Lord Cottesley picked up the candle and waved its flame before her face, close enough that its heat brushed her skin. She stared into the dark abyss of the mirror, willing herself to stillness, to the calm cool depths of a pond frozen over in winter. She'd never seen one, but she'd read about them.

He set the candle down. A moth flew up to it, flitting around in aimless arcs. He moved, tilting Gean Choo's head slightly to one side, his palm flat against her skull, impersonal, angling her neck towards the light. He tugged down the stiffened line of her collar.

Mrs. Edevane had only bitten her twice on the underside of her left wrist. Even though her neck was unblemished, he continued staring at her. Not at her eyes, but at some point around her head. Was something... was something wrong?

"Such young eyes," he said, a mocking edge to his voice. "Palms up on the table."

Gean Choo placed her hands as he'd asked, pressing down to stop them from trembling. The mark on her wrist wasn't that obvious, not like his own servants, who'd been scarred many times over, the tissue bumpy and reddish. But it was there all the same.

Mrs. Edevane had been quiet thus far, but now she spoke, the words coming out in a rush. "You needn't worry yourself over my Pearl. Besides, if she talked, who would believe her? Everyone here is so superstitious... What's the locals' word for ghosts, Pearl?"

"Hantu."

"And it's an entire industry, an obsession. Just look at Sago Street. Death shops crammed with incense and paper trinkets. Why—"

Behind her, Lord Cottesley sighed. A thud made her flinch. Gean Choo glanced down, blinking twice. He'd stabbed her with a penknife between the knuckles of her third and fourth fingers on her right hand. Blood poured out over the table, hot and red and sticky. There wasn't any real pain until she tried to move.

"My lord!" Mrs. Edevane exclaimed, her tone on the verge of censure.

He wrenched the knife out, and Gean Choo sucked in her breath, clenching her teeth as not to cry. Mrs. Edevane swooped down upon her and took hold of her fingertips, delicately kissing her hand, first the back and then the palm. When she released her, the skin had mended, though her flesh still throbbed and blood ran down to her wrist, untouched. Mrs. Edevane would never have wasted a drop at home.

"You put a hole in my housegirl," Mrs. Edevane said, raising her voice.

Lord Cottesley tilted his head, and the woman servant came up to Gean Choo, holding out a bowl of water and a cloth for her to wash. A slice of lemon floated in the water, though it was too big to be a finger bowl.

Was she the guest or the main course? She tried not to laugh. It must've been the shock of it all, because nothing about this was particularly amusing.

"Have you lost your appetite?" Lord Cottesley asked.

Mrs. Edevane scoffed, circled back to the settee, picked up her teacup, and cautiously sniffed it. Her face spasmed in a rictus of disgust, but she quaffed the fluid all the same, her throat making an elegant curve as she threw her head back to swallow. She placed the empty cup down on the table with a ring of resignation. "I killed a man the other night. It was perfectly to Code, my lord. Self-defence. He invaded my home, stole from me, shot me here"—she brushed her fingers against her ribcage. "Pearl was there, weren't you, Pearl?"

Lord Cottesley shook his head. "Unbound domestics. Consuming raw humans. Those we take into our confidence must ever be the right sort—humans who truly understand how the world functions. You're one step away from a security breach."

The effect on Mrs. Edevane was stark. She drew in her breath, shoulders high and tight, hands clenched in the fabric of her dress, cheeks flushed with rage, as well as rouge. For a moment, it almost seemed as if she were about to strike him.

But instead, she fell to her knees before him and captured one of his hands in both of hers, pressing his fingertips to her forehead. She murmured something, too low and fast for Gean Choo to catch its meaning.

He touched her hair gently, like a lover. He—

The female servant caught Gean Choo by her still-tender right hand, making her yelp, and dragged her away.

# CHAPTER 26

## A TRIBADE

### VERITY

*Monday, 16 May 1927*
*One night since last meal*

"I vow to never compromise the secrets that bind us, by act or omission. I will remember that I am but part of a whole, and as my kin survives, so do I. Above all, I vow to protect the security of our people and the sanctity of our bloodlines. Now and always, till the moment of my true death, do I promise to uphold and to enforce the tenets of this Code for the betterment of myself and my brethren. I—"

"That's enough." Kalon's fingers grazed down the side of her face, found her chin, and tilted her head to meet his gaze. "I'm satisfied you remember your covenant. Whether you observe it..." He shrugged.

"I would never allow my actions to compromise our security, my lord. Never." Her mouth was too dry. She swallowed. "The fact is, I have lived on this island for almost nine decades and not once—"

He released her. "Please come sit, Mrs. Edevane. I can't bear to converse with you like this."

She took a moment to collect her wits. A security breach—he wouldn't dare—her blood roiled at the very supposition. She went and took her seat, knees primly together, hands on her lap. Her mouth craved something warm and sticky.

He sat opposite and eyed her over the low table. "None of them are fixed, are they? Not your amah, not your driver, nor that brooding woman who runs your household. I've ignored it so far because I'm trying my hardest to be lenient, Mrs. Edevane. To be fair. Because that's what all of us want, isn't it? To be treated fairly, with dignity and respect."

"Fixed." A polite word to mean broken, brutalised, reduced to the barest parody of human life. There wasn't enough distance between them. She needed a hot bath to scrub off the invisible grease left by his words, leaving a stain upon her soul.

"Mine might be an uncommon household, my lord, but it's not a dangerous one. Each of them would sooner swallow their own tongue than betray my confidence." It was ridiculous she even had to spell it out. His predecessor would never have made such a fuss over nothing.

"Perhaps there's a way," Kalon said.

"A way for what?"

"A way I could trust you. To ensure you truly have the best interests of our colony at heart."

There was a chasm yawning under her, the trap beneath his words, but she couldn't see its shape. Not yet. "I always do."

"I believe I can rely upon you to be straight with me."

She bit her lower lip. "Of course, my lord."

"This widow act has served you well, but perhaps it has outlived its usefulness. You must tire of its pretence. You need security. A true partnership."

Her throat was so parched her tongue clung to the roof of her mouth. "You'll have to speak plainly, my lord."

"I'm proposing an alliance. Marriage."

It was a good thing she wasn't drinking as she'd have spat the whole mouthful in shock. "I beg your pardon?"

"I have a certain reputation for... efficiency."

More like brutality.

"But you—your ethics, your diet—speak to a crowd that appreciates such softer sensibilities. Such an alliance would go a long way towards assuaging those people's fears. Would give some weight to the assertion that I am not, in fact, an unfeeling monster. In addition, your pedigree; such an illustrious bloodline, to be sure. You should know you're still Benny's favourite fledgling, despite... circumstances."

She hadn't thought of the duchess in years.

No. That was a lie.

She blinked past the emotion threatening to well in her eyes, searching his face to ensure he was being serious, that this wasn't yet another test. There was no trace of mockery in those high cheekbones, that square jaw. If he were having her on... well, what would be the point? "My lord, I'm still in a state of mourning—"

"Over a figment? Please. Mr. Edevane never existed. You hid your paperwork well, I'll give you that. But surely there's no more need for pretence." He paused. "You must miss this. Conversation between equals."

"I'm your vassal."

"For now. But were you to be my lady, that would be something altogether different. A title and a link to one of the oldest bloodlines in the Occident."

The title mattered less than his bloodline. The things she could do. The people she could offend with impunity. Yes, that would be something different.

"You may have heard I am a tribade—" she began.

"Please. I don't care how you play with your food."

She had to push him to see how far he would go. "What if it's more than that?"

Kalon chose to misunderstand her. "You're not falling for Haywarde's youngest, are you? She's not your type."

Freddie's youngest, Miss Justine Skelford? Her face twisted.

"Is it simply that you prefer Asiatics?" he asked, watching her. "No. She horrifies you. Do you fear old age, Mrs. Edevane? The inevitable decay of beauty? It was Lawrence who'd approved her fledging, but I would've done the same."

"As is your prerogative."

"But I would've approved it for a different reason. Did you know she'd suffered from consumption prior to her undeath?"

She didn't see how this was relevant. "No."

"And now it seems all her symptoms have vanished. Don't you find that fascinating? Don't you wish we knew more about the fledging process, the changes the body endures post-rebirth? For instance, not all ailments can be cured that way. I've read of a man who'd been born blind, but sadly, he did not regain his sight after turning."

"It sounds like you want to dissect Miss Skelford."

He went on without contradicting her, "Do you suppose it's the nature of the ailment, or perhaps, the severity of the disease? Interactions with the bloodline of the sire?"

How was all this talk of fledglings and siring meant to entice her to say yes? Some people found it romantic, the idea of creating immortality, of playing God. Not her. "My lord—"

"You must forgive me, Mrs. Edevane. I've let myself get distracted from the matter at hand."

The matter at hand. No such luck that he'd forget about it altogether, talking himself into circles with his suppositions. A human woman, confronted with such an offer, might've recoiled at the thought of sharing a bed. Their kind were less prescriptive. With marriages lasting centuries, monogamy was the exception rather than the rule. Besides, the rebirth made certain acts, if not impossible, then at least impracticable. Men complained they'd drawn the shorter straw.

She had no fear of his carnal intentions, if he even possessed such desires. It was the fashion, in certain circles, to disavow all human weakness, lust included. He could be the ascetic sort. Daphne kept abreast of all that gossip, who was dallying with whom and so on. If there'd been talk about their new overseer, she would know.

No matter what he wanted, marital duties were unlikely to feature. But when one could heal from almost any injury, the sadists in their midst had become inventive. Bennesbrook, for instance, had a fondness for hot pokers. The sight of one still made Verity shiver.

In any case, his predilections didn't matter. Vampire or not, they still resided in a human-centric world and had to pay at least lip service to human laws. A marriage could ruin her. As her husband, he'd have unfettered access to her assets. Why, he could have her thrown into a madhouse on merely a word. Not that any human institution could ever hold her, but it was the principle of the thing. And she could say goodbye to tasting an unshackled body ever again.

She took a deep breath and braced herself. "Your offer is too great an honour, my lord. I simply can't accept."

His face didn't change from its expression of feigned tenderness. "My dear, you've been here so long, the heat's corrupted your sense of decorum. Don't tell me you're actually in love with a *human*." He said that last word like one might say corpse or child or animal, with all the derision of a dried-up old purist who'd never touched one not of the blood.

"Love? Of course not."

"Then I scarcely see the problem."

If she refused him, he'd take them from her—Pearl and Po Lam and Zaid, Cookie, and the boys—or worse yet, make her perform the binding herself. Her household wasn't perfect, nobody was, but they were hers, damnit, all of them were *hers*.

Spending another moment in his lair would simply drive her mad. What wouldn't she give to wipe that smirk off his face?

She needed time. Space. A long drink.

"It's such a momentous decision, I need a while to think about it. T-to divine my fortune." She wrung her hands. As if tea leaves could save her. "And I'm afraid, my lord, the night grows late. I really must go." If she stayed a single moment more, one of them was going to die.

As she turned to leave, he grabbed her just above the elbow. "I look forward to making plans with you very soon, Mrs. Edevane." He smiled at her, shadows lurking between the points of his teeth.

She returned the expression for a half-second, then shook her arm free from his grasp and strode towards the front door. Her head was light, the phantom press of his fingers still tingling upon her skin.

## CHAPTER 27

# IN EVERY WAY

### GEAN CHOO

*Monday, 16 May 1927*

**M**rs. Edevane remained uncharacteristically silent during the short drive back and all the way up the stairs. Gean Choo trailed behind her. This was the sort of emotional turmoil a husband was meant to console, but if there'd ever been a Mr. Edevane, the house bore no trace of him.

The mem sat at her dresser, reaching to undo the straps on her shoes before kicking them off into a dark corner of the room. Gean Choo went to fetch them, dusting them off and neatly placing them into a stack with the others.

When Mrs. Edevane reached up and pulled the pins from her hair, her yellow curls fell free. She ran her fingers through the tresses until every pin had been hunted down.

Gean Choo rubbed her right hand. It didn't ache anymore, and there was barely any mark left as a reminder. The entire evening held the sheen of the unreal, like some unpleasant dream, misremembered upon waking.

Mrs. Edevane fumbled with her purse, took out an apothecary bottle, and poured a sprinkle of pills into her palm, swallowing them dry. She patted cold cream all over her face and neck, then wiped it with a cloth, taking off her make-up. Once she was done, she turned to Gean Choo and spoke her first words since they'd left Lord Cottesley's. "Is that all?"

Gean Choo came closer, took the cloth, and wiped the excess cream from the side of Mrs. Edevane's nose. "That's everything, Mem."

"Quite," Mrs. Edevane said in a perfectly normal voice. She began to laugh, with a resonance and volume that belonged somewhere distant—in a novel, on a fog-blighted moor, whatever that was, in the driving rain, on a tower outlined by lightning. "Fuck them." She swept her hand across the dressing room table, casting aside hairbrushes, pots of rouge, powders, skin creams, and toilette water. Mercifully, none of the little glass bottles shattered, but the powder spilled, dusting the floor in a spray of rose-scented talc. "Fuck Cottesley and fuck the council! They can all rot in hell!"

Gean Choo's skin burned at the sound of his name. He'd taken Mrs. Edevane apart, ruined her equilibrium, and sent her home like this, furious and miserable. How dare he. How dare he! She'd have to lend whatever comfort she could.

"Speakers are all the same. Bullies. They think they can swan up to a person's home, snap their fingers, and take whatever they desire. And they expect us to bend over with a smile! Well, fuck him. Fuck all of them!" The mem's voice dropped to a whisper. "I won't be owned. Never again."

Mrs. Edevane slumped over the dressing table, hand pressed to forehead, eyes closed. "They're all cads, the lot of them. Oh, what shall I do, Pearl? What's to become of me?"

She began to cry, blood tears rolling down her pale, pretty face. Gean Choo fumbled in her pocket for a handkerchief. "Shh, Mem, please. It'll be all right." She proffered the handkerchief, which Mrs. Edevane took, dabbing her cheeks. What else could she do? She placed a hand upon Mrs. Edevane's shoulder, a merest brush of her fingers skating over the pale soft lace.

Mrs. Edevane grew rigid all at once under her touch, her tears subsiding. Gean Choo drew back. She'd overstepped. This wasn't her place. She wasn't... she'd never touched the mem before without invitation.

Mrs. Edevane seized her retreating wrist with uncanny strength and pulled Gean Choo onto her lap. Her face was blotchy, smears of blood still on her skin, eyes rimmed red.

Should she apologise? Try to leave her in peace?

Mrs. Edevane held her with both arms, balancing Gean Choo across her bony knees. She radiated cold, yellow light haloing her pale hair, leaving her face—bent over Gean Choo's—in shadow.

Mrs. Edevane lunged. Gean Choo opened her mouth to scream but was caught in a kiss, the mem's lips pressed against her own. Her mouth tasted of copper and some not entirely unpleasant combination of salt and waxy lipstick. Gean Choo froze, though her heart raced. Was she meant to kiss her back? Was that... was that allowed?

Her body wanted it. Wanted to be held again, wanted even the bite of her fangs, the sweet agony of that intimacy. Mrs. Edevane pulled away, her brows slightly angled as though uncertain, as though she needed reassurance.

Gean Choo would give it to her.

She reached up, wrapping her arms around Mrs. Edevane's neck, lifting herself up to return the kiss. She closed her eyes, burying her hand into the smooth, soft silk of Mrs. Edevane's hair, so much finer than her own, familiarising herself with the strange, cold touch of Mrs. Edevane's tongue.

A lifetime passed in those few seconds before she drew back. Had she been too forward?

Mrs. Edevane reached out, rubbing her thumb at the side of Gean Choo's lips. "Kalon would deny me moments like these. He would deny me of you—warm, vital, independent. That's a form of death, isn't it? To be alive, but unthinking. A fate worse than death."

Her eyes weren't colourless, they reflected all the colours—flecks of blue, green, hazel. Mrs. Edevane moved her hand, shifting it to clasp Gean Choo's neck, pressing up against her throat. The breath left her lungs in a gasp.

"If you were like them, this wouldn't startle you. Your heart would be steady, slow. Would you prefer that?"

Gean Choo tried to shake her head, but she couldn't move. "No, Mem," she squeaked.

"Neither would I." Mrs. Edevane released her grip, used her thumb to stroke the side of Gean Choo's neck before trailing her fingertips down, pressing her hand between Gean Choo's breasts, over her heart. "I need you tonight. Do you understand?"

Her heart leapt as if longing to pour the contents of her veins down Mrs. Edevane's throat. "I wish to serve you, Mem." She bit her bottom lip. "In every way."

Mrs. Edevane stroked her knuckles against Gean Choo's cheek. "Darling, you don't know how happy that makes me."

# CHAPTER 28

# HARD TO PLEASE

## VERITY

*Monday, 16 May 1927*
*One night since last meal*

Pearl shifted on her lap. At every point they touched, there was the heat of her, the weight, the twin rhythms of her breath and pulse. Verity stood, gathering Pearl in her arms, and lowered her onto the bed.

"Mem—"

A bruise was blooming on Pearl's neck. Well, she didn't know her own strength, even after all these years. "What is it, dear?"

Pearl reached down and removed her shoes, tucking them beside the bed. She rubbed her neck, her gaze self-consciously refusing to meet Verity's. "I don't know... I'm not very good—"

"Don't lie to me."

"It's not that I haven't..."

The rapid beat of her pulse was a pleasant reminder of how sweet she'd tasted. Verity leant down and slipped off her hose, dropping it onto the floor. She crawled on the bed until she reached Pearl and her deliciously fragrant veins. "Whatever you need to know, you'll learn, won't you?"

"Yes, Mem," Pearl whispered.

Verity undid the first fastening to her collar, her skin clammy beneath it, each stiff fabric button a torturous exercise in dexterity. Her brassiere was dark with sweat under the arms. Verity reached behind her and undid the clasps one-handed, sliding it off Pearl, along with the top half of her cheongsam. Her nipples were pinky-brown, soft beneath her finger-tips, gradually stiffening with a pinch. Pearl closed her eyes, parted her lips; she yelped when Verity pinched too hard.

"I suppose I'll never see you on that fur rug, but at least we can still have this." She stroked the girl's hair, following the curve of her skull. "Would you go back to... Where are you from again?"

"Fukien."

"Fukien. Why, they'd hardly recognise you. British-schooled, your accent a mélange of port tongues. Is that why you didn't go? After your father died?"

The poor thing was as silent as she'd been when meeting Kalon. Verity examined Pearl's hand. "Hmm. See that?" she asked, entwining their fingers. "Not even a scar. It must have frightened you to be the subject of such violence."

"I knew you would protect me." Pearl shyly met her eyes for a moment. They were deep brown, pupils blown with desire. Pearl raised Verity's hand, pressing her knuckles to her lips. She turned it and kissed Verity's palm before moving her kisses along her wrist, her arm, up to her shoulder, across her collarbone, to the sensitive arc of her neck. Verity moaned, her fingers clenching the bedsheets.

They kissed again. Gean Choo's mouth was soft and yielding, making Verity fight her natural instincts. The mouth held so many blood vessels close to the surface. She forced herself to be soft, to kiss without taking, even as her gorge rose at the thought of other mouths being here before her, other lips tasting what she now tasted.

Pearl drew back. "Mem, about before—"

Before what? Before Adam and Eve, before the Buddha, before they'd met? But Verity only said, "Yes?"

"Please don't ever... not when I'm asleep. I was asleep earlier this evening."

"Really?" Verity exhaled in a little laugh. "You were moaning loud enough, I thought otherwise. But as you like." She patted Pearl's hand. "I'll wake you next time. Satisfied?"

"Thank you." Pearl reached around her and undid a hook on Verity's dress.

Verity turned to give her greater access. "And while it's just the two of us, you might as well call me by my Chri—by my given name."

Pearl's fingers stilled for a moment. "I couldn't."

"Whyever not?"

"It's not right."

"It would please me. There. Now, won't you try?"

"Yes, M—Verity." Pearl crawled to the end of the bed, easing Verity's dress over her hips and removing the undergarments at the same time. She stroked Verity's skin with the ease of the initiated, bent her head to Verity's breasts, her hot wet mouth sending a shiver down Verity's spine as she fastened it on a nipple. How she hated her, that unknown, unseen woman who'd taken Pearl's innocence, who was there in every touch, every gesture. Hated her and longed to be her, to turn back the hands of time and demand her droit du seigneur.

Pearl tugged down the rest of her cheongsam and discarded it, remaining in her knickers.

Verity grabbed the soft, slim curves of her buttocks, slipping her hands beneath the fabric, her nails digging in. "You're beautiful." Still a little thin, perhaps, limiting what Verity could reasonably expect to take from her. Small-chested and narrow-hipped, suiting the fashions of the decade. She'd have drowned in a robe à la polonaise or a Victorian bustle.

"Thank you. But you're the true beauty here." Pearl wriggled out of her grasp and inched lower down the bed, all elbows and knees and upturned naked feet. She settled in between Verity's legs and paused with her hands on Verity's hips.

"I'm very hard to please," Verity said. "But you may try, if you'd like."

Hard to know what she was thinking behind those dark eyes. Pearl lowered her head, and Verity fell back on the pillow, determined, for once, to enjoy herself.

It wasn't at all bad. There was an aesthetic pleasure to be had in the shape of her, that sleek dark head between her thighs, her hands stroking Verity's hips, her tongue working industriously, so impossibly soft and warm and alive. But Verity's body was numb. Indifferent.

"Inside," she said, lifting her hips in imperious demand. Pearl complied with her fingers, and again, Verity sensed the ghost of that other woman. She could ask to know her name—their names?—but why torture herself and spoil the mood? She didn't matter, that other woman. She wasn't here.

Verity tugged at her arm. "Come up for a moment."

Pearl gently withdrew and shuffled up towards her, lips gleaming. They lay side-by-side, two spoons in a drawer.

Nothing worked the same after death. Pearl wasn't her worst lover, but she wasn't her best, and even her best had failed to move her. She'd tried, oh she'd tried, so many times—by herself, with her own kind, and with humans of all sorts, thralls and freewomen alike. Her flesh had proved stubbornly immune to influence, to any pleasure save that of the feast and the pipe. It was too bad, really. Duchess Bennesbrook should've warned her, but Duchess Bennesbrook was a cunt.

"I'm sorry," Pearl said.

"Don't be. Here," Verity said, pulling at the buttons on Pearl's knickers. "You have the advantage of me."

Pearl helped her, and together, they got her free of the garment, the last barrier between her skin and the surrounding air. Her hair below was just as black as the hair on her head, thick and curled like a shield of modesty hiding her pudendal cleft. Verity ran her fingers through it, then touched Pearl in earnest, parting her lips to find the shy head of her clitoris. She was slippery and wet, hot where she clutched Verity past her second knuckle.

"Good girl," Verity said, and observed her blush. Educated girls were her favourite; so eager to please. With her other hand, she held Pearl down by the hair, ruining the perfect line of her kiss curl, baring the smooth curve of her throat. She held herself above Pearl, admiring the rosy blush across her neck and breasts. The colour of desire.

Her canines lengthened, growing heavy like the weight of sin. Pearl's gaze went to them, transfixed, like the mouse watching the snake. And like the snake, she struck.

Pearl arched against her, clutching her shoulders. That only lasted a moment, and then she slumped back against the mattress. The taste of her was heat and bitterness, iron and salt. She whimpered, her nails digging into Verity's back, her poor heart speeding up, pumping warm spurts of blood straight into Verity's mouth.

At some point, she contracted against her, shuddered, and pulsed around her fingertips, trembling afterwards. Verity stilled her fingers, withdrawing when Pearl shifted, and continued to drink. Human women were so easy. Had she ever been that way?

She stopped when the flow decreased to a dangerous degree. It went against instinct, stopping herself before she had drained the girl dry, but she could do it, and do it easily; fuck Kalon for implying she couldn't. She kissed the wound she'd made, and it sealed beneath her mouth.

Feeding filled her with a pleasant glow like it always did, the promise of strength and renewal. She opened her hand and closed it. Power hummed through her veins. Newly fed, she could go anywhere. Do anything.

Pearl clutched the sheet, but Verity stopped her, grabbing her wrist. "Not yet. I'd like to look at you."

There wasn't any mess, because she wasn't some neophyte with half her meal seeping down her décolletage. Just a small, discreet scar on Pearl's neck, the elevated heartbeat, and unnatural pallor of her skin. Was it so very difficult to operate a camera? She was no painter, no artist, but she felt obliged to preserve something of this, the pleasing symmetrical lines of Pearl's youth, the soft arc of her belly, her breasts, the angles of her hips. Preserve it against the decay yet to come.

Pearl pressed her fingers against her neck, eyes suspiciously glossy. She stared at some dark corner of the room and took in deep breaths, her hand shaking where it touched the scar.

Verity laid next to her and nestled in close, pulling Pearl to her, petting her hair, stroking the soft planes of her back. Pearl sighed and turned towards her, their naked limbs entangling, her head pillowed against Verity's breast. Her heartbeat pulsed beneath Verity's fingertips, and Verity smiled as she closed her eyes, already counting the days until she'd taste her again.

# PART TWO

1928

# CHAPTER 29

## SHE NEEDS ME

### ENSEMBLE

*Gean Choo*
*1927 to February 1928*

The months passed quickly. Christmas, New Year, and Chinese New Year all rushed by in a flurry of sound and colour. Gean Choo settled into her new routine as though it had always been this way. The mem took her out to theatres, for long walks on Beach Road beneath the trees dripping with flame-red blossoms, and for midnight swims in the ocean. The latter were disquieting, with no way to ascertain what lay beneath the murky waves. They stopped after one hot December evening when the corpse of a sea turtle became stuck under one of the piers, the smell making Gean Choo vomit and Mrs. Edevane turn away in disgust.

Mrs. Edevane showered her with gifts: clothes, shoes, perfume, cosmetics. A little golden anklet hung with tiny bells. Makeup to hide the tell of scar tissue. Gean Choo still slept in her own room most days, but every month or so, Mrs. Edevane would summon her upstairs, into the velvet dark womb of her bedchamber. What a gift, to be so favoured. It meant Mrs. Edevane needed her. Wanted her.

She'd gladly drown herself beneath the weight of Mrs. Edevane's regard.

Mrs. Edevane didn't allow herself to grow as weak as she'd been that first night, when she'd stumbled straight into Gean Choo's arms. She had to be feeding from others since Gean Choo's veins were insufficient. There were some nights she'd walk downstairs dressed to death, telling Gean Choo not to wait up. Zaid or Po Lam would drive her to some unknown location, and she'd return mere minutes till daybreak, pleased and glowing and utterly wanton. Mrs. Edevane no longer faltered when walking downstairs, and she turned away Seok Eng's dinners more often than not. Now Gean Choo was the weak one, pausing in the middle of the hallway to catch her breath, sleeping late into the afternoon.

A wall grew between herself and Po Lam, impersonal and unassailable. Had she dreamed that strange intimacy they'd shared on the abandoned plantation? Po Lam was distant and cold around her, as if that night had never happened.

*Po Lam*
*Sunday, 26 February 1928*

MRS. Edevane was getting worse, and there was little Po Lam could do about it. There'd been more deaths, doubling from once a month to once a fortnight. Had she been careless enough to attract the notice of the police? Even if they investigated, they wouldn't believe the truth. A mem, killing off impoverished plantation workers and prostitutes? The latter would almost be seen as hygienic.

Why all these bodies? Why now? Maybe something had happened with Lord Cottesley. The body count had only started rising after that night.

Such an awful night. Gean Choo walking out of the house in that clinging red cheongsam. The ache in Po Lam's jaw when she'd gritted her teeth and burned at the thought of Mrs. Edevane touching her, and of

Gean Choo responding. Such dark, inconvenient thoughts. She'd taken the sampan out by herself, rowing into the black chasm of the night without purpose or destination, just to have something to do, to wear her body down to the point where it hurt to breathe.

Mrs. Edevane had deflected her attempts to discuss her appetite. Perhaps the situation was only temporary.

Perhaps it was a sign she should leave.

With the mem's latest victim, Zaid had only sighed, glanced up into the night sky, and muttered something under his breath. Then they'd gotten to work.

That had been Saturday night. On Sunday night, Mrs. Edevane had taken Gean Choo dancing. When they'd finished and Po Lam was driving them back, they were both giggly, Gean Choo flushed with alcohol and Mrs. Edevane flushed with blood. In the mirror, Gean Choo had given Mrs. Edevane a look—unguarded, soft, *grateful*. Po Lam's hands had tightened on the steering wheel, and she'd forced her gaze back to the road, to the texture of bitumen illuminated by headlights, forever leading away into the dark.

*Verity*
*Monday, 27 February 1928*
*Two nights since last meal*

VERITY RECEIVED Kalon's invitation with only three weeks' notice. Perhaps it'd been a deliberate slight. Perhaps not. The post was unreliable, there was no doubt about that. She took a penknife and split the edge of the thick cream envelope, her lips twitching at the coppery scent, faded but still present.

"Arse," she said, pulling out the card.

"Mem?" Pearl glanced up from the book she'd been reading, curled up on the study's settee. It was *The Age of Innocence* by Edith Wharton, and she was three quarters done. Verity should've told her not to waste her time since Newland was such a dunce.

She fanned her face with the card. "Never use blood as ink, dear; it makes one look morbid at best and insolent at worst." The scent didn't bother her as much as it could've because she'd stopped starving herself like a pathetic martyr. Why bother to be good when Kalon was a delusional lunatic who didn't care about her temperance? She might as well regain her strength until their next overseer arrived. They couldn't all be this troublesome.

Besides, she needed the energy to keep up with Pearl. It was impossible to keep going out, night after night, on an empty stomach.

And Pearl was so easy to please. She made Verity feel young again, and that was charming. An unexpected delight.

She placed the card on her desk, smoothed it out, and read it, her eyes narrowing with each line, a frown furrowing her brow. Beneath the invite was a more personal note:

*Let's talk further after the auction and set a date. October is a delightful month for brides.*

As if he held all the cards, like she'd just roll over for him as soon as he snapped his fingers. Wasn't her silence a sufficient answer? She'd started marking his gifts "return to sender." What did he suppose she cared for, his title? His rank? How very human. Well, fuck him. Fuck all of them! She'd sooner stake herself than bend to him.

There was one surefire way to put an end to it, and she wouldn't even have to commit the faux pas of refusing him. At least, not directly.

She looked at Pearl until the girl lowered her book. "He's holding a ball at his house on the equinox. Would you like to come? As my guest."

"But I'm your amah."

That was rather the point, wasn't it? Such a scandal would shut Kalon up once and for all. Verity stuffed the card back into its envelope. "If you don't want to go, you can just say so." Of course, she didn't actually intend to accept no as an answer.

"No... no. That is, I mean, I would like to go. Please, Mem."

"Verity."

"...Verity."

"Well! That's settled, then." Verity pushed back her chair and stood. "I have a dress you can have sewn up to suit you if you'd like. Ask Po Lam to take you to Madame Page's tomorrow. And ask for Madame Page herself, don't let her fob you off with one of her assistants. The dress is by Callot Soeurs."

"I think tomorrow is a scheduled day of leave for Po Lam—"

"Leave again? She's just had all of New Year's! Tell her to move it. I don't want this to be a rush job."

"As you'd like."

*Gean Choo*
*Tuesday, 28 February 1928*

Po LAM, predictably, was not thrilled with the idea of accompanying her through another long day of errands. "I'm sure you can swap your leave for another day," Gean Choo said. "Was there a particular reason you wanted today free?"

Po Lam kept her eyes on the road as she drove them both into town. "It doesn't matter."

Gean Choo could've borrowed a bicycle and not bothered Po Lam at all, but it made for a convenient excuse to find herself in Po Lam's company. "Have you been avoiding me?" she asked. Blunt, but she didn't have time to prevaricate.

"What? No," Po Lam said, frowning. "We've both been busy."

"I sometimes think of them. Lai Hock and his friend, their bodies floating in the ocean."

Po Lam pulled the car over to the side of the road, causing the vehicle behind them to honk loudly as they went around while the passenger yelled out something indistinct. Gean Choo glimpsed a reddened face in a white suit before the car sped away from them.

"Have you talked to anyone about that?" Po Lam asked, ignoring the press of traffic, the rickshaws, cars, and oxen carts redistributing themselves to flow around her.

"No."

"Good. If she ever thinks you've betrayed her..." Po Lam squeezed the wheel, then dropped her hands into her lap.

"There have been more, haven't there? Almost every fortnight, or thereabouts."

Po Lam leaned her arm against the steering wheel and hunched over it, her body half-twisted to face her. "Have you thought about what I said? About leaving?"

The word jolted into her like a shot to the arm. It had been so long since Po Lam had last told her to go. She smoothed down her skirt, her palms sweating. Wearing a dress the mem had bought for her, brushed cotton in a floral print. Stomach filled with the meal the mem's cook had prepared for her. Sitting in the mem's car, with the mem's housekeeper, holding a garment bag with the mem's silk tissue frock. "She needs me."

"She needs someone like you."

What did she mean, "like you"? Like an idiot? Like a lovesick fool?

She wasn't entirely an idiot. It couldn't last, could it? Mrs. Edevane was a vampire. She was rich. She was white. The gulf between them could not loom larger. Sooner or later, one of her own kind would sweep her off her feet, and that would be the end of that. But, oh, until then, she would do everything in her power to make this last, to burn it bright.

"I can't leave her," she said. "But I wish... I wish we could still be friends."

Po Lam stared at her, forehead furrowed, eyes dark under her unfashionably natural brows. She looked one hair's breadth away from snapping.

But she said nothing. Instead, she started the car again, inserting herself into traffic with reckless abandon, a near-collision with a rickshaw puller causing the man's passenger to scream, the rickshaw careening on one wheel before righting itself, no lasting harm done.

Gean Choo shrank into her seat and wished she'd held her tongue.

# CHAPTER 30

# MURDER FOREST

## GEAN CHOO

*Tuesday, 28 February 1928*

Madame Page clucked when she saw the dress. "The waist needs to be raised here, the armscye shifted. Meera? Meera, bring the clips." She glanced up at Gean Choo, who was taller by virtue of standing on a stool. "It won't be an easy job. The beading should be unpicked and resewn, here and here." She pointed out the problem areas, along the curve of the armpit and all across the dropped waistline.

Gean Choo pitched her voice to Po Lam. "What do you think?"

Po Lam hadn't looked at her since she'd emerged from behind the changing curtain, awkward and gangly in a pair of heels borrowed from the dress store. Mrs. Edevane's gown was sleeveless, currently falling to mid-calf, stitched all over with tiny glass bugles and foiled seed beads, forming a sunburst pattern over the chest. The fabric weighed heavily on Gean Choo's shoulders, as though she were donning the shiny, dry skin of some great naga.

Po Lam glanced up at her from her seat. The husband's chair, one of the girls had called it. The memory of that made Gean Choo blush for no reason. "Whatever Madame Page recommends will be fine," Po Lam said in English.

"When's your function?" Madame Page asked, attaching another clip to the folds of the dress.

"Our mem wants it by the seventeenth of March," Gean Choo said.

"Hmm." Madame Page paused with a pin in her mouth. "Meera! The diary!"

Her assistant brought over a large black book, exchanging it for Madame Page's bag of clips. Madame Page flipped through the book, her spectacles sinking low on her nose. "Yes, it'll be tight, but doable, I think. Can you come by the week before for a final fitting?"

"Of course."

Gean Choo went back behind the curtain to change, carefully stepping out of the dress as not to dislodge the clips. When she emerged, clothed again in her day outfit of white and powder blue, Po Lam had finalised the payment details and was ready to leave.

"Did you like it?" Gean Choo asked outside the shop. She'd reverted to Hokkien now that it was just the two of them.

"What?"

"The dress."

"I'm sure Mrs. Edevane will be pleased."

"That's not what I asked."

Instead of turning to lead them back to the car, Po Lam moved across the street, forcing Gean Choo to sprint in front of a rickshaw to keep up.

"This isn't the way back."

Po Lam glanced at her as if irritated to see she was still there. "I have my own errands."

"You didn't say."

"I'm telling you now."

They crossed three streets and came to an alleyway where the sunlight was scant, the buildings close together, the windows on the upper floors bristling with so much hanging laundry. Po Lam stopped by a nondescript door. "Wait here."

"Where—"

Po Lam rapped on the door. Someone poked their head out. Gean Choo only caught a glimpse of tousled hair, a Chinese man's face, and then he and Po Lam were gone.

She folded her arms and tapped her foot. There weren't any signs on this street. Some buildings were the back sides of shophouses, jammed together like teeth in a skull. A few doors down, a boy emerged to empty a slop bucket into the drain, but then quickly disappeared back inside.

It might've been ten minutes, maybe twenty, but eventually Po Lam reappeared with a cloth bag nestled under her arm, about the size of two large shoe boxes stacked together.

"What's that?" Gean Choo asked.

"Something I ordered."

They dodged traffic on the way back to the car. After the shadowed gloom of the alley, the glare of the sun set Gean Choo's head throbbing. The mem's habits were getting to her.

Po Lam placed the bag down by the back seat before getting in. "Do you remember what you asked me the first month you started working here?"

"Which question? I needed to know so many things."

"You asked me about your predecessor." Po Lam joined the flow of traffic, driving away from the town centre. The morning was hot and sticky, although the clouds coming in from the west looked heavy with rain. Mrs. Edevane would be disappointed if it was still raining when she awoke. She'd been so looking forward to taking a walk down by the ocean.

"You'd told me she was working for a new family in India."

Po Lam's face was serene, devoid of affect, someone might say; someone who'd spent less time around her. The set to her lip betrayed a certain bitterness. "The mem killed her. She's buried at Bidadari."

If Po Lam had lied once, she could be lying now, but that seemed unlikely. "Why are you telling me this now?"

"Because you still have a choice." A frown line appeared between Po Lam's brows. "Did you bury the wages like I told you?"

After paying Po Lam what she'd owed her, Gean Choo hadn't

touched her wages. They ought to be safe in a container under the big tree to the north of the tennis court. "Yes."

"Take them. Take them and go—Malaya isn't far enough, but Siam might be. Hong Kong or Amoy. Go back to your family."

Gean Choo winced at that last suggestion. She could never go back. If Po Lam ever found out about what she'd done... how she'd despise her. "What about you?"

Po Lam glanced into the car mirror, even though they were on a deserted stretch of road, its surface pitted with potholes, making Gean Choo's teeth shake. This wasn't the way to the house. "I can take care of myself," Po Lam said.

That didn't mean she had to. The world was hard on single women, on those without anchors, without families. "I don't like to think about you being all alone in that big empty house."

Po Lam's voice cooled by several degrees. "I'll be fine."

There was a wealth of loneliness there that Gean Choo couldn't touch. She shifted uneasily in her seat. "How did she kill her? My predecessor."

"How do you expect?"

"Was it an accident?"

"I'd been away that night. When I came back, she'd been dead for hours."

Perhaps it'd been unintentional. Mrs. Edevane still left bruises on Gean Choo from time to time. She didn't know her own strength and mistakes were inevitable.

"Where are we going?"

Po Lam tilted her head towards the back seat. "Do you know how to shoot?"

Gean Choo did not. "Are those... Your special order was a gun? Do you have a licence?" She bit her lip. It had been a stupid question; no one collected firearms from back alleys if they had a licence. "I don't need a gun."

Po Lam sighed. "What about that night, when those men broke into the house?"

"I wouldn't have been doing the mending with a gun strapped to my hip!"

"Maybe you should consider it."

The car slowed, then stopped. Po Lam had brought them to a wild stretch of deserted land. It might have once been a plantation, bearing the scars of abandoned dormitories and processing sheds, but the jungle had rolled over them all, wreathing the empty buildings with cloaks of green.

"Is this where we stayed that night?" Gean Choo asked. Everything looked different in the dark.

"No." Po Lam got out of the car and picked up the bag from the back seat, along with something else, black-handled, gleaming. A machete. "Come on. Let's try these before the rain comes."

Gean Choo was not dressed for a trek in the wilderness, and she certainly wasn't shod for one in her patent leather heels. She stomped out of the car, grimacing as her soles sank into the soft dirt. "Look at me. Look at me!"

Po Lam looked, her gaze lingering as it travelled from Gean Choo's impractical shoes to her chiffon-gabardine skirt, to the fussy bow on her blouse. Her eyes narrowed as she considered the pale bands of cicatrices on her neck.

She shouldn't have said that. Her cheeks blushed hot. She didn't always use paint because it melted off in the heat and persisted in the wash.

"We won't go far. Will Mrs. Edevane even notice if you ruin one outfit?" Po Lam asked with an unexpected note of bitterness.

She probably wouldn't, but that wasn't the point. Besides, her shoes were new. "I don't know what to do with a gun."

"That's why we're here." Po Lam started walking, swinging the machete before her to clear the way. There were signs this path had been used not too long ago, cut vegetation and parts of the ground trampled underfoot. Spiky grass brushed Gean Choo's ankles, needle-sharp. She slapped at her legs, trying to ward off the hordes of biting insects. She was doomed to itch after this frightful adventure. Mrs. Edevane loathed the smell of tiger balm.

The forest opened up a little into a clearing. The canopy overhead warded off the worst of the sun, cocooning them in the fertile green undergrowth. Up above, a monkey watched them from a branch, small hands curled like a human's, its bright eyes inquisitive.

Po Lam set her bag down and unpacked it, taking out two gleaming black handguns, scratched from use, the metal brighter along the edges. She picked one up and pressed a lever so that the front fell open, revealing an empty chamber. She loaded it, slipping in six cartridges one by one, then snapped it back together.

She raised the revolver, took aim at a tree in the distance, and fired. The sound was momentarily deafening. Above, the monkey screeched, bounding away through the canopy as a flock of birds vacated the area.

Gean Choo pressed her hands against her ears, willing them to stop ringing. Po Lam walked to her target, examining the damaged bark.

"You could've warned me!"

"I should've. I'm sorry," Po Lam said, walking back. She set the revolver down and picked up the other gun. This one had a shorter, stubbier barrel and lacked the round chamber. Po Lam glanced at her. "You can come closer. It's unloaded, see?" She turned the gun, displaying the space before the barrel and the void in the grip.

"Nothing's happened in almost a year. I don't think this is necessary."

"It'd make me feel better. To know that you're sa—that you can defend yourself."

Gean Choo wanted to laugh, but Po Lam looked so solemn, the dappled light bringing out glints of blue in her hair like a raven's wing. "All right. But if I let you teach me, I want something, too."

Po Lam stared at her blankly. "What?"

"Take me to New World park sometime. I've never been, and everyone says it's fun."

"Who's everyone?"

She'd read about it in a paper once. "Can we go?"

"Fine. After the gazebo's done."

That ought to be soon. After countless delays, the foundation had been poured and the frame was in. It was just waiting for the glazier to return. "All right."

Po Lam started with a lecture on safety, somewhat hypocritically. Gean Choo ought to have paid more attention, but her gaze kept returning to Po Lam's hands. The stubby, rounded nails, the tiny marks of everyday life, scabs and scratches in various stages of healing. She had a scar on the back of her left hand, jagged like a lightning bolt. How would those hands feel against her skin?

"What did I just say?" Po Lam asked.

Gean Choo gulped, her heart racing. "I should always treat any firearm as if it's loaded. Only point it at things I'm willing to destroy. Be aware that it will likely continue travelling past its target. Ah... don't put my finger near the trigger until I'm ready to shoot."

"Yes." Po Lam held out the pistol and went through its parts, labelling the barrel, the slide, the trigger. This was how one inserted a magazine. These were the safeties, one on the grip and the other beneath the hammer. This was the ejection port. And so on.

The gun was heavy in Gean Choo's hands and warm to the touch. Po Lam left her standing there and used the machete to chop down a string of vines, tying them around a tree twenty yards away in parallel lines to make a marker.

She came back and passed Gean Choo an empty magazine. "Do you remember how to load it?"

She did not, but Po Lam reminded her without berating her. She seemed... not relaxed, exactly, but less uncomfortable than she'd been in the town proper. Po Lam placed her skilled hands on hers, lightly touching her hips, her shoulders, adjusting her stance and then her grip. She was warm, so unlike the mem, the roughness of her calluses sending a tingle through Gean Choo's skin. Her breath brushed the back of Gean Choo's neck, making her freeze in place. Mrs. Edevane didn't need to breathe, except to speak.

Po Lam passed her a pair of wax earplugs and briefly took the pistol from her grasp so she could put them in. As soon as they were in, it was clear how loud the forest had been—the rustling through the trees, the susurrus of insects. She could still hear them, but everything was muffled.

Po Lam handed the gun over and put in her own earplugs. She'd been planning this, to have everything together, but what if Gean Choo had said no?

She almost laughed at herself. As if she'd have given up the chance to ask Po Lam for a favour. As if she would have declined any opportunity, however innocent, to have Po Lam touch her.

Her world narrowed to the strip of bark between the vines and the line of the barrel. She raised the pistol, leaning forwards, conscious of its weight and the position of her thumbs.

The noise was less shocking this time, because of the earplugs and because she expected it, but the pushback that ripped through her hands was new. She gritted her teeth, lowering the horrible thing at last, the acrid smell of gunpowder stinging her nose.

She hadn't hit the tree at all.

"Wide, I think. To the left," Po Lam said, pitching herself to be heard through the earplugs.

"How many do I have to do?" Gean Choo asked, hating the whine in her voice, but she was hot and thirsty and being eaten alive by mosquitoes.

"Until we get it right. Or until it rains. Whichever comes first."

Gean Choo would've prayed for rain, but that would've meant running through mud, and one could sprain an ankle that way. How terrible it would be to get stuck in this awful wilderness with Po Lam injured and having to figure out how to drive when she'd never done such a thing before.

It took her getting an entire magazine in a row within the boundary of the vines before Po Lam conceded she might have gotten the hang of it. The poor tree was bleeding sap from its many wounds, sticky and clear. Gean Choo slapped at a mosquito on her leg and her hand came away with blood.

They removed their earplugs, unloaded the guns, and packed up, then began walking back.

"How much do I owe you for all this?" Gean Choo asked.

"It's a gift."

"It's too much."

"It's in my interest to keep you safe."

Was it? Because they worked together or...? "I have a gift for you, too," Gean Choo said.

"Oh?"

"It's back at the house. Not here in like... murder forest."

"I thought you liked a little danger in your life," Po Lam said, her tone lilting.

Was she teasing her? Gean Choo wanted to see her face, but she'd fallen behind. A sharp bit of debris was stuck in her shoe. She bent down to dislodge it, and something rustled in the vegetation.

"Don't move," Po Lam said, her voice soft but edged with strain.

Gean Choo glanced up. Beside the path was a snake. Its head reared up a foot above the ground, placing itself at her eye level and exposing a pale-yellow belly, its back striated with darker bands. Its nose was softly rounded, a black tongue flicking out of its mouth, its hood almost as wide as her palm, long body coiled and only half-visible in the underbrush.

"Slowly back away," Po Lam whispered. "No sudden movements."

She wasn't sure if she could move at all. At least Po Lam hadn't made her carry anything because she would've dropped it.

Somehow, she found the will to shuffle back a few steps. The snake had had enough. It lowered its head and slithered away from the path, exposing the length of its body—two, maybe three yards?

"Are you all right?"

Her legs were wobbly and her hands were shaking. "Fine. What kind was it?"

"I don't know," Po Lam said. "Come on. Don't fall behind."

Gean Choo ran up to her and clutched her arm, forcing Po Lam to transfer her bag to her other shoulder, the one holding the machete.

She didn't care if she was being childish.

And if Po Lam minded, she didn't complain.

# CHAPTER 31

## AN ASS

### PO LAM

*Tuesday, 28 February 1928*

"I hate snakes. I hate snakes. I hate them," Gean Choo mumbled as they got into the car. Her knees bounced as if unable to keep still.

Po Lam reached for her canteen and passed it over. "Small sips."

The simple act seemed to soothe her. They were both quiet along the drive to the house. It began to rain, pounding across the shell of the car, the wipers waving madly. How differently things could've gone. The snake had been a king cobra, albeit a young one. Venomous. A snake like that had taken down a bull elephant somewhere in Malaya.

She had to spend a few minutes working on her breath, calming her racing pulse. If Gean Choo had died... if she'd had to gather her limp body in her arms, feeling the life draining from her...

She couldn't think about that. Was she going soft? Why now? And why *her*?

It was still raining when they arrived at the house, turning the walkway into treacherous slick tiles. Po Lam turned to her passenger. "Let's not worry Mrs. Edevane. She's already fretting about this party as it is."

"I won't say anything." Gean Choo brushed a bit of leaf from her skirt. "Can I give you the present now?"

"All right."

They both got out of the car. Po Lam put the machete away but brought the bag in with her. The sky was stormy grey overhead, but it was still daylight, not yet past three o'clock. Time enough to catch a few hours of sleep before the mem woke up.

Po Lam's dreams had become vicious as of late. Haunted by murderous intent, by the thought of turning on her mistress. Sometimes she crept upon the mem when she was sleeping, bracing herself to run a stake through her chest, only to find Mrs. Edevane wide awake, lunging from her slumber and tearing through Po Lam's throat.

Po Lam wasn't a killer, even though she was a kidnapper and a liar. But a person who enabled murder was just as guilty as the murderer themselves, weren't they?

She went to her room and unpacked the bag. Her hand hovered over the cartridge choices for a moment, then reached towards the smaller box. She loaded the revolver with six wood-core cartridges. The gun went into a sling she'd tied under the bed, out of sight, along with the ammunition.

A hesitant knock came at the door. "May I come in?" Gean Choo had changed for sleep, wearing a flimsy nightgown with a matching robe thrown over the top, an outfit that no self-respecting unmarried woman would dare to be seen in. She would've looked right at home in a brothel.

Po Lam swallowed. She nodded and glanced down at her hands. Anywhere but at her.

The bed sagged next to her as Gean Choo sat. Po Lam spied her robe in the periphery of her vision. The pink of a lotus blossom. Was her skin beneath as soft as it looked?

"I mended your shirt for you," Gean Choo said, shifting with a rustle of fabric.

Po Lam forced herself to look up, to accept the folded square of cloth being handed to her. "Thank you." Their hands brushed as she took it. She shook it out to give herself something else to focus on. Holding up the shirt, she went still.

"My sewing isn't the best, I know," Gean Choo said, her voice anxious. "I picked white thread because my stitches aren't even, and it's less obvious that way. I had to cover the stain, see?"

She'd sewn the sleeves back on, and they seemed sturdy. Embroidery covered the elbow of the left arm, white thread over white fabric. A four-legged animal, with a bushy mane and tail. A horse. "It's an ass," Po Lam said, because she could.

"What? N-no. It's your birth year. Year of the Horse. I asked Auntie Seok Eng—"

"I was just teasing."

Gean Choo bit her lip, her eyes narrowing, as if uncertain whether to believe her.

"What year were you born?" Po Lam asked.

"Monkey."

It was currently the Year of the Dragon, which meant Gean Choo was turning twenty. Po Lam's first impressions had been right. Gean Choo was definitely too young for... well, it didn't matter.

"Do you like it?" Gean Choo asked, a note of desperation in her voice.

"Yes. It's lovely. Truly." If Po Lam were more certain of herself, she would turn to Gean Choo and kiss her. People did that in poems and books, didn't they? Maybe then she'd stop pining over what she couldn't have. What she couldn't be.

She turned. Caught sight of the scar tissue on Gean Choo's neck. Crushed the shirt in her fist. "Thank you for mending this for me," she said. How easy it was to push her away. To see the hurt in her eyes, and to not care.

"Of course. It's no trouble." Gean Choo glanced out the window and heaved a theatrical sigh. "We should both get some rest. The mem will be awake soon."

Mem this, Mem that. "Yes," Po Lam said. "Wait. Take this." She handed her the pistol and a loaded magazine.

Gean Choo took them from her gingerly, distaste crawling all over her features, and left, closing the door behind her. Po Lam stretched out on the bed, stared at the white ceiling, and tried to think of nothing at all.

# CHAPTER 32

# RUN

## PO LAM

*Thursday, 1 March 1928*

Po Lam had almost finished the staffing calendar for April, but one nagging problem remained. She cornered Gean Choo one night, catching her just after the evening meal, a half hour before sunset. "You haven't confirmed your leave for Cheng Beng. Everyone else has their preferred dates." Seok Eng always made her arrangements early, and the twins were all too keen to spend time away from the house. Even Po Lam had transferred a little extra money in her last missive to her sisters, for all that she had cause to despise the intentions of the festival.

Cheng Beng was for families, for the filial to pay their respects to departed ancestors. Not for people like Po Lam, who could spout a million filial phrases and feel nothing but hollow.

Gean Choo set her bowl and chopsticks down in the kitchen. "I don't need leave, thank you."

Po Lam trailed after her to the walkway connecting the main house. "You didn't take leave last year, either. Aren't your parents buried in Tiong Lama?"

Gean Choo stopped in her tracks, almost making Po Lam crash into her. "How did you know that?"

"It's my business to know," she said, though she had no idea about the other servants' family histories, let alone where their ancestors had been buried.

Gean Choo stared at her, eyes flinty. Her gaze went towards the main house. "I'm not going."

"Why not?"

"I just—" Gean Choo looked away, hands clenched into fists by her sides, shoulders hunched. "I'm not. Excuse me, the mem's calling."

If a bell was ringing, Po Lam couldn't hear it.

*Saturday, 3 March 1928*

Two DAYS LATER, Gean Choo was sick.

The mem kept her distance. Seok Eng made soup for Gean Choo's fever and placed cool cloths upon her forehead with a solicitous care that Po Lam hadn't seen her display with the other amahs.

Gean Choo slept the first two days, but on the third, she asked for a book. Po Lam picked one at random from the study upstairs. When she brought it to her, Gean Choo's face crinkled with suppressed laughter.

"Should I get you another?"

Gean Choo pressed her fingers to her lips. "No, no. This should suit me quite well, I think." She set the book aside, with its back cover facing up. "Do you have time to sit with me? It's been ever so dull."

Po Lam hesitated. Gean Choo looked like death warmed up, her face pallid and eyes red with fatigue. She gripped her handkerchief in one hand, holding it at the ready in case of congestion.

"I'm sorry. The mem asked me to drive her tonight." Lucky Zaid. She needed to find more work for him.

"Ah. I wish you a pleasant time, then."

What was so amusing about the book she'd picked? It'd been an English text, its title innocuous. *Astrid Cane.*

Po Lam left her to rest. During Gean Choo's convalescence, the mem had been more shrill and more demanding than ever. One of the sprung bells rang even as Po Lam headed towards the kitchen. She'd crossed into the main house and was standing at the bottom of the staircase when the mem abandoned the bell and started calling out instead. "Po Lam! Po Lam, is that you?"

"Yes, Mrs. Edevane."

Her voice came from upstairs, querulous and petulant. "I'm out of pills. Do we have any more?"

"I'll check, Mrs. Edevane."

Po Lam returned to the kitchen and found Seok Eng washing the pot from her latest batch of blood tofu. "She wants pills."

Seok Eng scoffed and gestured with a sudsy hand. "Try that cupboard. She's been taking so many."

There was one amber bottle. Empty.

"I'll make more tomorrow," Seok Eng said. "Still heading out tonight?"

"We'll see." With the break in routine caused by Gean Choo's illness, Po Lam hadn't taken as much notice of the calendar as she'd ought to. She went to it now, taking it down from the wall and leafing through the wafer-thin pages. If Mrs. Edevane intended to dine that night, she was early. The one before had been the previous Saturday, a week ago.

Back in the main house, Mrs. Edevane was not pleased about the lack of pills. She sat behind her desk, pressing the back of her hand against her lips, closing her eyes as though pained.

"Should I get—" Po Lam began.

"No." Mrs. Edevane clasped her hands and raised her head, gazing up at her. "Is Pearl still sick?"

It took Po Lam half a second to parse the name. "Yes, Mem."

"Fine. We're going out, then." Mrs. Edevane still wore her night-clothes, a slip in dark rose and a matching robe, her feet bare against the floor.

"Would you like to change first, Mem?"

Mrs. Edevane shrugged, the chair screeching as she stood. "Why bother? I'm not in the mood to be fussy. Let's pick up a whore, then I won't even have to get out of the car."

Po Lam schooled her expression to stillness. So it was going to be that kind of night.

The car rolled out into the evening, down Meyer Road and across Kalang River towards Sago Street. The narrow roads were crowded with rickshaws, coolies, sailors, and a few men in nicer shoes, who were probably clerks or teachers. Mrs. Edevane didn't tend to feed in brothels. The older and more desperate streetwalkers were a safer bet, less likely to have someone mourn them or file a police report when they inevitably disappeared.

Mrs. Edevane rapped her knuckles against the car window. "This one will do," she said as they came up to a building, a red silk lantern hanging out the front. It was one of the nicer establishments, all its wares safely tucked away inside. "Find me someone fresh, would you?"

"Yes, Mem." The road was too congested to permit parking, forcing Po Lam to drive several streets away to find a quiet spot. She stopped the car and glanced in the mirror. The mem was drumming her fingertips against her arm, staring out the window, her eyes half-lidded.

If it'd been Gean Choo in the car, she wouldn't have left her alone, not at this time of night. But she closed the door on Mrs. Edevane without a second thought.

She walked back to the brothel. A carpet was rolled out the front, stained with beer. Bright music spilled out the door. Inside were three girls sitting in the entryway, all in colourful robes. Their short black hair was neatly parted down the centre, with blunt bangs cut across the forehead or waved to the side like Gean Choo's.

Po Lam didn't look too hard at their faces. They'd probably all been born poor, from a village not unlike her own. The back rooms were impregnated with the scent of steamed rice and fresh garlic, cheap perfume, and unwashed bodies. The walls were decorated with art, nudes of women reclining, fondling, and kissing one another, their skin as pale as a full moon, their husband indulgently gazing on.

The madam was solicitous. Ingratiating. Po Lam haggled over the call-out fee out of habit but handed over fifteen dollars, well over the nightly rate.

She picked a girl at random, who was probably in her twenties, face powdered white, slim in a yellow robe with pink flowers along the hem and sleeves. She placed her hand on Po Lam's arm, the sleeve of her robe falling back to expose the narrow bones of her wrist. They were shadowed by her chaperon, an older woman, plain, her waist thickened by the years. The woman held a paper fan, which she waved near her face, her skin shiny from sweat.

"The car's not far," Po Lam said in Cantonese.

Outside, a bunch of men flirted drunkenly with the girls flitting around the brothels, who called out to their potential customers in a range of tongues.

"You come as a set, love?"

A man's hand closed around the girl's elbow, making her cry out in shock. He was European, with a sun-weathered face and grizzled chin, wearing a sailor's striped jersey. A switchblade weighed down Po Lam's pocket, but she froze without even touching it, as though part of her brain had been turned off.

The chaperon wasn't so idle. She reversed her grip on her fan and jabbed the wooden handle in his face. Howling, he sprang back, hands cupped over his eyes. His friends rushed to his side. "You bitch! I'll fucking kill you!"

"Run!" Po Lam said.

They ran, dodging rickshaws, travellers, and other women until they rounded the corner and lost sight of the sailors. Po Lam glanced behind them, her hand in her pocket, closing around the reassuring solidity of the knife. She needn't have bothered. No one was following them.

The women spoke to each other in low voices that Po Lam couldn't quite catch. The younger one seemed mildly upset, but the chaperon said something that made the girl go quiet.

The car loomed in the distance, lamplight flashing off the familiar silver trim. Po Lam breathed a sigh of relief. She had to pull herself together before Mrs. Edevane noticed anything was wrong.

"Your tuan must be shy," the girl said. "Government?"

"It's my mem, actually."

"Oh!" The girl turned to her chaperon, and they exchanged looks.

"Is there a problem?" Po Lam asked.

"No," the girl said, relaxing by her side. "But Ma might've knocked off a dollar if she'd known it was a woman."

If she'd known everything, she wouldn't have let her go at all.

## CHAPTER 33

# ROSE

## VERITY

*Saturday, 3 March 1928*
*Seven nights since last meal*

The whore tried to kiss her in the car, but Verity held out her palm in a near-universal gesture to stop. "Let's get you cleaned up first," she said. "What's your name?"

"Rose, Mem."

She stank of sweat and sex, her pupils constricted into two tiny dots from an ebbing opium high, the collar of her tunic stained with white residue. Verity sat as close to the car window as possible and discreetly attempted not to retch as Po Lam drove them home.

Everything in this world was such an effort. Why couldn't she want normal things, like normal kindred? It would be so much easier to only maintain a blood harem. To never kill. Easier and safer, and far more palatable to the rest of polite society.

But being good was so, so dull.

After a tedious drive, Po Lam pulled into the garage. "Po Lam will show you to the bathroom and bring you up when you've washed. Don't be long," Verity said, glancing at the chaperon as she delivered this last bit of instruction.

The woman nodded.

Verity went to the drawing room, pressing a palm flat against her stomach when it growled. "Soon, you horrible beast," she murmured. Sitting down on the bench, she rolled back the piano cover and stretched her fingers until tension radiated down her arms. Settling her hands upon the ivories, she began.

She'd finished an étude and two sonatas and was beginning an elegy by Fröhlich when the door opened behind her, footsteps echoing on the marble. She didn't bother to acknowledge them and continued to play. Fröhlich had been such a sensitive man, one of Duchess Bennesbrook's favourites. Benny had been so terribly disheartened when he'd killed himself instead of allowing her to turn him.

Benny was such an emotional soul, and so spiteful when she put her mind to it. Why, that whole unpleasantness between them had been almost a century ago, and still, Verity remained unforgiven.

The soft tread of Rose's footsteps circled around to Verity's left side. At least she smelled better, albeit not quite like her namesake.

Verity played the last bars ritardando and held the final chord, letting the notes linger. When she slipped her foot off the pedal and lifted her hands from the keys, Rose softly clapped.

"Beautiful," she said with a shy smile.

"You're too kind." Verity rolled down the cover and replaced the dust cloth. "Come to the settee. Let's sit."

She took the middle of the sofa, forcing Rose to sit close to her. Po Lam had loaned her an old tunic and skirt outfit in faded green. Rose was older than Pearl, though probably not as old as Po Lam. She wore a dutiful smile, her face unwashed so as to preserve the integrity of her makeup.

"What would you like, Mem?"

Rose's hair was straight and cut short. Verity fingered the end of a lock, curling it around her finger. "I'd like you to sit still for me. Can you do that?"

"Yes, Mem."

If she was disturbed or surprised by Verity's request, she didn't show it. Verity pressed her thumb against the side of Rose's neck. "I want to kiss you. Here," she said. "All right?"

"Please."

Verity's stomach growled again, insistent. She pressed her fist against her abdomen, made herself feel it. Her gaze narrowed to a small section of Rose's neck. Her skin without the rice powder was darker than Pearl's. The mamasan probably let her out all the time to go shopping or whatever young women liked to do nowadays.

Verity pressed her palm against Rose's head, turning it to the side. Her scalp was hot and damp. Even as Verity watched, a bead of moisture rolled down behind her ear and soaked into the trimmed edge of her blouse.

Her pulse sounded like any other human's, currently moderato. Verity leant down and bit into it.

Rose yelped, a brief exhalation of air that melded into a sigh. She raised her hand, as if... as if to touch Verity, to press against her back or stroke her hair. Verity gripped Rose's arm, holding it by her side until she gave up on moving.

There was a bitter edge to her blood and the char of opium dross. Verity forced herself to drink anyway, each hot mouthful coating the back of her throat. After a few minutes, her blood sat heavy in Verity's stomach, causing it to roil. Rose's heart was still beating, but she couldn't manage another drop. The wound closed before her eyes, leaving behind a smear of blood on the girl's skin she couldn't bear to clean up.

Verity stood, swaying on her feet, releasing Rose and allowing her body to slump against the settee. She caught her balance and blinked. The world resolved itself into sharper focus. Everything was too loud—the tick of the new grandfather clock standing proudly in the foyer, the hum of the nightjars outside, the sound of Rose's breathing... for she was still breathing.

Verity walked over and tugged on the bell pull. She'd only waited a moment before Po Lam came up. "I'm done with the girl. You can take her back."

Po Lam went to the settee and rolled Rose onto her side. "She's not dead," she said with a trace of amazement.

"I wouldn't have asked you to deliver a corpse, would I?" Verity snapped. She pressed her fingertips to her temples. Her mouth was tacky, aching for the pleasant, sweet smoke of the pipe, but the tedious work to prepare it was beyond her at this current moment. How could Pearl be so inconsiderate as to make herself sick? Verity was growing attuned to her scent, could detect it even from here. Perhaps Pearl had fallen sick on purpose, as some sort of protest. Had Verity ever done her wrong? The whole thing was just grossly unfair.

Verity threw open the doors to the back verandah and walked outside, her lightweight peignoir billowing out behind her, and gazed up into the night sky over the ocean. Her skin itched as if ants were walking on it. Maybe Rose had taken something other than opium. Her world was so out of sorts tonight; she should've been sated, joyful, fulfilled for a brief moment in time.

Even the sky was wrong here, the crescent moon grinning like an empty smile instead of standing upright. In the garden, the fronds of the coconut palms waved in the breeze, reaching towards the heavens, tall and impossibly slender.

There had to be more than this, hadn't there? Some great mystery to unravel, some adventure to pursue. A glittering quest, like a vision in a storybook.

Some part of Verity was missing, and maybe she'd never get it back.

# CHAPTER 34

## YOU'RE EXQUISITE

### GEAN CHOO

*Saturday, 3 March 1928*

Gean Choo woke in a darkened room to the gleam of eyes sitting across from her bed. She tried to sit up, and then her visitor moved, standing, placing a cold hand on her shoulder.

"Don't exert yourself, dear. It's only me."

She laid back down. Her mouth was furred and bitter, unpleasantly dry. "I heard the car. Did you have a nice time tonight?"

Mrs. Edevane barked a short laugh. "It was tolerable enough. Missed you terribly, though."

"I missed you, too."

The back of Mrs. Edevane's hand pressed against her forehead, better than a wet cloth. "Fever's broken. Good. I'm certain you'll be right as rain in no time at all."

Her lips descended, kissing her forehead, her hand smoothing the hair back from Gean Choo's face, lingering in a caress. She stayed in the room a little while longer, her weight pulling down the middle of the mattress.

The memory lingered the next day, the sensation of being, for once, completely safe.

*Saturday, 10 March—Wednesday, 21 March*

BY THE TIME of Lord Cottesley's soirée, she was up and about. Unfortunately. She went back to Madame Page's for a final fitting and spent an embarrassingly long time staring at herself in the shop mirror, at how the dress hung from her shoulders, little pleats of silk chiffon in apricot and peach giving the appearance of river weeds drifting in water. Why couldn't Po Lam offer her a kind word or even a thoughtful look? The other woman had simply settled the bill and waited for her to change into her day clothes.

The equinox meant it'd been over a year since she'd first started working for Mrs. Edevane. She'd paid her back now in full. No one could say she'd not gotten her money's worth.

She didn't need to stay, but she couldn't walk away now, not with her dress already fitted and the gazebo not yet done. Maybe... maybe after...

On the night of the party, they started preparations as soon as the sun set. Gean Choo helped Mrs. Edevane with her hair and makeup before retiring to the servants' quarters to dress herself. She finished her hair in the bathroom, leaving the door open for ventilation.

She was holding up a mirror, peering into the glass to check for lipstick on her teeth when Po Lam passed by. "You look nice," she said, as though it pained her to admit it.

Gean Choo drew back, clutching the side of the sink to steady herself. "Thank you. Madame Page did a great job, didn't she?"

Po Lam's gaze travelled from her shoulders, down to the jewelled belt slung low across her hips, to the fluttering skirt with its dozens of cut chiffon waves. Mrs. Edevane had lent her a necklace, long strands of rose quartz to match the pink and apricot dress, and a gossamer-thin scarf to drape around her neck.

Po Lam reached into her pocket, pulled out her watch, and flicked open its cover. "You're leaving in fifteen minutes. Make sure your mistress is ready."

That was an odd way of putting it, given that Mrs. Edevane was mistress for them both. Nevertheless, Gean Choo slipped her lipstick into her matching purse, grabbed her shoes from her room, and hurried back into the main house.

Her shoes clicked over the marble flooring. It was easy to see what was so compelling about heels. The firm curves they made of her calves, the sway they lent to her hips. If only they weren't going to a party at all, but instead going dancing, somewhere private, like that first night when it'd been just the two of them beneath the stars.

She crossed the drawing room and walked into the foyer as Mrs. Edevane appeared on the floor above, a slender spectre in black and white. Slim black pants covered her legs, her chest trussed within a white silk vest and shirt, with a white bow tie. A black tuxedo jacket completed her ensemble, tailored to nip in at the waist, the shoulders narrow and feminine.

It was daring. It was dapper. It stole Gean Choo's breath away. She'd never seen anyone more handsome.

"What do you think, Pearl?" Mrs. Edevane asked, descending, one gloved hand on the staircase. Her shoes were patent leather, buffed to a shine.

"It's exquisite."

"'It's'?"

"You are. You're exquisite."

Mrs. Edevane alighted on the bottom stair and crossed to Gean Choo, then adjusted her scarf. She was still taller, despite Gean Choo's heels and her flats. When her gloved fingers grazed her skin, Gean Choo shivered.

"Keep this on, won't you?" Mrs. Edevane said, hands still on the scarf. "We don't want the others getting the wrong impression."

"What impression would that be?"

Mrs. Edevane pursed her lips. "That you're available. Come, let's not keep poor Zaid waiting."

Gean Choo took care not to bump her head on the car roof as she got in, to preserve her coiffure. The cream leather seats held a whiff of fresh polishing wax and solvent.

Mrs. Edevane talked most of the way. "In our society, one must pay attention to people's preferred mode of address. I know I can trust you to be polite."

"Of course, Mrs. Edevane."

"We don't have such rigid mores about sex as your government does with their antiquated views. So keep that in mind."

Gean Choo blinked. Whatever did she mean by that?

"And I believe you're already acquainted with Justine. She'll probably be there, too."

"Justine?"

"Miss Skelford."

Gean Choo's expression froze. "She helped me secure this position."

Mrs. Edevane sniffed. "She's Mr. Haywarde's fledgling."

Therefore, Miss Skelford was immortal now, too, and part of Mrs. Edevane's society? Gean Choo wanted to laugh. So much for never having to see her again.

When they rolled up to Lord Cottesley's estate, the cars were already parked two deep in the driveway. Zaid joined the rest of them, then held the door for Mrs. Edevane as she got out of the car.

"Don't have too much fun without us," Mrs. Edevane said when they parted.

"Yes, Mem." Zaid circled to the back of the house, heading towards the servants' entrance. Gean Choo stared after him. She belonged with him, with the other servants, not in the tiger's den.

Lord Cottesley's house sparkled with laughter and light, the noisy hubbub of several conversations being held at the same time. Silent servants moved like shadows between guests, carrying drinks, red liquid clinging to the sides of the empty glasses. The servants' faces were all the same, regardless of their race. That impassive stare, that seemingly peaceful mien.

Inside, were they screaming?

Gean Choo pressed her clammy palms against her hips. She shouldn't be here.

As they walked inside, Mrs. Edevane was accosted by a tall European woman in a jet-black gown.

"Verity, my dear, you look divine." The woman and Mrs. Edevane exchanged air kisses, one for each cheek.

She'd never heard Mrs. Edevane's given name spoken aloud before. It sounded pretty.

"I could say the same for you. Have you met my houscgirl? Pearl, come say hello to Mrs. Ainsworth."

Gean Choo risked a quick glance at the woman's face. Mrs. Ainsworth had a strong jaw that couldn't quite be tapered with powder and paint. Her eyes were lined with kohl, rouge blooming pink on her cheeks. Dark gloves elongated her hands, the left one bare, the right glittering with rings. "Hello, Mrs. Ainsworth."

"One of Miss Skelford's little flowers, are you? She's out on the ground floor verandah if you'd like to resume your acquaintance."

She'd avoid the verandah, then.

Mrs. Edevane's hand glided over her spine to the small of her back. "You should go mingle. I'll come find you later."

All her doubts about this night came flooding back. Mrs. Edevane was right; she was still her housegirl, after all. Her place was in the back rooms with Zaid. She shouldn't be up here, dressed like one of them. She didn't have the millions or the husband with millions that would rent her a second-grade place in this society.

Gean Choo smiled politely at Mrs. Ainsworth, though she wasn't looking at her, seemingly more preoccupied with speaking to Mrs. Edevane.

"—when you said 'a scandal,' you truly meant a scandal, didn't you?"

At least the house was not entirely unfamiliar. Lord Cottesley's blank-faced servants filled the hallways, arms burdened with trays of glasses, each wearing matching outfits of navy with bright white gloves. She stared at those a little too long. What an absurd novelty, people wearing gloves in the tropics.

Gean Choo was heading towards the back of the house when something pierced the squall of conversation—the soft cry of a baby, primal and despairing. She paused and the crying continued. Wasn't someone going to tend to it?

It couldn't possibly belong to a guest, could it? And if the servants had children, they'd be safely tucked away in another building somewhere. Gean Choo glanced around. There, in the distance, was the bulk of Lord Cottesley's guests, spread out around the downstairs living rooms and spilling out onto the verandah. She changed direction, going back into the hallways and finding a set of darkened stairs. She paused at the first one, straining her ears. The baby was still crying. She went up.

Gean Choo froze at the top of the stairs, uncertain of what she was seeing. Two women in colourful kebayas were seated on the sofas, their long black hair unbound and reaching almost to their hips. In the middle of them floated a—what had Zaid called them? A penanggalan. She had the head of a woman, floating in mid-air and reeking of vinegar, her heart, stomach, and intestines dangling from her neck. A thick oilcloth had been draped over the sofa to protect it from the viscera that continually dripped down her spinal column.

All three turned to look at Gean Choo as she paused on the stairwell. The sound of crying was gone, if it'd ever been there at all.

"Are you one of Lord Cottesley's? We could use another plate," one of the whole-bodied women said in Malay.

Gean Choo glanced at the empty platter on the cocktail table between them. It was unclear what had been served. The platter was draped with a banana leaf, decorated with vegetables cut into the shape of roses. Blood pooled in the hollows of the leaf, dark and cloying.

"Don't be rude, Mayang." The other woman patted the seat next to her. "Who's your master?" When she smiled, her teeth were too white.

Vampires were real. Hantu were real. What else?

She couldn't breathe. Couldn't move. One of the whole-bodied women stood and grabbed her arm, fingers warm to the touch. She stiffly let herself be led to the couch and sat with a jolt. She wanted to laugh—

monstrous, hysterical laughter—but instead found her voice. "I work for Mrs. Edevane."

The two women—pontianaks?—exchanged a look, and the penanggalan grinned, wide-mouthed and cavernous, revealing the shadow of missing teeth. Gean Choo tried not to stare at the *plink, plink, plink* of the penanggalan's dripping blood sliding down her yellow intestines.

"How lovely for you," Mayang said. "And how is Mrs. Edevane? Not still claiming to be a pacifist, is she?"

"I'm not sure she's ever claimed that."

The three monsters tittered with laughter. "How long have you worked for her?"

"A year."

"So long," the one sitting next to her said. "She pay well? Lord Cottesley would double it. I hear he's quite obsessed with her."

"I'm quite content in my employment," Gean Choo said, momentarily reverting to English. *Obsessed.* Lord Cottesley? She could picture them together now. How beautiful they would look, both so elegant and tall. A perfect matching pair. She could lose Mrs. Edevane faster than she knew.

"Spoken like one of them," the penanggalan said in Malay, the tip of her tongue running over her lips. "No wonder Mrs. Edevane picked you. Did she tell you why she left England?"

Vaguely. Not really. But Mrs. Edevane missed her homeland deeply, though she'd never said it in so many words. "I don't like to pry."

The pontianak sitting next to her patted her hand. "You should know she has a temper. She killed Duchess Bennesbrook's favourite, after all. That's why she had to leave."

Killed, how? And who was Duchess Bennesbrook? Po Lam had said... She'd said the duchess was Mrs. Edevane's sire. "We're all running from something, aren't we?"

The others laughed. "Spoken like a woman with a secret," Mayang said.

Gean Choo flushed, even though the pontianak had likely meant nothing by it. Could they somehow sense her shame? "I should go." She tried to stand, but a hand shot out and seized her arm, long red nails digging into her skin.

"Don't be so precious, we're only teasing," the pontianak closest to her said. Her breath was warm against Gean Choo's cheek. "You smell"—she inhaled, her nose pressing against the back of Gean Choo's ear —"delicious."

Gean Choo ripped her arm away. The pontianak hooked her fingers into Gean Choo's belt and tugged. The clasp broke, leaving the belt in the pontianak's hand and Gean Choo stumbling several steps back. She didn't pause to look behind her, dashing down the steps two at a time, followed by the sound of laughter.

She fled towards the lights, the noise, gulping in air, trying to calm the rapid hammering of her heart as she searched the crowd. They were mostly Europeans in dresses and suits, bow ties and cravats all done up tight, as though no one was bothered by the heat. There were members of a few other races wearing tunics and cheongsam or clothes of Western make.

At last, she found Mrs. Edevane, who was engaged in animated conversation with a red-haired woman and a man wearing spectacles. Beneath the warm electric glow, Mrs. Edevane's hair shone gold, the sateen of her vest pearly white.

Gean Choo moved towards her but was intercepted by a servant in navy livery. "Champagne, miss?"

The liquid in the glasses was bubbling, innocuously yellow. Gean Choo grabbed one, took a sip, made a face, and placed the glass on a nearby plinth. Even that small amount had made her cheeks burn.

A gloved hand seized her arm and she startled, but it was only Mrs. Edevane. "Having fun, dear?"

"Yes, Mrs. Edevane."

"Whatever happened to your scarf?"

Gean Choo resisted the urge to raise her hand to her neck. She must've lost it while fleeing downstairs. "I could go look for it," she said, even though the thought of running into one of those women again gave her pause.

"Oh, leave it. Let's adjourn to the ballroom. I'd like to dance."

A protest found its way to her lips but lodged in her throat as they left the room and moved to the other side of the house. She gazed upon the ballroom. The last time she'd been here, it'd been two rooms with a divider running between them, but now all the furniture had been removed and it was crowded with couples. Mostly men and women, but a scattered few men danced with men, women danced with women, and the odd couple where she wasn't quite sure of one or either party's sex. The band had set up in a corner: saxophones, trombone, pianist, and a drummer.

A big painting took up part of a wall, ten feet tall and twice as wide, a pale young woman barely covered by a winding sheet, her wild red hair streaming in the wind as she glanced to the side, baring the long arch of her throat, her eyes widened with fear. A skeleton in a tattered black robe held her close, one bony hand against her waist. There was something tender in the way he touched her, scandalously intimate, arresting enough to make Gean Choo blush.

"Mrs. Edevane, I'll embarrass you."

"Nonsense. You do remember your foxtrot, don't you? Never mind—just follow."

They'd covered all sorts of dances over the year. The waltz, of course, and then the foxtrot, the Charleston, and once they'd gotten to know each other a little better, even the tango. She did remember, but that wasn't the problem.

Mrs. Edevane led them onto the floor, weaving them through the crowd. The current song ended, but there wasn't much of a pause before the next song started. Gean Choo hovered her hands in the air, her mind going blank. Exasperated, Mrs. Edevane had to guide her: left on the mem's shoulder, right in her gloved hand.

The tempo was quick and her skirt spun out around her legs, despite the weight of the beadwork. She was soon flushed and breathing quickly, but Mrs. Edevane remained perfectly pale and cool to the touch.

They danced through three lively tunes before the band changed to something with a slower beat. Gean Choo could've died right then and been content. Mrs. Edevane stared at her, red lips slightly parted. She'd worn diamond studs tonight, each one glittering. Her perfume was a mix of rose and frangipani, something woodsy and warm underneath.

She was, without a doubt, the most beautiful person in this gathering of beautiful people.

"Mrs. Edevane..."

"Yes, Pearl?"

Gean Choo lowered her voice, even as they passed closer to the band, since she knew Mrs. Edevane's hearing was excellent. "People are staring at us."

She was the only non-European on the floor. There weren't even any Eurasians here, or at least, none whose features betrayed them. Bad enough Mrs. Edevane took her housegirl to a party and let her dress up like one of them, but this? Flaunting it in their faces?

If they'd gone to the Europe Hotel, she'd have been turned away at the door. No one here was so impolite, but their looks made it clear she was unwanted.

She didn't belong here. She didn't belong anywhere. She didn't—

"Let them stare. Let them look at what they can't have." Mrs. Edevane's nails dug into the sensitive flesh at her waist, her breath cool against her cheek. "The only good opinion you should care to cultivate is mine."

She clung to her, drowning in the cool pewter grey of her eyes, faltering beneath the weight of her attention. "Yes, Mrs. Edevane," she whispered like a prayer. The delicate lines of Mrs. Edevane's face were so lovely, it hurt to look at her, stealing the air from Gean Choo's lungs.

Of all the glittering people in this room, Mrs. Edevane wanted her. Needed her. It was enough to make her head spin.

The song ended and the band put their instruments down to take a break. Mrs. Edevane led her off the dance floor and briefly tugged off her glove to caress her cheek with her bare hand.

"I have a few more people to catch up with, but you'll come find me after, won't you, Pearl?"

"Yes, Mrs. Edevane."

She patted her cheek. "Good girl."

Gean Choo helped her tug her glove back on, and then Mrs. Edevane threaded her way through the crowd and was gone.

She needed air. She found a waiter offering coconut water and snagged a glass, polishing it off in one long swallow. Taking out her handkerchief, she gently dabbed at her hairline to blot the sweat, trying her best not to dislodge any of her makeup.

It was a little cooler outside, ceiling fans whirring above the crowds on the verandah. She handed her empty glass to another waiter, wishing she'd taken two.

"Miss Pearl Teo! Is that you? Why, I hardly recognised you."

Her heart lurched into her throat. Could she leave? Pretend she hadn't heard? No. It'd reflect badly on Mrs. Edevane.

Miss Skelford sat on a rattan settee next to a European man in a brown suit. She held a glass in her hand but set it down when Gean Choo approached. There was only a little liquid left in it, something dark and viscous. The man was drinking from a glass filled with pale amber. Gean Choo jerked her gaze to his face, briefly meeting his eyes, hazel and contemptuous. He was human.

Miss Skelford smiled. "Mr. Barrow, this is one of my former students, Miss Teo. I was just congratulating Mr. Barrow on his recent appointment to the legislative council."

Was she meant to respond? Congratulate him? It was bad enough that Miss Skelford had introduced her, as if she were someone worthy of being known.

As if coming to the same realisation, Miss Skelford held out her empty glass towards her male companion. "Why don't you fetch me another glass?"

His gaze burned into Gean Choo before he turned away, obliging her to sit. She took the chair opposite Miss Skelford instead of the one newly vacated.

"You said you'd write." Miss Skelford's lips were pink, her skin flushed with blood. She'd never have Mrs. Edevane's pale, smooth complexion, but she looked well, dressed in a dramatic sky-blue gown with rhinestones down the front. When she'd been Gean Choo's teacher, she'd had no issues with the sun. She must've been turned not too long ago.

"I'm sorry, Miss Skelford. I've been busy."

Miss Skelford had clearly gone on with her life, ascended even, to immortality. She probably didn't ever think of Gean Choo at all. If she did, perhaps it was with the faint nostalgia for a pleasant memory, completely guilt-free.

She probably slept like the dead.

"Oh, please, call me Justine if you'd like. You're not in school anymore. Is Verity treating you well? She must be. Just look at you." Her gaze fell to Gean Choo's bare neck, to the pale white scars on either side. Her smile grew pinched.

"Yes, miss." Gean Choo shifted uncomfortably, leaning her arm across her stomach. She ought to have eaten before they'd left. Her head was light, her stomach cramping. It couldn't have been that one small sip of champagne.

"I'm so glad. I know teachers, like parents, ought not to have favourites, but... well. We're only human. Or were," she said, laughing. Miss Skelford always had such a braying laugh, she'd almost forgotten. "You were always my favourite."

Those words shouldn't have warmed her, but they did. She'd always been weak.

The music had stopped some time ago. From the ballroom there came the sharp chime of cutlery being tapped against glass and the warm, resonant vowels of Lord Cottesley's voice: "...to thank you all for gracing my humble abode with your presence. After a disappointing start, it's proven to be a bountiful year. With no further ado, allow me to present the first offering for your consideration. Male, ten weeks; dam third generation, sire fifth. The very first time, ladies and gentlemen, that Haywarde has allowed this particular line to enter the market. A smooth, full-bodied flavour for a refined palate. Notes of green apples, copper, and petrichor—"

"What's he doing?" Gean Choo asked. Looking around, most of the other guests had abandoned the verandah to descend upon the ballroom, though a few small groups remained here and there, speaking in low voices.

"It's an auction."

"For what?"

Miss Skelford looked uncomfortable. When Gean Choo tried to rise, she grasped her wrist with her too-warm fingers. "I think you'd better not watch. For the sake of your nerves."

Gean Choo stared down at her hand until Miss Skelford let her go. In the other room, another voice was calling out. A female she didn't recognise, accepting bids.

"Do I have two hundred? Two hundred? To the Wakefields, in the back. Two-fifty?"

Gean Choo gripped the side of her chair and stood, waving away Miss Skelford's protestations. "I don't... I don't feel well."

"Of course. Perhaps a cool drink would help?" She flagged a passing servant. "Fetch a glass of ice water for Miss Teo, would you?"

"That's not necessary." Gean Choo turned towards the house.

Her former teacher grew still. "Dear," she began, a quiver in her voice, part horror and part longing, "you have a little something... on your dress."

Gean Choo tilted her head over her shoulder, trying to glance behind herself, to no avail. She ran her hand down the back of her dress and it came back sticky. She stared at her fingers, disbelieving, then glanced at the chair she'd been sitting on. If there was any blood, it had melded in with the dark pattern of the fabric.

"Oh," she said, her head spinning. This wasn't her dress to ruin. Callot Soeurs. What would she tell the dry cleaner?

Around them, the low murmur of conversations tapered off. Faces turned in her direction, hungry, hollow-cheeked, and none of them human.

She took a step back towards the garden. Miss Skelford slowly rose from her seat, something dark and delighted in her expression.

A breeze brushed past her, stirring her dress. She'd later swear Mrs. Edevane had appeared out of nowhere, coalescing from a cloud of black smoke into the shape of a woman. She gripped Gean Choo's arm with her cold, gloved hand.

"We should be making a move," she said airily. "Come now, Pearl."

She dragged her away from the verandah into the verdant dark of the garden, first moving in a brisk walk, then breaking into a run. Gean Choo struggled to keep up, her heels faring poorly over the damp grass. Glass shattered from a second-floor window.

"Run," Mrs. Edevane said, tugging on her arm as if she wasn't already running. "Don't look back."

A baby cried somewhere in the distance, soft and plaintive. Gean Choo's pulse thudded between her ears, seemingly louder than the slap of her soles, the gasp of her breath burning in her lungs. She'd never run so fast in all her life.

Mrs. Edevane led them around the outskirts of the house, circling to the driveway. Zaid was standing near the car beside another driver, the tips of their cigarettes glowing orange.

"Get inside," Mrs. Edevane said, shoving Gean Choo towards the door. "Start the car. Hurry!"

It wasn't locked. Gean Choo scrambled inside and flung the door shut before looking back. It seemed like half the guests were drifting out of the house, heading in their direction, dresses sparkling under the lanterns that lined Lord Cottesley's driveway, eyes gleaming with twin points of red, like a nest of crocodiles lurking at night. Miss Skelford slammed her hands against Gean Choo's window, face leering between two flattened palms. Her teeth were growing into points, her tongue scarlet and long against the glass.

Gean Choo screamed.

Zaid started the car, reversed, then lurched forwards. Miss Skelford lost her grip, stumbled, then ran after them, followed by the unearthly horde.

"Hurry!" Mrs. Edevane snapped.

At the end of the driveway, the guardsmen scrambled to open the gates, and the car rushed through them. They picked up speed on the open road, leaving Lord Cottesley's house far behind.

## CHAPTER 35

# BODIES AREN'T MEANT TO DO THAT

### GEAN CHOO

*Thursday, 22 March 1928*

Gean Choo turned away from the window, settling back into her seat. She shifted, trying to lean more on her hip. She hadn't put down a towel and was probably bleeding all over the cream leather interior.

Beside her in the back seat, Mrs. Edevane was hunched over as though in pain, rocking slightly, the black wool of her tuxedo jacket stretched tight across her back, crouched as far away from Gean Choo as she could be.

"Mem... Mrs. Edevane, are you all right?"

Mrs. Edevane glanced in her direction, her face twisting as she stared at Gean Choo without recognition. There was a flash of furrowed brow, of protruding cheekbones—*what was wrong with her mouth?* She moaned like a wounded animal and clutched at her head with both hands, trembling, her yellow curls slipping free of their pins and falling to hide her face.

"Mem, please—what can I do to help?"

Mrs. Edevane reached up and punched a hole through her side

window. The glass shattered outwards, raining down on the road. She shook the debris from her fist, the broken shards tinkling as her flesh rejected them, pushing them out from under her skin, the cuts closing without a trace.

Mrs. Edevane stared out the broken window and said, in a strangled whisper, "Pearl, I am two whiskers away from ravishing you right here and now, so for the Lightbringer's sake, *shut up.*"

She shut up.

When they arrived home, Mrs. Edevane didn't wait for her to get out but instead, came around to her side and threw open the door, grabbed Gean Choo by the arm, and dragged her from the car. She rushed them into the house and took the stairs two at a time, her fingers tight on Gean Choo's wrist, forcing her to keep up.

They didn't make it to the bedroom. The first door from the landing led to the study, which was where Mrs. Edevane shoved her, as though she were a floating market hawker throwing her wares from one boat to the next. Gean Choo stumbled and banged her hip painfully on the side of the desk.

Mrs. Edevane tore her gloves off with her teeth, scattering buttons, then shoved Gean Choo onto the rug, straddling her. Her nails blackened and lengthened into claws, monstrous and curling. She shredded the peach dress before Gean Choo could protest. Beads bounced across the floor, tiny chips of glass and foil that a servant would probably be sweeping up for days to come.

There was no time to brace herself. Mrs. Edevane was upon her, claws carelessly slicing her knickers free, a thin red line blossoming on her hip. Mrs. Edevane bent her head and lapped it up, then pulled Gean Choo's thighs apart and went to her blood-soaked folds.

She whimpered. It was not meant to arouse, even though it did. Mrs. Edevane was too focussed on her own desires that Gean Choo became an afterthought, an accessory. A vessel. At least her nails had retracted to their usual shape, though her grip was strong enough that Gean Choo could not even think of moving.

Her tongue could not harm her, though it was almost too much, too

hard, too quick. Voracious. She lay back on Mrs. Edevane's Persia
and wished for a pillow, for numbing cream, for a drink. This was no
supposed to be happening.

Mrs. Edevane's tongue was cold and flat and questing, like the
appendage of some horrid monster who had come to devour her.
Gean Choo couldn't move her legs, trapped as they were in Mrs. Edevane's iron grip. She was gruesomely aware that she smelled of coppery
blood and stale sweat and the faintest whiff of talc.

Her first taste seemed to soothe her, for Mrs. Edevane slowed her
frantic pace. She lapped at Gean Choo's clitoris and gently sucked it into
her mouth until Gean Choo squirmed and clenched her hands into fists.
Mrs. Edevane laughed. She was usually so fastidious about eating, but
now her vest was patchy with blood, her chin smeared red.

"Did you see their faces, Pearl? All wanting you... smelling you...
longing to taste you." She tip-tapped her fingers across Gean Choo's stomach, spider-like, up to her clavicle, and then cupped her face. "My sweet
little prize. My delectable Oriental flower." Her other hand pressed into
Gean Choo: two fingers, three, four.

Gean Choo rocked her hips, reached out, and pressed the heel of her
palm against Mrs. Edevane's wrist. "Mem, that's too much."

"Shh. Breathe out. That's a good girl. Relax."

Gean Choo breathed, writhed, whimpered, raised her head to stare
down between her own splayed legs. Strips of ruined silk hung from her
shoulders, fluttering with her breath. "What are you doing?"

Mrs. Edevane flexed her hand, adding her thumb. Gean Choo cried
out as she pressed down, almost to the knuckle. "I'm going to put my hand
inside you, and you're going to feel wonderful."

She had the awful, startling image of Mrs. Edevane's claws popping
out and shredding her from the inside. "Bodies aren't meant to do that."

"How old are you?"

Her birthday had passed, unremarked, on the twenty-fifth of
February. "Twenty, Mem."

"Old enough to know better. You can stretch, dear. How do you
suppose an entire baby could come out of you?"

to reassure her, it didn't. Childbirth was agonising
nger.

ng, Pearl." Mrs. Edevane unclasped Gean Choo's
bra⸺ free hand, pulling it down but not bothering to remove
it complete⸺ d fondled her breasts. Gean Choo was horrifically sensitive, with even a breath of cool air making her nipples harden. Mrs. Edevane pinched them both in turn. It was exquisitely awful and perfectly
delightful, and Gean Choo arced up against her, silently begging for
more.

"You really have no idea how gorgeous you are, you silly thing. I am
going to eat you up."

She lost track of time, floating on the eddies of Mrs. Edevane's patient
encouragement. All traces of frenzied need had left her, allowing her to
be kind, to show some consideration. Her lipstick was smeared, dried
blood flaking on her chin, pupils enormous in those colourless eyes,
dilated with wanting.

Mrs. Edevane pressed into her again, and Gean Choo screamed. The
mem didn't stop this time, pressing harder, pressure all around, like she
was fit to burst. She was going to... tear or something. It wouldn't work,
she didn't *fit*—

Mrs. Edevane eased inside her with a damp squelch, a terrifying slip
of flesh on flesh. Everything was too much. Mrs. Edevane loomed over
her, still in her tuxedo, the bowtie undone, lost somewhere during the
frenzy. Shadows clung to her. She was all teeth and vicious smile.
Dazzling. Triumphant.

Gean Choo couldn't move, couldn't upset this delicate balance.
Scarcely dared to breathe. She'd never been knifed before, but perhaps
this was alike, the instant unravelling of herself, the exposure of delicate
nerve endings to a whole gamut of sensations.

"Shh, don't fret. See? I knew you could manage." Mrs. Edevane's
smile curved on her face like a sickle moon. She did something with her
hand, flexed or tried to open it; all four fingers and thumb pressing up,
pressing out, making that dreadful stretch. Everything was too much—the
fullness, the proximity. How on earth could she be inside her and still feel

so cold? Gasping, Gean Choo curled her nails against the rug, pinpoints of light flashing like stars behind her eyes.

"Is this a first for you, Pearl?"

She fluttered her eyes shut and sucked her lips to moisten them. "Yes."

That seemed to delight Mrs. Edevane more than anything Gean Choo had ever done or said. "How wonderful you haven't been completely ruined." She curled her fingers again, making Gean Choo whimper.

"Mem—Verity, please. It's too much."

Mrs. Edevane leaned over and nipped at her ear. "You don't know how lucky you are."

Gean Choo inhaled sharply at the scrape of teeth against her skin.

"Do you think you can come like this? I think you can manage." Without waiting for an answer, Mrs. Edevane lowered her head again and kissed a path across her neck. Gean Choo rolled her head back and without thinking, bared her throat, something that would haunt her when she thought about this moment, when she touched herself, dreaming about it in the days to come.

Mrs. Edevane didn't bite her but continued downwards, grazing her teeth against her overly-sensitive breasts. She used her free hand to pinch, teasing Gean Choo's nipples until they were tender and aching, bringing her to the sharp side of pain.

"You're a little slattern at this time of the month, aren't you? If I'd known, I'd have looked out the clamps. Or clothespins, if we wanted to be barbaric."

Neither sounded particularly appealing, but she couldn't distract Mrs. Edevane from her trajectory. "Whatever you'd like."

Mrs. Edevane moved her hand again, and Gean Choo sobbed. "Quite right, dear," she said but bent her head and stroked her tongue against Gean Choo's clitoris.

She let out a strangled cry. She reached behind herself, seeking an anchor, some solidity, and found the leg of the desk, curling her hand around it. The ceiling in the study was corniced with peacocks and flowers, the central light hanging from a plaster rose. She closed her eyes and moved her hips against Mrs. Edevane's hand. The ache had gone beyond pain and had now morphed into a kind of fiery stretch. She tried and failed to avoid thinking about those knife-thin claws, black as midnight, opening inside her like a chrysanthemum blooming in a teapot.

Mrs. Edevane moved her head and replaced her tongue with her otherwise unoccupied fingers. She leaned back and swatted Gean Choo, right on top of her clitoris.

She cried out, tears forming in her eyes. Mrs. Edevane replaced her fingers, gentle now, soothing. She nudged Gean Choo's knee to the side with her elbow, leaned down, and bit the inside of her thigh.

Gean Choo screamed and shuddered, the puncturing agony of Mrs. Edevane's fangs giving her release, a helpless convulsion with her body clamping down around the enormous stretch of Mrs. Edevane's hand. She moaned, the arch of her back softening. Mrs. Edevane pressed down on her thigh, holding her leg open and splayed to the side as she drank.

Gean Choo couldn't move. She pressed her nails into the desk leg, the wood resisting her attempts to leave a mark. She rolled her head to the side to prove to herself that she still could. Breathe. Endure. Her pulse echoed too loudly between her ears, still elevated, still pounding. She squirmed every time Mrs. Edevane shifted her weight, her teeth lodged in her thigh like the hand still lodged in her sex. She was no longer in possession of her body, so she drifted like a wandering ghost.

She was still drifting when Mrs. Edevane retracted her fangs and kissed the incision to make it heal. She snapped back to herself when Mrs. Edevane flexed her hand.

"I'm going to withdraw now, Pearl, so you have to relax."

She was. She was relaxed, wasn't she? But when Mrs. Edevane moved, everything shot back into focus with startling clarity, like the shift from monochrome to Technicolor. She squeezed her eyes shut.

Mrs. Edevane's voice drifted over her. "Breathe, dear. Remember to breathe."

Gean Choo pressed the heels of her palms over her eyes and forced herself not to hold her breath. Mrs. Edevane rocked her hand from side to side, gently inching further and further away, until finally, the rest of her slipped out without any fanfare, leaving only the burning embarrassment of a gauche, wet sound.

She came again, weakly, when Mrs. Edevane cleaned her up, lapping at the spilled red of her menses, blithely unconcerned about the state of her clothes or her hair or the ruins of her makeup. Mrs. Edevane's brilliant white cuffs were hopelessly stained. She licked her hand, both sides, and then sucked her fingers one by one, staring down at Gean Choo with a self-satisfied expression.

"I think you should sleep upstairs tonight, Pearl. I may wish to fuck you again in the morning."

MRS. Edevane was gentler the next night, her lips soft against the back of Gean Choo's neck, her caresses unhurried. After she was done, she seemed in sufficiently high spirits that Gean Choo dared ask her a question.

"At Lord Cottesley's. The auction."

Mrs. Edevane sat by the shuttered windows, lighting a cigarette. The match flared, momentarily haloing her in its glow, chasing back the shadows beneath her brows. "What about it?"

Gean Choo pulled the sheet up to her chest and shuffled against the headboard. "He was selling... he was selling children. Babies."

"Youth has a certain cachet to it, yes. For various reasons. Easier to train, for one. And some say the blood of a child, gifted by a mother, is the most powerful of all."

"He was selling them."

Mrs. Edevane shrugged, tapping her cigarette against an ashtray. "It's perfectly awful, isn't it? Archaic. But your kind are just as bad. Po Lam would know."

"What do you mean?"

"She used to be a bond servant before I rescued her."

"A... pardon?"

"A mui tsai, dear. Oh, might as well call it what it was. A slave."

She couldn't imagine it. A mui tsai; little girls packed tight in the belly of a stinking ship's hull, enduring a cramped and nauseating journey by sea before stepping off the gangway and seeing the sprawling port of their new home for the first time. Being traded as little more than slaves, all to provide a rich family comfort and status.

It was commonplace. It was heart-breaking.

Po Lam had likely been between the age of six and ten, finding herself in a foreign land, a hostile home. Had she run away from her family and been snatched up by a trader? Or had her parents sold her?

The lives of girls were worth so little. Women were nothing more than meat, put upon the table for men to slice.

"But then, his party," Gean Choo began, "the auction... Why did you bring me there? Why—"

Mrs. Edevane finished her cigarette and climbed back into bed, placing her fingertips against Gean Choo's lips. "Shh. Don't fret. You were never in any danger. You know I would never allow such a thing to happen to you, don't you?"

The scent of tobacco clung to her hand. Gean Choo kissed her fingers, then took them into her mouth, one at a time.

Mrs. Edevane's grey eyes were half-lidded, her lips wry with amusement. She tugged the sheet from her. "Let's not speak of the horrible ways of mankind." She ran her fingertips across Gean Choo's bare skin from hip to breast.

She might not get another chance to speak freely. "Verity," Gean Choo began, the name still odd on her lips, even after all this time, "may I? I mean, would you like me to touch you this time?"

Mrs. Edevane drew away from her, a slight frown marring her face.

She'd said something wrong. It was only because after that first night, Mrs. Edevane had gently rebuffed all her attempts to please her, either with her fingers or her mouth or the friction of her thigh. Was she so very disappointing in bed?

"Is it because I did something wrong? I can learn, I promise—"

"It's not that."

"Do you... do you not want me?" Gean Choo asked in a whisper. Perhaps Mrs. Edevane missed the attention of men.

Mrs. Edevane chuckled. "You dear, silly girl. I want nothing else but you." She swiped her fingers between Gean Choo's legs, making her yelp, then sucked on them. Gean Choo's flow had lessened today, but she was still bleeding. Mrs. Edevane's gaze turned thoughtful. "The books probably didn't tell you, did they? Those Victorians, so deeply repressed. Certain things just aren't the same after Rebirth. Bodily functions." She gathered Gean Choo in her arms, pressing her lips against her neck. "I want you. All of you. I adore seeing you writhe beneath me. Feeling you come undone in my arms. I'll never tire of that."

Gean Choo's cheeks flushed with heat.

"But as for my own pleasure—ah, well." She stroked the side of Gean Choo's throat with her nail. "Blood is pleasure. And the pipe, sometimes, but in a different way. Do you understand?"

She wished she could bleed for Mrs. Edevane every day. "Yes."

"Good girl." A smile scudded across Mrs. Edevane's face like a cloud gliding past the moon. "Kiss me."

Gean Choo kissed her. Mrs. Edevane's mouth tasted of ash, bitter and dry. Her hands fisted in Gean Choo's hair and pulled her down, down into the sweet soporific abyss of the little death.

# CHAPTER 36

# NEW WORLD

## PO LAM

*Wednesday, 28 March 1928*

The gazebo was finally done. The frivolous thing glittered like some gaudy jewel on the hand of an aristocrat. Stained glass windows sat in a white frame, the ceiling panels completely clear. The interior was tiled in teal and pink, stuffed with smoking couches and pot plants on decorative plinths.

It was still afternoon when the last contractor packed up and left the property. Gean Choo fluffed a pillow and flopped onto one of the couches, shielding her eyes as she squinted up into the bright light. If anyone else had been watching, Po Lam would've had to discipline her for the presumption.

"Do you think it'll still look nice when the sun goes down?" Gean Choo asked.

Why should any of this matter? "I'm sure she'll be pleased with it," Po Lam said, even though Mrs. Edevane hadn't spoken about the project for months. It was entirely possible she'd simply forgotten about it altogether.

Gean Choo rolled onto her side, bracing her chin on her palm. "Do you remember that day in town? When we dropped off the dress?"

When she'd had to watch Gean Choo, multiplied by all the mirrors, scintillating in diamantés and beads and almost... almost looking like one of them. "Yes."

"And we took the guns to the forest? And then there was that snake—"

Po Lam shuddered. "It rained that day."

"And you said, when the gazebo's finished—"

"That we'd go to New World," Po Lam said. "All right. Let's go, then."

"Now?" Gean Choo sprang to her feet, all the lassitude leaving her. "But there's hardly any time!"

"There's time enough. You want to go or not?"

Gean Choo shot her a mutinous look. "I'll tell the others we'll be out."

WHEN THEY ARRIVED at New World, they paid the entry fee and walked in, Gean Choo staring wide-eyed at the colourful facades lining the entranceway with its row of light bulbs, not yet lit. They would miss all the main attractions: the theatre, the boxing, the opera. They had to leave before dark to be back in time for Mrs. Edevane.

"What do you want to do?" Po Lam checked her watch. They had maybe ninety minutes.

Gean Choo grabbed her sleeve and tugged. "Let's get some food."

They visited a few hawkers and ate as they walked—golden curry puffs, their contents steaming inside the pastry, and skewers loaded with fish balls like pearls on a string. Gean Choo drifted towards the market stalls next. She passed the cloth merchants with their bolts of bright silk and intricate batik, and went straight to a shop filled with stuffed animals and dolls, a multitude of eyes gleaming sightlessly.

She touched a furred arm, then another, and bit her lip as she considered two bears that looked identical with their amber glass eyes and stitched black noses, their paws highlighted in pale beige. The shopkeeper wandered up to them. "This one is very popular with children."

Gean Choo smiled at her but walked away without responding, forcing Po Lam to hurry to catch up.

"Let's go on the carousel," Gean Choo said.

The organ music was bright and cheerful, the painted horses gaudy and wide-eyed, mouths constantly sawed open by their jewelled reins. Gean Choo selected a white horse with violet and gold tack. Po Lam took the seat next to her on a chestnut bay with sculpted tassels on its bridle.

Other families climbed on board, mothers standing with their children, the smallest being relegated to the stationary carriages. There was one other couple, but most of the seats remained empty as they started to move. Did they look strange, adults partaking in this amusement? Their horses rose from the floor, the scenery floating by in a whirl of colour.

Gean Choo clung to her mount and stared out, seemingly fascinated by the swirl of the world around her, by the gilt edging and scrollwork carved into the ceiling. She was seated side-saddle, clinging to the pole for support. Halfway through, she turned to Po Lam and, over the music, said, "I've never been on one of these before."

"Oh." Po Lam hadn't, either, and was now regretting her choice to eat two helpings of skewers.

When the music stopped and they finally got off, Gean Choo pressed her palms together, bouncing on the balls of her feet. "Again? No, I know... the Ferris wheel!"

That meant more moving. Po Lam checked her watch. They still had time. And she'd promised, after all. "All right."

The wheel looked bigger the closer they came to it, adorned with terrifying little cabins. Perhaps this was not a particularly good time to admit she wasn't the best with heights.

The crowds were still light enough that they snagged a cabin to themselves. Po Lam groaned as it moved, the wheel pushing them along so the next cabin could load.

Gean Choo was already looking out. As they ascended, she pointed out the sights. "Don't those people look so funny down there? Like little dolls. And I didn't realise the carousel had another horse on the roof! That's so pretty."

Po Lam only listened with half an ear, swallowing down her nausea.

Gean Choo, leaning too far from her seat, stood for a better view, which promptly set their cabin to rocking. She quickly sat back down again. "Sorry."

Po Lam could endure this for five seconds, and so she could endure it for five seconds more. But she was never getting into one of these things again.

"This is so nice. Thank you." Gean Choo's hand reached out, covering Po Lam's before she could think to move away. Her fingers were soft, clean. A hand accustomed to leisure.

Perhaps that was unkind. Serving the mem was still work, even if she did it on her back—

Po Lam broke contact, digging her fingernails into her knee and squeezing. She tried to cover her actions with a cough. "You're welcome," she said a fraction too late.

When the wheel finally came down and an attendant released them, Gean Choo was unusually subdued. She glanced up at the bright blue canvas of the sky. "I suppose we should be getting back soon. Before we're missed."

"I need to use the bathroom," Po Lam said. "Will you wait by the entrance so I can find you?"

"All right."

She walked quickly through the park, dodging clumps of family units and young couples holding hands. It was growing late, and the crowds had begun to trickle in for the night.

She found the stall with the toys. The woman was helping another customer, so she jammed her hands into her pockets, shifting her weight from foot to foot as she waited. Finally, she gave up and picked up one of the bears by its outstretched paw, then thrust a few notes into the shopkeeper's hands.

The toy thumped against her leg as she walked back, finding Gean Choo still by the entrance, just where she'd left her. A Chinese man was talking to her, dressed in a Western-style shirt and tie, the knot loosened. He was leaning too close. They both laughed at something he'd said.

Po Lam swapped the bear to her other hand and came up behind Gean Choo, taking her arm. "We should go. It's getting late."

"It was nice meeting you," Gean Choo said with enough enthusiasm that Po Lam couldn't tell if it was genuine.

The man retreated, his smile strained. They headed back to the car.

"I'm sorry I took so long," Po Lam said.

"It wasn't long." Gean Choo glanced at the sky, still blazing with light. "I hope the traffic is good." She squeezed Po Lam's arm, her hand resting in the crook of Po Lam's elbow. "I had a wonderful time. Thank you for taking me."

They reached the car. Po Lam slid into the driver's seat, and then, before she lost her nerve, she held out the bear. "I thought you might—"

"Oh!" Gean Choo took it from her and squeezed the toy to her chest before setting it down to examine it. "I feel so selfish. I didn't get you anything—"

"It's really nothing—"

Gean Choo straightened, leaving the bear in her lap. "Or are you sending this to your family back home? I'm so sorry, I shouldn't have presumed—"

"It's for you," Po Lam said, her tongue clumsy. "If you want it."

Gean Choo touched the fur on its face. "I do. Thank you... thank you. This is..." She reached out and took Po Lam's hand, stroking her thumb over Po Lam's skin.

This time, she didn't pull away. "I know we couldn't stay long today, but maybe... maybe we could..."

Could what? She couldn't schedule them to take leave on the same night. Mrs. Edevane would want to know why. She could say it was her menses, perhaps, but that was no good, either. The mem would know if she were lying about such a thing.

"It doesn't matter. This was nice, with no crowds. We got a lot done," Gean Choo said.

They had. But maybe it wouldn't ever be enough.

# CHAPTER 37

## THAT THING

### VERITY

*Thursday, 12 April 1928*
*Three nights since last meal*

Verity was at her dressing table, still fixing her last earring, when voices drifted up from the foyer. She'd slept in for some reason, tossing and turning, trying to ignore the growing cramps in her belly. It'd been only a few nights since her last meal on some dockside whore, gin in her veins, barely palatable, but already she needed more. So much more. It was the stress getting to her, Kalon and his horrible demands. They still hadn't talked since the party.

She'd only seen him once that night. He'd come over and kissed her cheeks in front of everyone, his fingers like iron digging into her shoulders.

"How kind of you to bring a donation for the auction," he'd said, drawing her close, his breath against her ear, his smile sharp enough to cut cardiac muscle.

She'd hurried off to find Pearl, and it'd been for the best. If she hadn't reached her in time—

But she had. Everything had worked out just fine, hadn't it? And they'd had a bracing run to liven up the appetite. No harm done.

A horrible wail came from downstairs. Verity finished tying the bow on her blouse, then wandered down to see what all the fuss was about.

Pearl was standing in the foyer, a swaddled weight in her arms. The warm, slightly milky scent of a newborn was undercut by the fact that the baby needed changing.

Verity swung the front door open, but no one was there. She slammed it shut, then strode over and snatched a sheaf of papers tucked between the folds of the baby's swaddling cloth. She waved Pearl away as she smoothed it out. "For goodness' sake, go clean that thing up."

Pearl bent down to pick up a basket of spare cloths and tins of formula, and mercifully, took the infant away, her footsteps receding. Verity's eyes were glued to the pages. The first few fell from her grasp, fluttering to the floor: pedigree papers, the brat's sire and dam statistics, complete with height, weight, and blood types.

Her throat closed over. The gall of him. The audacity! He knew just where to cut her.

At the end of the stack, she found it at last—a single sheet of cream parchment, handwritten. Her hand shook, her face twisting in a grimace. The letters were formed in dried brown sepia, sloping evenly towards the left-hand side of the page. Not thrall blood; he'd used himself as the inkwell. Romantic, some would say, opening one's veins for such a prosaic cause.

Given the context, it was nothing less than a threat.

*My dearest Verity,*

Verity, not Mrs. Edevane—as if he already owned her, as if he had any *right*—

*I heard you'd had a sweet tooth in life. I set this child aside especially for the notes of burnt toffee in her lineage. Think of her as an early wedding gift, the first of many to come.*

*You'll forgive me the liberty of choosing the nineteenth of May as the date for our nuptials. I trust this affords you sufficient time to make the necessary domestic arrangements. You are welcome to bring your staff upon joining my household, of course, but I cannot, alas, accommodate unsecured individuals above the age of three.*

*I understand every bride wishes to look her best on her special day, and to that end, I have enclosed within a recommendation for a dressmaker.*

*I endeavour to be, now and forever,*

*Your most obedient servant,*

*K*

She let the note fall from her nerveless fingers.

This warm island with its swaying palms and fragrant plumeria was no longer a haven but a trap, waiting to spring. Not only did he expect marriage—perish the thought—but to dismantle her entire household, too?

Soulless automatons. That's all he wanted. From her as well. *Lady Cottesley.* The very thought of it made her cringe. A beaming hostess, a charming wife with no opinions of her own, voiceless, pliant—that was the only thing people like him ever wanted. What kind of life was that? She'd rather be flensed on some trumped-up charge than suffer the indignity of losing first her independence, then her soul.

She needed to make inquiries. Not directly. He would know, he would *know*, damn it. Meanwhile, she'd have to pretend all was well, to act the simpering bride. And then what to do about her things, her gowns, her books? That crate of Mother England's earth sitting beneath her bed? The people who'd come to rely on her?

She needed time to think. She needed—

Oh.

She needed a drink.

# CHAPTER 38

## ARE YOU ALL RIGHT?

### GEAN CHOO

*Thursday, 12 April 1928*

An unholy shriek echoed across the grounds, and Gean Choo ran back into the main house. Mrs. Edevane was poised partly up the stairs with one hand upon the railing, the other arm wrapped tight against her waist, her brows knitted into a frown.

"Mem—Verity? Are you all right?"

Mrs. Edevane laughed. "No. No, I rather think I am not." She raised her hand to her forehead, massaging her temples.

"Is there anything I could do to help?"

"Perhaps—" She turned and looked at Gean Choo as if seeing her for the first time, her gaze travelling from her crown to her toes, then back again. She made an uncertain gesture. "Make it stop."

"Pardon?"

"Make it stop crying. I don't care how you do it."

Gean Choo moved slowly, as if approaching a wounded animal. "Mem, I don't understand—"

Mrs. Edevane reached out and grabbed her shoulders, shaking her so hard that surely her teeth were about to fall out. "The baby, Pearl, for goodness' sake, the baby! Make it shut up. I have a headache."

There wasn't any crying, or at least, none she could hear. Mrs. Edevane released her with a little shove. Perhaps she'd meant nothing by it, but Gean Choo stumbled backwards, arms briefly outstretched until she fell down a handful of steps, landing in the lobby with a thud and a sharp burst of pain jarring her wrist and radiating all up her arm. The breath seemed to squeeze out of her lungs. Why was Mrs. Edevane staring at her like that? She glanced down at her skinned hand, red stripes scraped raw.

That wasn't her main problem. The pain burned through her hand, so consuming she could barely speak through it. "Mem," she said, tears burning at the corners of her eyes. She tried to blink them away. "Mem! I can't... I can't move my hand."

Mrs. Edevane's right foot had already reached the first-floor landing, and only her back was visible. For one breathless moment, it seemed she might actually keep walking, leaving Gean Choo to an uncertain fate.

She tried flexing her wrist again but had to stop as a white-hot spasm of pain shot down her hand and up her arm. "Please," Gean Choo called out.

Mrs. Edevane's fingers still lingered on the railing. Her hunched shoulders rose a fraction, then dropped. She turned with an explosive burst of movement, heels clacking down the stairs, each step sharp, like a staccato spray of gunfire. She crouched next to Gean Choo in a flurry of silk and took her arm, icy fingers probing around her elbow and down to her wrist. Gean Choo bit her tongue to hold back her scream, her mouth flooding with blood.

"Flesh is delicate, Pearl. I can't believe you'd be this careless," Mrs. Edevane said, her voice as cold as her fingers, impersonal. She undid the buttons on Gean Choo's cuff and rolled her sleeve back.

Hot tears ran down Gean Choo's face; she couldn't hold them back any longer. She kept her lips tightly pressed together as she nodded. "I'm sorry. I'm so, so sorry."

"Give me your handkerchief."

She fumbled around in her pocket with her left hand. Mrs. Edevane sighed loudly and reached into Gean Choo's dress to retrieve it. She spread the handkerchief on her knee and began rolling it into a tight cylinder.

"You've dislocated your wrist," Mrs. Edevane said. "I'll have to expose the bone to fix it, you understand?"

Part of her wished she hadn't called out. "Maybe... maybe I should go to a hospital—"

"Don't be ridiculous. Those butchers know nothing. And I can't have you useless for six months, recovering from a human surgery." She held up the rolled handkerchief. "Open."

Gean Choo hesitantly opened her mouth. Mrs. Edevane shoved the handkerchief between her teeth. The cotton was dry and rough, tasting of nothing.

There was no more discussion, no prevarication. Mrs. Edevane brought Gean Choo's wrist to her mouth and tore into the flesh. Gean Choo screamed into the handkerchief, which wasn't particularly effective as a gag. She glimpsed red slick meat and pale tendons. She was going to be sick.

"I did say I had a headache, did I not?" Mrs. Edevane reached down with her fingertips and did something with the bone. Everything went hot and white, a pain that refused articulation, that could not be spoken through, even if she'd tried.

Gean Choo must've passed out for a few minutes because when she came to, she was lying with her back against the marble, her wrist pressed against Mrs. Edevane's mouth. She wasn't drinking, but the flat of her tongue was ticklish against Gean Choo's palm and the underside of her wrist. Mrs. Edevane's eyes were half-lidded, her fingertips pressing so hard they'd probably leave bruises along Gean Choo's arm.

Mrs. Edevane would consume her if she could. Tear off strips with her teeth, gnawing through the stringy tendons, the pale ligaments. Crack the bones to reach her marrow.

Mrs. Edevane's thumb brushed against her wrist, over and over again until it hurt. There was something wrong about her face, a greyish cast to her skin, her eyes sunken and glinting red.

"Thank you, Verity," Gean Choo whispered, her throat hoarse from screaming. "Verity," she repeated. She had to coax her back, to remind her of her... humanity.

Mrs. Edevane dropped her hand, letting it flop against Gean Choo's stomach. She stood and turned in a whirl of chiffon, her heels clicking as she strode upstairs.

Gean Choo cradled her arm to her body and stared up into the glittering lights of the chandelier, reluctant to move from the floor, from what felt like safety.

# CHAPTER 39

# AH MUI

## GEAN CHOO

*Thursday, 12 April 1928*

The baby hadn't been left with a name. She was a girl, round-cheeked and impossibly small, even though her papers had said she was almost seven weeks old, her skin pink with newness, but already sporting strands of soft black hair across her tiny skull.

Po Lam had found an old wooden crate in place of a cot and had lined it with blankets and pillows until all the rough surfaces were covered. "Is she letting you keep her?" Po Lam asked, securing the makeshift liner with a length of cord, the baby held tight against her chest by a sling. The baby was quiet now, drowsing, seemingly unperturbed by Po Lam moving around.

"I don't know. Should I ask?"

Po Lam straightened, cupping her hand around the baby's head as she moved. "Best not to. Don't mention it, and she'll likely forget."

"Does she have a name?" Gean Choo asked, standing beside them. Her mother had tried, unsuccessfully, to give her a sibling. Perhaps they would've looked just like this, odd and round and strangely unlovely.

"Chun Mui, I think. Does it suit her?"

"It's perfect." The full version was too much for a newborn. Ah Mui would do for now. "What do you think, Ah Mui?"

The baby screwed her eyes up, opened her mouth, and began to wail. Po Lam patted her back.

"I'll make up a bottle," Gean Choo said, retreating to the kitchen. She read the formula instructions twice, heated some pre-boiled water on the stove, and dropped in a scoop of the creamy yellow powder.

She found Po Lam back in her room where she'd placed the cot. She was sitting on the bed with Ah Mui as the baby continued to cry. The sound set her teeth on edge. No wonder Mrs. Edevane had been so distressed. Gean Choo should've been more considerate. Perhaps then she wouldn't have had that accident on the staircase...

"Here," she said, proffering the bottle.

"Would you like to do it?"

She did not, but she sat on the side of Po Lam's bed anyway. It was the first time she'd touched Po Lam's bed. The experience was not quite what she'd imagined. And yet, she'd always wanted to be a baby amah, hadn't she? It was one of the most highly coveted jobs in any household, less strenuous and uncomfortable than many others. Fate had a way of perverting her wishes.

Po Lam put the sling over Gean Choo's neck. "Hold her like this." She demonstrated with one hand under Ah Mui's bottom, her head cradled in the crook of her arm. She passed the baby over.

Ah Mui was heavier than Gean Choo had expected, but at least her wrist appeared to be functioning normally. Mrs. Edevane had been right; she couldn't have managed a half-year convalescence, not with her dominant hand. She offered the bottle, and after a moment, the child latched on to it, that horrible wailing silenced at last. Her eyes were huge, endless brown and framed by long, thick lashes.

"The bottle and teat need to be cleaned thoroughly between feedings or she'll get sick," Po Lam said.

"You know so much about babies." Had Po Lam cared for children as a mui tsai? When she'd asked Seok Eng about the subject, the older woman had been no more forthcoming than Mrs. Edevane.

"I have three sisters."

And she was the eldest, too. "That explains a lot."

"Does it?"

"You're so responsible." Gean Choo gazed down at Ah Mui, who continued to suck, but was slowing now. She had such impossibly small hands, such a tiny nose and mouth. A thread of milky drool seeped from the corner of her mouth.

Po Lam blotted her face with a cloth. The way she looked at Ah Mui, her jaw relaxed, her posture unguarded, was so... odd. She'd never looked so disarmed.

"Will you give her to one of the day staff to look after?" Gean Choo asked.

Po Lam thought for a moment. "Auntie Seok Eng could do it. But she'll need attention during the night shift." She glanced away. "We'll both have to take turns with that, given our... other duties."

Gean Choo flushed crimson. "I don't know if I can be trusted with—"

"She's a baby, not an alien. They don't need much. Food and sleep, and someone to love them." Po Lam fixed her with a hard, expectant gaze.

Gean Choo found herself staring at Po Lam's lips.

The baby moved her head and coughed, spluttering. Po Lam showed her how to place Ah Mui against her shoulder to burp her.

The brass bell rang in the kitchen. Gean Choo's wrist throbbed. She handed Ah Mui back, and for just an instant, their hands brushed.

"Don't mention the child if she doesn't," Po Lam said.

"I won't."

The bell rang again. Ah Mui cried. If only she could tear herself in half, give one piece to Mrs. Edevane and the other to Po Lam, but Po Lam jerked her head towards the door. She went to bring her whole self to her mistress, leaving only her daydreams behind.

# CHAPTER 40

## HAS SOMEONE DIED?

### VERITY

*Sunday, 15 April 1928*
*Six nights since last meal*

The telephone call came just past midnight, startling Verity from her morbid contemplation of whether to strangle the baby to stop it from crying or to drown it. "Hello?" she all but snarled. She'd made barely any progress on her migration plans, let alone deciding what to leave behind. Whom to leave behind.

Static crackled along the line. "It's me," Daphne said, though it took Verity a second to recognise her voice. Daphne always spoke with such aplomb. She sounded nothing like that now, instead adopting a hushed whisper as if she were witnessing an execution. "Meet me in an hour. Not here. The sawmill. Don't tell your humans. Just come."

As Verity drew breath to speak, the line went dead.

Her first instinct was to ignore the latter part of Daphne's request. Not telling her humans would mean devising her own transport, and it seemed hardly worth the effort to sustain a mist form for the entire trip. But the urgency in Daphne's voice had been undeniable. That, and the fear. Whatever could frighten Daphne? Serene, dependable Daphne?

There were several sawmills nearby, but Daphne could only have been referring to the one adjacent to the ironically named Lavender Street, one of the foulest-smelling streets in the entire colony. At this time of night, it was utterly silent. Piles of logs loomed in huge stacks, almost as tall as the main building. Ramps and conveyor belts stretched from the ground up to the building, while lorries and cranes stood unmanned, reaching their tall spindly arms towards the sky.

The sharp scent of freshly cut wood always made her skin tingle. Even a blunt-edged beam could pierce a heart, were it handled with sufficient strength. There was almost zero chance of them running into another kindred here.

Verity solidified near the north side of the building. Falling back into her body was a relief, like loosening the last lace on a too-tight corset. Extended insubstantiality wreaked havoc on her proprioception, but it was the quickest means of getting anywhere.

Daphne kept her waiting fifteen minutes, then thirty. Verity paced, whatever good humour she might've possessed waning with each passing minute. She lacked the patience for pranks.

When Daphne at last deigned to show herself, words of censure were on Verity's lips, but they died when she met Daphne's gaze. She didn't even squeak a word of protest when Daphne reached out and enfolded her into a hug with trembling arms.

There was something wrong with Daphne's face. It was bare, with not even a hint of lipstick. Verity hadn't seen her bare-faced in years. "Gracious, darling, has someone died?" Verity asked with too much cheer.

From Daphne's expression, it was worse than that. "I haven't long." She glanced behind herself, both hands still on Verity's shoulders.

"There's no one here."

Daphne turned back to face her, eyes wide with fear. "You've done it this time. After that stunt you pulled... dancing? In his house? You should've seen him. He's out for blood, Verity."

"I really don't—"

"I've been trying to get word to you sooner, but I couldn't. He... he's done something to my servants. I think they're watching me. I didn't notice, not at first, but then..."

"Then?"

"Then I tasted one of them, and their blood..." Daphne dropped her hands and hugged her arms. "It doesn't matter. You have to run. It's not safe for you. Not while he's here."

"I'm making plans—"

"Make them faster!"

Verity stared at her. Daphne hardly ever raised her voice; she didn't have to, relying on her charm and wit to cut through the most vexing conversation.

"I can't stay long," Daphne said. "Write to me when you're safe. Don't underestimate him. You know what Speakers are like." She stepped forwards and kissed both of Verity's cheeks, her lips dry and cold, then took a deep breath and disappeared, floating away on the breeze like a veil of morning fog being scoured by the sun.

## CHAPTER 41

# I UNDERSTAND

### PO LAM

*Sunday, 15 April 1928*

The house was unusually empty the tenth day after Cheng Beng. Po Lam had marked herself down as absent for the entire afternoon, even though she had no family buried in the Straits and no intention of observing any commemorative rites. She'd scolded Gean Choo for her inattention, and the hypocrisy did not escape her. She couldn't really participate since none of her ancestors were buried here, but she'd sent extra money home and said all the right things in her last letter.

That didn't mean she believed her words. Her level of filial piety was like a bad paint coat—scratch it with a fingernail and it'd flake off. But why should she care? They'd abandoned her, not the other way around.

News travelled so slowly from China to the Straits, her own parents could be dead right now and she wouldn't know. Perhaps it was better that way.

She sat on the edge of her bed, oiling the spring in her switchblade even though it hadn't needed it. What had happened that night on Sago Street?

She'd choked. Panicked. She couldn't let that happen again. She—

A knock came at her door and she put the knife away. "Yes?"

It was Seok Eng's turn to mind the baby, so she'd expected to see her face, because no one, it seemed, was capable of looking after a child by themselves. But instead of Seok Eng, it was Gean Choo standing in her doorway.

"Would you go with me?" Gean Choo asked. She was dressed for dancing in a lemon-coloured blouse and white skirt, a pair of shoes dangling from her fingertips.

"Where?"

"To the cemetery. There's still time. The mem won't miss us."

Po Lam put her knife away and reached into her pocket, flipping open the lid of her watch. Four forty-five. They'd have to take the car and hurry. "What will you give me?"

Now it was Gean Choo's turn to be confused. "Give you?"

"In exchange. I'm meant to be on leave. You're asking me for hours of my time to visit the grave of a stranger—"

Gean Choo walked to her bed and sat next to her. She hesitated for a moment, her fingertips trembling against the whiteness of Po Lam's sheets, but then she wrapped her arm around Po Lam's shoulders and kissed her. Her mouth was soft, yielding. She felt small against Po Lam's chest. Fragile. Po Lam relished the warm pressure of her tongue, the powdery floral scent of her perfume. Her arm snaked around Gean Choo's waist. Her hands had touched no one, save to commit violence, for how long? Years. It almost broke her to know she could still use them for *this*.

Gean Choo pulled back. Her lower lip trembled. "I'm sorry. I didn't mean to... I only wanted—"

"Forget it." Po Lam's mouth still tingled. She fought the urge to wipe it. She stood and started walking towards the door. When she didn't hear footsteps, she turned back. "Are you coming? We should hurry."

THE CEMETERY WAS DOTTED over with the filial but tardy, knots of family members up to four generations deep paying their respects. Po Lam helped carry the assortment of grave offerings that Gean Choo bought from a hawker—rice, chicken, pork, fish, and a large, spiky pineapple. She brushed ants from the pineapple as they walked.

Gean Choo led them past the graves and tombs to a modest pair of markers. Po Lam helped her pull the weeds encroaching on the stone, and Gean Choo knelt by the markers, repainting over the engravings with a fine brush.

Po Lam glanced at the dates. Gean Choo's mother had died in 1918. The flu, most likely. Her father in 1927, only two months before Gean Choo had started working for Mrs. Edevane. No wonder she'd been so eager for a job.

Gean Choo struggled with a box of matches. Po Lam took over, the match flaring to life with one strike. Gean Choo dipped her incense into the flame, which licked up against Po Lam's thumb by the time the incense caught alight.

She shook out the match and focussed on the sting of the burn as Gean Choo bowed before the gravestones. This really was neither the place nor time for her to be thinking about that other flame, the heat of Gean Choo's lips. She bit the inside of her mouth to distract herself.

Gean Choo was suspiciously glassy-eyed when she turned away, which instantly quenched any thoughts of ardour Po Lam might've had. They tidied up the remainder of their offerings and walked back to the car in silence.

Inside, Gean Choo sat awkwardly with her knees pulled to her chest in the passenger's seat. When Po Lam reached for the ignition, she grabbed her hand. "Not just yet. Please? There's still time, isn't there?"

There were only five minutes before they had to leave. "A little."

Gean Choo hugged her knees to her chest, her shoes likely scraping the edge of the leather seats. She was clear-eyed but distant, her gaze focussed somewhere across the horizon.

What was Po Lam meant to do? Say something? Touch her? She shuddered. Bad enough they'd kissed. If the mem found out…

"We have to go," Po Lam said, although it was the last thing she'd wanted to say.

Gean Choo hugged her knees. "I know. I know." She rocked herself from side to side like a child. She was like one of those antique Japanese vases, the seams mended with gold inlay. Mrs. Edevane had one at the back of the first-floor corridor.

"You did your part. I'm sure your parents will be pleased—"

"My parents?" Gean Choo turned her eyes upon Po Lam. "My parents have every reason to loathe me."

"Why? Whatever you've done... I'm sure they can forgive you."

There'd been that gap of two months between her father's death and her employment with Mrs. Edevane. Perhaps she'd worked as a taxi dancer... or in a brothel.

There was a hint of hysteria in Gean Choo's voice, as though she were on the edge of laughter. "I can't take credit for my mother. That was just disease, like everyone else that year. But Pa? I killed him."

Patricides and matricides were destined for the lowest level of hell, the most severe punishment. "How?"

Gean Choo slumped back in her seat. "He craved the pipe. He sold the furniture, Mother's jewellery... even the books I'd borrowed from Miss Skelford. But he still had debts. Big ones. I prayed for him to die. And then, a week later, he was dead after smoking a pipe I'd prepared for him."

"How does that count as you killing him?"

"I wished ill upon him too loudly. Some evil spirit must've heard my thoughts." She gazed out the window, her teeth worrying the dry skin on her lips. "If the mem is real, if hantu are real, then other beings must be real too, mustn't they?"

"You don't know. Maybe the dealer cheated him, sold dross too concentrated."

"But I made the pipe for him. I should've known. Maybe I was careless with the dose. I can't remember."

"Were you drunk?"

"No!"

"Did you offer something to the spirits in exchange for his death?"

Gean Choo shook her head. "I had nothing to offer."

"Then if something had been listening, why would they have accepted your plea? Even ghosts need to eat. It wasn't your fault."

Gean Choo was silent for a while, arms wrapped around her knees. "I don't deserve this."

"Deserve what?"

"You being kind to me."

"I'm just being reasonable. Don't take on a sin you might not have committed." She had to say something else. Say something true for once. Truth demanded to be answered with truth. "For what it's worth," Po Lam began, "I understand."

There was silence for a time, broken only by the sound of birds flocking overhead and the distant chatter of families returning from gravesides. Gean Choo leaned over the gearbox, invading her personal space, and wrapped her arms around her, pressing her cheek against Po Lam's chest. Po Lam hesitated, overwhelmed by the weight of her, the insistent grip of her limbs, but eventually, she placed her hands over Gean Choo's back, completing the circle. Perhaps it was fate that Gean Choo's father had died. Destiny. It'd brought her here. Po Lam could be greedy, too.

The sun sank over the horizon as they sat there, joined, reluctant to break the spell. As Po Lam gazed up, finding the first star of the evening, it felt as though she were falling into that dark and endless void.

# CHAPTER 42

## AN ILLUSION

### GEAN CHOO

*Sunday, 15 April 1928*

They were late back to the house after leaving the cemetery, but Gean Choo didn't care. She couldn't stop sneaking glances at Po Lam while they were in the car. Po Lam, who'd said she'd understood. Who'd learned her worst secret and hadn't yet turned away.

What was this effervescent feeling, precious and rare?

Hope. It was hope.

When they reached the house, little Ah Mui's cries were audible all the way from the garage. "I'll get her." Po Lam sighed. "You'd better see to the mem."

It was full evening, the sky already pitch-black. Gean Choo hurried to the kitchen, trying to compose excuses in her head. A lorry overturned, blocking the road, a flat tyre, an existential conversation about one's deepest, darkest secret...

When she stepped into the kitchen, it already smelled of blood tofu. She startled when a woman walked in from the north side, carrying an empty plate.

"Hello, Miss Teo. Imagine seeing you here."

It was Koh Bee Leng from the lodging house, her lips curved into a triumphant smile. She placed the plate in the wash bucket and began to clean it.

"What are you doing?" Gean Choo managed after a moment.

"What does it look like I'm doing?" Bee Leng pulled out the clean plate and started drying it with a towel. "I've heard there's a new baby in the house. That's wonderful! Now you can be the baby amah. I can be the cleaning amah, the washing amah, the sewing amah... whatever the mem needs. It'll lighten your load. Don't get jealous already."

"I'm not." Gean Choo glanced at the bell board, which remained silent for now. "Listen. The mem. She's... dangerous."

Bee Leng opened a cupboard and put away the clean plate. "You're not afraid."

"That's not true!"

Bee Leng straightened. Wisps of hair had escaped from her bun, which she blew out of her face. "Why are you still here, then?"

Why was she here? It couldn't just be for the employment. Mrs. Edevane had saved her more than once, but hadn't she repaid her debt in blood many times over?

"I'll tell you. Just look at you!" Bee Leng said, gesturing to her, encompassing her dress, the heels she'd neglected to remove, her fashionably short hair. "You practically look like one of them."

It was one of the cruellest things Bee Leng might've said to her. The ringing of the bell stopped her from responding.

"What's that?" Bee Leng asked.

"It's the mem, asking for someone." She glanced up to check the bell's label. "In the study."

"I'll get it," Bee Leng said, and practically ran out the door.

All alone again. At least Ah Mui had stopped crying. Maybe she ought to warm her bottle. Gean Choo leaned over the stove, hand on the saucepan. The water remaining in it showed her reflection, dark and shadowy against the metal.

She didn't look anything like one of them.

She prepared Ah Mui's bottle, then brought it to Po Lam's room.

Po Lam had found an old rocking chair and was sitting there with Ah Mui, who took the bottle easily enough.

Gean Choo sat on the edge of Po Lam's bed. "Did you know we were getting a new amah?"

Po Lam didn't glance up from her charge. "No."

"It's Koh Bee Leng. From my old lodging house." When Po Lam remained silent, Gean Choo continued, "She doesn't know what danger she's in."

"Perhaps you should look to your own future before you seek to control others."

It sounded like the sort of thing a monk would say. Gean Choo didn't need a lecture. "She asked me why I was still here. I couldn't think. Why are you here?"

"Why is anyone anywhere?"

When Ah Mui finished the bottle, Po Lam placed her against her shoulder and patted her until she burped.

None of this was helping. Gean Choo turned to leave.

"Have you heard the story of the monkey and the moon?"

"What?"

Po Lam rose, still holding Ah Mui in her arms. "A monkey dangles from a branch, reaching towards a puddle that holds a reflection of the moon."

"And?"

"Just think about it first."

It sounded like one of those assignments given at the end of a long and hot week, when all the students were already languishing at their desks, faces sticky with perspiration and eyes upon the big clock at the front of the schoolroom. But Gean Choo couldn't help but answer, "The real moon is in the sky; the puddle is only an illusion."

She was rewarded with a smile, so quickly gone. "She stopped the thieves from hurting you. She took you from Lord Cottesley's house before his other guests could hunt you. You think she's keeping you safe."

"I'm not so bodoh to ever think of Mrs. Edevane as safe." The words tasted of hypocrisy even as they left Gean Choo's lips.

"Leave her. Come with me, and we'll leave her together."

*Together.* A tingle ran up her spine, a frisson of heat and yearning. "Ah Mui?"

"We'll take her, too. I have a friend in Alor Star. I'm sure he'd put us up for a few days."

Like it was that easy. Like she could just... walk away. "Come with you as your... travelling companion?"

"As my—" Po Lam bit off her words. "What matters is that we leave."

She stood in Po Lam's doorway like a dumbstruck fool. She didn't deserve this, didn't deserve a second chance at happiness. She didn't deserve anything more than the scraps of affection Mrs. Edevane inconsistently bestowed upon her. She was Teo Gean Choo, and she had *killed her own father.*

The sprung bell rang, high-pitched and insistent. The sound brought her back to reality, back to a world where things made sense.

"I have... I have to go."

Upstairs in the study, the phonograph was running with the needle up, the record spinning uselessly round and round. Mrs. Edevane sat at her desk with a book in her hand. She didn't glance up as Gean Choo entered.

"Oh!"

Bee Leng lay draped on the couch, boneless and pale of face. Gean Choo raced to her and felt for a pulse.

"You needn't worry yourself. She's quite alive."

Her pulse was there, but weak—much too weak. Gean Choo shook her by the shoulders and Bee Leng's head limply lolled back and forth. The scar was on her neck, shiny-new and delicate. Gean Choo recoiled from it.

"I don't think that's helping, dear."

She had to fetch Po Lam, or even Zaid. Bee Leng needed medical attention. She needed—

"Where are you going?"

Gean Choo paused with her fingers on the doorframe. "I have to call a doctor."

Mrs. Edevane waved her hand, closing her book with a snap. "She'll sleep it off. You did, after all. Besides, I didn't call you here for that."

"Mem, she's very ill—"

"You know, Pearl, when I set hours for my employees, I expect them to be adhered to."

"I'm sor—"

"The clubs all close at midnight, which is most inconvenient, and I'm obliged—" She paused for a moment. "One must make appearances."

"I didn't—"

"The thing is, Pearl. The thing is. I ask so little of you, do I not? And don't I give so much of myself in return?"

Gean Choo was silent. She dared drop her gaze to Bee Leng, whose chest continued to move slightly. She was still alive. "I'm sorry, Mrs. Edevane. It won't happen again."

"Verity."

"I'm sorry, Verity."

Mrs. Edevane gestured, and Gean Choo walked to her, heel to toe, heel to toe. Mrs. Edevane splayed her fingers against Gean Choo's breastbone, five points of smouldering ice against the heat of her skin. She bent her head and her nose brushed Gean Choo's hair. "You smell of incense."

"I went to the cemetery."

Mrs. Edevane pulled back and glanced at the clock on the wall. "I'm planning a little getaway. You must help me pack." She strode towards the door, grabbing Gean Choo's hand as she went.

Gean Choo glanced back at Bee Leng's prone form. So still. So pale. "Where are you going?"

"*We* are going—oh, it doesn't matter where."

"We?"

They'd reached the bedroom. Mrs. Edevane threw open the doors to one of her wardrobes, tossing clothes onto the bed. "Of course. You and Po Lam. The others will have to mind the house while we're gone."

The clothes offered no clues, furs mixed in with dresses of airy muslin. Gean Choo picked up a dress and folded it as Mrs. Edevane continued to add to the pile.

She filled three suitcases fit to bursting, then stacked them neatly against the wall. Once the clothes had been put away, Mrs. Edevane peevishly demanded her pipe. There was no clock in the bedroom, but the minutes slipped by like acid wearing down the enamel of Gean Choo's teeth, leaving the nerves raw and aching.

"When are we leaving?" Gean Choo asked.

"Soon, dear. Soon."

"Are we bringing the baby?" As soon as the question left her mouth, she cringed. Po Lam had said better not to mention it.

Mrs. Edevane paused with the pipe halfway to her mouth, her fingers tightening along its stem. "What good would that do? No, I think it much better left behind."

The edges of the room seemed to spin. The pale clouds of vapour were getting to her, even though she wasn't the one smoking. "I should check on Bee Leng—"

"Don't be ridiculous, Pearl. I can't cook this on my own."

She should've left anyway, told her to hell with it; but instead, she found herself reaching for another lump of opium paste.

## CHAPTER 43

## DO YOU LOVE HER?

### PO LAM

*Monday, 16 April 1928*

P o Lam found Mrs. Edevane in the study, staring at Bee Leng as though she wasn't seeing her at all. Po Lam rushed over and knelt, rolling Bee Leng's face towards her. Glassy eyes looked out at nothing and her jaw was slack. There was no pulse.

"Do you suppose there'll be trouble? She might've told someone where she'd gone." Mrs. Edevane's voice was distant, unconcerned, as if she were speaking of the weather.

Po Lam slowly rose to her feet. What had she promised herself? That she'd leave if Mrs. Edevane took one of them. If she attacked Seok Eng, or the gardener, or the twins, or Zaid. "How did it happen?" Po Lam asked.

"What?"

"Her death. How did it happen?"

Mrs. Edevane looked towards her, lips pursed, brows upturned. She was flushed with blood, standing tall and strong. The sort of woman who could walk around in plain sight, armed with her beauty and manners, her wealth and pedigree. No one would ever pick her as a murderer. She looked nothing like the pale, fragile creature Po Lam had nursed throughout the pandemic a decade prior. And she resembled even less the soft-spoken, generous woman of two decades past, who'd plucked Po Lam from a life of obscurity and pain, who'd bought her loyalty and silence with everything Po Lam had ever asked for. Money to send home, education for her nieces and nephews, tutors for Po Lam herself.

And all she'd ever required in return was for Po Lam to turn herself into clay. To let Mrs. Edevane shape her into a monster.

"You've never asked that before," Mrs. Edevane said.

"You've never done this before."

"Whatever do you mean?"

"She was one of us."

Mrs. Edevane stared at her as though perplexed. Then she broke out into a laugh, head thrown back, light brushing along the lines of her throat. A moment later the laughing fit stopped as quickly as it'd started, all gaiety leaving her expression. She gestured towards the corpse. "Clean this up."

Po Lam had not much to pack. Twenty years of service and very little to show for it. Not here, at least. She'd sent most of her wages back home, spread between three sisters and their ever-growing broods. She dug up what little remained from beneath the lantana bushes, shaking the dirt from the old tin with "Capstan" painted across the top in fading letters.

The effort wasn't enough to distract her from what she was leaving—whom she was leaving. Little Ah Mui would have to come with her. There was no question of abandoning her to Mrs. Edevane's cold, undead hands, but it would only make things harder when Po Lam sought her next lodging place, her next job, her next meal. Harder, but not impossible. She ought to change her name; maybe pretend she'd once been married. The thought sat uneasily in her stomach.

Her suitcase lay half-open on the bed. Her fingertips traced across the slight texture of Gean Choo's embroidery, of the horse she'd so carefully stitched out in her uneven hand. She stared at it for some time, then folded it and put it away with the others.

Someone knocked, then opened the door before Po Lam could answer. Gean Choo stepped inside, her face flushed, hair dishevelled. "You're leaving," she said, glancing at the open suitcase, the stripped mattress, the almost bare shelves.

"Yes. With or without you."

Gean Choo's gaze fell upon a stack made from thin sheets of yellow paper, adorned with bright red calligraphy. Po Lam swept up the talismans and scrunched them to the side of the suitcase, showing them less respect than she'd ought to. The Taoist priest who'd prepared them had certainly charged enough to give her pause. She withdrew the talismans and smoothed them out before neatly stacking them back in the suitcase.

"Are you sick?" Gean Choo asked, most likely unable to read them.

"They're not for me."

Gean Choo flinched and glanced away as if pained. She paced across the floorboards, fingertips buried in her hair as though she were trying to hold her skull together. "You were right. You were right, and now Bee Leng is dead."

"I'm sorry."

"She didn't... didn't even have a funeral! And we just threw her away, like nothing!" Gean Choo slumped onto the bed with a thump. She pressed her knuckles to her lips and made a noise somewhere between a moan and a sob. "I thought she wouldn't... that she wouldn't eat her own."

None of them were safe. "She's incapable of love. Surely you know that by now."

"That's not true!"

The beginnings of a headache pounded at Po Lam's temple with all the force of a ceremonial drum. She closed her suitcase and snapped the clasps shut. Gean Choo jumped at the noise like a startled deer in the woods.

"Come with me," Po Lam said. "We'll borrow the car, take it to the station. Catch the train to Bangkok. Or you could sail to Hong Kong, or Gwong zau, or... Amoy?"

Gean Choo's head had dropped into her hands, hair falling over her face. "I won't go home. I can't. And you know why."

"Somewhere else, then. What do you want, Teo Gean Choo? Where do you want to go?"

Gean Choo stood and stepped towards her, eyes dry, though her cheeks gleamed with tears. "I want you," she whispered. She moved. Tried to kiss her. It took everything Po Lam had not to crumble, not to yield to her, not to capture that sweet, soft mouth with her own and write over her memories of their first kiss when she'd been too startled to respond. She wanted her like a knife in the belly, like bamboo slivers beneath her nails, all biting pain and wretched agony, begging for the sweet void of release.

Po Lam shot out her palm as if she were being attacked, bracing it against Gean Choo's shoulder. "I'll give you everything I am, only—"

"Yes?"

"Only we have to leave. Tonight."

"Tonight!" Gean Choo stepped back, her hands twisting together. "I can't leave tonight."

Po Lam reached under the bed frame and pulled out the revolver, sticking it inside the suitcase.

"You still have that thing? You wouldn't... you won't hurt her, will you? Bullets don't work against her, anyway."

"I had these made. Wooden core, steel jacket." Of course, Po Lam had never tested them on a real vampire. And with luck, she never would. By the time things got so bad as to require violence, the odds wouldn't be in her favour.

Gean Choo gasped. "You have to promise me you won't hurt her. Besides, she said she was going away. She won't harm us."

Po Lam scoffed, "And you believed her?"

"Promise me!"

"If it's in my power."

"That's not a promise!"

"If you come with me, I won't," Po Lam said, because what else could she say? "But it has to be tonight."

Gean Choo moved again to kiss her, and this time, Po Lam let her. At first, it was awkward, hasty. Their teeth clicked. They each pulled back at the same time, then came together again. Gean Choo's arms wrapped behind Po Lam's head, her hands entangled in the short fluff of Po Lam's hair. She leaned her whole weight against Po Lam, pressing her against the wall, heels raised off the floor, her body a map of soft curves that Po Lam longed to explore at leisure. Her lips were plump and yielding, her tongue a shock of warm, wet heat.

Gean Choo grabbed Po Lam's hand at the wrist, placing it upon her breast, which rose and fell sweetly with her breath. Her eyes brimmed with tears, pleading.

There was a full hour of daylight yet. She'd dreamed of this, hadn't she? Dreamed of Gean Choo throwing herself at her. Dreamed of exploring those warm curves, those secret depths. And oh, she must've gone absolutely insane because disentangling from Gean Choo's grasp felt like cutting out a piece of herself.

"You must pack," Po Lam said, pushing herself off the wall and circling around Gean Choo to pick up her suitcase. "The sun will set soon."

Gean Choo sharply tugged on her dress to make it lie smooth. "Tonight's too late. We should wait until morning."

"Every moment you spend with her chips away a piece of your soul. Soon you'll have nothing left, and I won't stand by to watch. Not anymore."

Gean Choo pressed the heel of her hand against her forehead. "I can't just go! Please understand, I have to... I have to find some way to say goodbye."

"Write a letter and post it!" Po Lam hissed.

"I can't! I can't. She's done so much for me... please. Please understand." Her hands fluttered uselessly by her sides. "She said she rescued you."

"What?"

"She said you used to be a mui tsai."

Po Lam narrowed her eyes. "Did she, now?"

"It's true, isn't it? You owe her just as I do."

"I've repaid my debt, again and again."

"I thought, of all people, you could understand why... why I can't—"

"Do you love her?"

It took Gean Choo too long to respond. "I don't know," she finally whispered.

There was a tightness in Po Lam's chest, more constricting than the smallest vest. "I won't wait forever."

"I just... I can't go back to that—to being nothing! To meaning nothing."

"You were never nothing. Not then. Not ever."

"You're just saying that because you want me to leave."

Po Lam clenched her jaw so tightly, it sent shooting waves of pain into her skull. She forced herself to breathe out, to let her shoulders soften. "I've done terrible things. Kidnapped people. Led them to slaughter. I see their faces sometimes, in dreams, bloated and pale. Accusing." She dropped the suitcase, reached out, and touched Gean Choo's face, tracing her thumb against the soft velvet of her skin. "I thought if I could only save one person... if I could save you, maybe my life would mean something." She sighed, moving her hand to Gean Choo's shoulder, torn between the desire to embrace her or to shake some sense into her. "Why won't you let me save you?"

Gean Choo shuddered and stepped back. "Maybe I don't deserve to be saved."

There were so many things Po Lam could've said to her. That she was being deliberately blind, giving into fear; that she was misguided at best and an idiot at worst. "I can't make you believe otherwise," Po Lam said. But oh, how she wished she could. Wished she had the power to make Gean Choo feel what she felt. To see herself as Po Lam did, her impossible desires aside. How Po Lam wished she could say... but she couldn't. Her mouth kept speaking, disconnected from her brain. "You have to find that for yourself. Do you think *she's* going to give you that? Because of who she is? What she is?"

"No!"

"Then why are you choosing her over me?"

"I'm not—I just need a little more time and—"

Po Lam let out an exasperated sigh. It was like being forced to leave Shiuhing all over again but worse because now she had an adult's foresight and an adult's cynicism. No one picked her. No one ever picked her. Not her parents, not her former mistress, and not Gean Choo.

"Go to her, then," she said, each word burning her tongue like a curse. "Go to her like the running dog you are."

Gean Choo's expression crumpled as if she'd been struck.

Po Lam picked up the suitcase and brushed past her without looking back.

# CHAPTER 44

# I'VE GIVEN YOU EVERYTHING

## GEAN CHOO

*Monday, 16 April 1928*

What on earth was wrong with her? Was she absolutely insane?

The bell rang and rang, and she just stood there, frozen in the empty sterility of Po Lam's room.

She should run to Po Lam. Beg for her forgiveness. Tell her she'd made her choice.

But why did she have to choose at all? And how could Po Lam ever say that—that awful thing about her?

It wasn't fair. None of this was fair.

She'd served her entire year and more. She didn't owe Mrs. Edevane anything. Not her loyalty, not her faith, and certainly not her lo—

The bell rang so hard, it seemed the spring was sure to snap.

She roused herself from her stupor. Step by step, she went to the kitchen, warming a plate of blood tofu before walking to the main house. She could do this in her sleep. Had virtually done so on some evenings, exhausted beyond measure by Mrs. Edevane's strange hours.

This had to be the last time. She had to make this the last night, to say goodbye properly. To not run away as she'd done with all her other problems—

She reached Mrs. Edevane's bedroom sooner than she'd expected, standing in front of the door with the plate in one hand as she knocked with the other. What would she even say? How did one broach this sort of thing?

She worried the inside of her lip, probably ruining her lipstick, come to think of it. No... she'd ruined that on Po Lam.

Oh.

Oh dear.

Gean Choo wiped her mouth with the back of her hand, scrubbing violently. She felt around her pocket for a spare lipstick but found nothing. Maybe she'd left it in the servants' bathroom. She couldn't let Mrs. Edevane know—

"Enter."

She was really doing this. All right. Deep breath. She pushed the door open and stepped inside.

Mrs. Edevane was seated at the dressing table, wearing a midnight blue frock in crepe silk. The pleated skirt was tedious to press, and the beading around the collar had a habit of coming loose. She looked one part beautiful, two parts annoyed. At least she was fully dressed tonight, sparing Gean Choo the distraction of having to speak to her in her negligée.

When Gean Choo held out the plate, Mrs. Edevane waved it aside with a soul-weary sigh. Gean Choo put it down on the table next to the smoking lounge. She'd never been tempted before, but now she stared at Mrs. Edevane's smoking paraphernalia with mingled yearning and envy. Oblivion sounded almost sweet. "Mem, there's something I ought to... ought to say to you, I suppose."

Mrs. Edevane turned to face her dresser, even though the mirror was painted over. She reached behind her head and smoothed back her loose waves. "What is it, darling? Do you have a temperature again?"

She'd been sick maybe once the whole year, but Mrs. Edevane spoke as if she caught ill all the time. "No, Mem. It's just..." Gods, what was she saying? She couldn't do this. Po Lam was right; she should've written a letter. "I wish you hadn't killed Koh Bee Leng."

Mrs. Edevane dropped her hands and held out the hairbrush for her to take. "Why do you care? She wasn't your friend, was she? The way she talked about you, I hope to true death she wasn't your friend."

She didn't have to do this. She wasn't beholden to her for anything. But Gean Choo still walked over and took the hairbrush from Mrs. Edevane's outstretched hand, gently parting her hair. She brushed it out in sections. "No, we weren't friends. But she came here to serve you, and you killed her."

Mrs. Edevane huffed a laugh. "Well, she did serve me, didn't she? There, there; I would never be so careless with you. You do know I kill people, don't you?" she asked, her voice syrupy with condescension. "You must. You're no dullard, all evidence to the contrary, so don't try to pretend. It's never bothered you before, has it? Why now?" Mrs. Edevane twisted on her stool, a full half circle to face her, forcing Gean Choo to take a step back. "Is it because you knew her name? Makes it a little more real, doesn't it?"

Was that all it was? It couldn't be. All those other people had names, too—ambitions, desires...

"When you get to my age, you'll see these lives don't mean anything at all. What was Bee Leng doing with herself that was so important? Who would even miss her?"

The question stung. Who would miss Gean Choo when she died? "I'll miss her. And she had a mother, she had family, she—"

Mrs. Edevane laughed as if she'd said something amusing. "Oh, please. Miss her? Did you even know the first thing about her?"

Gean Choo's hand tensed around the hairbrush. "I know she didn't deserve to die."

Mrs. Edevane stood. "Deserve," she began. "Oh yes, let's talk about—" She froze, a flicker moving across her eyes. Her nostrils flared. Her hand shot out, seizing Gean Choo by the collar of her dress, dragging her in close. She inhaled again and her lips drew back in a snarl. "You reek of her."

Gean Choo's collar dug into the back of her neck. She ought to have rinsed her mouth out, washed her face... That damn bell! She hadn't thought. The permissions of concubinage only flowed one way, even when its centre was a woman and not a man. She'd known Mrs. Edevane would be angry, but she'd kissed Po Lam anyway and now she was going to die, all because she couldn't make up her mind. Was Po Lam going to be in trouble, too? No. Po Lam was gone. "It wasn't her fault. I was the one—"

Mrs. Edevane spun her around, slamming her back against the dressing table, the shock of it knocking the breath from her lungs. Gean Choo's hands shot out to support herself, upsetting knickknacks and ornaments, scattering jars and bottles all over the floor.

Mrs. Edevane leaned over, her knuckles still twisted in the fabric of her dress, digging in against her collarbone. She bent down until they were nose to nose. Gean Choo didn't dare look away, forcing herself to meet those wild and storm-filled eyes.

"You belong to me," Mrs. Edevane said, each word a millstone. "From your crown to your cunt, every inch, every hair upon your head. Do you understand me, child?"

Yes. The only correct answer to that was *yes*. But to her own surprise, she whispered, "I'm no child."

"Then you'll take your chastisement like a woman."

Mrs. Edevane released her and walked to the door, pressing it shut with a gentle click. Gean Choo rose, adjusting the line of her dress, massaging the redness where it had dug into her skin. There wasn't a second click. Mrs. Edevane hadn't locked the door, not that it mattered since she'd blocked the path to it, anger radiating from her so intensely it was almost visible.

The windows were probably useless, each one tall as a door, shutters facing the verandah, glazed on the inside. The glass sections were open, but the metal shutters were closed, scaled like armour to permit airflow but not light.

"I should kill you for what you've done, you know that? I've killed for less."

What she'd done? She'd stolen a kiss. Two kisses, maybe, counting Cheng Beng. "I don't doubt it, Mem—"

"Verity! How many times must I tell you?"

She couldn't bring herself to care about pleasing her right now, but she needed to. How else could she neutralise the situation? She ought to have been grovelling from the moment she'd been found out.

But Gean Choo had spent enough of her lifetime on her knees.

"It's really too bad," Mrs. Edevane said, walking towards her. "And here I thought we were getting along so splendidly, but then, why should I expect fidelity from a filthy Oriental whore?"

"You don't own me!"

Mrs. Edevane slapped her with a hand that was half claws, curving, black, and lethal. Pain stung her cheek, blood running down, warm and sticky. Mrs. Edevane leaned in and dragged her tongue over Gean Choo's face, sending a shudder down her neck. Her skin itched as it knitted itself together.

No. No. No. They were not doing this. Not now.

She took a step back towards the windows. Mrs. Edevane grabbed her with her left hand, the human one, using the claws on her right to slice through the buttons running down Gean Choo's dress. Each one plinked as it hit the polished floorboards, one rolling in a spiral before it came to a stop.

Mrs. Edevane was standing between her and the door. She tried to move backwards again, tugging against her grasp.

Mrs. Edevane raised her right hand. The skin at the wrist shaded up into something that was wizened, blackened, each claw six inches long and sharp as a stiletto. Gean Choo froze as they caressed her cheek, slicing through a few strands of her hair.

"I'd stay very still if I were you," Mrs. Edevane said, her voice hypnotic. She lightly traced her claws down from Gean Choo's face and snagged them on the collar of her dress, tugging it off her shoulders.

The whimper emerging from Gean Choo's mouth might've embarrassed her under other circumstances. The backs of Mrs. Edevane's claws seemed colder than her fingertips, raising gooseflesh over her skin.

"Very still," Mrs. Edevane admonished.

The dress fell to the floor, leaving her standing there in only her brassiere and knickers. She hadn't even bothered putting on her shoes.

Mrs. Edevane released her arm, her heels clicking as she circled her. A vulture surveying the feast.

Gean Choo ran for the door. It wasn't locked. She threw it open and dashed down the hallway as though she were running for her life.

She probably was.

The door between the hallway and the landing was still open. The chandelier gleamed ahead in all its ostentatious finery, crystals throwing rainbows about the foyer.

She was almost at the stairs when a cloud of black smoke swirled about the landing, creating a breeze that ruffled the lace hem of her knickers. She stopped so abruptly, it jarred her knees, then shot out a hand and braced herself against the wall to stop herself from falling.

The smoke coalesced and reformed from the legs up into Mrs. Edevane, left hand on her hip, a delicate sneer on her beautiful face.

The hallway behind her opened out directly onto the verandah. Gean Choo turned on her heel to run back the way she'd come.

Mrs. Edevane seized her around the waist, mercifully, with her human arm. Gean Choo squirmed in her grasp. "Let me go! Please—"

Mrs. Edevane dropped her so abruptly that she fell, a lance of pain shooting up her elbow as it hit the floor. Mrs. Edevane grabbed her ankle, fingers like a ring of ice. She dragged her down the hallway, on her belly, back to—back to her bedroom.

Gean Choo twisted in her grip, kicking. She stretched out her hands, seizing upon the doorframe of the study, and clung to it for dear life.

Mrs. Edevane gave her a sharp tug, making her shoulders ache in their sockets. "Don't be silly, Pearl. Or do you want to lose a hand?"

She wouldn't. But when Gean Choo looked back into those soulless eyes, she couldn't be sure. "I abjure thee," she said. "The Lord our God strike you down, fiend of hell!"

Mrs. Edevane rolled her eyes. "Sorry, darling, but that doesn't always work, not even for so-called believers."

"Help," she whispered, before turning it into a shout. "Help! Fire!"

Mrs. Edevane gave her ankle a hard shake, and with a despairing sob, Gean Choo released her grip on the doorframe. The mem dragged her down the hallway as if she were nothing more than fallen prey. Once inside the room, Mrs. Edevane finally released her ankle. Still on the floor, she scrambled backwards to put space between them. Her belly was red from the friction of being dragged, but she couldn't feel it. Not yet.

Mrs. Edevane leaned against the door and locked it, then threw the key, which sailed across the room and fell somewhere behind the armoire.

"When I was a neophyte, if a slave misbehaved, one would cut off a toe. Then, if they persisted, a finger. Or perhaps an ear." She strode towards her. Gean Choo continued shuffling backwards until the edge of the bed dug into her back. Mrs. Edevane leaned in and smiled, her teeth gleaming white, dimples in both cheeks. "What should I take from you, I wonder?"

Gean Choo had to tilt her head back to look at her. To look at the way the light touched her hair, bringing out the gold in it, to look at the jewels trembling from her earlobes—platinum-set sapphires.

She was awful.

She was magnificent.

She was going to kill her.

"I've given you everything," Gean Choo said, half a retort, half a plea.

"Oh, darling, no!" Mrs. Edevane tittered. "Don't think so little of yourself. At your age, you should be a mother. Wouldn't you like that? Another brat to call your own?"

Gods. What was she even saying?

"I once bred a line five generations deep. That last daughter..." Mrs. Edevane whistled in musical admiration. "Divine. But they all went in a flood, and I never tasted her like again." She leaned down and Gean Choo cowered, pressing her spine against the bed frame. Mrs. Edevane entangled her fingers in Gean Choo's hair, tilted her head back, and kissed her.

The shock of Mrs. Edevane's ice-cold lips went straight between her legs, as if she wasn't already embarrassingly wet. She squirmed, her thighs squeezed together. Mrs. Edevane bit her, drawing blood, the weird metallic taste of it making her gag and then moan when the mem gently licked the wound closed.

Mrs. Edevane released her. "Get on the bed."

Gean Choo raised a trembling hand to her mouth—to wipe away the waxy trace of Mrs. Edevane's lipstick, to bite down on her own fingers to stop herself from screaming—she surprised herself by doing neither and said, calmly, "Say 'please.'"

Mrs. Edevane rolled her eyes. "Really? Fine. *Please* get on the bed, my slant-eyed little slut."

The bed was between herself and the window. Without letting herself think about it, she turned and dove under the bed, sliding past the valance and shimmying under, her heartbeat loud between her ears as she blindly crawled into that velvet darkness. Her outstretched hand hit something. A box.

From behind her, Mrs. Edevane tutted. "Only monsters live under the bed." She bent down and lifted the valance, letting in the light. Her face looked strange turned to the side. She reached out and grabbed Gean Choo's foot. "Come now, no more games—"

Gean Choo twisted so she was facing up when Mrs. Edevane dragged her out. She pulled back her arm and threw what she'd found in the box— a fistful of dirt, black and gritty beneath her nails.

Mrs. Edevane dropped her and Gean Choo ran to the windows, struggling with the clasps on the shutters. She pulled this way and that, leaning to put all her weight behind it. When the first one wouldn't budge, she went to the next, and then the next.

They wouldn't open. They just wouldn't open.

# CHAPTER 45

# THE KISSES AND THE CLAWS

## VERITY

*Monday, 16 April 1928*
*One day since last meal*

"Why must you test me like this?" Verity asked, grimacing as she brushed soil from her face and collar. Her precious supply of homeland earth was limited, seeing how the Powers That Be were determined to prevent her from setting foot in London ever again. Did the girl have no decency at all?

Pearl turned to face her, still rattling the window with one hand. Dirt smudged her cheek. Even that was oddly endearing, a perfect frame for that soft, wounded expression, eyes wide, the delicate arch of her brows pleading.

"There's nowhere to run," Verity said, advancing upon her. "Don't make me cross."

Pearl backed against the window, palms braced against Verity's bookshelves. She seemed poised to try for the door, but Verity was done playing. She seized Pearl around the waist and threw her onto the bed. Pearl hit the coverlet and rolled for half a turn. Verity didn't let her get up. She was upon her, one knee pressing her weight into the small of Pearl's back as she pulled the elastic on Pearl's brassiere and sliced through it with her claws. Her knickers met a similar fate, buttons popping off the side, the thin cotton tearing down the seams. Then Verity gritted her teeth and forced her hand to revert to normal. Four fingers and one thumb. Soft.

Kalon's insufferable infant took the opportunity to cry in that moment, audible even half a house away. Pearl stiffened beneath her.

Verity reached between Pearl's legs without further preamble, slipping three fingers into the warm, wet heat of her. Pearl buckled, her muscles bearing down against Verity's fingers. She sobbed as if she were dying.

Verity shifted, lying down beside her and pulling her into her arms. She continued to work her fingers in and out, her thumb outside making small circles against Pearl's clitoris. "Shh, dearest. There's a brave girl."

Pearl pushed against her, hand pressed along the outer curve of Verity's ribs, dirt black beneath her nails. "Mem—Verity, please."

"You don't know how much it pains me to show you anything but kindness. And I have been kind to you, haven't I?"

Pearl stared blankly at the far wall, heat radiating from her neck. She was so absurdly fragile, it would take no effort at all to finish her.

"Everything ends. Isn't that what the dharma says? So even this. Even us. Let yourself go and come for me. You still remember how, don't you? Of course you do. Show me how much you need me."

She disrupted their connection for a moment, slipping her fingers out. Pearl's body clenched around her as though reluctant to let go. She rolled Pearl onto her back. Her chest bore the marks of where the brassiere had dug into her, straps and wires and the faint outline of O-rings. Tears clung to her eyelashes. Her breath came quick and sharp, her lips lush and soft like bruised plums. Verity traced the shape of her face with her gaze, the lines of Pearl's wide, flat nose and broad cheekbones half-hidden by pads of fat. Her eyes gleamed like polished blackwood, pupils almost indistinguishable from the iris in the dark.

"Should I go down on you? Perhaps that would be better, wouldn't it?"

"Oh, Verity, please, don't—"

Verity moved down the bed and folded Pearl's legs up and to the side.

She lowered her head and licked from the bottom of Pearl's slit to her clitoris. Even on bloodless days, her taste wasn't unpleasant. Kind of musky and bitter, a little salty. She'd been too preoccupied last time to pay much attention, but now she experimented, varying the pressure, the patterns, gently sucking the clitoral hood into her mouth to see if it would make Pearl jump.

It did.

She slipped her fingers in again, one at a time, until they were all liberally coated. She left three in Pearl's cunt and pressed a fourth finger lower, lower… there.

Pearl's squeak of horrified indignation was muffled. She held a pillow to her face, clutching it with both hands, her knuckles white. She had a birthmark on the inside of her left thigh in the shape of a hare. Or perhaps a rabbit.

Verity eased into her past the first knuckle, then the second. Around her ears was the hot pulse of Pearl's blood. It took no small effort to keep her mouth soft, her teeth hidden. The things one did when one cared deeply.

It was fortunate she'd spent several human lifetimes learning to be patient, because Pearl refused to come for the longest while, even when Verity crooked her forefingers, hitting that mass of spongy tissue. Pearl writhed, trying to get away. Verity was obliged to dig her fingers in along her thigh, holding her steady despite her softly mouthed protestations.

"Please, Verity, I can't give you what you want—not tonight—"

Verity raised her head from between Pearl's legs. "As soon as we start with the 'not tonight,' it becomes not any night, and then where would we be? Don't you want to be a good girl who comes for her mem?"

The hitch in Pearl's breathing suggested she did. Her slight chest rose and fell. She was absurdly pretty laid out like this, flushed red down to her breasts, the kind of arousal that couldn't be faked. Verity shifted her weight for a better view, holding herself over Pearl. "I suppose I should drag you down the hallway more often," she murmured and nipped Pearl's ear.

"No."

"Why ever not?" She stilled her fingers for a moment, sinking into the feeling of having Pearl's muscles squeezing all around her, that endlessly snug, warm sensation of being exactly where she needed to be.

"You frighten me," Pearl said and moaned when Verity began moving again, so audibly wet, it was obscene.

"Fear is a kind of passion, isn't it? Don't lie to me, pet. You wanted me that very first night. Wanted it all—the kisses and the claws."

Her eyes were empty mirrors. If only Verity could see herself in them, find a surface that could hold her image. She wrapped her spare hand in Pearl's hair, pulled her head back, and kissed that soft and fragile neck— gently, not breaking the skin. Not yet. She closed her blunt incisors around a nipple, holding on a moment longer after Pearl gasped, straining away from her.

"If you want this to be over, then touch yourself. I'm otherwise a little preoccupied," Verity said dryly, one hand still in Pearl's hair, the other with fingers embedded in both her holes, stroking in and out in hard, sharp motions. She waved her thumb over Pearl's clitoris as encouragement and smiled with all her teeth when Pearl squirmed.

Pearl obligingly snaked her hand over the plane of her stomach, sliding over her mons. Her eyes fluttered closed when her fingers found their place.

"No, dear. Eyes on me."

Pearl's eyes snapped open with a kind of desperation. She was close. Verity leant down and plundered her mouth, moaning when Pearl's body arced up against her. She ought to have undressed, to feel the delicate slip of skin upon skin, but this was nice, too—Pearl's nudity against the rumpled silk of her third-best frock. She was so warm. So human, with all that meant; all the fragility and the weakness and the sickly miasma of death ever-present.

She raked her teeth over Pearl's bottom lip. Pearl whimpered, the sound stirring Verity's hunger. She was close to snapping before Pearl did, her stomach insisting it was empty, all evidence to the contrary. Something about the way Pearl writhed beneath her made Verity ache to devour her, as though she were a witch in a fairy tale.

When Pearl finally gave up and shuddered, pulsing around her, heartbeat spiking allegro for just a moment, it was all worth it for the gasp in her breath, for the way she convulsed and gripped Verity's fingers with all that blood-engorged muscle. Her back made a lovely arc, rising off the sheets. Pearl would always be worth it. How loose her limbs looked afterwards, all the tension wrung out of them. How Verity envied her. How she loathed and craved her all at the same time.

When Verity moved to lie next to her, rolling Pearl towards her so they faced one another, Pearl's lips tasted of salt and then of herself. Her mouth was frozen under Verity's, unresponsive.

"I hate it when you upset me, Pearl. It always makes me feel awkward and out of sorts."

Pearl's face was empty, eyes flat like tarnished pennies.

"You are so precious to me, darling. Why must we fight? I know we've both said harsh words, but let's put that all behind us. A new start." She wrapped her arms around Pearl, kissing the crown of her head, lips against the unnatural, smooth slip of her hair. She moved lower, across her cheek, below her chin, and finally, down to her neck.

Verity pierced her with all the solemnity and longing of a sommelier uncorking the rarest vintage. Pearl's breath escaped in a whine, and she pushed, rather feebly, against Verity's shoulders. It was better, really, that they'd fought. All that poison leeched out into the open, leaving the blood pure. Verity drank greedily, her soul filling up with warmth, with power. Feeding was always better from someone who loved you. And obviously, deep down, Pearl loved her.

She really hadn't meant to let little Bee Leng die. Such things happened, sometimes. But to save Pearl from that fate, she made herself stop early, even though it went against her every instinct.

Yet another sacrifice that was sure to pass unnoticed.

She withdrew from Pearl's skin, kissing the wound closed. There was plenty of blood to spare. She'd restrained herself admirably.

Pearl slumped against her. She was limp and flushed and still so very naked, trembling in her arms like a bird in a cage. La jeune fille et la mort. The sight of her touched all of Verity's poetic sensibilities.

She eased Pearl's weight from her, laying her down on the pillows. It was just as well she'd curbed herself, as the girl remained unmoving. If she hadn't the heightened senses that permitted her to perceive Pearl's breath, her heartbeat, she might've been unnecessarily concerned. Pearl's eyelids fluttered as she struggled to focus on Verity's face.

"Shh, darling. Don't exert yourself. Go to sleep."

She tried to defy Verity, as she'd tried to defy her in everything else that night, but eventually, she lost the fight and surrendered to sleep.

# CHAPTER 46

# THE HOOK

## GEAN CHOO

*Monday, 16 April 1928*

Someone was humming. Gean Choo tried to move, but her limbs were heavy and unresponsive. She took in a breath, held it for the count of three, then released it. The canopy of Mrs. Edevane's bed hung over her, as deep and dark as the eighteenth level of hell.

Her head pounded. She needed water, clothes.

Ah Mui was still crying. Po Lam was really gone, then. And, well, why shouldn't she be? She'd clearly made the right choice. The choice Gean Choo had been too oblivious to make.

No. Not oblivious. She'd known the signs. What was it, then? Was it the shoes, the clothes, the dancing?

It wasn't any of that. It was the way Mrs. Edevane touched her, kissed her like she needed her—and she did need her. Or at least, someone like her. That was the magic, the lure, the hook; to be held as if she'd never be let go.

Gean Choo struggled to raise her head off the pillow. Mrs. Edevane was in the bathroom with the water running, the door slightly ajar. She could leave if she had the strength.

She tried to roll over on her side, and a sharp pain shot through her neck. She whimpered despite herself, pressing a hand over the scar tissue. Even that small effort left her depleted.

The water stopped. Footsteps. She closed her eyes, pretending to be asleep. Ah Mui had stopped crying. What did that mean? Was Zaid back? Had the child just exhausted herself, poor lamb? Or... or had something made her stop? The water was still running, but that didn't mean anything. Not when the mem could turn herself to mist.

She had to get up. Get out of bed. Get downstairs. Cross the garden. Into the servants' quarters.

The whole sequence of events seemed impossibly long, as cruel and pointless as being asked to pick lentils out of a hearth.

*Ah Mui needs you. GET UP.*

## CHAPTER 47

# YOU NEED ME

### VERITY

*Tuesday, 17 April 1928*
*Zero nights since last meal*

Pearl's breathing shifted, indicating she was awake. Verity flicked the ash from her cigarette, tapping it against the ashtray. Her throat itched for the soporific sweet clouds of the pipe, but she doubted Pearl's hands were steady enough for cooking, and damned if she would do it herself. She maintained a staff of seven, and the fact that none were in a position to serve her at this moment was abysmal.

She leant back in the window seat, relishing the cool night air brushing over her covered shoulders. It was really too bad they hadn't gone out dancing like she'd intended. It hadn't rained once. She still had to keep up appearances, after all, in the midst of orchestrating her flight from the settlement and negotiating a safe harbour in Hong Kong. Immigrating was stressful at the best of times, and this certainly wasn't the best of times.

She was at her wit's end.

"Have a nice rest, dear?"

Pearl shifted. She gripped the sheet, trying to pull it free from its mitred corner, trembling with the effort. How precious.

"No, don't cover yourself. I prefer you better this way. Nothing between us."

Kalon's accursed brat began crying again. Verity groaned, reached across, and tugged sharply on the servants' bell. Why wasn't someone getting that?

Pearl turned her arm so her hand lay over the edge of the bed. She pressed her fingers against the mattress and pulled, inching herself closer to the edge.

Verity exhaled in a ring of smoke. With tortuous slowness, Pearl managed to get from one side of the bed to the other. She tumbled over the edge and rolled onto the floor. She lay there for some moments, as if catching her breath, before righting herself. She started to crawl.

There was an aesthetic appeal to the view this afforded. The bared thighs, the slight curve of her bottom, the shadow between her legs. The jut of her shoulder blades, the dip of her spine as she moved, painfully sluggish.

Verity ran her tongue over her lips. "Where are you going, my pet?"

Pearl found the door and reached up, fumbling with the handle. It rattled as she tested it, the whole frame shaking.

"Stop that. You're making such a racket."

Pearl choked back a sob. "Ah Mui—I have to go—"

"Don't be ridiculous. Po Lam will see to it."

"She's not here."

Verity inhaled on her cigarette and then exhaled. "A lover's tiff? Tch. What do you think you'd do about it, then? Fall halfway down the stairs, most like. You're not in a state to mother anyone."

Pearl mumbled something under her breath, an indistinct mix of English and Chinese.

"What was that, dear?"

"I said, fuck you, Mrs. Edevane."

Verity stood. She walked to Pearl, looming over her, blocking the light. Pearl, still crouched, stared back at her defiantly, but that changed when Verity seized her by the throat and lifted her, slamming her against the door. Pearl wheezed, hands scrabbling at Verity's arm, her toes desperately seeking purchase and finding none, feet dangling above the floor.

"You are really trying to vex me tonight, Pearl, and I'm ashamed to say it's working," Verity said, her arm outstretched. Now she found herself needing to gaze up to meet Pearl's eyes, those foreigner's eyes, glazed with terror and frantic with existential dread. "You might think that because my blood runs colder than yours, I have no heart, but the opposite is true. If anything, I feel too deeply, love too much."

Pearl's face was taking on a queer shade of puce, which wasn't at all appealing.

"You simply don't understand—how could you? You don't know the depths of my torment, the everlasting hunger, twisting like knives impaling my flesh, an empty throat like swallowing ground glass. The constant need, the dependency of it all, the heartache. It's more than any sane person could bear."

Pearl's pulse skittered and she flailed, nails scrabbling ineffectually at Verity's grip. Verity glanced down at her cigarette. The tip was still smoking. She pressed it just above Pearl's left breast, grinding it in. Pearl writhed, her heels making dull smacks as she kicked the door.

Verity flicked the cigarette away and glanced at the mark. Perfectly circular.

She released her. Pearl tumbled to the floor, hunched over. She gasped in air like a dying fish, one hand cupped over the burn. Verity couldn't watch; it was all so dreadful.

She found another cigarette and lit it. Her head was buzzing tonight, and she was so beside herself, she couldn't think straight. Her arm ached. She shook out her wrist, rolling her shoulders back. She flicked the cigarette, the ash drifting away on the slight breeze that ran through the room.

If only insolence burned as easily as flesh.

She dropped the cigarette into an ashtray and went back to Pearl, drawn by her scent and the seductive beat of her pulse. Pearl scrambled back from her. Verity caught her hair in her fist and turned her until Pearl was facing away, struggling to free herself. Verity pressed her fingers between Pearl's legs, stabbing into that slick and heated flesh.

Pearl's back arched against her. She was on her knees, reaching behind her head, groping against Verity's fist in her hair.

"Tell me you want me. Tell me you need me." Verity withdrew from Pearl and brought her palm to her mouth, spat, the phlegm pink, clotted with blood. She tucked her thumb in tight against her fingers, making her hand small, and pressed her fingertips against the eager cleft of Pearl's sex.

The first few sounds from Pearl's throat were groans, indistinguishable as language. She coughed and managed to make herself heard. "No," she said, then kept saying it, as though it were some magical incantation that would turn Verity into dust.

"Tell me," Verity said again, and inched in a little further, the thud of Pearl's pulse all around her, the warmth of her flesh fever-hot, crushing down around Verity's fingertips. Verity pressed her blunt incisors against the back of Pearl's neck and Pearl moaned, her knees giving out. Verity travelled with her until Pearl lay face-down, flush against the rug, only her hips raised in silent acquiescence.

Verity rolled Pearl's head to the side. Her cheeks were flushed, eyes glazed. A tear trembled at the bottom of her lashes. "You need me, Pearl, don't you? That's why you stayed, isn't it? Because you want me. You love me." She pressed in a little further, and Pearl jerked against her, hands reaching behind herself to push Verity away.

"I don't love you," Pearl said in the damaged voice of prey, breathy and frail.

"Don't lie to me. I can't abide a liar." She moved her hand, drawing out and then back in, slipping a little deeper with each thrust.

Pearl whimpered, squirming against her, sweat beading on the small of her back. Verity pressed her tongue against that hollow and had to force herself not to bite.

"Verity, please, I can't—" She was actually crying, her body trembling with the force of her sobs. Her flesh squeezed around Verity's hand, buried now to the hilt of her fingers.

"You can, dear," Verity said, releasing her hair, finding it within herself to be kind. She stroked the engorged head of Pearl's clitoris and pressed kisses against the back of Pearl's neck, only using her lips, willing herself to be soft, to soften for Pearl. The girl sobbed and wailed and writhed beneath her, fingers outstretched by her sides like claws, curved and empty.

Verity eased her way past the last of Pearl's resistance and buried herself to the wrist. She shifted her thumb and used the back of her knuckles to stroke the spongy little bit of flesh along her anterior wall, flexing her hand to find the right spot. Pearl struggled under her, legs thrashing. Verity was obliged to lean her full weight against her to hold her down. Her pulse echoed through Verity's fingertips, allegro, so intimately close they could've been sharing the same heart. She nuzzled her nose against Pearl's neck. "Shh. Don't cry, sweetheart. Tell me what I want to hear."

Pearl shuddered, her palms flat against the floor, outstretched, as if searching for something. A loose nail, a broken bit of floorboard. Verity had seen this all before, but for poor Pearl, there was nothing in reach that could conceivably be made into a weapon.

Pearl's hands stilled. Verity rewarded her with a flick against her clitoris from her other hand, with the delicate slow process of gently flexing her fist, withdrawing slightly, then pushing back in.

Pearl moaned.

"Words, dear. Use your words."

She sobbed, stubbornly mute.

Verity grazed her nail against the outside of her folds, stretched around her wrist. "Pearl."

Her breaths were wet and trembling, choked with snot. As if she didn't understand the favour Verity was granting her, the honour of her magnanimity. "I need you," she said, tensing around Verity's hand.

"Good." Verity kissed the open shell of her ear, stroked her from without and within until the breath caught in Pearl's throat.

"I want you."

"I know," Verity said, rubbing her fingers on either side of Pearl's clitoris, keeping her touch light, until she gasped.

"I—"

"Yes?"

Pearl's hips pressed against hers. Verity moved her free hand and gently rolled Pearl onto her back. She did not want to be moved, hissing and whimpering, crying out at the change in pressure. Her face was a mess, glazed over. Verity worked her gaze down her body, squeezed her nipples into hard peaks, and ran her fingertips against the dip between her ribs before reaching down again for her clitoris. The sight of her, stretched and open around Verity's fist, was so primal and timeless, so deeply alluring. Not that she'd ever admit it. It would only give her airs.

Pearl gestured weakly, three fingers crooked.

Verity leant down until their noses almost touched.

"I love you, Verity," Pearl whispered, then raised her chin and kissed her.

It was Verity who moaned against her mouth, who melted above her, kissing her again and again. But it was Pearl who came for her, bearing down around her hand, legs splayed open and spasming, her heartbeat accelerating to a delightful crescendo. Verity rocked with her, whispering all sorts of sweet nothings. Such a good girl, a brave girl, an obedient whore who'd do anything for her mistress. She kissed Pearl's hair, working down to her neck. She lay with one arm wrapped around her through the after-shudders, and then slowly, delicately, eased her way out.

Her fingers ached. But she regretted nothing.

She gave Pearl one last kiss against her forehead and stood. Lying on her side, Pearl curled up around herself, knees drawn tight to her chest. Verity left her there and washed her hands. Pearl had left a damp patch on her skirt, so she changed clothes, still doing up her cuffs as she walked back into the bedroom.

Pearl hadn't moved, unless it was to hug herself even tighter. Verity went over and shook her. "Pearl. Time to get up."

Pearl still didn't move. The waves had fallen out of her hair, which hung over her face in damp, greasy tangles.

Verity rolled her eyes and picked her up. Pearl yelped, struggling in a blind panic, the back of her hand catching Verity beneath her jaw. Verity dropped her and Pearl's dead weight thudded as she hit the floor. "What is the matter with you tonight?"

Pearl curled her limbs in close, like a crab retreating into its shell and simply sobbed with the mindless, inarticulate fervour of a small child.

Verity breathed in, tasting the air. It held a hint of copper. "I think you owe me an apology."

Silence. Nothing but the choked sounds of Pearl trying—and failing—to stem her crying.

"Pearl. Don't make me cross again."

"I-I'm sorry," she whispered.

"Louder."

"I'm sorry, Verity."

"What are you sorry for?"

"For being rude to you."

"And?"

"For trying to run."

"And?"

Pearl drew in a breath. "I can't say I'm sorry for kissing Po Lam. Because I'm not. I'd do it again. So—"

Verity scarcely felt herself shift, it was that fast. She pounced on Pearl, pressing down on her, claws digging into Pearl's shoulders, drawing blood. The girl opened her mouth to scream, but all that came out was a gasp. Verity shook her, and the back of Pearl's head banged against the floorboards. She longed to bite, but couldn't trust herself. If she fed now, she'd tear her throat out.

She couldn't bear that. Not again. Verity dropped her, transformed back, brought her hands to her mouth and sucked on her fingers as she paced the floorboards. She tried to focus on the repetitive thud of her footsteps instead of Pearl's sobbing. She was—fuck—infected. With feelings.

"Fuck," she said. "Fuck. Fuck!"

She couldn't stand to be in the same body with herself. She was corrupted. Disgusting. Even her voice had the edge of hysteria. "For pity's sake, if you don't stop snivelling, I shall lose my temper!"

Pearl gasped in a few more breaths, clutching her bleeding shoulders.

Her eyes were bright in the dark, gleaming with tears, her face a glossy mess. Blood dripped down her fingertips, fragrant and hypnotic. Verity's mouth watered. She brought her knuckles to her mouth and gnawed on them. She couldn't bear the taste of Pearl's blood on her lips.

The little brat filled the relative silence with an answering wail.

It was all too much.

"I'm not done with you," Verity said. "Stay right there. And don't bother getting dressed."

She transformed with a shiver, turning herself to mist. Then she was out through the shutters, enveloped by the deep velvet of the night sky, consumed by the darkness that welcomed her home like a daughter.

# CHAPTER 48

## PROOF

### PO LAM

*Several hours earlier*
*Monday, 16 April 1928*

No one challenged Po Lam when she drove away in Mrs. Edevane's car. The warm night air streamed in through the open windows, bringing with it the scent of frangipani and damp earth.

She should try again. Make Gean Choo see reason. But where was reason where the heart was concerned?

She shouldn't try again. She'd made her case, done her part. If Gean Choo was still blind, that wasn't her thread to mend.

But if Po Lam had meant to leave for good, she would've taken Ah Mui.

She parked a few blocks from Lord Cottesley's house and walked the rest of the way. When she arrived, the servant on duty came over, blinking owlishly at her lack of vehicle.

"Miss San. You're not expected."

"I don't have an appointment," Po Lam said. "But it's important."

"Your mistress isn't here."

"No. It's about her."

The guard turned without a word. He went to the gates, drawing them back on silent hinges, and Po Lam walked through.

There was a new topiary in the garden, a bird with wings outstretched, taller than a man. When she approached the back door, another servant came to greet her, leading her inside.

The house interior was brightly lit, a gramophone playing somewhere. Jazz. Po Lam's footsteps echoed as she walked through the receiving rooms to the back verandah.

The lord of the house was nowhere to be seen. Instead, a Sikh man in servants' navy and a white turban rose from a chair and greeted her. "Miss San, my name is Ranjit."

Po Lam eyed him. They'd never met before now, but one of Mrs. Ainsworth's servants had named him as the person in charge of his master's household. An unenviable position, given the rumours about Lord Cottesley.

"I have business with your tuan," Po Lam said.

"I'm afraid he's not here. But rest assured, I'll relay anything you might care to say to him."

Their communication might even be synchronous. Some servants could do that if they'd been blood-bound long enough. For all her flaws, Mrs. Edevane had never subjected her to such an affliction.

"Very well." Po Lam took in a deep breath and exhaled slowly. It was better Lord Cottesley wasn't here. Perhaps she'd even make it out alive.

"Would you care to sit?" Ranjit asked, indicating the settee.

"This won't take long," Po Lam said, still standing. "I have proof Mrs. Edevane has been killing her prey."

Ranjit watched her, unblinking, his eyes vacant and calm beneath two dark brows. "What proof?"

Po Lam reached into her pocket and pulled out a notebook. She flipped through its pages, holding them out to show him. "I have records from 1908. Dates, places, and times. The later ones were all rowed out to sea, but we buried the early ones in unused plots or old plantations. If you need physical proof, you'll find it there."

"May I?" Ranjit asked, holding out his hand.

Po Lam hesitated before she handed the notebook over.

Ranjit flicked through it. He stared at one page where Po Lam had done her best to sketch the woman from Sheik Madersah Lane, the weathered lines of her face, the too-loose blouse, her missing teeth.

Ranjit lowered the book and tilted his head slightly, as if he were listening to a voice she couldn't hear. When he spoke, there was something different about his intonation. "You must understand, to the others, this will look like heresy, the word of a disgruntled servant against their mistress. My lord can't just bring this to them."

"He doesn't have to. Isn't he the council's voice in this settlement? Doesn't he believe me?"

He shifted his attention back to her. "I believe so." Despite his words, he took a match from his pocket, struck it, and pressed the flame to Po Lam's notebook.

She bit her tongue to stop herself from crying out. The fire devoured two decades of work, the thin pages dissolving into ash.

"In a colony such as ours, there will always be atrocities," Ranjit said, his face orange in the glow as the flames licked higher. He dropped the smoking remains of the book, and it hit the verandah tiles with a puff of sparks and ash. Another servant rushed over to sweep it up.

"So your lord will do nothing?"

Ranjit paused. "He'll do what he must."

*Nothing, then.* Po Lam turned to go, and Ranjit's hand descended on her arm with a grip like iron. "My lord wishes to extend an offer of sanctuary to you," Ranjit said without loosening his grip.

Sanctuary? More like slavery... or the slaughterhouse. "I must decline." Po Lam slid her free hand into her pocket.

Ranjit snapped his fingers and more servants spilled onto the verandah, closing in on her. All were broad of shoulder and had at least half a head of height on her.

Po Lam drew her hand from her pocket and shoved it in Ranjit's face, talismans fluttering from her clenched fingers, yellow slips covered with red calligraphy. He lurched back with a snarl, releasing her as he raised his arms to shield his eyes.

Po Lam moved one of the slips to her other hand and brandished the talismans as though they were torches driving back the night. The servants stumbled in their haste to get away. One man knocked over a decorative crystal bowl, flowers and water spilling onto the floor as it shattered.

Po Lam backed away. Once she reached the doorway, she turned and ran, the talismans snapping against her palms as she sprinted down the driveway.

At the gates, the guard cowered from her outstretched hands. She leaned in closer to snatch the keys from his waist. He whimpered as he turned his face from her, something dark moving along the veins that bulged and pulsed beneath his skin.

She let herself out, locked the gate, and tossed the keys down the road. She didn't rest until she was back in Mrs. Edevane's car, making such a sharp turn that a dust cloud formed in her wake.

# CHAPTER 49

# THE RULES

## VERITY

*Tuesday, 17 April 1928*
*Zero nights since last meal*

The Sago Street brothel was doing a busy trade at this time of night. It was one of the nicer establishments that kept its girls indoors, away from prying eyes, instead of parading them in chairs out on the street.

A few shops down, one or more of the funeral parlours was holding a wake, tables crowding the streets, the air thick with incense, faces garish orange beneath the light from paper lanterns. The noise was awful—ritual clanging, the wailing of mourners. The phrase, "loud enough to wake the dead," came to mind.

She'd bear with it, just this once. It served her purpose, after all.

The sound wasn't loud enough to chase away that errant itch, that horrible gnawing feeling that connected her back to Pearl. The girl's presence in the world existed as a slight tug upon the tendons of her soul, the knowledge that Pearl was alive and somewhere towards the east, not too far away.

She'd been careless. Such a bond came at a price. It meant she'd grown too attached, too indulgent. Well, it was time she proved to herself she didn't *need* her. She didn't need anyone. She wouldn't be bound to a mere mortal.

She was Verity Josephine fucking Edevane, and she was going to fix this.

Verity stayed in her mist form until she was past the front doors, then reformed in the entranceway. She didn't need an invitation to enter, not in a public place that welcomed all with coin to spend.

Her appearance startled the madam and a European who seemed too young to grow a beard. Another john trudged downstairs, his trousers not yet fastened. He didn't even pause to whisper, "demon," but simply whipped out a pistol and shot at her. The madam screamed, dropped to the ground, and scurried towards the doors, followed by a handful of girls and their clients.

The shot hit Verity's shoulder, forcing her to take a step back. She growled low in her throat. The bullet forced itself from her flesh, pinging when it hit the floor.

People ran. A gale howled through the building, slamming the doors shut. They rattled in their frames as the crowd rushed at them, trying and failing to pry them open.

Verity picked her way through the herd at leisure. Firstly, she tore off the shooter's head, as if tearing through a wet paper bag. Then her claws made quick work of the other johns, slicing through arteries and severing veins. The madam and the girls she drank, sinking her fangs into their necks or their slim, upturned wrists, discarding their bodies one after the other.

The last girl ran, leading Verity down dingy, cramped corridors. Hunger had fled, but still she craved more, chasing that savoury richness, the salt and the sweetness. She wouldn't find what she was looking for here, but damned if she didn't try.

She caught up with the whore in the alleyway out back, draining her against the wall before ripping out her throat.

She'd made a mess of herself. Gore stained her chin, dripping onto her dress. Even the best dry cleaner couldn't save this silk.

She wandered back inside. The noise had drawn curious onlookers from the street or the brothels next door. Someone saw the carnage in the entryway and ran out, screaming.

The blood drying on her skin cooled both her appetite and her mind. Each of her one hundred and eighty-three years weighed down on her like fruit hanging from the tree of knowledge.

She headed upstairs. The rooms were all empty, save one. Verity stopped in the doorway, a jolt of unwelcome recognition shocking her through the bloodlust. Emiel stood in the middle of the room, pulling his shirt over his head. When he was dressed, he looked at her, his jaw dropping. "Verity! This is no place for a lady."

His companion was slumped face-down on the bed, lacking a heartbeat. "I thought you were such a stickler for the rules."

Emiel grimaced. "She's not dead." The whore failed to stir when he nudged her with an elbow.

She saw Emiel for what he was—undisciplined. Pathetic.

He'd only had one tonight. How many had Verity killed? Fifteen? Twenty?

She shoved the corpse to one side and dropped onto the bed, the frame creaking under her weight. Emiel jumped, squeamish, as if afflicted by some superstition that made him fear the corpse and her outstretched arm, which had flopped onto the floor, vaguely pointing in his direction like an accusation.

Verity's head sank into her hands. She'd only wanted to forget. What was so wrong with that? But everything about this whole sordid affair made her miss Pearl even more.

"Look, Verity... when I see our lord, I won't tell him about this."

She sat up straight. "This? You're the one killing your lays."

Emiel scowled. "It was an accident! And just, well..." He gestured at her. "Look at you!"

Verity didn't have to look. The scent of blood and despair was all over her, as miserable as a one bob bottle of claret. "Let's not tell him."

Emiel laughed shrilly. "Are you insane? This will be front-page news tomorrow morning."

She had a plan for that, didn't she? She always had a plan. But no, this time she hadn't thought, hadn't planned... only hungered. Driven by her appetite like a beast in the night.

She stood and paced. Kalon would have to fix it for her. That was his job, wasn't it? Secret societies were always shooting each other. Yes. That would be it. Some sort of turf war tussle. The police were overworked at best and deliberately incompetent at worst. It would blow over. News always did.

No. She couldn't delude herself. Kalon would hold this over her, using it as leverage to make her comply...

She ought to let the whole place burn.

"I haven't seen you this worked up since oh-two," Emiel said. "It's your new girl, isn't it? I heard—"

She stopped and fixed him with a glare that could've melted steel. "What did you hear?"

He swallowed, his Adam's apple bobbing. "It's nothing... Just, I know how you get so particular about your girls. You're not the only bloodsucker who's had her, you know."

"Who?" Verity asked before she could stop herself. It was impossible to have a past here when everyone insisted on knowing everyone else's business.

He told her.

The world closed in on her like a velvet curtain collapsing, drowning her with a tinny whine, like the sound of a mosquito at night. Emiel kept talking, but she couldn't hear him. She couldn't hear anyone.

She dissolved into mist and drifted out through the shutters, back into the night. To the hunt.

Only this time, her prey wasn't human.

# CHAPTER 50

## I'M COMING

### GEAN CHOO

*Tuesday, 17 April 1928*

Gean Choo didn't move for a long while.

It was easier not to move, not to think. Her burn throbbed and her wounds stung. Even the skin on her stomach had been rubbed raw.

Perhaps this was what death felt like. A thousand little insults all adding up to a lethargy she had no interest in preventing.

She hadn't meant to provoke her. The truth had just spilled out, urgent and hot. Saying it had felt good at first, like pricking a blister.

There was a spider building a nest in the northwest corner. It seemed absurdly important that she reprimand the others about cleaning this room more thoroughly. Some superstition seemed to keep them from wanting to spend too much time in Mrs. Edevane's bedroom.

And weren't they right?

Far in the distance, Ah Mui began to cry again. It was honestly a testament to her lungs that Gean Choo could still hear her from all the way over in the main house. Where was Zaid?

Gean Choo rolled onto her side, winced, and sat up. The room spun for a moment. She hunched over and pressed her forehead against her palms, ignoring the awful creep of blood trickling down her arms.

Everything hurt in that dull, aching kind of way that always followed a feeding, but worse this time. She could still feel the press of Mrs. Edevane's hand around her throat, the flaring burn of the cigarette, blackening to ash where it met her skin. Her head and throat throbbed with a dull ache, echoed by the ache between her legs. Her hand drifted to the back of her skull, brushing over the sticky tangle of blood matting her hair.

Ah Mui continued to cry. Po Lam must really be gone for her to be crying for so long. Gean Choo wished her well, truly.

She could've been halfway to Penang by now, if only she'd listened.

She unfolded herself and shifted her weight to her knees. She grabbed the leg of a side table for support and pulled herself upright. When she tried to let go, she staggered and rested against the wall for a moment while she caught her breath.

She couldn't blame it all on Mrs. Edevane. She'd provoked her. And she'd known—known for a long time now—what Mrs. Edevane truly was. Inhuman. Would she expect sympathy from a tiger?

She just looked so normal, most of the time, it was easy for Gean Choo to forget. To ignore her true nature. And Mrs. Edevane had eventually stopped, hadn't she? She'd wanted to continue, to keep hurting her, but she hadn't. She'd chosen to leave instead, to leave her house instead of allowing herself to do more harm.

That had to mean something, didn't it?

Ah Mui cried in fits and stops. "I'm coming," Gean Choo muttered, shuffling from one piece of furniture to the next.

Still bleeding, she made it as far as Mrs. Edevane's dressing room. She took perverse pleasure in borrowing some of Mrs. Edevane's silk wraps and winding them around her shoulders and arms. She found a white cotton nightgown that was mostly opaque and put it on, tying it around her waist. The neckline was a bit low, but the thought of the others seeing didn't bother her. *Only Po Lam.* And that would never happen now, so it was fine, wasn't it?

She was fine. She was always fine. She had to be.

Against all the strictures of her hygiene lessons, she slipped into the adjoining bathroom and drank water straight from the tap, slurping it from her cupped hands. It would serve her right if she caught some awful disease. She dabbed cool water over her burn and sucked in her breath at the sting.

It was a good thing the main house held no mirrors, for she couldn't bear to look at herself right now. It would've been like looking at a stranger.

She went back to the bedroom and tested each window, but they were all fastened tight. The scent of frangipani reached her through the shutters, but the tree might as well have been on the other side of the moon.

She wanted to scream. She and Ah Mui were probably of the same mind in that regard.

The armoire was hardwood and refused to move. She stuck a shoe-horn beneath it, sweeping for the key, but the only thing she found was the desiccated husk of a lizard.

She made her way back across the other side of the bedroom and tried the door. The handle rattled under her palm. When she put her eye to the keyhole, she only saw the hallway wall. There was no such luck that Zaid would be randomly walking by.

She glanced at the ventilation slats in the wall above the door, dragged a stool over, and climbed up. The screws holding them in place were facing this side, the whole panel tall enough she could wriggle through in a pinch.

Now she just needed a screwdriver.

That didn't seem like the sort of thing Mrs. Edevane would keep in her room, but in the dressing table drawer, she found a metal hair stick. Pulling off the long, dangling ornament, she was left with a piece of blunt metal shaped like a letter opener.

She climbed back onto the stool but was still too short to reach the panel. The dressing table was already in disarray, with half its contents swept off, and the rest met the floor with a satisfying crash. What would the houseboys think if they saw her now?

They'd probably think the same thing as before—that she was a running dog of the white man. Woman. They all thought that.

Even Po Lam.

She stacked the stool on top of the dressing table, balancing it precariously on the too-smooth hardwood. Now she was finally tall enough. The hairpin was not a particularly efficient screwdriver, but she made do, moving the dressing table under the other side of the ventilation panel once she'd finished with the left side.

When all the screws were gone, she pried at the panel with her fingers. Someone had painted over it and the wall both, which made it reluctant to part, but as she tugged, hairline cracks grew in the paint. It gave way with a creaking groan and fell out, leaving a hole in the wall about a foot high and three feet wide.

Gean Choo dropped the panel and raised herself on tiptoes, sticking her head into the corridor. No one was there.

She dropped her heels back and rested for a moment, summoning her courage. She'd come this far. Just one step more, and she'd be out. The nearer it came to sunrise, the more dangerous this room became. Mrs. Edevane would have to come back to shelter for the day, and when she found what Gean Choo had done...

She shimmied through the hole, head-first. Once half her body was through the other side, she twisted awkwardly, clinging to the ledge until she dropped down on her feet, her knees jarring with the impact.

Gean Choo ran all the way downstairs and out. It was raining again, water drumming along the covered walkway leading to the servants' quarters. Ah Mui was crying, but it sounded different. Wrong. Almost like—

She reached the kitchen. Ah Mui wasn't crying at all, instead placidly sucking her thumb, her eyes wide. She seemed relaxed and content, gently rocked in the arms of a woman Gean Choo had never thought to see again.

"Hello," Bee Leng said. Water dripped from her clothes and her long, unbound hair, plinking as it hit the tiles. The hand not holding Ah Mui swirled a pan of formula on the stove, and she grinned with a mouthful of white teeth. "Care for a snack?"

# CHAPTER 51

# SORDID LITTLE SECRETS

## VERITY

*Tuesday, 17 April 1928*
*Zero nights since last meal*

Justine's house only had lights on across the ground floor. The driveway sported a lonely car, her blue Morris. Verity coalesced on the upstairs verandah and tried a door. It opened without resistance, supernatural or otherwise. She'd visited Justine before, and the invitation still held.

Inside was a guest room, unused and sterile, the mosquito netting tied back around the empty bed. She left it and wandered into the hallway.

The walls were lined with photographs, each one a different graduating class—girls in white shirts and dark pinafores, stern women of varying ages. And Justine, a pleasant smile on her face, growing older as the corridor neared the stairs. Verity looked for Pearl among all those grey faces but couldn't find her.

Was she really doing this? Kalon would just love the opportunity to make an example of her. He wouldn't get that much skin from her flayed corpse, not like his last victim, whose broad back had yielded a clean piece almost large enough to cover a cushion.

Footsteps approached. Justine flicked on the light and sucked in her breath. "Verity! Goodness, you gave me a fright, standing there all alone in the dark."

Verity glanced down at the drying blood crusting on her arms and décolletage. It pulled atop her skin when she moved her jaw. "What's wrong? Am I not presentable?"

Justine blanched but recovered. "Remember the five As. Accountability, access, alternatives, advertence—"

Merely the sound of her annoying nasal voice made Verity's decision easier. "I think it's a little late for that." She gestured to the portraits. "Where's Pearl?"

"Your Pearl?" Justine dabbed at the bloodsweat forming across her brow with a handkerchief. "She's... she's not here. She never finished her classes with us."

"Why not?"

"Oh, you know... The family was a hardship case on scholarship. They put her to work instead of leaving her in school. I went to her father in person and begged him to reconsider, but..." Justine shrugged.

"Did you offer her a position?"

"What, me?" Justine pressed a palm to her breast as though incredulous. "You must understand, I didn't have the patronage I do now. My household was small. To give her a job would mean firing one of the others, and some of them had been here for ten years."

"But you offered her one, anyway."

Justine fiddled with the buttons on her cuff. "Well, yes. It was the least I could do for my star pupil."

Verity dragged her finger over a photograph frame, which came back coated with dust. "You need to retrain your houseboy."

"Yes... yes, of course."

"Why didn't she accept your proposal?"

Justine's gaze flicked from one end of the corridor to the other, as though she were judging the distance to the nearest exit. It wouldn't matter; a neophyte like her could never hope to outrun Verity, gorged as she was. "I... I suppose it didn't suit her—"

"It wasn't because you'd been fucking her since childhood?"

"I beg your pardon?"

Verity wiped her finger against her bloodstained dress. Justine's chest rose and fell as though she'd forgotten she no longer needed to breathe. "I believe you heard me."

"Whatever you've heard, Mrs. Edevane, I assure you, it simply isn't true." Justine wrung her hands. "Sad to say, we all have enemies in paradise, purveyors of cruel gossip. A lady's reputation never remains unchallenged."

"You're saying my Pearl's a liar?" She'd never thought to ask Pearl about the matter, of course, but Justine didn't know that.

Justine hesitated. "It's a known fact that young women can be prone to all sorts of fantasies. Hysteria." She gestured towards the stairwell. "Please, come downstairs and partake of some refreshments, or at least sit. I'm sure this can all be cleared up by—"

"How old was she when you started?"

Justine paused, staring. Her lower lip trembled. "I won't be interrogated like this in my own house!"

Verity reached out, snatching her by the arm, claws extended and digging all the way in as she knocked Justine down. Justine gasped in pain as Verity pinned her to the floor.

Verity couldn't let this go. Fuck the Code and its consequences. She'd just have to avoid getting caught. "I'm feeling gracious tonight. Tell me what I want to know, and I'll give you a quick second death... or let me carve every word out of you until you're as limbless as a penanggalan. So, what's it to be?"

"Is this a test? Another hazing ritual for the neophyte, is that it? Or a sick joke—"

Verity sliced off Justine's ear. It would heal soon enough if she'd been well-fed, but Verity didn't intend for her to enjoy a long convalescence.

Justine clamped her hand over the bloody hole, eyes wide with shock, her body going limp.

An utterly human response.

Verity dragged her into the guest room and shut the door behind them.

"Everyone takes lovers, Mrs. Edevane. How dare you judge me! You're not immune to their charms yourself—"

So she had some fire in her, after all. "How old was she?" Justine was on the floor, hand still clamped to her head. Verity prodded her with a foot. "Come, now. I'm not known for my patience."

Justine sprang to her feet. "You're such a sanctimonious hypocrite. You really think you'll get away with this? He'll flay you. Burn you. Tie you to his balcony and leave you there, waiting for the dawn. Why throw eternity away over this... over her? Over some trumped-up slut who'd fuck a dog if it'd promised her a better life—"

Verity moved without thinking and struck Justine across the face, snapping her head to the side with an audible crack, four thin lines etched across her cheek, dripping red. It took Justine a moment to twist her neck back the right way.

"You've insulted canines the world over by comparing yourself to them," Verity said in a perfectly normal voice. Despite that, she burned with coiled energy, claws itching to rend, to maim.

Justine raised her hand to her face and stared at the blood on her palm as if she'd never seen the stuff before in her life. "You don't want to do this. We're the same."

Was Verity losing it? Hallucinating? Had she really just said...?

"I don't fuck children."

Justine gagged as if the obscenity had physically hurt her. "She was twelve. They marry their daughters off at that age all the time! Don't you remember how it used to be?"

"Times have changed."

"Have they? You know how mature she is. She seduced me. She insisted over my protests. Did you know, when a working girl that age is taking a client for the first time, they call it 'trying out the flower.'" She said this in the whispered tone of a confidante, as if imparting a gem of knowledge, and grinned, vicious and triumphant. "I was her first. I taught her letters and sums, and then I taught her everything she had to know to be a woman—"

Verity had suffered enough. She twisted her hand into Justine's hair, pulling her head back. Justine lashed out, trying to kick her. Verity reached into her mouth and tore out her tongue. Blood poured forth, bright red and fresh. Verity wrinkled her nose. "Dipping into the good vintage tonight? And here I thought you were so loyal to dear Kalon's principles."

Justine was still trying to speak but only produced a garbled, incoherent noise. She twisted at the end of Verity's grasp, her flat, human nails clawing towards Verity's eyes.

Verity evaded her with ease. "I know I said I'd finish you quickly, but I've changed my mind. I'd rather take my time." She smiled. "After all, the night is still young."

SHE WANDERED DOWNSTAIRS SOMETIME LATER, her clothes sticky with Justine's blood. It was like Vendée, 1793, all over again, but not in a bad way. Justine had held out surprisingly long for such a weak lineage, but that was all for the better. There was something vaguely nostalgic about the complex perfume of vampire blood, even from such an unaged vintage. Forbidden fruit always tasted the sweetest.

She walked into the sitting room, then froze. Merde. She'd fucked up.

Justine's sire was making himself at home on a smoking lounge. "Justine, I was just wondering where you—" Freddie lowered his pipe, his face obscured by a cloudy haze. His mouth hung ajar.

Justine hadn't been quiet. Had he only just arrived? Why hadn't she anticipated this? Now she'd have to kill him, too. But Freddie proved a greater challenge than Justine. He fumbled in his pocket as she reached for him, uncorked something, and threw it in her direction. Instinct made her duck, but a few hot droplets splashed against her hand, burning her flesh down to the bone.

Who the fuck was so paranoid and audacious that they carried genuine holy water on their own person?

Verity shrieked loudly enough to rattle the windows. She grabbed

Freddie's wineglass and poured its contents over her hand, hissing as the blood coated her wounds.

Her skin was trying and failing to close. She needed something more. Someone more.

Freddie had long since gone, taking advantage of her distraction to run. Instead of chasing after him, Verity headed down the hallway, following her nose to where one of Justine's servants had hidden himself in an armoire. When she opened the doors, he tumbled out, his screams hurting her sensitive ears.

Verity tore into his neck, bathing her hand in hot, arterial blood. That helped, a little. She drank some, but it had that strange, metallic aftertaste common to all thralls.

She dropped the human, tore open his rib cage, and ripped out his heart, squeezing the pulp of it all over her hand. When she gently poked at her skin, it seemed to be all intact.

She'd only suffered a few drops. Imagine what the whole vial could've done to her.

She slumped next to the human, or what remained of him, and examined herself for scarring. There was a small mark on the inside of her wrist, but nothing serious. Still, she owed Freddie recompense. She'd not been marked since the night of her death, and damned if she'd think of him every time she looked down at her hands.

A clock chimed in the hallway six times. Practically daylight. She'd have to bunker down in Justine's house of horrors, hoping that Freddie didn't send one of his ghouls to finish her off.

She went upstairs, following the scent of orange blossom water and pomade to Justine's bedroom. She checked that all the shutters were lowered, the windows fastened, and the bed curtains in place. Instead of a normal frame, Justine apparently slept in an oversized, elaborate coffin, its walls made of lacquered blackwood. How dramatic.

She confirmed the latch worked from the inside, then slipped into it, wincing as her toes touched the padded satin lining. When she pulled the lid shut, the sound echoed around her with a final, solemn bang.

It was just a box.

A silly, grandiose box.

There was no native soil beneath Justine's bed, not even the wrong kind. The absence gnawed at her like a canker. On top of that, she couldn't even raise her arms without hitting the lid. Verity shuddered and silently rocked herself to sleep.

## CHAPTER 52

# A MONSTER

### GEAN CHOO

*Several hours earlier*
*Tuesday, 17 April 1928*

Gean Choo held her arms out. "Please, give me the baby."

"What, no apology? No greeting? Go on... ask me if I've eaten."

Bee Leng still looked human. Mostly human. Her irises were red as blood, her nails two inches long, shaped to points. Gean Choo couldn't help but stare at them, curved around Ah Mui's tiny body. Her shirt was mottled and soaked through, seaweed clinging to one shoulder.

"I'm sorry. I should've tried harder to explain to you—"

"You didn't try at all!"

Ah Mui started crying at the sound of raised voices, and Bee Leng jiggled her against her hip, shushing her. "Go make yourself useful, baby amah, and fill the bottle."

Gean Choo moved, keeping Bee Leng in her peripheral vision. The milk was too hot. She filled the bottle and screwed the lid on tight, then ran the tap over the bottle, turning it so that the milk would cool evenly.

"You waste water here, also. I thought it was only people you threw away."

"We thought you were dead."

Bee Leng looked down at Ah Mui and made a silly face. The baby smiled back at her, reaching up one dimpled arm. "Me, too. I suppose my period wasn't just late, after all."

Everything finally made sense. Bee Leng must've been pregnant when she'd died. They hadn't known, hadn't bothered to bury her with the appropriate rites, and so when Zaid had tried to toss her into the ocean, she'd awakened as a pontianak.

"What did you do with Zaid?" Gean Choo asked.

"Is the bottle ready or not?"

Gean Choo tested it on the inside of her wrist, then handed it over. Ah Mui eagerly drank. If she were concerned with being handled by an undead woman, she showed no sign of it.

"Zaid?" Gean Choo asked again.

"I did what any woman in my position would do." Bee Leng grinned, her teeth stained crimson. "Just like your Mrs. Edevane did to me, and just as I'm going to do to you."

Maybe Gean Choo should've been afraid, but fear was beyond her emotional palette at this moment; she could only muster up exhaustion. "What will you do with Ah Mui?"

Bee Leng glanced down. "She's only a useless girl, but it could be fun to have a daughter. Mama can take care of her when I'm out hunting."

Ah Mui would be safe, then. Or at least, as safe as she could be while being raised by a predator. "For what it's worth, I'm truly sorry."

"Your word is cow's piss."

The pontianaks from Lord Cottesley's party had seemed light on their feet. She couldn't outrun Bee Leng, not for long.

And part of her didn't want to. She deserved this. She'd lied by omission, and an innocent woman had died. Women, counting all the ones before. If her death could shift a line on the scales, why fight it?

"May I hold her, please? I'd like to say goodbye. I won't run. There's nowhere for me to go."

Something in Gean Choo's face must've made Bee Leng take pity.

She passed Ah Mui over, who began to wail as soon as she'd left Bee Leng's grasp.

"Shh," Gean Choo said, shifting her grip as Po Lam had shown her. "I've got you. I'm sorry it took me so long, but I'm here."

"That's enough. Put her down."

"Just one minute more—"

"Enough!"

A kitchen wasn't really a safe place to leave a baby. Gean Choo settled for placing Ah Mui down in a corner, on the floor, where she couldn't roll off a table and hurt herself. Her limbs flailed in the air like an upturned turtle, and she screwed up her eyes, preparing to cry again. She gripped Gean Choo's finger with one chubby fist.

It was too much. Gean Choo gently pried her finger free and stepped away from the child. Bee Leng placed herself between Gean Choo and the door, her breath hot against the back of her neck.

"We don't coddle when we bite like your English do. Though from the looks of it"—her nails lightly scratched at the cicatrices around her throat—"maybe they don't, either."

"Just do it," Gean Choo snapped, jerking her head away. She resisted the urge to press her palm over the throbbing burn.

Bee Leng hesitated a moment more. "Wait. Are you pregnant?"

She could lie. It might even save her life. But for how long, and to what end? "No. You don't need to do anything special with my corpse. I promise not to haunt you." She giggled. The whole idea was so absurd, as if the kings of hell would permit a patricide to wallow in limbo, instead of receiving their deserved eternity of torture. She sobered up. That was one aspect of the afterlife she sincerely hoped wasn't true.

"Get on the counter."

"What?"

"I don't like to bend over when I eat. It gives me a pain in my neck."

Gean Choo turned to look at her unsmiling face. "But you're dead."

Bee Leng scowled. "So? You think because I'm dead, I can't suffer? Get up."

Someone more sensible would've fought back, would've died on her feet. Had Gean Choo ever been that person? Maybe once. Not now.

She slid up on the countertop. It pained her to bring her feet up, but once Bee Leng was done, her blood would probably be everywhere and there'd be more for Seok Eng to worry about than a little dirt in the kitchen. She laid herself flat as though the counter were her coffin, staring at the white moths circling the light. Their wings made shadows as they passed over, distorted and looming.

Bee Leng leaned over her, casting a shadow. Gean Choo screwed her eyes shut. She'd try not to scream too much. She didn't want to disturb Ah Mui.

Bee Leng opened the folds of Gean Choo's robe just enough to bare her stomach, her breath hot and dry against the exposed skin. Gean Choo pressed both her palms over her mouth, wishing for something to bite down upon.

Nothing for long seconds. The tick of a clock. The bark of a neighbourhood dog. And then, Bee Leng groaned like the creak of a boat running aground.

"I don't know… I don't know if I can do this." Bee Leng staggered, reached for a cooking pot, and leaned over it, coughing up a stream of black, stinking blood.

Gean Choo slowly sat up and gazed down at herself to make sure all her organs were still in place. She jerked the front of the dressing gown closed. "It probably gets easier," she said. "I've seen other pontianaks around here. Maybe one of them could help you—"

"I don't want to be helped!" Bee Leng dropped her head into her hands and cried red tears of blood, just like Mrs. Edevane had. The sight of it made Gean Choo queasy. Bee Leng shoved the pot to one side, the rattle of it as loud as a gunshot, and slid down onto the floor, her back against the kitchen cabinet. "I never asked for this. I don't want to be one of them. I want to *not be dead*."

"I'm sor—"

"Do you know what Zaid said? When I crawled over the side of the boat, dredged in seaweed and stinking of fish? You know what he said to me?" The tear trails running down Bee Leng's face matched the colour of her eyes.

"What?"

"He cried for his ma. A grown man like him, a killer also... He cried like a little boy and begged me to spare him. And I did. I lied before. I couldn't do it."

If Gean Choo were a heroine on the moors, she'd go to her and hug her, offer her a shoulder to cry upon. But she couldn't bear to touch anyone right now, not even Bee Leng. There was nothing she could say, no word she could think of that might offer some comfort.

They might have sat there for eternity in some sort of uneasy truce if the door hadn't swung wide open.

"Get down!"

Instead of obeying, Gean Choo looked over. Po Lam was standing by the door, both hands on her revolver, aiming it at Bee Leng. Her white shirt was a beacon shining through the darkness of the night.

Bee Leng sprang up and yanked Gean Choo off the kitchen counter, so quick Gean Choo lost her breath for a moment. Bee Leng wrapped her arm around Gean Choo's shoulders, holding her tight like a human shield.

"Don't move," Bee Leng said. "Drop the gun."

If Po Lam was concerned by this turn of events, she showed no sign. "If you want that, I'll have to move."

"Fine! But slowly."

With exaggerated care, Po Lam leaned down and placed the gun on the floor, her other hand upheld, palm facing out.

"Kick it here."

The gun skittered across the tiles, coming to rest against Bee Leng's foot, though she didn't bother to pick it up.

Gean Choo glanced down, then wished she hadn't. Bee Leng's sharpened nails were black against her skin, coming up to rest lightly on her neck, forcing Gean Choo to press her head back as far as possible against Bee Leng's shoulder.

"What do you want?" Po Lam asked, her hands still raised.

"I want you to forget about me. Forget you ever saw me," Bee Leng with Gean Choo towards the door. She waved Po Lam to slowly backed into the kitchen, not taking her eyes off the two of them.

"What about her?" Po Lam asked.

Gean Choo accidentally stepped on Bee Leng's foot as they were shuffling. Bee Leng hissed, tensing her arm. There was a flash of pain and then the warmth of blood running down the hollow between her clavicles.

Bee Leng stopped moving. Her gaze flicked to Gean Choo's neck, pupils enormous. She ran a red tongue over cracked lips.

Ah Mui, still on the floor, started to wail. Bee Leng moved her attention onto the baby for just a moment.

Gean Choo had resigned herself to death only a few moments prior, but that had been before she'd seen Po Lam again. Now everything was different.

She slammed her elbow back, connecting with Bee Leng's ribs. If she'd tried this with Mrs. Edevane, it would've gotten her nowhere, but Bee Leng exhaled with a soft gasp of surprise and let her go.

Gean Choo stumbled forwards, her hair falling over her eyes for a moment. The revolver boomed, so loud in the confined space that her ears perceived it more as pain than sound. Bee Leng screamed, a high-pitched, inhuman wail, and Po Lam fired again.

Bee Leng was still upright, staggering forwards. She peered down at her chest, at the two blackened holes seared into her tunic. Her blood had spattered against the wall behind her, dark brown like flecks of paint, but even as they watched, the wounds in her chest began to close.

Po Lam dropped the revolver, ran, and grabbed something from the cutlery drawer. She seized Bee Leng's hair and bent her face-down over the kitchen counter. Something glinted in her other hand. Not the gun. A skewer.

"Wait. Stop!" Gean Choo cried out. "She hasn't killed anyone. She doesn't deserve—"

Po Lam centred a metal skewer over the back of Bee Leng's neck and hammered it in with the butt of a meat cleaver. The wooden handle thudded with a dull smack, like the sound of Seok Eng julienning ginger. Po Lam raised her hand and brought it down again. And again.

Bee Leng went limp. Po Lam carefully turned her head, checking her eyes. They were brown again, glazed over and unseeing. Po Lam lowered Bee Leng to the floor, turning her head so as not to dislodge the makeshift nail. She remained limp, though her chest appeared to move slightly with her breath.

Ah Mui was screaming. Gean Choo ran and picked her up, holding her tightly, though her arms trembled.

"What a mess," Po Lam said.

Gean Choo laughed, forcing herself to stop after a few moments. She ought to have been dead several times over tonight—the first moment Mrs. Edevane detected Po Lam on her lips, her trachea crushed by Mrs. Edevane's fist, Bee Leng's nails disembowelling her on the kitchen counter. To find herself still alive was, all things considered, a disappointment.

"You didn't listen to me," Po Lam said. "If this is going to work, you have to trust me."

What was "this"?

"I didn't know you were coming back."

"What's wrong with your voice?"

Gean Choo didn't answer the question. "She wasn't going to hurt me," she said. "She couldn't." Her ears still felt dull and strange, as though stuffed with cotton wool.

"Go get changed. It's two hours until sunlight, and we need to leave." Po Lam picked up the revolver, put the safety back on, and reloaded it with cartridges from her pocket. No hello, no further questions. She didn't seem entirely surprised to have seen Bee Leng standing, lying, and all the stages in-between. If this sudden reappearance phased her, she didn't show it.

"Shouldn't we do something with her?" Gean Choo asked. "Bandage her wounds?"

"A gun can't kill her, and the skewer's long enough she can remove it herself when she wakes up." Po Lam inclined her head towards the hallway. "Worry more about yourself. We should hurry."

Po Lam had only been on the estate for five minutes, and already, they were disagreeing. Gean Choo ought to have been grateful she was here at all.

She went to her room and set Ah Mui down on her bed. She handed the stuffed bear to her, and Ah Mui wrapped her fingers around the toy's paw for one moment, then dropped it to the floor and started to cry.

Gean Choo sighed and placed the bear in her bag. "You can have it again later. Later!"

Ah Mui continued to cry, but she ignored her and reached into the very bottom of the clothes chest, searching out the plain white shirt and black pants she'd brought with her. It was time to leave everything Mrs. Edevane had ever given her—the shoes, the dresses, the jewellery. She left those first earrings lying on top of the nightgown, gold and red upon the white.

It didn't take long to dress and pack, and to hold Ah Mui over the latrine. In the bathroom, she stared at herself in the mirror. Her whole neck should've been a bruise, some obvious sign besides the redness in her eyes. She looked so disappointingly normal, apart from the narrow gashes of claw marks. Had she imagined the force of Mrs. Edevane's rage? Surely, she was exaggerating. Surely, Mrs. Edevane hadn't meant her real harm.

But then her gaze fell to the small burn mark below her collarbone, and she wasn't so sure.

On her way out, she stopped to look at Bee Leng's body, still unmoving. "I'm sorry," Gean Choo said. Was Po Lam right about Bee Leng's survival? How could she be certain? Had she done this before?

Outside, a figure was standing by the car. It took Gean Choo a moment to recognise her as Po Lam. When she did, something seemed to pop in her brain, filling it with a frisson of giddiness like bubbles bursting in a champagne glass.

Po Lam wore a pantsuit of Occidental make in pale cream, a jacket slung over her shoulder, draped over her fingertips. Her tie was a dull gold colour, knotted tight over the soft sleek hollow of her throat. A watch chain looped from one of the buttons on her vest to a small pocket. Po Lam plucked out the watch, consulted it, and frowned at her.

"You can't take the train looking like *that*," she said, dismissing Gean Choo with one word. "If Mrs. Edevane asks, she'll be looking for two women and a baby, or perhaps an amah and a baby. Not..." She gestured. "Go change. And pack enough clothes for the next week."

How stupid of her. She hadn't even thought.

Gean Choo dressed and repacked her suitcase. It was different this time, as if she were playing some childish game, pretending to be a married woman—for what else would people see upon looking at the three of them? Married to *Po Lam*. Something burned inside her at the thought of it.

Po Lam had the motor running by the time she came back wearing a dress and hose, a scarf draped loosely around her neck to hide the bandages. Gean Choo threw her bag into the back seat and slid into the front of the car, Ah Mui on her lap, swaddled in her sling.

Neither of them spoke until they'd driven a good ten minutes. It was still dark, the traffic light at this early hour.

"Thank you," Gean Choo said. "For coming back."

"It's not over yet," Po Lam said, but she seemed to relax, sinking further into her seat. "Did Bee Leng hurt you?"

"Hmm?" Gean Choo touched her fingertips to her neck. "N-no. I'm fine."

That didn't seem like the right thing to say. The atmosphere in the car grew uncomfortable, and Ah Mui began to fuss. To distract her, Gean Choo sang a lullaby while the car purred onwards into the dawn hours.

# CHAPTER 53

## I'M LEAVING

### VERITY

*Tuesday, 17 April 1928*
*One day since last meal*

Verity's day passed uneventfully in Justine's coffin. She woke when the sun set, pushed back the lid, and opened her eyes, her eyelashes struggling to separate from the glue of dried blood. Gore crusted her face and décolletage. Frankly, she needed a bath.

And a drink.

Freddie had gotten away the night before, hadn't he? Assaulted her and ran. She couldn't stay here. It wasn't safe.

But she also couldn't bear her own smell, caked in Justine's viscera and that of the human she'd dragged from the armoire. The corpse would be stinking in the tropical heat if someone hadn't cleaned up. Which wasn't likely since Justine's death would've freed any bloodthralls by now. They'd probably all vanished, taking the silverware with them, if they'd been sensible.

Verity staggered into Justine's bathroom and bumped her hip on a cabinet, scattering little toiletry bottles onto the floor. There wasn't a bath, just the usual water trough and scoop.

She found soap and cleaned herself up as best she could, leaving her ruined clothes on the floor, turning the water pink as it sluiced over the tiles. Back in Justine's room, she picked a dress and threw it on. Justine favoured pastels even though they clashed with her complexion, so nothing in her wardrobe matched Verity's midnight-blue shoes.

She had to think of her future. Had to move. It was impossible to stay here under Kalon's watch. He'd ruined the whole island and the peninsula.

No matter. It wasn't as though she'd put down roots. There were other corners of the empire still open to her. Perhaps some place with a longer night. Canada? Why not? She could use a change in scenery.

She had a nagging sensation of... something. Guilt? Yes, perhaps that was it. Not over Justine, of course, but before... She'd behaved insensitively. It'd been just the shock of it all, the betrayal. Not only Pearl, but Po Lam, too? What was she meant to do with that?

It was so very awful not having anyone to trust, no one to turn to.

Well, she'd just have to make things right. She had to swallow her pride and apologise to Pearl, to make sure her burn healed cleanly. And then... then they could talk about expectations. About standards that should've needed no explanation. And then—

She opened the shutters and dissolved herself with a shudder, seeping out through the slats and into the garden. A wind buffeted her as she floated above the ground. There was a sound behind her, a whisper perhaps, imperceptible over the croaking of frogs and the whirring of insects.

Something happened to Verity that had never happened before; she fell back into her body, resuming solidity with a force that knocked her back, sending her sprawling in the damp grass. Dew soaked her skirts and wet her palms.

She smelled him before she saw him, that cologne he always used, sandalwood and tangerines. She scrambled to her feet.

"My, my. You have been a naughty girl."

She whirled to face him. Kalon waited at the edge of Justine's elevated verandah, carelessly elegant in a dove-grey suit, hands in his pockets, standing five steps above her.

"Good evening, my lord." She used her sweetest voice, though her fingers trembled. Why had she returned to human form? Had he done something to her?

"I must deplore your timing, Mrs. Edevane, since it compelled me to postpone a meeting with the governor. Still, I always have time for you. Even when you've put me in such a pickle," he said, not moving.

Had he come alone? She breathed in, filtering out the scent of rain and wet earth, the distant rot of the corpse she'd left somewhere on the ground floor.

It was just him.

"That's your job, isn't it, my lord? To ease ruffled feathers."

"I could have you staked for what you've done."

She took a step towards him, then another. He might be her senior in the council's eyes, but she was his elder in years. She had to hold onto that, even as her blood demanded she bow to him. "I won't be your problem for much longer. I'm leaving on the earliest ship. India. Hong Kong. I hear Sierra Leone is picturesque this time of year."

"It won't be enough. Not this time."

"She was a monster." Verity didn't have to exaggerate the snap in her voice, the derision. She'd gladly kill Justine Skelford again.

"We're all monsters, my dear Mrs. Edevane."

He'd not moved an inch, even as she'd advanced upon him. They stood separated by twenty feet of damp lawn.

"Speak for yourself," Verity said. "We're the ones bringing civilisation to all corners of the—"

She moved without completing the sentence, willing herself to disappear, to scatter into particles finer than ash. She was already drifting away when Kalon barked out a single word. "Stop."

It happened again. She coalesced violently as if thrust into a too-small box, falling in a tangle of limbs, the air squeezed from her lungs. Her outstretched palms hit the ground with jarring force, shooting pain through her arms.

Kalon's footsteps echoed on the steps like a heartbeat. Largo. He'd lied to her. Lied to everyone. The whole lot of Speakers were liars—his sire, the entire damn bloodline.

She wasn't immune to his voice. She never had been.

Beneath the stars, his eyes gleamed red. "Sleep."

## CHAPTER 54

# TWENTY YEARS OF HELL

### PO LAM

*Tuesday, 17 April 1928*

They'd taken the northbound express train heading to Penang, spending the layover in KL eating dinner. Po Lam's back stiffened whenever she felt eyes upon them, but most of the time it was only women cooing at Ah Mui and complimenting the baby on her manners. The child seemed unscathed by the tumult of the day.

It was an hour past sunset when the train began moving again, clacking rhythmically as they picked up speed. They were in a second-class lounge, Po Lam making a show of reading a newspaper. Her layers upon layers of clothing fitted her like armour. If she'd been travelling on her own, this would've been a harder role to sell—the ambiguous softness of her face, the timbre of her voice—but the others provided such camouflage as she'd never expected. They were like the words to some secret spell of invisibility, her pretty wife holding their quiet baby. This was what she'd been missing. A foil, the yin to her yang. Did other people feel like this all the time? Pleasantly unremarkable, without the need to justify their appearance, their mere existence?

She massaged her watch chain, worrying the links between her thumb and forefinger until metal and flesh became one. If only she could do the same with this suit. But it was all an illusion, nothing more. Gean Choo had made her no promises. She couldn't expect... It didn't matter if she wanted—

Gean Choo was pointing out the city lights to Ah Mui, whose head was beginning to nod. The scene was so sickeningly domestic, it seemed needlessly cruel that it'd all have to end when they reached their destination.

Maybe part of it didn't have to end. But she wouldn't be holding her breath, waiting for Gean Choo to give her a proper answer.

Po Lam shouldn't even be here; she would've been safer on her own. Mrs. Edevane could always find a new handler. But one of her girls? She wouldn't let her go this easily.

Gean Choo was nodding off along with her charge, and Po Lam shook her awake. "Time for bed."

Someone had obligingly brought a small cot to their sleeping cabin, which had two bunks fitted across the width of the cabin, one atop the other. The window was ajar, permitting the relatively cool night air to seep in. Gean Choo laid Ah Mui down on the cot as Po Lam sat on the lower bunk, retrieving her suitcase.

"Do you need help changing your bandages? I brought fresh ones. And Mercurochrome," Po Lam said.

Gean Choo straightened and glanced at the door. "No, thank you. I can manage."

"Do you have your pistol?"

"I'm not taking a gun to the bathroom!"

"Bring my knife, then. Just in case."

She took it, along with the bandages, although she didn't look happy about it. The cabin door squeaked as she pulled it shut.

She was gone for a while. Po Lam had half made up her mind to search for her by the time Gean Choo returned, looking pale, her neck freshly wrapped, bandages extending down to her arms from what Po Lam could see of them under her dress. Gean Choo went to check on Ah Mui, who was asleep, then turned her back to Po Lam and changed from daywear to a white nightdress. She did it modestly, the nightdress going on first before she shimmied out of the day dress, revealing nothing but the lines of her bandages.

"She hurt you," Po Lam said, biting down all the words she'd have preferred to say.

Gean Choo turned back, smoothing her hands over her nightdress. "It's nothing." She flushed. "I just don't want them to scar."

"What happened? With the mem."

Gean Choo wrapped her hands around her arms, winced, and shook her hands free, as if to disavow her reaction. "Nothing happened."

"If this is going to work, we can't go on keeping secrets from each other."

Gean Choo reached over and played with the toggle at the bottom of the window shade. She stared at it, her lip quivering. "I provoked her," she whispered. "I knew it would make her angry, and I said it anyway—"

"Said what?"

Gean Choo's face went bright red as she twisted the fabric of her nightdress. She looked so painfully, profoundly uncomfortable that Po Lam wished she could bite her tongue, take back her needless line of questioning. But then Gean Choo sat on the other side of the bunk, its frame creaking, and turned to face her. "I said I wasn't sorry I'd kissed you. I said I'd do it again." She leaned in a little closer. "May I?"

It was Po Lam who reached up, closed the distance between them, brought Gean Choo's face to hers. She'd meant to make the kiss tender, her mouth soft, but Gean Choo kissed her like one or both of them were dying. Gean Choo straddled her, fists scrunching up the shoulders of Po Lam's shirt. She leaned her full weight against her, pinning Po Lam against the cabin wall. Her kisses meandered from her mouth, ran scatter-shot down her neck, trailing heat across her skin as her fingers fumbled with the buttons of Po Lam's vest.

Po Lam placed her hand on her hip. Gean Choo sucked in a breath, drawing back with a hiss of pain. Po Lam took her hand away. "Is that sore?"

Gean Choo shook her head. Her hair lay limp and greasy across her face, head tilted down to leave her eyes in shadow. "It's just a bruise. I'm fine."

"Where else?"

Gean Choo blew the strands of hair from her eyes with a sigh. "I told you, it's fine."

"Maybe I should take a look—"

"No!" Gean Choo shifted her weight, sitting upright. "There's really nothing to worry about. Let's not talk about the before times, if only for a while."

Po Lam crinkled her eyes. "The before times. Is that what we're calling it now?"

"What else would you call it?"

"Twenty years of hell."

Gean Choo flinched. "Oh, don't say that! There was music, and dancing, and books. So many books that it would take a lifetime to read them all."

"It came with strings."

"You think I don't know that?"

Po Lam chose her next words carefully. "You said you provoked her earlier. But nothing you could've done excuses her from hurting you."

"You don't know what you're talking about."

"Why are you protecting her?"

"I'm not!" Gean Choo leapt from the bunk and stood with her back half-turned from Po Lam, arms wrapped tight over her chest. The little cabin didn't have much room to spare, but she'd managed to wedge herself in the corner farthest from Po Lam.

"She's not here. You don't have to talk as if... as if she'll know."

Gean Choo's voice was choked with tears. "If I make her the villain, what does it mean? If what she did was wrong, I let her do it. And I should've known better. I'm old enough to know better!"

In the village half a day north of Po Lam's birthplace, there'd been an old glassworker who made bowls and cups, but also ornaments, little figurines of animals and people. There'd been a crane among his wares, wings outstretched and poised to take flight. Gean Choo had that fragility about her, that same mix of brittleness and strength.

Po Lam stood and offered her hands, palms facing up. Gean Choo stared at them, wide-eyed and distant. She had the look of wildlife in headlights. Then, all at once, she threw herself into Po Lam's arms and buried her face in Po Lam's shoulder. Po Lam slowly, carefully, placed one hand on the small of Gean Choo's back. She flinched, but then gradually relaxed.

When her posture had softened, her breathing still too quick, but her eyes dry, Po Lam spoke in a low voice, the same tone she'd used to cajole women to the slaughter. "What do you need right now? If it's space, I could leave the cabin—"

Gean Choo dug her nails into Po Lam's arms. "No! Please don't leave me. Not at night."

"I won't. You can let go now."

Gean Choo relaxed her grip, but she didn't move from the circle of Po Lam's arms. "I don't know what's wrong with me. I'm sorry."

"Nothing's wrong with you."

Gean Choo tilted her face to look at her. "I don't want to live like this anymore. I don't want... I don't want to be afraid all the time."

How could she let that statement lie? It wasn't her place to say anything, but she said it all the same. "Fear can be helpful. Some things should scare you. But not the person who says they love you and demands your love in return."

Gean Choo's breath caught in her throat. She stared at Po Lam as if she were one of the eighteen disciples or a manifestation of divinity. Her eyes were the eyes of all the women Po Lam had ever killed.

The cracks in her ran deep—deeper than just her time with Mrs. Edevane. If Po Lam stayed, if she tried to hold this together, whatever this was, it would mean living with those scars, accepting them, and loving their bearer all the same.

After all, who among them had lived to adulthood unmarked? Not Po Lam. And not, it seemed, poor Gean Choo.

"Are you running to me? Or just running from her?"

Gean Choo gazed at her as though wounded. "To you. Only to you."

"I want to believe you."

It would be so easy to fall into her, to open her heart again. And why shouldn't she? Didn't she deserve happiness, someone who wanted her? Gean Choo leaned into her, one hand on her arm, lips half-parted. It would be the most natural thing in the world to spin her around, press her against the wall, wrists captured in one hand. Wedge a knee between her legs, lift the hem of her nightdress, all the while listening as Gean Choo's still-damaged voice whispered immodest surrender.

It would be so easy, so right. Hadn't she suffered enough? Hadn't she fought for her, been ready to kill for her? Hadn't that bought her the right to know peace?

"When was the last time you slept?" Po Lam asked, hearing her voice as if from far away. The voice of an elder sister, not a seductress.

Gean Choo dropped her grasp and stepped back, trembling with a whole-body shudder of revulsion. "I've slept enough. I want—"

Po Lam refastened the top button of her vest. "We should have this conversation when we're away from the peninsula. Away from her."

"Is it just talk you want from me?"

"No. But if we're to do this, we should do it under better circumstances."

Gean Choo's shoulders slumped. A complicated mixture of emotions flitted across her face before it returned to a carefully studied neutrality. "You're right, of course," she said, but her voice sounded off, the words stilted.

Exhaustion meant Po Lam couldn't manage Gean Choo's disappointment in addition to her own. "We should get some rest."

Gean Choo was slow to move, but eventually, she scrambled up onto the top bunk, using the bottom bunk's railing for leverage. The springs squeaked as she settled her weight.

Po Lam changed and switched off the light before sliding onto her own bunk. She stared into the velvet darkness and thought of broken vases, their cracks limned in gold.

## CHAPTER 55

# TELL ME WHAT YOU WANT

## VERITY

*Tuesday, 17 April 1928*
*One day since last meal*

Her head throbbed with an unceasing ache. Verity woke up to find herself prone, staring into a circle of wooden rafters, each beam converging upon a central point. Frogs croaked from somewhere outside. She was lying on something flat and unyielding, her scapula finding no comfort from the hard surface.

It was impossible to move her limbs, as if the body she inhabited wasn't entirely her own. She was in some kind of round hut, the walls raw brick and unadorned. A row of naked bulbs hung overhead in a line, the light yellow and glaring. She was strapped to the gurney, or table or whatever, restraints around her biceps and ankles. Her hands, lying atop her stomach, were cuffed.

There were grates set in the floor to ward against flooding, or perhaps to make clean-up easier when Kalon flayed her alive. Maybe both.

To her left, the light gleamed over a rolling metal cart with multiple shelves. On the top shelf was a tray of tools. Scalpels. Pliers of various shapes. A bone saw.

The straps around her were tight, made of leather. She badly needed to itch her nose but had no means of doing so. She could only stare up into the cobwebbed darkness of the rafters, at the shadows made by the light.

Review the facts. Kalon had wanted something from her. He'd been willing to trade marriage in order to get it, a move that would've offered him scant social advancement. All that talk about her reputation, her supposed ethics... it wasn't worth this investment, surely.

She didn't have anything of equivalent value. If he'd wanted to make an example of her, she'd be the centrepiece of another party, a public staking... or a pyre, if he were feeling particularly vindictive. Perhaps she was still headed for that fate.

What did he want? Information? No. All her gossip was third-hand these days. Wealth? Certainly not.

She couldn't think. She couldn't think, and now she was going to die, and it wasn't fair, it wasn't—

A door creaked from above. Verity would've stiffened had she the muscle control. Instead, her limbs remained limp, perfectly relaxed, as if she were already dead.

Sandalwood and citrus. He had blood on him, the merest drop. The smell of it made her teeth ache. He made no effort at concealment. His footsteps rasped, each one like the death knell to Verity's funeral. The stairwell was completely blocked off by a wall, ensuring she couldn't see him until he was almost right beside her.

"Oh, Verity. Look at what your folly has wrought."

There was no blood visible, but she could smell it all the same. Perhaps it clung to the sole of his shoe, the hem of his trousers. Light flickered across his face, his expression amused and eager and entirely too smug. He turned away for a moment to roll up his sleeves and don an oilcloth apron, standing with his back to her as he secured the straps.

"You can speak if you'd like, but no profanity. You know I hate that."

She took in her first breath since she'd woken up, which pressed her chest against the restraints. She was still in Justine's yellow seersucker dress, which was not an outfit she'd have chosen to die in. "This isn't to Code."

"No. On that point, you're quite right." He fished a notebook from his pocket, and laid it out next to the scalpels, along with a pen and a small round object that might've been a pocket watch. "But the charm of these backwaters is that hardly anyone is watching."

She kept breathing, even though she only needed air to speak, and tested the restraints by expanding her chest as far as it would go. It was no good. She'd never break these.

"That woman who manages your staff came here. Sold you out. Talked all about your sordid history—so earnest, so sombre. As if I hadn't already known." He laughed, short and sharp, a mere exhalation of breath.

"What did you do to her?"

"Nothing you wouldn't have done yourself." He picked up something from the tray, hummed, then set it down again. "You know, I really have to thank you."

"Thank me?"

"If Haywarde hadn't called me in such a frenzy, I might've had a harder time convincing the others you'd committed a capital offence. I do wish you'd been a little less carefree with Miss Skelford, however. There wasn't much left to dissect."

He picked up the stool from next to the instrument tray and brought it over to Verity's left shoulder before taking a seat. His apron was long-sleeved, covering most of his suit. He clasped his hands together above the table and smiled down at her, eyes sparkling, reflecting the golden gleam of the light.

"This isn't... this isn't like you, my lord. You've always played by the rules, always done the right thing—"

"Are you so sure? Perhaps I'm simply better at faking it than you are." Kalon turned away and came back with a scalpel and a watch. He flipped the cover on the watch, holding it in his left hand. With his right, he held the scalpel like a pen and used it to flick the hair from Verity's face. A few strands met the blade and were cut free. He brushed them away with the heel of his palm.

"Tell me what you want."

He met her eyes for a moment. "I want you to feel everything."

The air stirred above her face when he moved his arm. The first touch of the blade was sharp, stinging. It sank into the delicate skin of her forehead as if her flesh wasn't even there. He made one sinuous cut, then lifted the scalpel, the blade stained crimson. Blood trailed down the valleys of her face like tears. She blinked rapidly when it rolled into her left eye, momentarily blinding her.

Kalon pressed a button on the watch. The scalpel clattered upon its tray. He turned back to Verity and stared intently at her forehead. His thumb moved, clicking the watch again, and he glanced down, went to his notebook, and scribbled something.

She still couldn't fucking move. "Am I your experiment now?"

"Greenwood's hypothesis, Mrs. Edevane." He smiled, the light glinting off his teeth.

That sounded vaguely familiar. Some nonsense about combining bloodlines. Impossible.

At least her forehead no longer itched. Verity shifted her gaze to look at him. This rather crude hut was such a change from his usual surroundings. He must've really lost it with all this playing at mad scientist, creating his own Frankenstein's monster.

The elders among them sometimes grew strange and ornery in their old age, eschewing the draw of society to live solitary lives and pursue unconventional interests. Was Kalon suffering from the same ennui? He wasn't old enough to use that as an excuse.

"I don't have a talent," Verity said. "You're wasting your time—"

"Do you really think dear Benny would've risen to her position without the benefit of some advantage, however small? Think, Verity. What secret could your bloodline possess?"

Something clunked on the tray. He'd put the scalpel down and was wielding something that looked a bit like a pair of secateurs. "My lord, there's nothing. We can't Speak, we don't commune with animals. I've never seen Benny turn into a cloud of bats—"

"Yes, yes," he said impatiently. "Teagle. Do you remember him?"

Only vaguely. She'd been newly dead at the time, barely cognisant of all the kin who claimed some distant relation. If she recalled rightly, they shared a great-great-grandsire. "Wasn't there some scandal with an elder? Lenore something—"

The sound of Kalon's teeth grinding together was audible. "He lost his arm in a boating accident."

"That's right." The blood had dried on her face, stretching like paint upon her skin.

"He regrew it within the year."

"Did he? I never saw him without it." Cold realisation settled around her, like a monsoonal sumatra dumping its first lot of rain. Teagle had regrown an *arm*. In a year. Could any other bloodline claim such vitality? "My lord," she pleaded, "there's no evidence that what you claim can be done—"

"No evidence *yet*. Perhaps you'll be the first to prove otherwise. Wouldn't you like that? There's immortality for you—the prestige of a new discovery." He picked up her right hand and placed her index finger between the jaws of the cutter.

"What you claim isn't possible; there's simply no point. If this were doable, don't you think we would have destroyed ourselves long before now and—"

"You know what? I think you should participate. It's only fair, after all."

The pressure lessened on her finger. He moved the cutters, bracing one of the handles between her left forearm and torso, while still holding the other handle. The mouth of the cutters pinched her index finger at an angle. "I know the position's a bit rubbish, so you'll have to squeeze really hard to get it right on the first try. You understand?"

"This isn't going to work, Ka—m'lord, please, you're a man of reason, you have to see that—"

"Squeeze," he said.

Her arm jerked against her body as if moving of its own accord. The jaws of the cutter snapped. Verity screamed.

The cut hadn't gone through; instead, it caught on bone. Kalon sighed, took hold of the cutters himself, and finished it. The pain was like a burn, like the touch of the sun. She tried to cover the wound with her other hand but still couldn't move. The cut oozed blood onto her dress, a great red stain spreading like spilt ink.

Kalon picked up her finger and popped it, nail and all, into his mouth. His teeth crunched audibly upon bone, his face twisted in a grimace of disgust.

The chest strap was too tight. It was a good thing Verity didn't need to breathe because she couldn't consume enough air. The lights blurred together overhead, shimmering, distorted. The open wound on her hand appeared pulpy, abhorrently naked, as though ashamed of being revealed to the world.

Kalon swallowed. He opened his book again, laying out his watch and a fresh scalpel. He peeled back the sleeve of the apron to reveal his forearm and drew a thin line of red upon himself before clicking the watch.

Her hand bloody well hurt. Verity gritted her teeth against the pain, trying to ignore the insidious itching as her flesh attempted to repair itself. How long did it take for one to regrow a finger?

She wouldn't let him keep her like this, siphoning blood from her, cutting off her limbs one by one. Having to obey him, like a human, like a *thrall*... If it was too cruel a fate for her servants, it was certainly too cruel for her. Having to listen to his voice droning on and on, day in and day out. She'd rather kill herself. But Kalon's torture room had a significant dearth of sharpened wooden implements upon which to impale oneself.

Kalon watched his arm, and then the clock. His brows remained furrowed.

"I told you it wouldn't work." After all, she'd drained Justine dry and had seen no lingering benefit from it. But then again, Haywarde's line was weak. Talentless. "You think with all the inter-kindred squabbling that someone hadn't tried this already? Tried it more than once? With multiple bloodlines? My lord, this is pointless. If you'd—"

"Perhaps it's a matter of quantity. A leg, say, not a finger. Or maybe it's solely found in the blood, not the flesh. In which case, multiple transfusions might do the trick," he said, seemingly addicted to the sound of his own voice.

"You're grasping at straws."

"I'm presenting my thesis. With the spirit of scientific inquiry, the intelligent man ought to be able to explore all the unknowns of the universe."

The watch clicked again and his fountain pen rasped upon paper. Kalon picked up a cloth and blotted his forearm, the fabric turning red.

"Tell me something," Verity said. "What were you hoping to gain if I'd said 'yes' to your proposal? You clearly didn't need a wedding to have me flat on my back."

Kalon pursed his lips, as if her innuendo pained him. "I'd hoped you'd fall for my winning personality and, over time, agree to participate willingly."

"Really," she said, not even trying to keep the sarcasm out of her voice. "You could've just ordered me to do it. You think I'd have chopped off parts of myself and fed them to you as part of some delusional ritual?"

Kalon turned to her with an expression that she might've labelled "tender" under different circumstances. His fingertips grazed the side of her face, making her skin crawl. "The art of holding power, Mrs. Edevane, is in avoiding its use. Besides, in this scenario, we'd already vowed to be one flesh."

"I don't think that phrase means what you think it means."

He moved his hand, drawing away from her. "Your line has been killed before, but it's notoriously difficult. I once saw a file recovered from a hunter's nest in Rome, suggesting that consecrated water was the best offence." He reached below the instrument tray to one of the lower shelves on the cart and pulled out a pair of thick black gloves. "I admit, I never thought I'd get the chance to test the veracity of those claims."

On the tray with the rest of his instruments was a clear glass bottle, about the size of a hip flask. Donning the gloves, he twisted off the cap and set it aside, next to a thick brush ending in a thin point, the sort the Chinese used for their calligraphy.

He leant over the table, drawing close to her ear. "I'll stop if you beg me," he whispered in a low tone that traced phantom fingers down her spine. "Beg me to stop."

She didn't know if she could manage it, whether it counted as movement or speech. She gazed at Kalon's cheek, calculating distance, velocity. She took aim and spat.

The spittle landed squarely on the side of his nose, sliding down his face. He let it sit there a moment, holding her gaze, before reaching for a handkerchief to wipe it away.

Kalon straightened up again. The brush went into the bottle and came out wet. He hovered the brush over her head. Verity tried to move her neck and found she could go so far as to skim her cheek against the table.

Kalon pushed his free hand against her crown and repositioned her in place. "Don't move," he said, sounding vaguely annoyed. A single bead of clear fluid trembled down the lengths of the bristles, poised, hovering, ready to drop.

She could move. She could move? But then—

"You could've had everything," Kalon said. "You could've had me."

The brush descended and made a contemptuous little flick across her brow bone.

When she thought about this in the future, she would remember it as the most painful moment of her existence, even after several lifetimes of skirting around stakes and sunlight, of extricating herself from over-zealous hunters and internecine politics. Agony consumed her with white-hot intensity, brighter than the evening star. Verity screamed like she was dying. The pain was a live thing, burying itself into her flesh and digging all the way through to her skull. The brush descended again, touched coarse bristles against one delicate eyelid. Vision fled her right eye. Something wet dribbled down her face, vitreous humour mingling with traces of holy water, burning fresh lines of pain down her cheek.

"Oh... my mistake. I've been a bit careless with my canvas."

him. Fuck him, fuck him, *fuck him*. If she ever got out of this nightmare, she was going to make such a mess of him, they wouldn't be able to scrape his remains off the walls.

He dipped the brush into the bottle. When he swished it in the liquid, pale pink chunks of flesh contaminated the bottle, briefly clouding the water before settling to the bottom in a layer of grisly sediment.

There was a faint sizzling noise when he brushed her left brow bone, her eyebrow crisping, the hair fibre searing down to the root. She kept her remaining eye shut, as if that thin layer of skin held any protection against the liquid fire he was gleefully dripping all over her face.

"Shh. There's a good girl." He blotted her forehead with a piece of fabric. It spread some of the water, burning new patches of previously untouched flesh. She keened like a banshee.

The relative silence afterwards seemed all too much. Her face burned as though it were on fire. Her diaphragm pressed up, reflexively breathing; the body, in a panic, no longer remembering if it was dead or alive.

She barely noticed Kalon change over his tools and strip off the gloves. His footsteps circled around to her right, his bare fingers tapping at the inside of her elbow, searching for a vein. She glanced down as he inserted a needle into her arm, depressing the plunger on a vial of clear fluid.

He wasn't wearing gloves, so it couldn't have been—

"It's only an anticoagulant," he said. "Nothing to worry about." He set the watch again, then laid it down, taking a seat by her left side.

It was almost too bad he'd eschewed conversation, though she'd never admit it. Without his barbs to respond to, she was left with her own thoughts, running in circles—*I'll kill him, I'll kill him, I'll kill him*—and the continuing burn of her face warring with an insane itch as the skin struggled to reform.

It was almost a relief when the watch gently chimed. He came back to her right side and inserted a fresh needle into the crook of her arm, tying it down with a strip of gauze. Her blood left her body in a traitorous line, via a thin clear tube dripping down into a glass beaker.

"This may take a while. Don't worry," he said, patting her shoulder, "I'll send someone in to keep you company." He thumbed the watch again before slipping it into his pocket, then hovered over the table, his stare boring into her good left eye. "Don't. Move." He enunciated it so she could hear the capitals. He turned from her and took off the apron, placing it on a hook before disappearing through the door, his footsteps echoing in the stairwell.

He'd left her alone.

## CHAPTER 56

# NO ONE ELSE

### PO LAM

*Wednesday, 18 April 1928*

They entered Province Wellesley in the morning, stopping at Butterworth to change trains. The next express to Bangkok didn't leave until the afternoon. Too late. Far too late.

"We can't wait that long," Po Lam said, pacing at the side of the station, parallel to the track. Staying still was simply not an option. Perhaps it'd been something Mrs. Edevane had said once upon a time, some rare instance of vulnerability she'd shared with Po Lam. Waiting meant death. She could feel the truth of it.

"It's daytime," Gean Choo said. "She wouldn't... It's safe now."

Po Lam tossed a glance in her direction. "If you believe that, you must truly be an idiot," she said, making no attempt to soften her words.

Gean Choo flushed.

Po Lam shouldn't have said that, but before she could find the words to form an apology, Gean Choo spoke again.

"We could take a walk. Stretch our legs. We've plenty of time."

They didn't. Not really. But what else could they do? She hadn't even bothered inquiring about ships leaving today. She couldn't do another journey by sea. Her first still gave her nightmares from time to time. The sounds. The smells. The tang of salt on her tongue, the endless rocking, the bile that rose up when—

Gean Choo placed a hand over her arm. "We'll be all right," she said and squeezed.

Po Lam wished she could believe her.

They passed an hour meandering, Gean Choo keeping up a stream of bright patter about nothing—the weather, their breakfast, Ah Mui, circling back to the weather when clouds gathered over the horizon. They stopped for lunch at a coffee shop, paying a server to make up Ah Mui's bottle. She bounced the child on her knee, making silly faces at her until the baby smiled.

Po Lam's chest ached when she looked at them. It was absurd, really, how much she wanted this—her. Them. Together. It wasn't healthy to want something that much. It wasn't safe.

Those traitorous thoughts kept lurching to the forefront of her mind, unwanted visitors she couldn't bury. Wouldn't it be perfect, though? Someone to come home to. Someone to be her home.

She sipped her coffee. The shop was crowded with workers and one or two families. She and Gean Choo were overdressed for the venue. Sometimes it was as if she'd lived her whole life like that. Never quite right. Never quite enough. Never fitting in.

Ah Mui pulled at the cufflink on Po Lam's shirt. Po Lam undid it and handed it over, watching the child play with it for a moment until Ah Mui raised it to her mouth, obliging Po Lam to snatch it back before she swallowed it.

They took a direct route to the train station, neither of them talking in the afternoon heat, and boarded their next train with plenty of time to spare. It was only another twenty-seven hours or so to Bangkok, and... then what? They kept delaying any talk about the future, but they couldn't delay it forever.

Ah Mui stared around the train car, wide-eyed, mercifully quiet. She hadn't quite caught up to the idea of sleeping during the night, but neither had anyone else. They were all tired and irritable, toilworn. Po Lam flicked open a newspaper and disappeared behind it, the print refusing to settle before her eyes, marching away like ants.

The train moved, the platform falling away. They had a measure of peace for the next two hours; Gean Choo even managed to doze a little, her weight falling against the headrest of her seat, her jaw slack. The steady motion of the train suited Ah Mui, who also slept, her tiny hands losing their grip on the sling that swaddled her against Gean Choo's body.

Everything was perfect... and then it wasn't.

The train's brake screeched, engaging with a start that made Po Lam drop her newspaper. A man stumbled and almost lost his footing in the aisle, needing the help of another passenger to stay upright. The ever-present hum of conversation grew louder, punctuated by cries of consternation.

"What on earth—"

"It's not an elephant, is it? Oh, Father, I would so love to see—"

"Can't believe we'll be late again—"

It was still light outside, with sunset a good few hours away. Po Lam's hand went to the paper talismans in her trouser pocket. They'd worked on the thralls, but Mrs. Edevane would be another matter. She needed her gun.

She stood, taking down their luggage from the overhead storage rack. No one was watching as she slipped the revolver from her bag and into the holster beneath her jacket. Her back stiffened at the sound of male voices shouting from outside.

Passengers clamoured to the windows, striving to see the cause of the disturbance. Gean Choo had roused herself, though she was not quite awake yet, blinking at the scene before her.

A woman shrieked, then thudded, as she collapsed in the aisle. The other passengers immediately surrounded her. "Mabel?" a man called out. "Mabel! It's her wretched nerves. Does anyone have smelling salts?"

Ah Mui fussed in Gean Choo's arms, sniffling at first before breaking out in a full-throated wail.

Po Lam clamped her hand on Gean Choo's shoulder. "Come on," she whispered. "We're leaving."

Gean Choo was still rubbing sleep from her eyes. "But we're not at a station. What happened?"

Po Lam shook her head. They had to inch by the knot of bystanders—two Eurasian men and a European, plus the fainting lady and, presumably, her husband. Gean Choo muttered apologies as she squeezed past, pressing Ah Mui close to her. The baby's crying helped clear the way until they'd reached the doors of the cabin.

Outside, the late afternoon sky was clouded and grey, the ground wet. Po Lam's shoes splashed against the mud.

A group of rail attendants and other crew members were clustered around the head of the train. A shirtless worker, his back heavy with corded muscle, lurched away from the track and hunched over, vomiting up his lunch.

"What is it? What's happened?" Gean Choo asked. Before Po Lam could stop her, she broke away and approached the crowd, forcing Po Lam to follow.

Some poor soul had been struck on the tracks, and the force had shorn his head clean off his body. It stared up into that grey sky, blood pooling below it. He looked young, his brown forehead smooth and clear. Pretty, too. Mrs. Edevane wouldn't have complained too much if she'd brought him home for supper.

The body was a good ten yards distant, looking strange and disconsolate without its head. Blood had splashed the railway track, mixing with the puddles, painting the whole scene red.

Ah Mui wailed. Po Lam nudged the back of Gean Choo's leg with a suitcase to get her attention. "Let's go," she said. It wasn't prudent to expose children to so much death.

They left the crowd of railway workers, moving closer to the cabin. Someone was crying on the train. The little boy who'd asked about elephants, maybe.

"We should get back," Gean Choo said. "I'm sure... I'm sure we'll start moving soon, and then—"

"No," Po Lam said. Go back? After an omen so clear, the heavens might as well have been shouting at them?

"But—"

"No!" Po Lam tried to soften her voice. "Who knows if they'll be ready before nightfall? We must be moving by then."

Gean Choo glanced longingly at the train, probably thinking of all it represented—order, safety.

But it was all a lie. Mrs. Edevane could easily kill them in a crowd, the laws of her kind be damned. She wasn't meant to upset the delicate balance, to alert humans to her presence, but when did she ever play by the rules?

Beyond the railway line, roads and the rooves of buildings peeked through the trees. They headed towards them, Ah Mui still red-faced and tearful. How many stations had they passed this afternoon? They were probably still in Province Wellesley.

The sounds of city life grew louder—the rumble of motorcars, the cries of hawkers. An ordinary afternoon on an ordinary day.

She picked a road a little way off a major thoroughfare. It was nigh on evening, on a weekday—imperfect timing, but it would have to do.

As luck would have it, she spotted a perfectly suitable mark just pulling into their side street. She dropped the suitcases, then pulled out her billfold and counted out some notes, wadding them up in a separate roll, which she stuck in her pocket. "Wait here," she said to Gean Choo.

"But—"

Po Lam was already moving, one hand below her jacket. Up ahead, a European couple were alighting from their red Austin. Their Malay driver held the door open for the lady until she got out, taking her husband's hand. They walked off in the direction of the shops.

The driver came around the opposite side of the car, about to get back in. Po Lam approached him. He didn't notice her until she was almost on top of him.

She pressed the muzzle of the revolver against his side and wrapped her hand around his mouth, holding him tight against her. "Don't move," she said. "I have a gun."

His gaze dropped to it, catching the gleam of metal. He tried to say something, but she didn't let him.

"I'll give you twelve hundred for the car. You (
employer as compensation, or you can take it and st
else. I don't care. But if you scream or make trouble, 1 m .
you understand."

His eyes closed in resignation as he nodded.

She lowered her hand from his mouth, grabbed the bills from her pocket, and thrust them into his fist. He stared at them, his jaw dropping. He'd probably never touched a thousand-dollar note.

"Go on," Po Lam said sharply.

The notes disappeared into his sleeve, and he ran without looking back.

Po Lam holstered the gun and adjusted the line of her jacket. She glanced at Gean Choo and waved her over.

Gean Choo took the suitcases and came. "I can't believe it," she began. "You... he—"

"It'd take too long to find a hire car." Po Lam consulted her watch. Six-forty-five. Almost dark. She took the suitcases from Gean Choo's nerveless grip and stowed them in the back.

"You've cost that man his job. He might have children—"

"He can still work, can't he? And he was well compensated. Get in."

Gean Choo braced her hand on the doorframe, trembling. "Would you have shot him?"

Probably not. Knifing him would've drawn less attention. Po Lam eyed her over the car bonnet. "I didn't have to."

"I know, but—"

"It's done," Po Lam said. She stripped off her jacket, revealing the revolver holstered by her side, and slid into the car. After a moment, Gean Choo did the same, closing her door with more force than was strictly necessary.

Po Lam would've burned down the whole world to keep them safe. Gean Choo opened her mouth to speak, but Po Lam wasn't done.

"No one matters. No one else, except—" Po Lam's hands tightened on the wheel, and she clenched her jaw shut.

she were braver, she'd have finished that sentence. Just one little .d. Why was it so hard?

Because she was weaker than she needed to be. Because she couldn't stand being rejected again—it would end her. If she couldn't have what she wanted, then at least she could pretend a little longer. Didn't they say ignorance was bliss?

She started the car, the engine roaring to life, and pulled away as the sun sank below the horizon.

# CHAPTER 57

# NOT THIS TIME

## VERITY

*One day prior*
*Tuesday, 17 April 1928*
*One day since last meal*

I t could've been another trick, something to throw her off guard so he could come back in and gloat. *Did you think you were going to escape? Blah, blah, blah.*

She flexed her toes experimentally. Her feet moved back and forth, side to side. When she tried to tense her hands, the cuffs made a small clink. She stopped, listening for returning footsteps, but no one came.

Maybe by ingesting part of her he'd done something to dilute his own control, inoculated her against his gift—the very opposite of what he'd been trying to achieve. Ironic.

The "how" didn't matter; it only mattered what she did with this moment.

Some tiny, rebellious part of her didn't want to move. What if he came back and was even angrier with her than before? Then again, there wasn't much more he could take from her. Her vision. Her beauty. Would she heal? Maybe not this time.

It was tempting to settle down in her rage, to give in to the fury, which was the only thing distracting her from the pain. But all that would have to wait until she escaped somewhere safe. If she could ever feel safe again.

Right, then. She tugged on the restraints holding down her ankles, trying and failing to lift her legs. Next, she tried rocking her weight, in case she could tip the table over and potentially break it, but it failed to move, possibly bolted to the floor.

This had taken no more than a few minutes, but each minute weighed on her like hours. The lights glared overhead, too hot and bright. She had to hurry. There was no knowing when he might come back.

Her hands were cuffed to each other, but not to the table, the needle still sticking out of her right arm, draining her. She could move them to either side and towards the ceiling. The instrument tray was still out of reach unless she had her left hand free. Then there was a chance—a small chance—she could lean over and touch it.

She waved her cuffed hands straight up into the air but couldn't reach the naked lightbulbs hanging overhead. There was nothing else within range. Well, that wasn't quite true.

There was always her. She was a weapon, an instrument of destruction.

Verity shivered.

She wasted twenty precious seconds waffling back-and-forth upon the subject. Her hands would heal once the coagulant wore off, and her stump already itched. She wouldn't be without an index finger forever, but the same couldn't be said about her eye.

Verity raised her cuffed hands to her face. If she did this, she'd have to break the joint at the very base of her thumb. The cuff was solid steel, without any give.

She was going to need so many drugs by the time she was done.

Verity shuffled her hands close to her face. At least Kalon hadn't taken her teeth.

*Oh, shut up. Stop thinking about him.*

She placed her left thumb into her mouth and bit.

Her jaw wasn't strong enough to get a clean cut on the first try. The pain seared through her, a fresh wave of it, her mouth filling with the awful sweet-salt-savoury bliss of her own blood. She probably wasn't meant to enjoy the taste quite this much.

Once she'd finally gnawed through the last strip of her skin, she spat out the offending digit, and it skidded somewhere on the floor. She ought to burn it, in case Kalon used it for one of his horrible experiments, but she didn't have the time.

She tried the cuff. Still too tight, even with blood slicking the metal. Well, no sense in dawdling. She had to lunge for her bleeding left hand, sink her teeth around the remaining bulk of metacarpal, and tear it from its meaty throne of flesh.

Her hand slipped out like a greased pig. She rested for two beats, then forced herself to stir, ripping out the needle from her right arm. Blood ran freely down her elbow, dripping over the table. She reached out, crimson-sticky fingers slapping over the edge of the instrument tray. She avoided the calligraphy brush and the bloodied cloth, instead reaching for a scalpel, fumbling to grasp it between her index and middle finger. It was surprising, really, how much one missed a thumb when it was gone.

The cuffs didn't have a particularly complex lock. A bit of fiddling with her makeshift shim and her right hand was free without having to resort to self-mutilation. It was just as well. Her head was light; the stress of this ordeal was getting to her.

With her hands free, it was a simple thing to grab the cutter from the tray, the same one Kalon had used to take her finger, its jaws red with blood. She cut through the rest of her restraints and slid off the table, swaying, then clutched it for support, leaning heavily. She needed a good hot bath and a couple of young women, but neither was in sight.

As desperate as she was to leave this chamber of horrors, she paused to put on a glove and pick up the bottle of holy water, opening it and holding it carefully in her mangled left hand, fingers pressing it tightly against her palm, the cutters in her less-damaged right. Both hands throbbed, as though they each had a separate pulse of their own.

It was finally time to leave.

The stairwell was poorly lit by a single, flickering bulb, throwing

,ainst the exposed brick. Something crunched underfoot as she
ra.. ᵉ stairs.

As she neared the top, the door opened, letting in a faint beam of light, Kalon silhouetted against it. His eyes widened when he saw her and he opened his mouth. Whatever he was planning to say, she couldn't ever let him say it.

She swung the bottle, throwing the liquid onto his face. One of his arms moved up to shield himself, and the water hissed as it touched his skin. Kalon's beautiful voice erupted in a howl. Parts of his arm sloughed off, the skin melting as if she'd just simmered him in a pot for twelve hours. His naked ulna gleamed creamy white.

Verity lunged while he was still standing there, trying to move his jaw, half his chin liquefied away, exposing his teeth. She'd never seen anything more revolting. She smashed the cutter into his face, once, twice, a million times. There was no finesse, nothing graceful about what she was doing, only the raw desperation to never hear his voice again.

Even when he'd fallen—first to his knees, then to the ground, his face a pulpy mess, his tongue unrecognisable—it wasn't done. Verity seized him by the ankle and dragged him down the steps, letting the remains of his face schlep in an undignified trail of gore down the staircase, each footstep loud, echoing. In the chamber, she rolled him over, sat on his chest and used the bone saw to take off his head, her right hand clutching the handle, left on top to stabilise it. Her grip was so sticky with blood, it kept slipping.

Right up until the end, he kept trying to vocalise, but whatever it was, she couldn't make out the words.

"There, there," she said as she sliced through his spinal column. Her vision stuttered in and out, eyes stinging with blood. His head came loose from his body, the saw clattering when it hit one of the grates. After it was done, she hugged her knees to her chest for a moment and rocked, making a dull noise at the back of her throat like a suppressed moan.

VERITY ROUSED herself sometime later and trudged up the stairs, finding herself in a secluded corner of Kalon's garden. When she approached the kitchen, humans scattered at the sight of her. Admittedly, she didn't look her best, her finger and thumb still regrowing with a horrible itch. When she reached out and grabbed a fleeing woman, draining her with neither delicacy nor appreciation, her right index finger finished its ascension and popped into place, skin shiny-pink and tight with newness.

She found the storeroom and fetched a kerosene can before returning to the chamber. It was almost a shock to find his body still there, unmoving. She poured fuel all around it. A match reflected orange against the pool of blood surrounding him. When she dropped it on the corpse, it burned blue for a moment, flames leaping up to cradle the exposed light bulbs, glass breaking from the heat.

She trudged back into the night. Her trembling hand, thumb halfway grown, drifted up to touch the ridges of scar tissue on her cheek. Would Pearl even recognise her? With her beauty gone, would she still want her?

Where was Pearl, anyway? That little tugging at the back of her mind directed her attention somewhere north. Distant. Far too distant.

She'd fucking left her. After everything Verity had done for her, everything she'd sacrificed, everything she'd endured—

Her face burned with unceasing agony. It was fortunate she didn't need to breathe, because she couldn't, not in that moment. Her legs wouldn't support her weight. She grasped one of the columns on Kalon's verandah, leaning against it. Her vision went red, black, red.

Someone was going to die for this.

# CHAPTER 58

# YOU PROMISED

## GEAN CHOO

*Wednesday, 18 April 1928*

Gean Choo found the strangers' car less comfortable than the mem's, but despite that, she'd managed to doze a little, only waking when Po Lam shut the door with a thud. The lack of weight against her chest made her breathless for a moment, until she glimpsed Ah Mui swaddled against Po Lam's chest.

Po Lam unslung Ah Mui, handing her back, along with a fresh bottle and a canteen of water. Gean Choo rubbed the sleep from her eyes, stifling a yawn as Po Lam started the car. They'd parked outside a row of shops, their signs difficult to read in the dark.

An hour later, they were still on the road, somewhere distant from civilisation, the way now bumpy and filled with potholes. Ah Mui had spent the last dozen miles crying, fraying all their nerves, and only now seemed to doze off into a restless sleep.

The train had probably overtaken them long ago. Why had Po Lam been so adamant about not continuing their journey? It didn't make sense. The roads were a far cry from the sleek lines of the track.

That poor dead man. His poor family! Suicides were condemned to wander across their own plane of hell, hounded by the winds of sorrow. Would his mother pray for him?

Her eyes burned with tears, and she blinked them away. She stretched and curled her toes, doing her best not to stare into the darkness just outside her window. The sounds were all different at night, with virtually no traffic and more wildlife, or at least it seemed that way. She shivered as a monkey screeched somewhere far above them. Unlike Singapore, the peninsula had not yet lost all its tigers.

She glanced at Po Lam, at her hands clenched on the wheel, at the firm set of her lips. They'd barely spoken since getting into this car. "Do you mean to drive all night?" Gean Choo asked. "You need rest."

"I'll sleep on the next train. We should find the nearest station, closer to morning. The track should be clear by now. And then—"

"And then the train to Bangkok."

"Correct." Po Lam took her eyes off the road for a second, glancing at Gean Choo before she looked back at the road. "Would you want to stay with me? You and Ah Mui?"

Gean Choo inhaled, exhaled, her mind dizzy. It didn't seem the sort of question that deserved just a yes or no answer. "Are we having the conversation you said you didn't want to have until we were in Siam?"

"No," Po Lam said. "We're not in Siam."

"Then I don't know."

It was hard to tell in the dark, but Po Lam looked as if she didn't know whether to be exasperated with her or not. Then her expression changed, flicking to the mirrors. Her foot came down heavy on the accelerator and the car leapt forwards with a growl, pressing Gean Choo against her seat.

Something moved up ahead of them. A shadow, a spectre... Gean Choo screamed, "Stop!"

The darkness before them coalesced into something with a shape. A face. Mrs. Edevane stood in the middle of the road, hair unbound and wild, feet bare, her pale dress dark and clinging with blood. She stared them down, unmoving, even as the car jounced along the dirt road towards her.

The headlights picked out the gleam of her eyes. Something... something was wrong with her face. Skin wasn't meant to look like that, as if some malicious spirit had reached out and turned half her flesh to clay, reshaping the contours of her brows, the bridge of her nose. Darker red flesh reached tendrils down her cheek, fractured now by tributaries of raised scar tissue.

Monstrous.

Mrs. Edevane reached out her hand, palm upturned. *Come with me.*

Gean Choo screamed again.

The car flowed through her as though she were nothing more than a cloud, an illusion. Ah Mui was crying. Gean Choo twisted in her seat, glancing behind. There was nothing there save for the shadows of trees and the empty stretch of road disappearing behind them.

"Stop," she said again. She reached for the wheel. It was heavier than she'd expected. Po Lam jerked it from her grasp. The car zigzagged, throwing her against the side door, Ah Mui's crying reaching a fever pitch. Po Lam finally managed to straighten the car before it skidded to a halt.

She needed a second to catch her breath. But beside her, silent and grim, Po Lam was already reaching for something wedged between her seat and the door.

"No," Gean Choo said, when she realised what Po Lam was holding. "No! Let me talk to her. You promised me, you *promised*—"

Po Lam raised her revolver, aimed, and fired.

Glass rained down, shards rolling into the cabin. Gean Choo clutched Ah Mui to her chest, covering her with her arms.

It took her a moment to see what Po Lam had seen. Mrs. Edevane, caught in the headlights, the wind teasing out her unbound hair. Mrs. Edevane pressed her fingertips against her sternum and then held them before her eyes, staring at them as though in wonder.

Po Lam shot her again. The sound would've been deafening if her ears hadn't already been ringing. This one hit Mrs. Edevane's shoulder, jerking her back.

She staggered.

Fell.

Gean Choo's hand shot to the door handle. She opened the door, then took off the baby sling, sweeping the empty seat for glass before placing Ah Mui down.

"What are you doing? Get back in the car!"

Gean Choo ignored her plea, as Po Lam had ignored hers. She had to see this through to the end.

On the deserted stretch of road, Mrs. Edevane was groaning, sprawled out on her side, one palm pressed over the bullet wound in her chest. Gean Choo approached slowly, shoes crunching along the dirt path, and stopped a good twelve feet away.

She stood frozen, certain she'd made a mistake. It was hard to tell at first because the fabric was ruined, torn and soaked in blood, but wasn't that one of Miss Skelford's dresses, the waffle fabric in pale yellow? Why was she wearing that?

Mrs. Edevane swivelled her head towards her. "You left me." Her voice was hoarse and broken, taut with pain. Black blood poured from her gunshot wounds, dripping over her hand and down her arm. Her face was riddled with scar tissue, the skin fused and melted around her eyes and tracing down her cheek. On her forehead, the flesh had worn so thin as to reveal the veins beneath, pitted and textured like dried durian.

Gean Choo had never seen anything like it. "I'm sorry you're hurt, Mrs. Edevane."

The mem's breath came out part wheeze, part hiss. Was she... laughing? Mrs. Edevane stretched out her hands, digging her fingernails into the dirt. She dragged her weight across the road, crawling inch by torturous inch towards Gean Choo. "Come here," she said. "Come here and show me how much you love me."

"Walk away from her. Please."

Gean Choo glanced behind. Po Lam had stepped out of the car, both hands on her revolver, slowly advancing.

Mrs. Edevane lifted her head. "This is all the thanks I get from you, San Po Lam? I took you in when no one else would. I protected you from your former mistress. I raised your entire family out of poverty—"

Po Lam raised her arms and took aim.

# READER'S CHOICE

To save Mrs. Edevane: continue reading.

To save Po Lam: skip to chapter 64, page 393.

# SAVE MRS. EDEVANE

# CHAPTER 59

## SAVE MRS. EDEVANE

There was no time to think. She simply acted. Whether from fear, love, or some strange mixture of the two, she couldn't tell. It simply was.

Gean Choo lunged, pushing Po Lam off-balance. The shot went wide, sailing harmlessly over Mrs. Edevane's shoulder.

Po Lam staggered upright, staring at her in open-mouthed shock. "This ends tonight!" she snapped and raised the revolver again.

Gean Choo threw herself in the way, standing before Mrs. Edevane with her arms outstretched, facing Po Lam. "No! I said stop!"

Rain started falling, softly at first, but then whole sheets of water came down as though some god had upended a bucket over the world. They were all soaked in only a few moments, the road turning to slurry beneath their feet. She didn't dare glance behind to check if Mrs. Edevane was still alive.

Po Lam didn't lower her arms. "Why?" There was so much pain in that single utterance, it was as if Gean Choo had flayed her alive. The rain plastered her hair to her head and her vest and shirt against her chest, revealing the small, flat buttons of the undergarment beneath.

Gean Choo didn't know why, couldn't explain it in a way that would've satisfied Po Lam in that moment, and left all their hearts unbroken. "I can't let you kill her," she said. She backed away and crouched, turning to Mrs. Edevane at last, confident that Po Lam would not shoot when there was the chance to injure them both. Mrs. Edevane—her mistress, her lover, her superior in every way that mattered—raised her eyes, one whole, one blind, to Gean Choo, her lips slightly parted.

"You foolish girl," Mrs. Edevane said, her voice husky and low. She stretched out her hand and traced the curve of Gean Choo's cheek. Her fingers seemed colder than usual.

Gean Choo slipped her hand against Mrs. Edevane's palm, lacing their fingers together. "Please don't die." She upturned her hand, offering her wrist.

"No!" Po Lam pushed Gean Choo aside until her fingers wrenched free from Mrs. Edevane's grasp. Quicker than she'd thought possible, Mrs. Edevane reached for Po Lam with a snarl, lunging as though her body had been one big coil waiting to strike. Her arm curled around Po Lam's chest and there was a horrible, strange noise like Po Lam's ribs were breaking. She sank her fangs into Po Lam's neck and the revolver dropped from nerveless fingers.

Gean Choo screamed. Her eyes locked with Po Lam over Mrs. Edevane's shoulder. Po Lam's accusing stare went glassy, then blank, then dropped altogether as her head slumped.

Gean Choo fell to her knees and fumbled in the mud, her hand closing in on something hard and metallic. She almost recoiled from the feel of it, that heavy and alien steel. The rain made it slippery and foreign in her hands, the barrel wavering as she raised it.

Mrs. Edevane dropped Po Lam's body. She wiped her chin as she rose, tall and regal, unbowed by the sleeting rain. "Pearl, darling, don't be squeamish now. You made your choice, didn't you? The right one."

All of this was wrong. She was wrong. She couldn't fix this. Couldn't go back. What had she done?

Her tears mixed with the rain streaming down her face, each droplet like a shard of glass pinging against her skin. Her arms shook. She squeezed the trigger, but nothing happened. A jam, maybe, or perhaps she wasn't meant to let it get wet—

Mrs. Edevane plucked the revolver from her grip and threw it away. She gazed down at Gean Choo with a smile on her face, the right side twisted with scar tissue. She began to laugh, quietly at first, then working herself into a crescendo, her head thrown back, water sluicing down her pale, long neck.

Blood ran from Po Lam's body, pulled by gravity towards them. Mrs. Edevane didn't seem to notice, but Gean Choo cried harder when the flecks of pinkish dirt touched the knees of her skirt.

The rain washed the hole in Mrs. Edevanc's—in Miss Skelford's dress, the water streaming down pink-tinged. Tiny splinters of wood pushed out from the wound in her chest as her skin began to heal over.

Mrs. Edevane crouched and took her hands, bringing Gean Choo's knuckles to her mouth, kissing them. First the left, then the right.

"Sweetheart," she said, her voice breathy, a lounge singer's croon, "no one has ever done anything like that for me before. I'll never forget this."

"Please, just let me go. The baby and me... we'll never bother you again, we won't tell anyone, I swear—"

"Go? Go where? You must understand, you saved my life. I can't just let you go with such a debt hanging between us."

Gean Choo bowed her head. Saved her life by paying for it with Po Lam's. "There's no debt, Mrs.—Verity, I absolve you. There's nothing more between us—"

"Nonsense." Her tone was brisk and sharp. "Why can't you just say it, Pearl? Say you want me. You need me." The ruins of her face softened. "You love me. Why else would you choose me over her?"

It was hard to breathe with her throat wracked with sobs. She didn't know. *She didn't know.* Why had she saved her? Who in their right mind would want this?

Mrs. Edevane was still holding on to her hands. She upturned the left, kissed Gean Choo's palm, and then her fingers, one by one. "We've a long night ahead of us. I know you won't begrudge me this one small bite."

She'd offered herself freely, but that had been before Po Lam's lifeless body had fallen from Mrs. Edevane's arms. Now she leaned away, tugging backwards, but Mrs. Edevane held her wrist close and wrapped her other arm around Gean Choo's waist.

She had to love her, surely. Why would this be happening if she didn't love her? How else could she justify this nightmare?

Mrs. Edevane released her wrist, reached up, and turned Gean Choo's head to the side, baring her neck, then bit. The pain was a relief and a release. Here, at last, was something she could let herself feel.

Ah Mui was crying again. Wait... She had to lull her to sleep, to silence. Mrs. Edevane hated the sound of crying. Ah Mui didn't know any better; she was only a baby. *She didn't know—*

## CHAPTER 60

# THE CRUELTY OF LIFE

## VERITY

*Thursday, 19 April 1928*
*Zero nights since last meal*

Pearl slumped in her arms, unconscious. Verity hadn't taken too much, as Pearl still hadn't recovered since the last time. At least that deceitful Po Lam had been good for something, providing enough nourishment for them to make it back to civilisation where Verity could feed again. Those bullets had been frightful, like molten lava. Whatever evil Kalon had injected into her veins surely hadn't helped.

She set Pearl down in the back seat of the car, making sure her arms were all inside before she closed the door. Pearl's head flopped against the seat, her heartbeat almost inaudible under the rain.

That little brat was still crying. Verity paused by the side of the car and turned her damaged face towards it. The baby sniffled and quietened in the face of this perceived threat, then started again.

They were out in the middle of nowhere. No cars, no livestock, not even the distant rattle of the train.

Verity reached down and picked up the child, then unceremoniously dumped her by the side of the road. If she were lucky, someone would find her. If not, well... such was the cruelty of life. It was still a better fate than growing up to be one of Kalon's slaves.

She brushed glass from the driver's seat before getting in and starting the car, turning it around. The vision in her right eye was getting worse. At this rate, she'd be completely blind before sunrise. No time to waste, then.

She glanced back at Pearl, seeing her for what could be the last time. Her tousled hair, damp with rainwater and tears. The plumpness of her cheeks, the soft pillow of her lips.

If she couldn't find a way to reverse the damage in her sight, she'd need people she could trust completely. Not another Po Lam. Humans with unimpeachable loyalty.

Thralls.

# CHAPTER 61

# THE ONLY CHOICE

## GEAN CHOO

*Thursday, 19 April 1928*

Perhaps Gean Choo had already died and gone to hell, waiting for one of the ten kings of the underworld to assign her punishment. Maybe she hadn't killed her father, but she was certainly responsible for Po Lam's death.

She saw the moon, once or twice. It was almost full, bloated and glowing. Like something in a dream. Was she dreaming? Please, let this be a dream.

She must've fallen unconscious at some point, for when she woke up, she was in a bed. Not Mrs. Edevane's bed. There were no drapes here, just crisp white sheets, and the sharp, chemical smell of paint.

She tried to sit up and whimpered at the pain lancing through her neck. Her tongue was unpleasantly furred, like the inside of a used pipe, a migraine pounding at her head. She reached up and touched her hair. Bone dry. Had she slept through a whole day?

The unfamiliar room was richly furnished, the floors hardwood, the furniture the same. Two large beds sat side by side, the other one empty, its covers thrown back. The next room over had a little sitting area with stuffed sofas and armchairs, a writing desk, and even a separate dining set.

The cocktail table held an array of shopping bags, overflowing with delicate tissue paper and jewel-toned fabric.

Beyond the sitting area, glass-panelled doors stood open to the night, curtains billowing in the breeze. The air held the tang of salt. Someone had painted the glass all black, defeating its purpose.

That explained the smell.

"You're awake. I didn't want to head off without seeing you."

Gean Choo forced herself to sit up. Mrs. Edevane stood in the shadow of one of the screens, a sleek narrow shape in wide-legged pants and a black blouse. When she stepped into the light, Gean Choo gasped.

The damage she'd seen the night before was even more shocking once illuminated. Both of Mrs. Edevane's eyes were milky, not just the right one. The deep-set eye sockets and stretched scar tissue made her resemble a corpse—desiccated, vile. At last, her appearance matched her heart. As if sensing her scrutiny, she reached behind her head and flipped a gauzy black veil over her face.

"I need to make a few calls before we leave," Mrs. Edevane said. "We'll take the next ship to Hong Kong."

No, Gean Choo wasn't going on a steamer; she had to take the train to —oh. An invisible fist squeezed her heart. She imagined it turning to pulp.

"There'll be..." Mrs. Edevane paused, her head swivelling to face the curtains, "five of us."

Gean Choo glanced to the other side of the room. She hadn't seen the man standing there, so quiet and still. He looked at her with the same empty eyes shared by Lord Cottesley's servants. A thrall. Two more men stood on the balcony, facing the ocean, hands clasped behind their backs. "You promised you'd never own a thrall," Gean Choo said.

"Ha!" To her surprise, Mrs. Edevane brought her knuckles to her face. Was she... crying? She wiped her hand across her eyes. "Well, needs must, dear. I'm in need of good help right now, as you can see."

"Where's Ah Mui?"

Mrs. Edevane fiddled with the edge of her veil. "The child? I dropped her off at the orphanage. A ship is no place for a baby."

"Which orphanage?"

She waved a hand vaguely. "The boys saw to it. I'm not so familiar with Penang."

Penang... they'd backtracked a little, now southwest of where the train had stopped. Mrs. Edevane must've loaded her onto a ferry at some point, but she had no memory of any such event. "I'd like to see her."

"We don't have time for this, Pearl. I'm a bit impaired at the moment... and not through any fault of my own!"

Mrs. Edevane's injuries were damning, indeed. Here was proof she could be hurt, could be changed. How fragile she'd looked, despite her monstrosity. Was that it? Was that why Gean Choo had tried to save her?

She'd been wrong. So, so wrong... and she hadn't even paid the price. She'd ended two lives with her stupidity—Po Lam's and Ah Mui's. Three, counting Bee Leng. Her list of sins grew steeper by the minute.

"If you so desperately want to be a mother, we'll pick up a new child in Hong Kong. No more infants, though. We'll get one who already knows how to stay quiet. Would you like that? A girl, maybe. It's always easier to find families trying to get rid of those."

It only confirmed what Gean Choo had already known. Their lives were interchangeable, meaningless to their employer. Mrs. Edevane didn't even seem to care that Po Lam was gone, that she'd killed her. That Gean Choo had killed her, tearing an enormous void into the fabric of the universe. Had Mrs. Edevane just left her? Probably. Left Po Lam to rot on the roadside or to be savaged by wild animals as though it meant nothing, as if she were nothing.

Gean Choo sat back down on the bed, that strange new bed in this bland, sterile room. It seemed impossible for her to be here, still alive and breathing. Obscene.

"Shh, Pearl, please," Mrs. Edevane said, the bed creaking as she sat next to her. "Hong Kong is so lively and gay. You'll love it there, you really will. A new country, a new view—a new start for both of us, darling. Don't you worry about a thing. Your mem will take care of you, just like you took care of her."

Gean Choo stared at her through the veil, at those filmy, sightless eyes, the red ropes of scar tissue across her forehead. "Did you... do something to me? Did you make me save you?"

The smile froze on Mrs. Edevane's face. She smoothed her hand over the coverlet, her lips pursed. "Would you like me to tell you it was impossible to resist, that there's some corruption in your blood, some taint I've placed there by virtue of our proximity? How the choice wasn't yours to make?

"The truth is, I couldn't say why you stayed. I'm grateful, don't misunderstand me, and touched by your loyalty, but also... I can't explain it. Not in a way that you'd like. Love acts in mysterious ways, doesn't it? And I do so love you, Pearl, you must know that. It's only natural you should love me back."

"I don't love you."

Mrs. Edevane laughed, short and sharp. "Don't be ridiculous." She stood and groped her way along the wall, outstretched hands tentative, spidery. She found the writing desk, sat beside it, and picked up a telephone receiver.

"Wait!" Gean Choo made up her mind. "I-I'm hungry. I haven't eaten all day."

Mrs. Edevane lowered the receiver, turning towards her. "After the ordeal you put me through, I can't bear to have you out of my sight. Out of my—" Her jaw clenched. "One of the boys will bring something back for you." She gestured, and the closest man came over to them. Mrs. Edevane turned her attention back to the telephone, speaking to the operator.

The man looked at Gean Choo expectantly. He was an Indian man, about as old as her father would've been, dressed in a khaki-coloured uniform. Had it hurt? When Mrs. Edevane had done... whatever it was that had turned him into this?

She couldn't save him. She couldn't even save herself.

"I'd like something fermented, if you can find it," Gean Choo murmured. "Stinky tofu, or noodles with belacan."

The man bowed and left. Mrs. Edevane made her calls, and Gean Choo slid back against the pillow, staring up at the ceiling. She could do this. She *had* to do this.

It was the only choice left for her to make.

ONCE THE MAN WAS GONE, leaving just the two others on the balcony, Gean Choo padded towards the door in her stockinged feet.

Mrs. Edevane placed her hand over the receiver and lowered it, turning her head. "Pearl," she snapped. One small word imbued with so much venom.

When Gean Choo stepped away from the door, Mrs. Edevane returned to her phone call.

Her meal arrived sometime later. She ought to have been too nauseated to eat, but instead her mouth watered at the savoury aroma.

Mrs. Edevane was not so pleased. "That stench! Take that outside."

Gean Choo sat at the small balcony table, flanked by looming thralls. A breeze wafted the curtains behind her. The night sky was beautiful, wasn't it? Tears blurred her vision. She blinked them away.

They were only one floor above ground level. She eyed the thralls. They eyed her back. How quickly would they move? She couldn't risk it.

When she'd finished, leaving a good amount of pungent shrimp paste in her abandoned bowl, Mrs. Edevane was still on the phone. "No, I told you, just put it through to the King Edward Hotel. The one in Hong Kong. That's right. I know, but it's only temporary—"

Gean Choo walked past. "I'm taking a bath," she announced to the air, since Mrs. Edevane was paying her not the slightest bit of attention.

Someone had brought up her luggage. Rifling through it, Gean Choo only found the softness of clothing. Mrs. Edevane must've removed her pistol.

She closed her eyes, clenching her hands to stop them from shaking. She could do this. She could.

Gean Choo stripped her bed of its sheet and took it into the bathroom, then started the water in the enormous English tub. The sound was loud, echoing against the tiles. The faucet was polished to such a mirror gleam that her reflection stared back at her, distorted.

She shook out the sheet, then twisted it neatly into a rope, working fast. She glanced around the bathroom. There was a central light fixture, but it would be awkward to reach. There was also a hook set into the wall, around waist height.

She knotted the sheet around the hook, then tugged. It seemed secure.

The tub was halfway full. Was Mrs. Edevane still on the phone? Impossible to tell with the sound of the water, but she couldn't turn off the tap just to check.

She knelt on the tiles and slipped her head into the cloth loop. It had a fresh cottony scent, crisp and clean. Clean in a way she could never be again.

She clasped her hands behind herself. Maybe she ought to have bound them. Maybe—

The tub was almost full. Once it started overflowing, the sound would change, and eventually, the water would soak into the rugs outside and draw Mrs. Edevane's attention. She had to stop stalling.

Gean Choo closed her eyes and let herself fall.

## CHAPTER 62

# FOR YOU

### VERITY

*Friday, 20 April 1928*
*One day since last meal*

I t was just past midnight, but already Verity longed to sleep for a thousand years. So much still to plan, to do. How she loathed maritime travel, the indignity of it all. She'd be compelled to travel as cargo, guarded by her thralls as she dreamt the dreamless sleep of the dead. It was the safest way to avoid sunlight and unpleasant questions.

She'd need new thralls when they arrived in Hong Kong. These ones seemed, well... they were adequate. She didn't have Kalon's gift, nor the fine control that came with practise.

She ought to have eaten his tongue, but no, she couldn't have, even if she could've persuaded herself to do something so disgusting. Even if his theory had been correct. The holy water had taken care of that.

In the end, what had it all been for? Those years of deprivation, of starvation, of weathering the social stigma from not toeing the party line. It had been worth it before, when every snub had meant she was doing something right, taking a stance, holding her ground.

She wasn't ashamed to admit she'd had a little cry after it'd been done, bathing her failing eyesight in blood until all she could see was red. Scarlet, crimson, rose... then nothing but black. The boys had stood by and watched, stoic, silent, uncaring. She'd been crying for them, for the awfulness of the whole matter, and they hadn't even known it.

Everything had crumbled to ash after that night, that awful night when she and Pearl had fought. If they hadn't fought, then nothing bad would've happened. The killing spree. Justine. Kalon getting his hands dirty.

So she was already in quite a mood when Pearl locked herself away and refused to answer. She banged on the bathroom door. "Pearl, come and open the door this instant!" Verity punched through the door's frosted glass panel, shards chiming as they hit the tiles. She groped for the locking mechanism.

Humidity blanketed her skin as she opened the door. Her footsteps broke the rhythm of running water, splashing against the wet floor. She ran and hit her shin against the tub. That damnable noise—she couldn't think. She groped around the bath and turned off the taps.

"Pearl... what have you done? You little fool!"

She found her at the far wall. Pearl was warm and floppy, with the limpness of a fresh corpse. Her makeshift noose tangled in Verity's hands as she struggled to free her.

Verity patted her cheeks. "Wake up. Wake *up*." Could she still swallow, or would blood only run down her chin? An irrational burst of laughter bubbled up to Verity's lips. How could Pearl do this to her? How could she choose the void over a lifetime of being cosseted, cherished, loved by her?

She knelt on the wet tiles, one hand braced against the back of Pearl's skull, cradling her like a child. She'd never done this before. In the almost two centuries since her Rebirth, she'd never wanted the burden of a fledgling, that awful unbreakable thread connecting another soul to hers. Kalon would know what to do, but Kalon...

Well, fuck.

She brought her own wrist to her mouth, tore her skin with her teeth, and pressed it against Pearl's lips. "Drink, damn you. Drink!"

Her blood drained out, plinking as it dripped onto the tiles. Maybe she wasn't strong enough; maybe there was something wrong with her, something missing. Nonsense! Idiots fledged all the time. Maybe the problem was Pearl. Maybe she was already gone, vacating her body as though she had somewhere else to be.

What had Kalon said about fledging, curse his name? *Not all ailments can be cured.* Had Pearl damaged herself irrevocably? Would Verity be raising a monster from the dead, condemning a soulless cripple to eternal life? No. No, she couldn't believe that.

Verity shook her by the shoulder. "Pearl, darling, listen to me. I can fix this. I can fix you. Only drink, sweetheart, taste me—don't you know what an honour I'm offering you? You'll be the heir to a great line, descended from Duchess Bennesbrook herself. We'll have parties again, we'll have dancing—all those glorious nights, year after year, century after century. Don't you dare leave me, Pearl! Don't you dare! I gave you everything! I killed for you! You don't know—how could you know?—the crimes I've committed for you."

Tears rolled down from her wounded, useless eyes, sliding along her cheeks and dripping off the end of her chin. "Only for you, darling. Everything I ever had. For you."

# CHAPTER 63

## EPILOGUE

Y ou wake in a pile of limbs like a penitent in the fifteenth layer of
hell. They flop this way and that as you climb out from the
middle of them, unable to trace each body to its adjoining head,
there are so many.

Sightless eyes stare back at you—men, women, neither. They're
clothed, but their clothes are torn, collars ripped and buttons missing.
Some of them look as though they've been savaged by wild animals, their
throats bloody gashes of brutalised flesh, red and ugly with broken skin
ragged at the edges.

Your head pounds like the skin of a temple drum.

You push the nearest bodies away, clearing a space to stand. The room
is unfamiliar, lush with textiles, the white walls decorated with blood
spatter.

Your stomach clenches. You press a hand over your mouth, forcing
yourself to breathe. Haven't you been breathing? Your palm comes away,
rust-like flakes of drying blood covering you to the elbows. You stare at
your hand as if you've never seen it before.

Outside the room is a huge skylight, open to the stars. Downstairs, an
indoor fountain, Psyche pouring water as Eros watches on. You stagger to
the edge of the railing.

The stars seem dim compared to the electric light flooding this house, this mansion. The lights are too bright, making rainbows at the corners of your vision. Everything seems too sharp, too real. The tiny hairs on the back of your hands. The pores of your skin, enormous and grotesque.

You smell her before you see her, some indefinable mix of damask rose and honey threaded with the coppery undertones of blood. It makes your throat ache.

"Darling, you've decided to join us! I was beginning to worry."

A European lady waits for you at the bottom of the stairs, her yellow hair shining beneath the lamps. She raises a glass to you in welcome, the liquid inside gleaming red. Despite your full stomach, your mouth waters. You descend the staircase, one step at a time, so as not to trip over the hem of your too-long nightdress. It was white, once, but is now stained crimson throughout.

"Oh, sweetheart, you smell like such a mess." The woman reaches for you, grasping the air before finding you. Slim, cool fingers trace their way all over your face, as if relearning your features by touch. Dark glasses obscure the woman's eyes. She wets her thumb and wipes it over your lip.

You lunge for her, teeth snapping shut over empty air.

She clucks. "Don't be so ungrateful. I gave you plenty of that already, didn't I?"

You scowl, but perhaps she can't see it.

"The fright you gave me... You're lucky I found you when I did."

You raise a hand to your throat, tentatively touching the soft flesh. It seems no more fragile than usual. You remember the sound of running water, but everything beyond that is a blur, a roar, a picture you once knew that has now become meaningless, broken into its constituent parts. Don't you have... a baby? Don't you have a friend—

A man walks by with a glass on a tray, filled with the same red stuff, and you take it. Your hand trembles so badly that liquid almost sloshes over the rim. The woman raises her glass, and you, as if drawn on strings, meet hers with a clink.

"To your new beginning, Pearl."

You drink, holding the glass with both hands to steady it. Is that your name? "Pearl." It doesn't sound right, but the woman says it with such conviction, it must be right.

Your mind is like a record player with a worn needle, years slipping away in seconds. Now you stand in the middle of a vast, gleaming room. Images move on glass panels on the walls, complete with sound, though you never see a gramophone. People flit past like butterflies, all dressed so scantily their mothers would be ashamed to see them. Life goes on all around you, the endless noise and whirl of colour. You are the centre of the kaleidoscope, a static point. Unwilling to move and unable to change.

The woman, sheathed in a body-hugging dress of fuchsia—the colour so bright it assaults the eyes, hem abbreviated to mid-thigh—holds you on a crowded dance floor, her face veiled in black lace, the damage beneath no more odd than any of the other oddities around you. "What are you thinking, Pearl?"

Thinking? You don't think anymore. Something is wrong. Missing. You rub your neck from time to time, expecting to find contusions, tenderness. The smooth, unbroken skin is almost disappointing.

Everything is glass these days, from the endless screens to the floor-to-ceiling windows. You expect the woman to be more circumspect about the sun, but at a touch of a button, the glass darkens and transforms into a surface like opaque, black marble.

She presses you against the window at night, the city spread out in lights so far below, the distance nauseating, unfathomable. She pierces your neck with her teeth, and you sup at her wrist, forming a loop with no end. Ouroboros devouring its tail.

You think you love her. You think, if this is love, you don't know anything.

The woman holds you in the bleak hours preceding sunrise and says, "Isn't this world a marvel? Eternal day, a playground for the imagination. Why, we can visit London without walking a mile. Isn't that something?"

You nod, although none of those words make sense when strung together. You drift, on the edge of consciousness, and consider, not for the first time, how nice it might be to see the sun. The real sun, not some fancy picture on a glass screen. Feel warmth on your skin, something to drive away the cold. Can it still warm you, after all this time?

You wonder.

# SAVE PO LAM

# CHAPTER 64

# SAVE PO LAM

The shot flew true, piercing Mrs. Edevane's cheek. She jerked back, crying out with a moan of pain like a dying animal.

Even near death, even crippled and scarred, there was something entrancing about her. Hair soft and wavy where it wasn't matted with gore, eyes large and colourless, the right one filmed over with white. Even the fresh striations of scar tissue on her face were somehow compelling. How on earth had she injured herself so badly that not even blood could heal her?

"Pearl," she said, hands outstretched. She groaned and coughed, blood oozing black from the corner of her mouth. "My Pearl. Come here."

"I'm sorry, Mrs. Edevane. I can't."

Po Lam stood, training the revolver on Mrs. Edevane, not moving her gaze.

"Isn't this enough?" Gean Choo asked softly in Hokkien. "Do we have to—"

"We do. I'm sorry." Po Lam gestured towards the car. "Back seat," she said with no further explanation.

Gean Choo went to the car and opened the back door. Ah Mui was still crying. She shushed her absently as she fumbled around in the footwell, her hand closing upon a wooden stake and a mallet.

She stared at them, her eyes refusing to focus. Po Lam must have taken them from her suitcase at some point after procuring this car, perhaps when Gean Choo had been asleep. She'd been planning this from the start.

When Gean Choo returned, Mrs. Edevane was hunched over, black blood oozing from the exit wounds in her back.

"Fuck you, San Po Lam. I should've sent the flesh merchants to take your sisters, bought them to make some old madam flush with cash. Or fed on them myself... Do you know how much blood is on your hands? How many women have died because of you? Do you think this makes you better than me?"

"No, Mem," Po Lam said, her aim not wavering. "But when you're dead, I'll still be alive."

Gean Choo nudged Mrs. Edevane with the head of the mallet, rolling her onto her back. She hissed in pain like a startled cat.

"Pearl, my beautiful Pearl, you've always wanted the best for me. I know it. Look at me! I'm harmless. Wounded. I even killed for you! You know why, don't you? Look at what I'm wearing!"

"It's a nice dress," Gean Choo said.

"I killed Justine for you, you selfish cunt! You don't know what hell I've been through tonight! I gave everything I had to avenge you!"

For once, she didn't think Mrs. Edevane was exaggerating. "I'm sorry you've suffered, Mem, but I didn't ask you to kill her."

The headlights cast ghastly shadows, insects fluttering in their beams, the shape of their wings enormous across the ground. The scar tissue on Mrs. Edevane's forehead gleamed red in the light.

There was still a pull between them, a thread unsevered. It would be so easy for Gean Choo to move. Offer up her wrists. Comfort her. Make it better, somehow.

But that was the lie. She couldn't make Mrs. Edevane better. She couldn't change her, couldn't save her—but she could do this for Po Lam. And Ah Mui.

And for herself.

"I thought I loved you," Gean Choo said. "You made were capable of feeling something other than ownership."

Mrs. Edevane's left eye snapped to hers. Her voice was ⌐ ⌐ than the meltwater at the bottom of the icebox. "No one will ever love you as much as I have."

"I hope you're right, Mrs. Edevane. I couldn't survive another love like yours."

"You think killing me will free you? It won't. I'll be there in every shadow, in every longing touch, every whispered endearment. I'll be with you till the day you *die*."

"I understand if you can't," Po Lam said. "You can give me the stake—"

"It's all right. I'll do it."

Cicadas called through the night. The air was damp and warm, pregnant with rain. Gean Choo circled around to Mrs. Edevane's side, drawing closer.

Mrs. Edevane groaned and coughed up blood. One of the bullets had gone neatly through her cheek, exposing splinters of teeth. Her eyes—one damaged, one whole—stared into the sky above, darting to the side as Gean Choo's shoes crunched on the dirt road. "You love me."

Gean Choo shifted her grip on the mallet, ignoring the way her arm trembled, her nerves singing with anticipation. "For what it's worth," she said, positioning the stake above Mrs. Edevane's chest, the mallet in her other hand, "I did."

It took more than one strike to sink the stake deep enough between Mrs. Edevane's ribs. Gean Choo would never forget the sound of her shrieking, incoherent with rage. When the stake met her heart, Mrs. Edevane's jaw yawned wide in her last brutal scream. Her body dissolved into ash, forcing Gean Choo to step away as the wind picked it up and blew it back into her face, making her blink the grit from her eyes. Her shaking hands dropped the mallet, and when her knees gave out, unable to support her own weight, Po Lam caught her and held her close as the heavens opened up and drenched them both with rain.

# CHAPTER 65

# YOU WERE RIGHT

## GEAN CHOO

*Thursday, 19 April 1928*

That night, Gean Choo didn't dream. In the morning, they continued to Alor Star, eventually finding the shophouse of Leong Yuen Kwai, Po Lam's old friend. Yuen Kwai was a middle-aged uncle with thinning hair and nicotine-yellowed teeth, but most importantly, he didn't ask too many questions. At least, not in Gean Choo's presence.

After they'd shared a meal and he and his family had gone to bed, Gean Choo found herself in the alleyway behind his grocery shop, sharing a cigarette with Po Lam. The heat coiled in her throat, dry and warm. She exhaled and watched the smoke ascend, curling up towards the heavens.

"How are you feeling?" Po Lam asked. "I thought you had a nightmare during that last stretch."

Gean Choo handed the cigarette back. "Yes, but it was just a dream." One where Mrs. Edevane was still alive and justly furious that she'd tried to kill her. Though it seemed she'd been more upset by what Gean Choo had said than by what she'd done.

Po Lam inhaled, leaning back against the wall, one knee bent to rest the sole of her foot against the brick. She exhaled, her face briefly wreathed in smoke. "I'm sorry about what I said before. That night... before Bee Leng came back."

It had only been three nights ago, yet it felt like a lifetime. The indelible sting gripped her for a moment, sharp and cruel. *Like the running dog you are.* "You were right."

"That doesn't mean—"

"You were right about the mem and I. About a whole lot of things, really." If she thought about it too hard, she might cry, and she couldn't do that to Po Lam. She pressed her fingertip against the bandaged burn above her breast, driving in hard, twisting on the release. Po Lam might've broken her promise about never hurting the mem, but it'd been wrong of Gean Choo to demand such a promise in the first place. She'd been wrong about so many things.

"You still miss her," Po Lam said, her tone making it just shy of a question.

Gean Choo shrugged. How strange it'd been, the sick descent of the stake driven in by her own hands, parting flesh with an absurd ease. The way she'd screamed, that last resentful glare, still disbelieving, with its unvoiced question, *how could you leave me?* "She'll never kill again. You've brought peace to her victims."

Po Lam exhaled sharply in a laugh. "That would be cold comfort to their families if they even knew."

Gean Choo covered Po Lam's fist with her hand. "You can't help them now, but you saved me. That's got to count for something."

Po Lam's gaze dropped to their joined hands. Gean Choo let go, her face flushing in the dark.

"We should try to find a lodging house tomorrow," Po Lam said. "Something more permanent."

She'd said "we." But maybe she'd meant for herself and Ah Mui. "Of course. I don't want to be a burden on you or your friend."

Po Lam was silent. The ash dropped from the end of her cigarette, forgotten.

She'd said something wrong again, and now Po Lam was angry with her. What had she...? Could Po Lam still want her, after everything they'd done? After everything she'd seen?

"I don't care where you live," Gean Choo said, "but I want to be there if you'll have me. I want to be with you."

Po Lam's face was half in shadow, cast by the lone streetlight. She dropped the stub of the cigarette and ground it beneath her foot. "I asked you a question, just past KL. Do you remember?"

"I remember." How could she not? It'd been all she could think about on the long tedious stretches of green forest and blue sky. *Are you running to me? Or just running from her?* "There's nothing to run away from anymore," Gean Choo said. "And I'm done running. Unless it's you I'm running to. I still want you. If you'll have me, after... after everything." She'd slipped into English because it was easier to sort her thoughts that way, to say it with precision.

"Tell me again," Po Lam said still in Hokkien.

Gean Choo bit the inside of her mouth and translated her words, more haltingly this time, feeling the weight of each one as it left her lips. Po Lam made her wait for a response. She stood there, long and lean in the moonlight, reminding Gean Choo of her first impressions—that of a young scholar, the hero of an opera.

Po Lam cupped Gean Choo's face with one hand. "I want you too, Teo Gean Choo. And I agree. It's time we stop running and start living."

# CHAPTER 66

# I'VE NEVER BEEN SO SURE

## GEAN CHOO

*Thursday, 19 April 1928*

They'd displaced the Leongs' daughters and were sharing their room on the first floor above the shopfront. Ah Mui occupied the Leongs' old cradle, quietly snoring. Gean Choo shut the door softly behind them, so as not to wake her or their hosts.

"You have no idea how long I've been waiting for this," Po Lam said in a breathy whisper. She leaned forwards, pinning Gean Choo against the door as she kissed her.

Gean Choo melted beneath her attentions. She was already embarrassingly wet, unable to bring her feet together because of the pressure of Po Lam's knee wedged between her own. "How long, then? Since that first day?"

Po Lam drew back. "What?" she scoffed. "After you were so late?"

"It was the riots. No one could predict—"

Po Lam pressed a finger against her lips. "The dress shop. The first gown fitting."

Gean Choo gasped. "Madame Page's? But you seemed so bored, so disinterested—"

"That was the intention. Too much flattery and you'd put on airs." She smirked as though she were only teasing.

"For me, it was..." Gean Choo brushed her fingers up Po Lam's arm. "When you told me to leave, a few days before Mrs.... You were so concerned. I knew then you really cared about me."

Po Lam's hands wandered under her shirt, so warm and firm. She was clay beneath those hands, soft and yielding. Po Lam unhooked the brassiere she couldn't quite stop herself from wearing, even though she'd changed back into her plain old shirt and pants. She ought to give it away.

"You've drifted," Po Lam murmured, her hands going still. "Is this too much?"

"No, no. I want this. You."

Po Lam kissed her neck, softly at first, sweetly. Then when Gean Choo moaned, pressing her fist over her mouth to muffle the sound, Po Lam kissed her harder, grazing her teeth over the criss-crossing white lines of scar tissue. Gean Choo moved her head, tilting it back to provide access. It was so instinctual by now, it took her a moment to realise Po Lam had stopped again.

The wavering candle flame reflected gold in Po Lam's eyes, casting strange shadows all around her.

Gean Choo straightened her neck. "I'm sorry. I didn't mean... Sorry."

"What are you even sorry for?"

For existing. For hurting her. For the reactions she couldn't yet control. "Everything."

Po Lam ran her nail over one of the scars, and Gean Choo almost came from that alone, her knees buckling. She made a wretched, desperate sound, and Po Lam slipped her hand down her trousers and stroked her through her knickers. It pushed her over the edge, and she came, shuddering, burying her head against Po Lam's shoulder for the shame of it, her ears hot and her stomach vaguely nauseated.

Po Lam allowed her to rest there for a moment before gently pushing her back. Gean Choo leaned against the door, still catching her breath. Her nerves sang, undone, her soul naked although she was fully clothed.

Po Lam sank to her knees before her.

"What are you doing?"

"Reminding you there are other roads to pleasure." Po Lam unfastened her waistband. At Gean Choo's nod, she pulled, stripping her pants. She glanced up before unbuttoning her underwear, the rasp of her calloused fingertips sending shivers down Gean Choo's spine. It seemed pointless to keep her shirt on, so she undid that herself and slipped off the brassiere along with it.

She fought the urge to cover herself from Po Lam's stare. "What?"

Po Lam's gaze fixed on the bruises on her hips, on the insides of her thighs. They were purplish, small ovals marking the shape of phantom hands.

Gean Choo's lip trembled. She wouldn't cry. She wouldn't. She braced herself for censure, for a well-deserved "I told you so."

Instead, Po Lam said, "You're stronger than you know."

It seemed gauche to refuse a compliment, but she couldn't acknowledge it, either. She just couldn't. So she said nothing; nothing when Po Lam pressed kisses across each bruise, starting with her hips, then working her way across her thighs, and then on the inside. She said nothing when Po Lam gently traced her hands along her hips, nothing when she smoothed her thumbs over the soft plane of her belly, and nothing again when Po Lam leaned forwards and pressed her hot, wet tongue against the core of her.

She sighed, though, shifting her weight as she angled her hips up. Po Lam pierced her with a finger, so slow it was tortuous, leaving her protesting with a breathy whine. She squirmed, silently begging, and flushed when Po Lam glanced at her. It was strange and awful to be seen like this, to have her hunger laid bare, every inch offered up for scrutiny. Po Lam added another finger, and then another, and Gean Choo sank down onto them.

For a while, there was nothing, save for the sound of their breath and the wet rhythm of Po Lam fucking her with her tireless tongue and blunt fingers. She was probably being greedy, letting her do all the work. Po Lam wasn't even undressed.

Po Lam paused and drew back. "Is this what you wanted?"

Yes. Oh, yes; notwithstanding that what she wanted could fill an encyclopaedia's worth of pages. "Can we swap? I'd like to undress you."

The pause lingered. Po Lam withdrew, easing out of her with a gentleness that made her mourn her presence. "All right. Bed?"

Not trusting herself to speak, Gean Choo nodded. They moved their pallets together and tumbled onto them. She found Po Lam's mouth, kissed her again, tasted salt and musk cut through with smoke. She fumbled with the buttons on Po Lam's shirt, then stripped it from her, revealing the little vest underneath. Her body was just as she remembered it from the night of the invasion—pale from never seeing the sun, hard from hauling around bodies for Mrs. Edevane.

"What's wrong?"

Gean Choo pressed her knuckles to her lips, needing the distraction of her teeth biting into them. "Nothing. Just a thought."

"About?"

"The past. Forget it."

Po Lam frowned. "If you're not ready, we don't have to—"

"We do! I mean, I'd like to. If you'd like to. I don't want to give this to her, too."

Po Lam studied her for some time. Perhaps that was her way of grounding herself. "If you're sure."

"I've never been so sure."

There was nothing less attractive than admitting to one's current lover that one was thinking of one's past lover. Gean Choo leaned down and kissed Po Lam's neck. The skin was soft, unmarked. She wanted to ask, but she couldn't. Not now.

*Stop thinking about that. Stop it.*

"Can I take off the little vest?" she asked.

"I'd rather you didn't."

She moved her hands to Po Lam's waistband instead, pausing there as a question until Po Lam inclined her head. She loosened the fabric belt and slipped the pants down over Po Lam's hips, then moved her hand over Po Lam's clothed waist. Po Lam gasped, but not in a good way.

"Ticklish?" Gean Choo asked.

"A little."

That deserved further exploration, but not now. Not tonight. This thing between them was fragile enough as it was. Maybe one day they'd be comfortable enough she'd know how to tease without offending... but not yet.

She slipped her fingers beneath the waistband of Po Lam's underwear and Po Lam lifted her hips off the bed to help ease them off. Underneath, her hipbones jutted out, sharp and defined. Her sex was obscured by a triangle of black curls, softer to the touch than she'd imagined.

"Would you like me to—" Gean Choo began.

"Not inside."

"All right. Mouth?"

"Yes, but same thing."

Gean Choo glanced down and parted Po Lam's folds with her fingertip. She glistened, her inner folds shading to mauve. Her clitoris looked swollen, purplish red. Gean Choo slid her finger up and brushed against it, watching Po Lam's eyelashes quiver against her skin. She lowered her head and kneaded the firm curve of Po Lam's ass, pressing her against her mouth. She was bitterness and musk, burnt char and salt. Gean Choo's own wetness slid down her thigh as she focussed on the inhalation of Po Lam's breath, sharp at times, growing more unsteady. Po Lam's fists clenched in the sheets before she reached out and stroked Gean Choo's hair, her head thrown back to reveal the long line of her throat.

Gean Choo closed her eyes and dug her nails into her own thigh. The movement of Po Lam's hips rocked her, too. Po Lam shifted, digging her heels into Gean Choo's back, locking them together. Gean Choo reached up, running her hands over the little vest, sliding fingertips over bare thighs and hips. She curled her knuckles, rubbed one between Po Lam's folds, and was rewarded by the heels digging deeper into her back. She couldn't bear the way Po Lam looked at her, as if she were drinking her in; adoring, as if she were worthy of adoration.

Po Lam was almost silent when she came, a seismic tremor quivering beneath Gean Choo's tongue, all flushed skin and delightful abandon. Her limbs slowly relaxed, gradually releasing her from their confines.

She pulled Gean Choo up and pressed her against her collarbone, her skin clammy with sweat. Her fingertips drew spirals through Gean Choo's hair, her heartbeat pulsing beneath Gean Choo's questing hand.

Gean Choo forced herself to move, to touch the softness behind Po Lam's ear. The fuzz around her hairline was almost as soft as Ah Mui's. She had a freckle on her left side, closer to her spine.

Their legs were tangled together, one of Po Lam's hands pressed against the small of her back. She was almost drifting to sleep when the friction of Po Lam's knee between her legs made her startle awake.

"Still hungry?" Po Lam whispered, her lips against her ear.

Gean Choo shifted in response, spreading her legs, pressing up against Po Lam. She luxuriated in that warm slick slip between them, stroking Po Lam's calf with the top of her foot.

"What do you want, Teo Gean Choo?"

The words stuck in her throat. One of the moths tried to settle against the glass of the oil lamp but jerked away at the last moment from the heat. It flew away, disorientated, then tried it again, with the same result.

Po Lam nipped at her ear, and Gean Choo turned back.

"I want you to be rough with me. If you'd like." She worried at her lip, wishing the oil lamp was brighter. It was hard to interpret Po Lam's look, that subtle line between her brows.

"Rough, like... pull your hair? Speak cruel words to you?"

"Yes, and yes? Maybe?"

The silence between them had all the heaviness of the air before a thunderstorm. Gean Choo scarcely dared to breathe, knowing it was filling her lungs with something wrong.

Po Lam sat up so suddenly it caused a breeze. She reached over and delivered a stinging slap, right between Gean Choo's legs, against her sensitive folds, sending a thrilling shock of pain all the way down to her toes. "Get up."

Gean Choo was apparently too slow to react. Po Lam circled around to her side of the pallets and dragged her up by the arm, spinning her around and shoving her against the wall. Gean Choo shot her palms out to brace herself, and the impact sent a jarring shock all the way to her elbows.

Po Lam kicked her legs apart, landing stinging blows against her calves. She twisted her hand into Gean Choo's hair, pulling her head back, making her body bend in an arch.

When Po Lam spoke, it was like they'd wound back the clock to three nights ago. "You think you're so much better than us, walking around in your lace and ribbons. The mem's favourite. Her little whore." She reached down between Gean Choo's legs, sliding in without preamble, making her gasp from the sudden raw stretch of it. "But while you've been letting her fuck you"—she began to move, her fingers pushing wide with each thrust, unbearably tight—"you've been longing to have my mouth on you. My hands on you and inside you." She changed her angle, curling her fingers. Gean Choo gasped and then sobbed as if someone had turned on a faucet inside her, breaking the dam of bitterness that had calcified over her wounds.

Po Lam's voice softened, although her thrusts did not. "You said you wanted this."

"Yes. I've always wanted you." She tried to turn, to catch Po Lam's eye, but the hand twisted in her hair kept her facing forwards.

Po Lam's breath was hot against her ear. "Then show me." She released her hair, wound her arm over Gean Choo's hip, and found her clitoris—her pearl. Po Lam's arms made a cage around her. Gean Choo sank down on her heels, caught by the rhythm, by the way Po Lam just seemed to know her inside and out. She crossed her arms against the wall and leaned her head against them, tears running freely down her cheeks, unashamed, her whole body thrumming with an unbearable lightness.

"Come for me, Teo Gean Choo." She repeated the invocation twice, as if she were saying a prayer. She needn't have bothered. Gean Choo was already there, had been teetering on the edge for so long that she pressed both palms over her mouth to stop herself from crying out. Po Lam stroked her through it, right to the point where more touch became unbearable and Gean Choo squirmed in protest, words failing her.

Po Lam stopped and placed her hands lightly on Gean Choo's hips.

Gean Choo turned, threw her arms around her neck, and sobbed against her collarbone. It was as if Po Lam had pierced her with a needle and all the evil thoughts were draining out of her. She imagined breathing in clear air and breathing out smoke, shedding the ills of the past year and beyond.

Po Lam held her patiently, as if she had nothing else to do and nowhere else to be.

"I'm so selfish," Gean Choo said, drawing back. She wiped a hand across her face. "That felt amazing. You're amazing. Can I do something for you?"

Po Lam dropped her hand, entwining their fingers. "Not right now. We'd better catch some sleep while we still can." She tugged her back into bed. Gean Choo didn't need further encouragement. She was boneless, tender. She could've slept for a year and not woken up.

Despite her words, after extinguishing the lamp, Po Lam remained sitting up at the edge of the pallet instead of lying down to sleep.

Gean Choo forced herself to stay awake just a while longer. "What's wrong?"

"I'm just... thinking."

Gean Choo sat up a bit straighter. "Do you want to talk about it?"

Po Lam settled down and rolled over in the dark, leaning on her elbow, light from a streetlamp catching the gleam of her eyes. "Yes, but not now. Maybe in a few hours?"

"All right."

Surely, she couldn't sleep with that hanging over her, drowning her with guilt. It'd been too early, she'd been too selfish. How could she have asked for something so foolish without even thinking of—

# CHAPTER 67

# NO MORE SECRETS

## PO LAM

*Friday, 20 April 1928*

According to her watch, it was two a.m. and she couldn't sleep.

She watched Gean Choo for a few minutes, the way her eyes flickered beneath her lids. Another nightmare? She didn't seem distressed, and Po Lam didn't want to wake her unless it was necessary. They'd had little enough rest over the last few days.

Ah Mui was sound asleep. She'd fed and taken her to the chamber pot around midnight, and with luck, she'd sleep through till morning.

She crept downstairs in the dark, walking on the far side of the steps instead of the middle to reduce the chance of them creaking. After all the kindness the Leongs had offered them, she had no intention of waking the family before dawn.

She stepped out into the back alley and fumbled in her pocket for a cigarette. It took her three attempts to light it, but then the smoke curled away from her, heat filling her throat.

She had to figure out what to say. How to say it. She had to do this right.

Killing Mrs. Edevane had been the easier task by far.

SHE'D LONG since finished her cigarette by the time Gean Choo found her, tip-toeing around in bare feet, a lit candle in her hand.

"You're here," Gean Choo said, her voice a whisper, even though there was no one else around.

"I said I wouldn't leave when it's night."

"People have said a lot of things to me and never meant it."

"I'm not people."

Gean Choo finally stepped out of the doorway, closing the door behind her. A thread of wax dripped down the candle, pooling in the metal holder. "You said you wanted to talk."

"Wanted" was a bit strong. "My mistress before Mrs. Edevane was... short-tempered. Heavy-handed with the cane."

"I'm so sorry."

One of the marks had never completely faded, a thin line beneath her ribs. One could only see it if the light hit the skin at a certain angle. "I swore I'd never be like that."

"You're not," Gean Choo said and tilted her head to the side. "Did you enjoy what we did before?"

"You know I did," Po Lam whispered, her voice hoarse. She'd enjoyed it too much. The way Gean Choo had shuddered against her, whimpering; the sob in her voice when Po Lam had taken her hard and fast. That soft, helpless cry when she'd hit her.

She wanted to hear that again. What did that make her?

"Listen to me. I enjoyed it, too. Very much so." Gean Choo reached out and tucked a lock of hair behind Po Lam's ear. "As long as we don't touch each other in anger, if we both want this, then there's no harm in it. It's like... playing pretend, isn't it? But I won't... I'm sorry. I shouldn't have asked. It's too soon, I was selfish—"

Po Lam reached out and grabbed her free hand. "I'm glad you asked me. I want to know everything about you. No more secrets."

"No more secrets," Gean Choo whispered.

They stared at each other. Gean Choo's expression was so soft. She didn't deserve to be gazed upon like that, as if she were capable of being loved. She was responsible for the deaths of so many innocent lives, so many families ruined at Mrs. Edevane's behest. And for what? For money, for comfort, for the safety of never being beaten again. But what Mrs. Edevane had done to her was far worse. She'd turned her into a monster.

Maybe that was why Gean Choo wanted her. Because she was attracted to monsters.

"What are you thinking?" Gean Choo asked.

"That you... that you shouldn't want this. You shouldn't want me—"

"I do. I love you, San Po Lam. And I want you so badly, you have no idea." She rubbed her thumb against the curve of Po Lam's jaw, leaned in and kissed her, messily, her hand entwined in Po Lam's hair, pulling just a little too tightly.

"I love you, too." It'd be easier if she didn't. But the thought of ever leaving Gean Choo again was unbearable.

"Let me take care of you. You've spent all your life looking after others. Let me look after you now." Gean Choo walked Po Lam against the wall, reversing their position from the other night. She set down the candle and straightened, undoing the first few knot buttons on Po Lam's shirt.

"We're in the street," Po Lam said.

"There's no one here." Gean Choo reached down and cupped Po Lam between the legs, stroking her through the fabric of her pants. Po Lam hissed, her eyes fluttering closed.

"You can be quiet for me, can't you?" Gean Choo's lips curved into a smile, her teasing fingers nowhere near close enough to satisfy. Po Lam needed contact, needed friction, and she needed it now.

Gean Choo didn't tease her for long. She loosened and unbuttoned Po Lam's clothing just enough to have access, then lowered herself into a squat, holding Po Lam's legs for balance.

Po Lam widened her stance to make it easier for her, then leaned her head back with a groan when Gean Choo's tongue made contact. Her mouth was so soft, it was almost too much. She placed her palm against the back of Gean Choo's head, holding her in position—not that she needed any encouragement.

She rocked her hips, trying not to think about the awkward questions she'd have to answer if one of the Leongs woke up or happened to spy them out the window. She could be quiet. *Was* quiet, save for the soft wet sounds their bodies were making that she couldn't control. This was almost everything she'd ever wanted, since that day at Madame Page's, since the Ferris wheel, since she'd let herself hope, for once, for a happy ending—

She snapped her hips forwards with a hard jerk, her hand fisting in Gean Choo's hair. She bit the inside of her lip and tasted blood, froze. Lassitude gripped her body, melting in its post-orgasmic haze. She had nothing to worry about. No more wrapping wounds in double layers of gauze so the smell wouldn't carry. It was another small freedom upon a lifetime of freedoms.

Gean Choo leaned her head against her thigh, pressing a kiss to her skin. Somewhere, a dog barked. She covered Po Lam again, doing up her buttons, raising her pants back into position. Po Lam shifted her weight. Her thighs would burn tomorrow, but it had been worth it.

She drew Gean Choo up beside her, kissed her and tasted herself. "We should go inside."

Someone passed by the mouth of the alley on a bicycle. They didn't bother glancing in their direction, but Gean Choo still stiffened beside her. "All right."

Upstairs, Ah Mui was mercifully still asleep. They tumbled onto their pallets, the candle making their shadows flicker against the walls. Gean Choo undressed and straddled her, skin tinted orange in the semi-darkness, her shoulders and upper arms crossed with thin red lines of claw marks, the wounds on their way to healing. Po Lam reached up and ran her hands down her sides, trying not to read too much into it when Gean Choo leaned forwards into her touch.

Gean Choo grabbed one of her hands and led it down between her legs. "I'm burning for you. Can you feel it?"

She could. When she slipped her fingers inside, Gean Choo leaned her head back, exposing the paler white scars along her neck. Maybe they'd fade in time, along with the bruises on her thighs. And if they didn't, then maybe the sting of the memory would fade.

Gean Choo rocked her hips against her. Po Lam reached up and fondled a nipple, then pinched it, pressing harder until Gean Choo gasped.

"Is that too much?"

"Maybe? Almost, but... don't stop. I'm so sensitive," she said, her voice breathy, eyes unfocussed. "I think... I think I'm due to bleed again."

That declaration would've sent her into a panic just a few days ago, but now it was of no more concern than if Gean Choo had said she thought it would rain tomorrow. Po Lam moved her hand to Gean Choo's other breast. "Is that why you're insatiable?"

"No. I'm just making up for lost time—"

They had so much time. Now she could finally permit herself to think beyond the next few hours and imagine the kind of life they might have together—a quiet, respectable life, doing honest work, sending their adopted daughter to school...

Gean Choo leaned over her, resting her weight on her elbows. She snatched the edge of the pillow with her teeth and quietly screamed into it, her whole body shuddering as she squeezed around Po Lam's fingers. Po Lam waited for her to go still and then withdrew, bringing her hand to Gean Choo's mouth. Gean Choo obediently licked her clean, her tongue hot and wet and so very soft.

They fit together in a way that felt right; Gean Choo sprawled against her shoulder, her breath warm against Po Lam's neck, their bare legs entwined. Maybe it was right—their kind of right, and no other. They were two broken pieces of pottery, the jagged edges lining up with each other, making a shape that wasn't altogether whole.

Her hand pressed insistently against Po Lam's hip. Po Lam covered it with her own.

"I'm not tired," Gean Choo said.

"You should be. It's"—Po Lam leaned over and fumbled for her pocket watch, flipping it open—"almost dawn. Still enough time to nap before Ah Mui wakes us all." She stretched a bit and blew out the candle, the smoke wafting blue-grey towards heaven.

"San Po Lam?"

"Yes?"

"Do you think, after everything, we deserve to be happy?"

After all this, no matter what work they found, she'd have less to send home to her sisters. But they'd manage, somehow. They had to. "I think that anyone who says otherwise can go fuck themselves."

Gean Choo giggled.

"What?"

"I've never heard you swear," Gean Choo said.

"I'll stop when Ah Mui is old enough to understand."

"Are we really doing this, then?"

She understood. What would they tell their neighbours? Should they change their names, pretend to be blood kin? That was almost worse than the truth. "If you want," Po Lam began slowly. "I know it's not ideal. We can't get married. I'm not a man; I can't give you the right kind of family—"

Gean Choo pressed her fingers against Po Lam's lips. "I don't need the world to see me as a wife in order to care for you. I'll keep your house, warm your bed, and raise our daughter. I'll be your partner, at work and at home. If you'll have me," she whispered, dropping her gaze, suddenly shy.

Po Lam seized her hand, squeezing it. "Are you..." It seemed silly to say it, awful to presume. It seemed impossible that Gean Choo was here, that she'd chosen her, that she'd continue to choose her. Some small, traitorous part of her whispered not to believe it, that it was a trick, that everything could change on a whim, and she had to guard her heart against the inevitable betrayal.

Gean Choo curled her knuckles against Po Lam's cheek. "I'm asking if you'll be mine."

The thought of belonging to someone should've felt like a cage, but it didn't. Not when it was Gean Choo. "I will," Po Lam said, dizzy with relief, with the strange sensation that she was falling, even though she lay perfectly still.

Gean Choo pressed forwards and kissed her, then pillowed her head against Po Lam's shoulder. It was too warm to sleep this close, but Po Lam didn't have the heart to move, instead, holding her as if to never let go again.

## CHAPTER 68

## EPILOGUE

*Monday, 1 January 1934*
*Penang*

Ah Mui cried on her first day of school, and the sound shot straight to Gean Choo's heart. She crouched, wiping the girl's tears with a handkerchief. "Shh, shh. I know, dear heart. But you'll enjoy learning things, I promise, and you'll make new friends. Here's one of the ladies who'll look after you. See, she's not so scary, is she?"

One of the nuns came over and leaned down until she was near eye-level with Ah Mui. "Hello," she said in passable Hokkien. "What's your name?"

"Say 'hello,'" Gean Choo prompted.

"'lo," Ah Mui said, in a small voice.

The nun straightened up and smoothed the line of her veil. "She'll be calmer once she's settled in." She held out her palm, and after a moment, Ah Mui took her hand. Gean Choo watched them both until they'd disappeared behind the corner of the building.

"It's hard seeing them off, isn't it? But they'll be all right."

Gean Choo turned to look at the speaker. Siu Hung co-habited with another woman a few blocks down from them, and they'd adopted a daughter around Ah Mui's age. Gean Choo hadn't yet summoned the courage to inquire about the nature of their relationship. Before meeting them, she hadn't understood how starved she'd been for company, for the sight of another family that resembled her own, if only on the surface. Siu Hung and her friend were former silk workers, having crossed the ocean during the Depression.

"Yes, I'm sure you're right," Gean Choo said, though her chest still tightened at the memory of those hard wooden desks, lined up in rows, the way chalk dust seemed to cling to the air. If it'd been her decision, Ah Mui would still be at home, if only for a few years longer. But Po Lam had disagreed. Ah Mui needed an education to get ahead in life—the Depression had shown them how quickly things could change. They'd still fought about it all the same. It was the only thing they'd ever fought about. Well. In recent memory, anyway.

"See you this afternoon," Siu Hung said, waving as she left the school grounds.

Gean Choo ought to leave, too. Ah Mui would be fine. Standing there worrying about potential futures wouldn't do any good.

She stopped by the marketplace on the way home, and then returned to the shophouse where they lived. Po Lam was in the backroom, surrounded by piles of boxes. A shipment had come in just the previous day. Leaning towers of cardboard hemmed her in on either side as she sat at a tiny desk, a ledger open before her. She'd taken to wearing glasses that constantly slipped down her nose, and no longer reminded Gean Choo of an operatic hero, but of the thoughtful scholar who counselled the hero to think before they leapt.

Over the years, Po Lam had stopped seeing any shadows, hantu, like the woman who'd been on the road that night Lai Hock had invaded the house. Perhaps they'd never been real, some manifestation of guilt leading her astray. Or perhaps they were shades who'd been appeased by Mrs. Edevane's death.

Gean Choo ruffled her hand through Po Lam's cropped hair until

Po Lam set down her pen, momentarily taking off her glasses to rub the bridge of her nose.

"Thank you for taking Ah Mui to school. I know it couldn't have been easy for you," Po Lam said.

Her throat closed over. No, it hadn't been easy. "I bought mangosteen." An indulgence, but they could afford it, couldn't they? It'd been so long since she'd tasted one.

They perched on a row of boxes together, and Gean Choo sliced through the thick, purple skin of the fruit with a knife. She pried off a plump, white segment and slipped it between Po Lam's parted lips before taking a piece for herself. The juices burst on her tongue, an explosion of sweetness and tart acidity, exquisitely delicious.

Like life. Sometimes sweet, sometimes sour. Luckily for them, it had mostly been sweet.

They took turns feeding each other, Po Lam's fingertips lingering against her lips. When the last of the fruit was gone, Gean Choo caught Po Lam's wrist and kissed her fingers, sucking the juice from them, watching how her eyes darkened.

She led Po Lam upstairs, walking slowly, exaggerating the sway of her hips with each step. A ray of sunshine fell across the landing, painting the room in a warm yellow glow. Po Lam caught up with her outside their bedroom and grabbed her by the waist. She turned and lost herself in the heat of Po Lam's lips and hands, in the touch that sent her pulse racing. Here was her heart, her home. She could sink into this moment forever and never leave, never grow weary or restless.

*Everything ends.*

*She* had said that, and someday it would, for they were but mortal. But not yet. If the world could extend its hand to her a little longer, she'd make the most of each moment, each day, each stolen second of happiness.

They'd earned it.

# HUNGRY FOR MORE?

Read the bonus third ending in the free ebook *Save Yourself* when you sign up to join my mailing list. You'll also be notified of giveaways, new releases, and receive personal updates from behind the scenes of my books.

Go here to get started:

go.lianyutan.com/subscribe

## MAY I ASK A FAVOUR...

Thank you for joining Verity and her servants in *The Wicked and the Willing*. If you loved the book and have a moment to spare, I would really appreciate a short review on the page where you bought the book. Your help in spreading the word is gratefully appreciated and reviews make a huge difference in helping new readers find the novel.

Go here to find a store page:

go.lianyutan.com/watw

Thank you!

# ACKNOWLEDGEMENTS

This book needed so many hands to pull it together and I'm incredibly grateful to everyone who stepped up in my time of need. As always, I'm so grateful to my wife, my first reader, who has patiently weathered the burden of living with a newbie creative and who is my best friend and confidante. You inspire me to be a better writer; a better person. You are my whole world. I love you so much.

With heartfelt thanks to my beta readers: Anders, Juliana and Eva Wong Nava, author of *The House of Little Sisters*; and to my sensitivity readers: Adelyn of pipsqueakreviews, Ashlee, and others.

I'm deeply grateful to Tim Barnard for reviewing an entire draft for anachronisms, and to all the other academics and history enthusiasts who kindly lent their expertise. Of course, all remaining errors are my own.

Thank you so much to Emily Woo Zeller for her amazingly nuanced performance on the audiobook. It brought tears to my eyes and almost made me change my mind about which ending I consider to be my favourite. Maybe it'll change your mind, too.

Thank you to Veronica, Heather Rose Jones, the Alpennia discord, the Server Baru Cormorant discord and the Indie Authors Ascending discord for help with specific questions, and to Carolyn for much-needed assistance with character names, language, and culture. I'd also like to thank my dad for further cultural assistance and family stories from history.

Epic fantasy character Baru Cormorant from Seth Dickinson's *The Masquerade* series was a huge influence on my decision to pick up this project. You can read more about how much I love those books on my website, lianyutan.com.

Thank you to my fellow authors, both in lesfic and dark romance, for your companionship, wisdom, and memes. Thank you to my editors, Silvia's Reading Corner and Lawrence Editing.

And to all my readers, thank you for taking a chance on me, for giving me your time, your reviews, and your support. I appreciate each and every one of you.

## OTHER BOOKS BY LIANYU TAN

Novels:

- Captive in the Underworld: A dark lesbian romance novel

Short stories/bonus content:

- Breathless: An F/F Hades and Persephone short story
- Save Yourself: The Wicked and the Willing bonus content

# ABOUT THE AUTHOR

Lianyu Tan has always been fascinated by the darker side of love: obsessive yearning and monstrous desires. She usually writes dark lesbian romance with a fantastical twist. She is the author of *The Wicked and the Willing*, an F/F gothic horror vampire novel set in 1920s Singapore, and *Captive in the Underworld*, an F/F dark fantasy retelling of the Hades/Persephone myth.

Lianyu is Malaysian Chinese Australian and lives with her wife in Australia. She loves to hear from readers. You can reach her as follows:

- Email: lianyu@lianyutan.com
- Website: lianyutan.com
- Subscribe to newsletter:
- go.lianyutan.com/subscribe
- Facebook: go.lianyutan.com/facebook
- Twitter: go.lianyutan.com/twitter
- Insta: go.lianyutan.com/insta
- Goodreads: go.lianyutan.com/goodreads

Milton Keynes UK
Ingram Content Group UK Ltd.
UKHW021043290224
438644UK00001B/29